The
Necessary
Beggar

Tor Books by Susan Palwick

Flying in Place

The Necessary Beggar

The
Necessary
Beggar

Susan Palwick

A TOM DOHERTY ASSOCIATES BOOK
New York

TOR®

THE NECESSARY BEGGAR

Copyright © 2005 by Susan Palwick

This book is printed on acid-free paper.

Edited by Patrick Nielsen Hayden.

A Tor Book
Published by Tom Doherty Associates, LLC
175 Fifth Avenue
New York, NY 10010

www.tor.com

Tor® is a registered trademark of Tom Doherty Associates, LLC.

Library of Congress Cataloging-in-Publication Data

Palwick, Susan.
     The necessary beggar / Susan Palwick.— 1st ed.
        p.   cm.
     "A Tom Doherty Associates book."
     ISBN-13: 978-0-765-31097-2
     ISBN-10: 0-765-31097-X
     1. Exiles—Fiction.   I. Title.

  PS3566.A554N47 2005
  813'.54—dc22

                                        2005041919

First Edition: October 2005

Printed in the United States of America

0 9 8 7 6 5 4 3 2 1

for my mother

CONTENTS

Acknowledgments *9*

1   Timbor   *13*

2   BODIES   *25*

3   Darroti   *57*

4   ROOMS   *68*

5   Timbor   *100*

6   NAMES   *111*

7   Darroti   *143*

8   HONORS   *187*

9   Timbor   *219*

10   CUSTOMS   *231*

11   Darroti   *263*

12   BLESSINGS   *274*

13   Timbor   *306*

ACKNOWLEDGMENTS

The seeds of this novel were planted by Valerie Fridland's anecdote about beggars in Turkey and by the Rev. Sherry Dunn's homily on the Parable of the Wedding Banquet.

Sharon Walbridge and Helen Palwick provided helpful comments on the first draft of the manuscript.

Rick and Natalie Michaelson introduced me to the National Automobile Museum, a wondrous place even for those of us who don't normally pay much attention to cars. The 1936 De Soto actually exists, in all its creamsicle glory: stop in and visit it if you're ever in Reno.

My husband, Gary Meyer, read each chapter as it emerged from my printer. He cheered me on with both praise and corrections, and also proofread the final manuscript. He is my first and best reader and staunchest support, and makes the lonely business of writing infinitely more companionable.

My indefatigable agent, Kay McCauley, has consistently helped me maintain my morale, sanity, and sense of humor.

My editor, Patrick Nielsen Hayden—and all the other fine folk at Tor—turned this manuscript into an actual book. I am particularly indebted to Patrick for his excellent editorial suggestions, to his assistant Liz Gorinsky for patiently answering questions, and to Dawn Antoline for careful and thorough copyediting.

Many thanks to you all!

The
Necessary
Beggar

I

Timbor

All of us were dumbfounded when Zamatryna-Harani insisted on the old customs for her wedding. The only thing that surprised us more was the marriage itself. Zamatryna had always been stubborn, but she had been stubborn about fitting in, about claiming this new place as her own. Or so we thought; she had been pondering the old ways for years, as you will learn, but she told no one. She kept silent out of love, and the family suspected nothing.

How could we have suspected? She was only six years old when we were exiled from Lémabantunk, the Glorious City, and sent to this strange dry place. She was still at the stage when little girls keep pet beetles and delight in memorizing epic poems, hobbies they put aside soon enough. If we had been allowed to stay in our home—home, I still call it that; this is not home yet after all these years, and I think it never shall be—Zamatryna-Harani would soon have moved on to geometry and horticulture, disciplines which are of course intimately linked, and the beetles, replaced in her affections by birds or toads or badgers, would have been freed to feast on the flowers she had planted.

But we were not allowed to stay there. My youngest son, Darroti-

Frella Timbor, was exiled for killing a Mendicant—a woman, no less—which was a terrible thing, an unheard-of thing. To kill anyone is horrible, but to kill a Mendicant is inconceivable. For Mendicants by definition have nothing, and they are helpless, and they are honoring the Elements. None of us understood how he could have done it, or why. He couldn't answer when we asked him. He told us he didn't know. He told us he had been drunk. And indeed, my poor Darroti was often drunk, but he had never been violent.

The dead woman was Gallicina-Malinafa Odarettari, the daughter of the third cousin of the second wife of the Prime Minister. She was twenty years old, only one month into her year of service as a Mendicant. It was a terrible death. The most grievous acts may be forgiven if the transgressor repents, and if the victim forgives: but the dead cannot forgive. The souls of the dead live on, as trees or birds or flowers, but they can no longer speak to people to say *I forgive* or *I burn in vengeance.* They live in a dimension parallel to the one where people live, but unbridgable by speech.

And so we were sent into a dimension like that too, into exile, knowing that we would never be able to return. There is of course an infinity of dimensions, and the Judges who sent us here did not know what this one would be. They knew only that it was a place where we could live, but where we would find no one who spoke our own language, for that is how the dead must exist also. They knew only that it was a place from which we could not return, as the dead cannot return. It was a hard punishment, but fitting.

They did not know that we would land in a refugee camp, in the middle of a desert, in a state called Nevada, in a country called the United States. I have thought about this often, after everything else that has happened. In Lémabantunk one would never think to question the Judges, or to ask how they know what they know. But now I ask questions I will never be able to answer. If no one has ever spoken to the Judges from these other dimensions, how can they know that none are utterly uninhabitable? For certainly I thought at first that we would never survive in this parched place, and sometimes it seems a miracle that we have. And yet everyone must feel that way, who is torn from a known, loved land and sent into darkness.

I do not know what pained Darroti most: his own guilt, or the fact that he had exiled his family. For of course we do not abandon each other, even or especially in disgrace. That is a Law: a Law of Hearts, not simply one of Judges. It is one of the many ways in which our own world differs from this one. And so when Darroti went into exile, we did too: I—his father Timbor—and his brothers with their families. My oldest son, Macsofo, brought his wife Aliniana and their three children, the boy-twins Rikko and Jamfret and the girl Poliniana. My middle son, Erolorit, brought his wife Harani and their daughter Zamatryna. I was glad then that my wife Frella had died of fever six years before, for as much as I missed her, I do not think she could have borne our fate. She was never a strong woman, either in body or mind. I loved her despite her weakness, and my love for her helped me understand Macsofo's love for Aliniana, whose unending wailing grief was a trial to all of us; but I was relieved that Frella was at peace, as we adults were not. What became of Darroti, on whose behalf we had come here, you will soon hear. It pains me to speak too much of it, even now.

The children fared better, of course, and Zamatryna, the oldest, seemed to do the best of all. If she remembered the bejeweled streets and glittering waterfalls of Lémabantunk, the festivals and flowers, she never gave any sign. Instead, once we had emerged from the bleakness of the camp, she became a little American girl. She insisted that we call her Zama because her real name was too long; she kept pet plastic dolls and memorized insipid television jingles about underarm deodorant and automobiles; she acquired a distressing interest in watching young men in cumbersome body armor symbolically slaughter each other on fields which could have been used for more important things, like growing beets.

She also received the highest grades in her mathematics classes, and loved poetry, and delighted to help her mother and auntie in the garden. One cannot completely deny one's heritage. I suppose there are American girls who do these things too, but we all get our talents from somewhere. Zamatryna got hers from Lémabantunk, from her parents and foreparents who grew in that soil.

And yet, since we were in exile and always would be, I had to hope that she would thrive here. I could not wish upon her the homesickness that I, and my children and their wives, felt daily, hourly, like the throbbing of a cut whose edges will not close. And so I delighted for Zamatryna-Harani when she fit in, when she went to her high-school prom looking like an underwear advertisement, accompanied by a young man who—to the horror of the older relatives—had made a great show of giving her mutilated foliage. I still do not know how she could work in the garden in the morning and accept a gift of dead blossoms in the afternoon, but it showed that she had become an American, and so I knew that I should be happy. I dutifully rejoiced for her when, in college, she was adopted by a group of other young women who wore upon their clothing the letters of a language no one here ever speaks, and who devoted tremendous energy to acquiring similar insignia worn by young men. I was pleased for her when she began to date Jerry-the-football-player, an earnestly polite young man who, even when he wasn't wearing his body armor, looked like a collection of tree trunks lashed together. He was a very important football player; the insignia he gave her were the envy of all her friends. I didn't think that she would go out with him for very long. None of us thought so. We saw no poetry in Jerry, and he trampled plants where he walked—although he tried not to, for Zamatryna's sake—and his acquaintance with mathematics was purely functional,

a matter of the ledger books he studied. Aliniana, of all people, became very fond of Jerry, and left off her sniffling long enough to
predict sadly that Zamatryna would break his heart. I think Jerry
expected this himself. There was no doubt that he worshipped
Zamatryna, but he always seemed to be holding his breath around
her, as one does around a wild, rare creature one does not want to
startle.

Imagine our surprise, then, when she announced that they were
getting married. And imagine further our surprise when she told
us that her wedding must include the Blessing of the Necessary
Beggar: a ritual she had never witnessed from a land which she
would never see again, and whose streets and scents she surely
could barely remember.

This is the custom in Lémabantunk, and among all the people
of Gandiffri, the Land of Gifts whose capital Lémabantunk is. A
week or so before you are to be married, you go into the streets of
your city, or into the countryside if you do not live in a city, and
you find a Mendicant. Of course this rarely takes long, because all
men when they reach eighteen must spend a year as a Mendicant if
they are to be admitted to the Temple as adults. Women have begun to demand to do it, too: they say it is not fair that men should
receive special religious privileges, and I think that is true, but it is
also true that the streets are more dangerous for women, although
not nearly as dangerous as where we live now, in these United States.
Gallicina-Malinafa Odarettari was one of the first female Mendicants. We learned after her death that she had been seeking her
family's approval for years. Since our exile, I have often wished that
she had not received it, although I was pleased, back home, whenever I saw a woman begging.

The tradition of the Necessary Beggar dictates that you choose
the first Mendicant you see, for this person is a blessing, an embod-
iment of the Elements, who has been put in your path for this purpose. Some people cheat: they go in search of Mendicants they

already know, or they put out word about the wedding to ensure that their favorites will be waiting on their path. But you are not allowed to choose any relative closer than a fifth cousin; this is very bad form, and bad luck for the marriage.

Once you have found a Mendicant, you bow very low to that person, and you say, "Please grace my wedding, to remind me of the ground of my fortune."

The Mendicant bows back and says, "I will grace your wedding, to remind you always of the gifts you have received."

And then you take the Mendicant home with you. You feast the person, dress him—well, they are nearly always male—in fine attire, put him in the airiest room with the softest sleeping mat. You do this for a week before the wedding. On the day of the wedding itself, the Necessary Beggar is at the head of the joyous procession; he sits on a litter decorated with live flowers in pots, and the groom and his friends (and the bride and her friends, if they are strong) carry it into the Temple, and everyone sings, and anyone who is not carrying the litter claps and rings bells, and the Necessary Beggar waves and smiles, the way presidents and football players do in parades here. And once the procession is inside the Temple, the Necessary Beggar climbs down from his litter and moves among the wedding party and the guests, and everyone gives him a very fine gift, and the bride and groom give him the costliest gift of all. People have been known to delay their weddings to save for the Beggar's Gift, although I think this foolish, too much like the United States. The point of the ritual is to show hospitality to a stranger; it is a reminder of civic duty and also a fertility rite, since parents must show hospitality to their children, who arrive as squalling strangers. Welcoming the Necessary Beggar is a symbol of welcoming the rest of the world. And most strangers, of course, appear at your doorstep when you have not had weeks and months to prepare for them, although babies are the exception. If we immediately love our children more than we love other visitors, it is because we have had more notice of their arrival, more time to train ourselves to love them.

But weddings are symbolic, and they are parties, and so they have grown into a display which does not bear much relation to the everyday discipline of inviting weary, dusty travelers to share a cup of tea. The Necessary Beggars are given wild, outlandish gifts: not just warm cloaks and sleeping mats and homely kettles, but wondrous articulated statues, pet peacocks and snakes and antelope, costly carpets woven with gold thread and beads of lapis lazuli.

Once, we are told but cannot prove, the most prized presents were not things, but gifts of self. There is a beloved story, very old, about a couple who gave the bride's sister—with her permission— to the Necessary Beggar; for a year after his service as a Mendicant, the deed said, she would bring him sweet cakes every evening, and fan him with fragrant boughs, and dance for him. It is thought that she knew him, or had seen him, and was already in love; at any rate, that year ended predictably with another wedding. And the bride and groom strained and fretted over what gift they might give that would be finer than the one that had comprised their courtship, and at last they decided that they themselves, both of them, would spend the first year of their marriage waiting upon the needs of their Necessary Beggar. But at the end of that year, their Necessary Beggar had fallen in love with the new wife's sister, who several times had helped them cook for him, and so there was yet another wedding, and the new couple and the old decided that all four of them would wait upon the latest Necessary Beggar. And so it went, year after year, always ending with another wedding and a larger circle of graciousness, until at last the entire village was waiting upon a Mendicant they had had to journey far into the countryside to find. And because there was no one left in the village for this latest Necessary Beggar to marry, all of them—scores of people by then, if not hundreds—packed up their belongings and moved to the next town over, that he might find a wife and continue the tradition. And at last, after years and years of this, everyone alive was part of the web, and they named themselves a country: Gandiffri, the Land of Gifts.

It is a story we tell our children. I do not know if it is true. I always wanted it to be, and hoped that by telling it, we might help make it true. But too many of our people are grown satisfied and inward, and certainly it is easier to give carpets than to give oneself.

So. The Necessary Beggar receives these gifts, whatever they are, and then he performs the wedding ceremony. The bride and groom stand before him, in the presence of everyone they love—except the dead, who are lost to them—and he recites a blessing: "For what you have given me, your errors and those of all your kin are forgiven. For charity heals shortcoming, and kindness heals carelessness, and hearts heal hurt."

It is a very ancient blessing, very holy. It has the power to assuage many crimes, for after it is spoken, anyone in the crowd who bears a grudge against anyone else is obliged to seek out that person and say, "I forgive you in the name of the Necessary Beggar."

These customs have great power among the living. They cannot reach the dead, who attend their family weddings—if they do so at all—only as finches or caterpillars or leaves, who cannot speak in human tongues. There is another story, older even than the one of how Gandiffri earned its name, about how once the dead could speak to us, and why they can no longer: the Great Breaking, we call it, the rift between the worlds of the present and the past. It is a very sad tale, and it reminds me of my poor Darroti. I did not like to tell or hear it even before our exile, and now the very thought of it hurts me. You will excuse me, then, if I do not tell it now. You will learn it soon enough, for it is part of the larger tale told here. And if that tale ends happily at last, I still have learned that all the mending in the world cannot heal some broken things. Could the dead gossip with us over breakfast every morning, still we would miss them, for life is more than speech.

The Great Breaking is why we always bless and thank our food before we eat it: for anything, fruit or flesh, may contain the spirit of some beloved person. We must believe that the dead delight to feed us, lest we starve, but we must also pay due reverence. And so coming to America was hard for us adults, for every television commercial of someone gobbling unblessed potato chips, unhallowed ice cream, made us blanch. The first time we saw a television set, at our friend Lisa's house, it was playing an ad for Smuckers jelly in which children smeared the stuff on pieces of bread and stuffed themselves, while animated fruit danced across the screen. We stared, aghast, although little Zamatryna immediately began humming the tune the cartoon fruit were singing.

Lisa had gone shopping for food to feed us, and was not there to explain this atrocity. "They didn't bless the bread or the fruit stuff," Macsofo said, somewhat wildly, and Erolorit, frowning, suggested that perhaps the first piece of bread and jelly had been blessed to include all the others. "But they didn't bless the first one either!" Macsofo said, to which Erolorit countered that maybe they had, and we just hadn't seen it. Macsofo shook his head. "Brother, what good is a blessing no one sees?"

Harani was in the bathroom, vomiting. Aliniana cried for a week. The children were puzzled but willing to adapt, and soon developed an inordinate fondness for Smuckers jelly.

At first we blessed all our food, as we had at home. But soon enough we stopped. It is easier to bless food you have grown and made yourself, and we still bless the yield from our own garden; but supermarket food rarely seems sacred here. Aliniana and Macsofo buy the parve Jewish food whenever they can find it, and Erolorit says prayers over entire bags of groceries, and Harani over the stove. But the children became good American consumers who could not eat just one Pringle, and who rarely remembered even to bless the first one. I remember Zamatryna-Harani, when she was eleven, pulling a bag of popcorn out of the microwave and telling her uncle Macsofo, "You want me to bless each *piece*? Are you *crazy*?"

"You would bless each ear of corn," Macsofo said, "but all the kernels may not be from the same ear. You can bless the bag, but say something about the different ears of corn. That will be good enough."

Zamatryna was already eating. "Too much work," she said, around a mouthful of hot popcorn. "Uncle Max, if the popcorn were haunted, I'd know."

"How? How would you know? How can you be sure?"

"I'd know," she said, rolling her eyes. "It would be, like, scary popcorn. This isn't scary popcorn."

Macsofo looked pained. "The dead are not frightening, Zama-tryna. The dead love us. You have been watching too many horror movies."

Zamatryna stuck her arms out straight in front of her and began lurching around the kitchen. "Night of the Living Popcorn," she said, in her best horror-movie voice. "Woo-woo-wooooo! Would you just chill?"

"You are not listening to me, Zamatryna. I am saying that the popcorn does *not* have to be scary to contain the spirits of the dead. The popcorn loves you. You should thank it."

Whereupon Zamatryna laughed so hard she choked. Then she gave Macsofo a hug and said, "If the popcorn loved me, I'd know that, too. Really I would. It's just, like, popcorn. If it's dead people, I'm helping them be alive again by digesting them, okay?"

Macsofo nodded. "Exactly! But you should thank them for feeding you!"

Zama shrugged. "Or they should thank me for giving them a body again. I'm going to go do my English homework now. I have to write a poem."

Zamatryna-Harani loved popcorn at least as much as she loved poetry. She loved movies and shopping malls as much as she loved math; she loved the Gabbing Girls, the latest teen lip-synching sensation, as much as she loved gardening. She was a good American child.

And so we were all of us stunned, when she told us that her wedding must be performed by the Necessary Beggar. Even Alini-ana was stunned, and it was from her reminiscences of Lémaban-tunk that Zamatryna had grasped the importance of the custom in the first place. Certainly I had never told her of it, for I knew bet-ter than to impose old ways upon her in a new place. Her parents had told her about their own wedding, of course, for little girls al-ways ask for such stories, but they had never thought for a moment that it would occur to her to follow the tradition. Our headstrong, assimilated Zama, with her letter sweaters and her laptop computer and her cellular telephone, instructing Jerry not to buy her a dia-mond ring, but instead to give the money he had saved to a Neces-sary Beggar? What kind of American child was this?

Jerry was the only person who didn't seem a bit surprised. "It's just like her," he told me, much later. "That's why I love her."

The problem was how to achieve what Zamatryna had com-manded. For, of course, the United States does not honor its beg-gars. They are not empowered to perform marriages. They are considered curses, not blessings. And there was the further diffi-culty that Nevada, where we lived, had just passed the Public Nui-sance Act of 2022 commanding that no one was to live on the streets, and the Reno police had plucked all the homeless people they could find up into county transports and had taken them away.

That is why the entire family, plus Jerry and Lisa, wound up climbing into Lisa's SUV and driving to the first place in America we had ever seen, eleven years before: the place, I suppose, where the story of Zamatryna's wedding truly begins.

2

BODIES

The door into exile was blue, and it shimmered. "Don't be afraid," the child's mother told her, but Zamatryna-Harani, standing in the Plaza of Judges in the somnolent warmth of high summer, was afraid anyway. The Plaza of Judges was vast, paved with smooth gray granite stretching away on either side into a distance that could have held fifty houses. Along the edges of the Plaza rose stone statues ten times taller than a grown man, the stern images of all the Judges who had ever ruled upon the fates of the citizens of Lémabantunk. The child could hear bees somewhere, although nothing grew on the Plaza; above everything stretched the sky, serenely blue. In front of them was the door, a different, more dangerous blue.

Zamatryna-Harani's nose itched, but she didn't scratch it. With one hand she clutched her little bundle of things, and with the other she clutched a fistful of her mother's skirt. She was afraid to let go of either one, lest something—her things, her mother, herself—be left behind. Her mother couldn't hold her hand, because all of the grown-ups were carrying possessions: cooking pots, bags of clothing, sleeping mats. Their hands were full and they wore bundles on their backs. All of them looked like Mendicants, but it was no honor.

Zamatryna didn't want to go away, but she knew they had to, because all the grown-ups said so. Twenty days ago, Uncle Darroti had done something terrible, and now he cried all the time, and Grandfather Timbor and Uncle Macsofo and her parents wouldn't leave him, and she and her cousins couldn't leave them, so they were all going together. Her twin cousins Rikko and Jamfret, who were only a year younger than she was, pretended it would be a splendid adventure, but she knew they were only boasting. She had heard Rikko crying one night, while Jamfret tried to comfort him. Her other cousin, the baby Poliniana, three years younger than Zamatryna, had cried openly, in front of all the grown-ups. Poliniana's mother, Auntie Aliniana, had cried too, and Zamatryna's parents had told her she could cry if she wanted to, that no one would laugh at her. But she hadn't felt like crying, not then. She had felt like being very quiet.

That had been after the first Family Council, where the adults had had long, worried discussions of how best to go into exile. Most of the time, Family Councils were about boring things like how much rice to buy or what color the new curtains should be, and children weren't included. But everyone was included this time, because what had happened was so important, and would affect them all forever.

And so the family gathered in their inner courtyard, and sat on the ground in a circle, and drank tea, and tried to plan. They were having the finest weather of the year, with clear skies and warm breezes. Small lizards basked on the walls, among the honeysuckle vines, and hummingbirds hovered above the sweet blossoms, drinking the nectar. Zamatryna tried very hard to pay attention, although she would rather have been playing with her pet beetles or memorizing a poem. She had been working on learning the *Epic of Emeliafa,* the woman who had first learned to plant gardens. She loved the poem, with its vivid descriptions of loam and weeds and the first tender green shoots of the pea plants.

She forced herself to mind the grown-ups, but as hard as she listened, exile was far more difficult to imagine than Emeliafa's first harvest of lettuce. The family would be living somewhere else, but no one knew where, and Zamatryna, who had been born and lived her entire life in this house, tried to think what it would mean. Would it be like being at her friend Lalli's house? Would it be like playing hide-and-seek under Grandfather's carpet stall in the Great Market, except that you would live there forever?

But every time she asked a question, the adults said only, "We don't know," and she grew more and more confused. No one who had been in exile could report back to advise how it should be done. The Judges said that no two Other Worlds were the same, although they promised that all were habitable, an infinity of welcomes. There was no way to plan a life in a place you couldn't picture, but the family had to try. And because they did not know where they were going, knew only what they were leaving, the Councils turned into endless discussions of what they should bring with them.

Zamatryna's father, Erolorit, wanted to shield his brother Darroti from any further shame. He favored wearing their best things, so that wherever they arrived, the people there would think they were just visitors on vacation, rather than the family of a criminal sent into disgrace. "But we will not be on vacation," Grandfather Timbor had pointed out quietly. "We will be in exile. And we do not know if there will be other people there at all. So we had best bring what we will need to live."

"But then we will look like Mendicants," Uncle Macsofo had said, frowning. "We will be claiming a position of honor we do not have, and—"

Grandfather Timbor stopped him with a raised hand. "We will be Mendicants in fact. It will be no pretense. We will need to ask for many things to live in this other place, if there are people there to ask at all. And if there are not, we must bring as much as we can of what we would ask other people to give us."

Macsofo still looked worried. "It does not seem right. It seems a mockery to act as if we are Mendicants ourselves. We are going there because a Mendicant is dead now."

At which Auntie Aliniana let out a little wail, and Uncle Darroti—who had not stopped weeping since the fragrant dawn when the City Guard had found him, clutching a bloody knife and swaying over the fallen body of the Mendicant woman—gave a low moan, the whimper of an animal in pain. Zamatryna's mother, Harani, put a hand on his arm and said gently, "We have to be able to talk about this, Darroti, even if you cannot tell us why you did it. You know we love you. You know we will not desert you. But we cannot keep silent about this thing, because it has changed our lives."

"I should have killed myself," Darroti said thickly. "That is what other people have done who have been found in such shame. I should kill myself now. That way the rest of you could stay here. That way—"

"Enough," Macsofo said, his voice sharp. Zamatryna saw his hand trace an X in the air, a quick slashing movement; it was the signal adults used to tell children to cease whatever they were doing, or to stop speaking, to remain silent. Her uncle used it now without thinking, even though his younger brother was no child. Darroti had been speaking madness since the Judges' sentence. Macsofo and Erolorit had been forced to take turns guarding Darroti to keep him from harming himself. "No one wants you to die, Darroti," Macsofo said impatiently now. "That would not comfort us, and it would not bring Gallicina-Malinafa back. It would only be a deeper pain and a more terrible disgrace, for you know full well that the Judges' sentence must be served, and were you to cheat them—"

"I would be serving the sentence." Darroti's voice was dreary, already lifeless and terrible. Poliniana, Zamatryna's sweet baby cousin, crept next to him and took his hand, stroking it as if it were an animal, but he acted as if he did not even know she was there. "I would go into the exile of death."

"We will not let you go there," said Erolorit, his voice gentler than Macsofo's. "We will not permit it, and if you love us, you will stop talking this way."

"I am a fool and a coward."

Zamatryna's mother shook her head. She looked as if she wanted to join Darroti in weeping. "You are our kin, Darroti, and we love you. If you go into the changelessness of death you will always be in the pain you carry now; in exile you will still be alive, and may grow happier. We do not know, after all, that this new place will not be a paradise. And our home is each other, not these walls."

"That is right," Grandfather Timbor said crisply. "And it is fitting that we go away as Mendicants, for a Mendicant has been killed and sent where no one can speak to her anymore, and we are following her fate, although we remain alive. And in any case there is no way around it. We must bring anything we think we will need, as much as we can carry, because we do not know what will be waiting for us."

"Then we should carry nothing," Macsofo said, "because all we can truly bring with us is our names."

"A cooking pot is its own truth," Grandfather Timbor said mildly.

So then there began the discussion of what, of all the things they needed to live, they should take with them, since they could not carry everything. Aliniana stopped crying long enough to say that they should bring food, flour and tea and other things that would keep, but the others disagreed. "We cannot carry enough food to live on for long," Erolorit said, "and if there is no food in exile, we will not live long anyway. We must assume that there will be food, and merely bring things in which to cook it."

"But we might not find the food right away," Harani said, frowning.

After some minutes of discussion, they decided to bring enough food for three days. "And seeds," Zamatryna said, "so we can plant things if there is good soil," and everyone praised her excellent suggestion, and she was proud.

"And several types of clothing, because we do not know what the weather will be," Harani said.

"And cloth for tents, and sleeping mats," said Macsofo with a sigh.

"And you men must bring your prayer carpets," Aliniana said.

"I want to bring my pretty slippers," Poliniana said. She was still holding Darroti's hand. "The ones with the jewels on them, that Uncle Darroti gave me for my birthday when I was small."

All the grown-ups except Darroti smiled, although Zamatryna didn't know why. "They no longer fit you," Aliniana said. "You outgrew them long ago, little one."

"I want to bring them anyway. They're beautiful. That's why I've kept them. And I love them because Uncle Darroti gave them to me." Darroti blinked then, and wiped his eyes with the hand Poliniana wasn't holding, but still he didn't smile.

"You shall bring your slippers," Grandfather Timbor said quietly. Thus it was decided that each person would be allowed to bring one small precious thing, one memory of home, even if it were not useful. The rest would be decided by necessity, as well as they could guess it.

And so now they stood in the Plaza of Judges, staring at the blue door. No one had come to see them off; that would only have made it more difficult to leave. Farewells had been quiet, friends coming by the house to hug them, to share a meal, to say prayers. They had given away their furniture and wall hangings, their fine festival clothing. The Judges would choose who would live in their house now.

Zamatryna had let all of her pet beetles out of their delicate reed cages, wishing each one well as it flew away. It had been difficult for her to decide what one thing to bring with her. At first she had thought she would bring one of her books of poetry, but there were so many that she could not choose, and anyway they were already in her head, except for the portion of the *Epic of Emiliafa* she had not yet learned. She worried that she would never be able to learn any more, never hear any poems again, but then she realized that she could ask the adults to recite poems for her, since they had memorized them, too, when they were small. She thought about bringing one of her beetles, but beetles didn't live very long, so she freed them instead. Finally, she remembered what Poliniana was bringing, and chose a doll that Uncle Darroti had made for her when she was much smaller, and he was still happy. She was a little ashamed not to have thought of it right away.

A doll, clothing and bedding, extra shoes, a loaf of bread. That was her bundle. She squinted at the blue door, wondering when they would walk through it. It was only wide enough for them to go through single file. They had been standing here too long.

"Let's go," Grandfather Timbor said, and Aliniana whimpered and fell to her knees. Macsofo and Erolorit got her up again.

"Alini," Macsofo said, gently enough, "you have to walk. I cannot carry you and carry the cooking pots, too."

She nodded, looking ashamed. Her children were whispering among themselves. Darroti stood a little apart from all of them, his eyes closed. Grandfather Timbor went over to him and said, "I will walk next to you until we reach the door. I will go through first, and you will follow me, and the others will follow you. Do you understand, Darroti? Yes? Very well. Come along, children."

And so Timbor led them. Zamatryna was afraid to look at the door; she looked at the ground, and recited over and over to herself, "My name is Zamatryna-Harani Erolorit. Harani is my mommy; Erolorit is my daddy. My name is Zamatryna-Harani Erolorit." Macsofo had said that they could only bring their names with them, and she was afraid that unless she kept her name uppermost in her mind, she might lose it.

Her mother went through the door. Zamatryna, now clutching the back of Harani's skirt rather than the side, followed. The door was cool and tingly; it smelled like seaweed and lightning. Zama-tryna felt rather than saw the Plaza of Judges wink out of existence behind her. In front of her was a long blue tunnel. She felt the hair standing up on her head, felt her cousin Rikko behind her, mur-muring a lullaby, a rhyme sung to babies, and just as she realized that the tunnel in front of her was empty, that Timbor and Darroti and her mother were no longer there—When had she let go of Harani's skirt? How could she have let go of her mother's skirt?—she took a step and found herself, impossibly, surrounded by a jostling crowd of people. "My name is Zamatryna-Harani Erolorit," she whispered to herself, simultaneously bewildered and awash in relief that she still remembered her name.

But that comfort was short-lived, because she couldn't see any-thing. All these other people were taller than she was, and they stank. Was that her mother in front of her? But no, her mother's skirt was blue and this was brown, and it smelled like shit and sweat. It was too hot here, much hotter than it had been in the Plaza. There was no moisture in the air; Zamatryna drew gasping breaths and found herself choking on dust. People were calling out in languages she didn't know, a babble of tongues. Where was Harani? "Mother!" she called, and somewhere she heard her mother's thin voice in answer. Now she heard Timbor calling, and Macsofo and her father; she saw Rikko through a gap in the mass of bodies and darted to him, taking his hand. He squeezed her fingers very hard.

"Zamatryna, where is my brother? Where is my sister? Jamfret! Poliniana! Where are you?"

"I hear them," Zamatryna said. She wasn't sure she did, but she didn't want Rikko to be more afraid. "We're all here, I'm sure we are, we'll find each other, don't be scared."

"Family, move to the side," someone called. Was that Timbor? It had to be someone from her family, because she understood the words. "Wait until we are all together again!"

So the children stopped, while the other bodies flowed around them, until finally they were gathered once more as a family. Macsofo had lost or cast aside one of his bundles so that he could support Aliniana, who seemed to be in a swoon. Darroti had put down his own bundles and stood hugging himself, his face clenched. Everyone else was pale but unhurt. "Well," Timbor said drily, "at least we know that there are other people here."

"I cannot breathe," Aliniana said, clawing at her husband's shoulder. "I cannot breathe, I cannot—"

"You can," Macsofo said. "You are. You're breathing, or you couldn't speak. Breathe more slowly, Alini, so you do not faint."

Zamatryna looked around. In front of her, going through a gate in an ugly fence made of thick metal wire, were the jostling people among whom they had arrived. Through the fence she could see low, dreary buildings made of wood and cloth. Behind her, from the direction in which they'd been walking, she saw very strange buildings, high and square, sitting on four round wheels. Were they carts? But they were metal, except for their roofs, which were dull green cloth stretched over poles. They looked so heavy, and there were no horses or people to pull them. Now she saw that each one had a tiny house with a door and windows attached to the front of it.

She didn't understand these carts. What kind of land was this? She looked down and saw herself standing on hard dirt, light brown and dusty. Nothing grew where she stood, although in the distance she could see low green bushes. There were no flowers anywhere. On the horizon were mountains, brown and rolling; some of the farther ones were blue, capped with white. But there were no trees, and everything was flat for a long, long way—for huge distances on either side, spaces that could have held ten, twenty, a hundred Plazas of Judges—until the mountains began far off. The mountains shimmered in the parching, brutal heat of this place, much as the door into exile had shimmered on the Plaza.

Suddenly there was a grinding, bellowing noise; they all jumped, and Zamatryna grabbed her mother's hand. One of the strange carts with the little house attached to it was moving, going away from them much faster than a person could walk. Stinking smoke came from the back of it. They all stared. "How does it do that?" Rikko said. "Nothing is pulling it. Is it alive?"

"It looks like a built thing," Erolorit said, frowning.

"It's ugly." Poliniana was very definite. "I don't like this place. I want to go home."

"Hush," Macsofo said, and knelt down to hug her. "We can't go home. This is home now."

"Hay hay yoo hall owe ear? Hay!" Someone was calling from the ugly gate; they turned and looked. Two people were waving and pointing at them, and one was also speaking. "Yoo thair. Whoo air yoo? Whitzer naemez?"

They stared. They had no idea what the person was saying. They stood and blinked, until finally the person left the gate and trudged toward them. "Is he ill?" Harani said. "What's the matter with his skin?"

"The other one is like that too," Timbor said, and indeed, both of these new people had the ugliest skin Zamatryna had ever seen, pale pink and blotchy. The man walking toward them wore green clothing, the same color as the covering of the grinding cart that had just gone away. His hair was the color of carrots. He carried a piece of wood with a piece of paper held to it with a small metal bar. He came within a few feet of them and then stopped.

"Hall owe," he said. He was smiling. "Will come." He looked at Zamatryna and knelt on the ground. "High let oil gull," he said. Zamatryna saw that his eyes were the precise blue of the sky, and her own widened in wonder. "Hoo air yoo fokes?"

"I'm sorry," Timbor said, "but we do not understand you."

The pale man stood up and scratched his head. He was frowning now. "Yoo air knot omen lust," he said. "Wear air yore pay pairs?"

"I'm sorry," Timbor said again, shaking his head.

The pale man walked closer to Timbor and showed him the piece of wood with the piece of paper on top of it. Zamatryna, curious, stood on her tiptoes to peer at it too, and saw a list of words, two or three words per line. Each line had a mark next to it. It was a poem! Maybe this pale man had put the mark next to each line when he memorized it.

When he saw that she was looking, he held the paper a little lower so she could see it more easily. Then he began flipping pages. There were three pages of poetry. All the lines had marks next to them. Zamatryna wondered why he still had to carry the poem with him, if he had learned it all.

He scratched his head, flipped through the pages of the poem again, and gestured at them: follow me, come with me. "Should we go?" Harani said.

"We have little enough choice," said Timbor, but he sounded more cheerful, and Zamatryna herself was less afraid than she had been. It was hard to be afraid of someone who memorized poetry.

So the ten of them followed the pale man to the gate, where he called out in his own language to another man, a darker man who looked more like Zamatryna's family. The pale man showed the dark one the poem, and they spoke among themselves for a little while, very quickly, and then the dark man smiled at Zamatryna and everyone else and began saying things. He said a lot of things, in a lot of different ways. Zamatryna didn't understand any of them, and each time Timbor said, "I'm sorry, but we don't understand you," the dark man looked more worried. Finally he turned to the pale man and shook his head, holding up his hands in a gesture of resignation, and then the pale man called someone else over to the group, and showed that person the poem, and they all talked together. They talked together for a long time, frowning and gesturing and looking at the pieces of paper, while Zamatryna and her family stood in the sun, getting more and more hot and thirsty.

Susan Palwick

At last the pale man sent the others away, and then he gestured at them again: follow me. He led them around the edges of what looked like a city of those ugly buildings made of cloth and wood. Zamatryna saw other people moving in the streets of that city, people who were dark like them. Most of them wore torn, threadbare clothing. Many had bare feet.

"It's a city of Mendicants," Zamatryna heard Macsofo murmur to his wife. "This must be a very holy place, dearest. Don't be afraid."

But the pale man didn't lead them into that city. Instead he led them to a large cloth building which stood by itself some distance from the city. He took them inside, where it was slightly cooler and where there were some strange narrow beds on legs, although not enough for everyone in the family. He made gestures which meant, Zamatryna could tell, stay here. Stay here. This is where you will live. Harani began to unpack her bundle, but the pale man held up his hand and shook his head. Maybe this wasn't where they would live, but then, what were the beds for? Macsofo tried to go outside, but again the man held up his hand. Were they prisoners?

More people came in at last. Two men brought more beds. A woman—the first Zamatryna had seen, a pale blotchy woman with hair like straw—brought warm rice and also water, which Timbor blessed. *Souls of the dead, thank you for succoring us, that we may remain among the living.* It comforted Zamatryna to hear the familiar words, and if the rice was bland, the water was wonderfully cool. All of the new people smiled at them while they ate the sparse meal, which seemed like a feast after the long, strange day.

After that, they sat there for a long time. The first pale man wouldn't let them leave, although when Jamfret made gestures indicating that he had to relieve himself, one of the other people took him outside. "There's a little building where you go," he said when he came back. "It smells. Will we have to stay here forever?"

They sat and sat. Zamatryna amused herself by silently reciting her favorite sections of the *Epic of Emeliafa.*

And when the shoots came up
She greeted each one by name
For she knew them already as old friends:
Hello, sweet peas, hello carrots, hello parsnips!
Greetings my wonderful melons! Hail rutabaga!
Welcome if you are the spirits of my ancestors,
Welcome if you are the spirits of strangers,
Welcome if you contain no human spirits at all,
But only the souls of green growing things.
You shall feed my family, you shall feed the world,
Every year you shall die and come to life again
And you will give us life, and we will revere you.

Finally some new pale people came, wearing white coats and odd metal necklaces. They smiled at the family, but when they gestured for Timbor to sit on a stool so they could poke and prod him, when one of them put the ends of her necklace in her ears and then put the necklace's pendant, a silver disk, against Timbor's chest, Zamatryna grew frightened.

"It's all right," he told her. "It doesn't hurt, little one." And he said to all of the others, "We must do as these people say, for if we struggle against them, they might put us back outside the gate, where there is no shelter or water."

So they stood quietly, watching. When the woman took the disk away, she smiled and then made funny blowing sounds, taking deep breaths and gesturing at Timbor. Timbor, looking bemused, imitated her, and the woman smiled and nodded and put the disk back on Timbor's chest, and then against his back.

"It doesn't hurt," Timbor told them all again. "It's a very odd ceremony, that's all. I'm sure they would find ours strange, too."

The woman in white performed her necklace ritual on all of them. Rikko and Jamfret competed to see who could make the funniest blowing sounds when they took their deep breaths. Macsofo scolded them—"You must not make fun of our hosts, children!"—but the man in white laughed. When it was Zamatryna's turn, she couldn't help but flinch a little bit, but the woman smiled and said something that sounded friendly, although of course Zamatryna couldn't understand it.

But none of them liked the next part at all. The woman in white had Timbor sit on the stool again. She put on gloves made of pearly-colored stuff that stretched. Then she took Timbor's arm and pulled the cloth of his tunic up over the elbow. She cleaned Timbor's arm with a pungent liquid, even though it was already clean, and then one of the other people wearing white tied a rubber string above Timbor's elbow. And then they took a silver needle connected to a tiny bottle and put it in Timbor's arm until blood came out.

All the children started to cry. "What are you doing to my father?" Erolorit yelled. "Stop it!" Zamatryna could tell that he would have rushed over to try to stop the people in white, had Harani not held him back.

"It's all right," Timbor said again, although his voice was less steady than it had been. "It only hurts a little bit. I don't think they are trying to harm me, although I wish I knew what they were do-ing."

They took three tiny bottles of blood from Timbor's arm. Then they wiped the place where the needle had been with more liquid, and put a paper bandage with pictures of animals on it over the wound. "Now it doesn't hurt at all," Timbor said with relief. The people in white smiled and nodded and gave him two little cakes to eat, and a glass of orange liquid. "See," he told the family cheerfully, "a blessing. Perhaps we are trading blessings. Maybe that is what the blood is." He blessed the food and drink before he ate them, and be-cause the pale people had brought a jug of the juice and a bag of the little cakes, he blessed them all at the same time.

Because, of course, they all had to go through this ceremony, too. Aliniana nearly fainted when she saw her own blood going into the tube, but the people in white clucked and patted her and gently turned her head away, and she recovered. When it was Rikko's turn, one of the people in white took out a puppet and made it dance to distract him. "I didn't even feel it," he boasted when they were done. "Those sweets taste good. I'd do it again, to get the sweets."

Zamatryna was last, but she was less afraid than she had been at first, because everyone else seemed fine. She got to look at a new puppet, a blue dog with floppy ears and a floppy tongue, and indeed she didn't even feel the needle, and the sweets were very good.

It was growing dark outside by the time the people in white were done with their strange rituals. The pale man turned on lanterns which shone without fire; each contained a miniature sun held in a round glass bottle. But these suns gave no warmth, and it was getting colder. Poliniana began to shiver, and Macsofo opened his bundle to get out a winter shawl for her. The pale man, the first one they had met, who had now been with them all afternoon, smiled at Macsofo, but his smile quickly changed into a frown.

Brows knitted, he stared at the bundle. He held up his hand and strode over to the bundle, and pointed.

Zamatryna craned her head to see. There were some little insects coming out of the bundle, aphids from the garden. She saw the top of a carrot sticking up among folded clothing: Macsofo must have picked carrots from the garden that morning, and some aphids had come along too.

The pale man shook his head. He looked very unhappy. He scooped up Macsofo's entire bundle and then, to the horror of the family, he stepped on two of the aphids that had begun to crawl across the ground. After he had killed them, he bent and picked up their bodies, and then he left the building, carrying Macsofo's bundle with him.

"How could he do that?" Harani asked. Aliniana was whimpering. "How could he just kill them? They might have been the souls of the dead!"

"Our dead mean nothing to them," Darroti said, his voice toneless. It was the first time he'd spoken since arriving here; he had gone through all the rituals without saying a word, and refused the sweets the people in white offered him.

The pale man came back without Macsofo's bundle. A new woman in white came with him, wearing the stretchy gloves, and looked at everyone's head and skin. When she was done, she smiled and said something to the pale man, but he shook his head and gestured for each bundle to be opened.

"Are they going to steal our things?" Jamfret said. "All of them?"

"We must do as they say," Timbor said, although he looked drained and gray. "They have given us food and drink and shelter. We must have faith that they do not wish to rob us."

And so Zamatryna bent, her back to the pale people, and undid her little bundle. Here were two winter tunics and two summer ones, two pairs of leggings for each season, a warm shawl, some soft leather boots. Here, tucked inside one boot, was the wooden doll Uncle Darroti had carved for her, with its dried-berry eyes and fuzzy woolen hair. Here—what was this?

Crawling out of the top of the other boot came a beetle, dazzling yellow and orange. It glowed like a jewel in the dim light. Zamatryna's heart leaped. It was Mim-Bim, her best, her biggest beetle, the one she had taught to jump through paper hoops for treats of sugar-water and rose petals. She had let it go; she had watched it fly away. But it had come back. Mim-Bim had come back and hid among her things, to come with her into exile.

And the pale people would kill the beetle if they saw it, as they had killed the aphids.

She had to hide it. But how? She gently picked it up and concealed it among the folds of her tunic. "Don't let them see you," she whispered, although not even the brightest beetle could understand speech. "Stay where you are, Mim-Bim. Don't come out!"

She heard footsteps behind her, and turned to find the pale man smiling down at her. He took her things—although he patted her arm as he did so—and divided them as he had divided everyone else's. The small store of food they had brought was in one pile, along with the seeds; clothing and prayer carpets and other soft things were in another, and tools and cooking pots—anything with a hard surface—in a third. Poliniana's slippers were in the second pile; he hesitated over Zamatryna's doll, but put it there too. Then he pantomimed scrubbing and washing the clothing, folding it, and giving it back to them.

"It's already clean," Aliniana said. "We washed everything before we left! It still smells of soap. Don't these people have noses?"

"Peace," Macsofo said wearily. "Do as they say." Now the woman in white showed them a pile of clothing she had brought, ugly green pants and shirts. She gave each of them a set; she pointed to their own clothing, and then pointed to the pile. She held up a sheet and shut her eyes, and the pale man mimed getting undressed behind it.

They did as they were told. Behind the sheet, Zamatryna managed to transfer Mim-Bim from her tunic to the pocket of the new pants, which were far too large for her and dragged comically on the ground.

The pale woman put all their clothing, and the carpets and the slippers and the doll, into a shiny green bag made of very thin stuff. She put all the food into another. She left the hard things where they were, and left the tent. The pale man motioned for them to sit down, and then someone brought them more rice, with stringy meat and tasteless vegetables in it, and more of the fruit drink they had been given after being stuck with the needles.

When they were done eating, the pale man turned down the lanterns so that the room was only very dimly lit, and pantomimed sleeping. And indeed, Zamatryna found suddenly that she was wearier than she had ever been. Still wearing the ridiculous clothing they had been given, they all crawled into their narrow cots, and Timbor murmured evening benedictions to bless them all. But

Zamatryna, though she was so tired, could not sleep. She felt for Mim-Bim in her pocket, and let the beetle crawl out to explore the world under the rough sheet and scratchy blanket. In the dimness, she could see the pale man sitting by the door. When he saw her looking at him, he smiled and gave her a little wave, and pantomimed sleeping again. She turned her back on him, flipping over to face the other way, and pulled the covers over her head.

There was Mim-Bim, shining like a little lantern. Pretty thing! It wouldn't live much longer, but Zamatryna could at least try to save it from the boots of the pale people.

As she watched, the beetle began walking in an odd pattern: up a few inches, a diagonal down, up a few inches, a diagonal back to where it had started. Zamatryna stared. She had never seen a beetle do that before. But Mim-Bim repeated the pattern, over and over. X. The beetle was tracing an X.

X for silence. "I won't tell the pale people about you," Zamatryna whispered, nearly soundlessly lest anyone hear. "I won't let them crush you."

Still Mim-Bim continued the dance. X. Up, down and across, up, down and across. X. Did that mean that Zamatryna couldn't tell anyone about the beetle, that she had to keep it completely secret? X. But why? And how had the insect learned human gestures? X. Had going through the door into exile changed it that much? But Zamatryna herself didn't feel so very different.

X. She fell asleep watching the beetle, watching and wondering. When she woke up, after no dreams she could remember, her head was above the covers and her body ached from the strange bed. She blinked, remembered where she was, remembered everything that had happened, and ducked under the covers again. Here was Mim-Bim, tracing the same pattern. Zamatryna picked the beetle up and put it back in her pocket. Since it knew gestures now, she hoped it would have the sense to stay hidden.

The pale man from the night before no longer sat at the door;

someone else was there, a man equally pale but with brown hair and darker eyes, who smiled at them. Someone brought them breakfast, a bitter hot drink and more of the orange juice, and dry granules to soak in milk. Someone else brought their clothing and the carpets back. "Oh, thank goodness," Harani said, and hurried over to the neat piles. Aliniana followed with more energy than she'd yet shown here.

"This soap smells terrible," Aliniana grumbled, holding one of Jamfret's tunics to her nose. "And the color's faded! Did they ruin everything?"

"Never mind. At least we can get out of these ridiculous garments and back into our own."

"Some of it," Aliniana said grimly. "This is too small for Jamfret now! They shrunk it! And where's our food, and the seeds? Did they bring that pile back too?"

The food and seeds were gone, and only some of the clothing they had so carefully chosen to bring with them was still wearable. Some of it was faded, some shrunk. Some had developed holes where none had been before. The prayer carpets had kept their colors, for they were costly things, but Poliniana's beautiful slippers were oddly bent, missing some of their jewels and beads. Zamatryna's wooden doll had been robbed of its eyes and hair; her mother handed it back to her with a sigh. "I'm sorry, sweet one. I'll fix it for you when I can."

"It's all right," Zamatryna said. She felt very grown up suddenly, and she knew what to do. She carried the wooden doll to her Uncle Darroti, who sat hugging himself on his bed, his face working, and placed it on his lap. "She lost her hair and eyes, Uncle. Will you make new ones for her?"

He didn't look at her. He stared into the air above her head and said tonelessly, "I don't know how."

"Yes you do, Uncle. Of course you do! You made them the first time."

"That was at home. I don't know how anymore."

She touched his hand. It was very cold. "You'll learn," she said. She began to climb into his lap, because once he had liked it when she did that, but he didn't respond, didn't unfold his arms, still didn't look at her. It was like climbing a tree, except that tree branches bent when you climbed them, and Uncle Darroti didn't bend.

"Zamatryna," her father said quietly. "Don't. He doesn't want it."

She got down again, feeling scolded. "I wanted to help. I thought—"

"I know. Come here." She went to Erolorit, and he bent and picked her up and held her for a long time, as he had not done since she was much smaller. "I know you were trying to help," he said into her hair. "You are a sweet, kind child, and your uncle loves you, but he cannot show it right now. He cannot show it to anyone. You must not be angry at him or upset with yourself. He is sick, and we will all try to make him better, but I think it will take a long time. Do not be upset. Can you go play with your cousins?"

But she didn't get the chance, because new pale people came and gestured for the family to follow with their things. This time they were taken deep into the ugly city and brought to another of the cloth buildings, much smaller than the one where they had been before. It had ten cots crammed into it, so close together that they had to crawl over each other if someone wanted to get up in the middle of the night. Their building was surrounded by others, each of which also held too many people, none of whom spoke any language they could understand. Little white houses stood between the buildings; they were the places of relief, made of hard shiny white stuff. They stank, but at least the ground was mostly clean.

A short distance away was a much larger building filled with tables, where three times a day they ate their food: plain, dull stuff, plentiful enough but tasteless, good only for keeping life in the body. Grandfather Timbor blessed it before each meal, his voice nearly inaudible over the uproar of voices around them. Zamatryna had never seen so many people in such a little space, and she never grew used to the smell. Babies could be bathed every two days, but anyone who could walk was only permitted to take a very short shower once a week, because water was too precious here to waste. The stink of bodies was everywhere.

That stink never faded. They spent fifteen long, strange months in the ugly city. If indeed it was a city of Mendicants, as Erolorit had claimed, it never felt sacred. The pale people in green were kind enough, but would not let them leave. They spent most of their time at school, studying English.

The children learned it most easily, and Zamatryna was the quickest of all. Nearly fluent after a year—a feat the Americans considered remarkable—she became the interpreter for the family. What a relief it was to be able to communicate with something other than gestures!

They learned that they were in the desert to the north of Reno, Nevada, in a camp built to accommodate refugees from other places, places torn by warfare or decimated by plague. Their neighbors in the camp had fled persecution, famine, and chaos to seek asylum in the United States, the wealthiest country in this world. These were the lucky ones, who had been able to leave their countries at all. Most of them had friends and family they had left behind, whom they would try to bring here once they became established in America. Once they would have been able to come here more easily, but the United States had been attacked on its own soil, ten years before Timbor's family arrived, and no longer trusted people who were not already Americans. Even getting to the camp was difficult: many people were turned away at airports, sent back to their own countries. And sometimes people in the camp were sent back, when their pleas for asylum were rejected.

The Army, the people in green, guarded the camp to make sure no one escaped to live illegally in the United States. That was why the camp was in the middle of a desert, for even if someone escaped, there were miles of harsh landscape between the gates and the nearest town, or even the nearest reliable source of water. But people from outside came into the camp: teachers, doctors, social workers, linguists and lawyers, ministers and church volunteers, all the people who wanted to help the refugees stay in the United States, even though they weren't Americans yet. Zamatryna liked the teachers, who told her how smart she was. She didn't like the doctors, who stuck needles into her, or the linguists, who kept trying to find out what language her family spoke. Some of the church people were very kind, but others told her that her family's blessings were no good, that everyone had to use the same blessings their church did. It was very strange, because the different churches had different blessings, too. But at least all of these people, the ones she liked and the one she didn't, wanted to help the refugees stay in the United States.

Her teachers told her that there were other people who didn't want the refugees to stay in the United States. Some of these people were very angry. They couldn't come into the camp. They couldn't get near the camp. The Army kept them away. The teachers and doctors and social workers had to come into the camp in Army trucks, or else in cars or vans surrounded by Army trucks and guarded by Army guns, because if they tried to come alone, they would be hurt by these others. A social worker and two nurses had been killed before the Army set up that system.

The people trying to help the refugees were called the Do-Goodniks, or Nicks for short. The people who hated them, who hated both the refugees and the Nicks, were called the Nuts, although there were different degrees of Nuts; not all of them were violent. Some only waved signs and wrote letters. But some Nicks also only waved signs and wrote letters, rather than coming into the camp to help the refugees.

The Nuts didn't call themselves Nuts: only the Nicks called them that. The Nuts called themselves Patriots, and called the Nicks Traitors.

Nut could also mean an edible seed. Nick could also mean a notch, or a small cut. English was a very confusing language. Patriot and Traitor, at any rate, seemed to have only one meaning each.

Zamatryna wasn't happy in the camp. She liked learning English, even though it was so confusing, and did well in her lessons, but there were too many people here and too many problems, both inside their tent and outside it. Having everyone in the family crowded into one room was extremely wearing. They all grew snappish, their love for one another strained, and Zamatryna had a private problem, one she was afraid to share with anyone.

Mim-Bim refused to die, as any ordinary beetle would have done at the end of the summer. The insect lived through the fall and the winter, surviving on bits of lettuce and rice and canned fruit that Zamatryna sneaked into her pocket in the dining tent. Mim-Bim lived in her pocket, always, allowed out only at night, when it traced Xs under the bedcovers. It traced Xs in her pocket, too; she could feel it. Silence, silence. So she had to keep Mim-Bim a secret, even though she longed to ask some adult what all of this meant. Clearly Mim-Bim was something other than an ordinary beetle, but whom could Zamatryna consult about this oracle, when the insect so obsessively demanded secrecy? The creature who had been a beloved pet became a dreaded burden, and yet one Zamatryna was afraid to discard. If she stepped on Mim-Bim, or refused to feed the beetle, she would be no better than the Americans. Each morning when she woke up, she yearned to find that she had accidentally crushed the animal in her sleep, for then surely she would be forgiven. But each morning it was still alive, still tracing its constant figure.

And then there were the problems outside their tent: an illness that swept through the camp, leaving Zamatryna's family untouched but killing five babies; perpetual fights between people from rival tribes or faiths or nations; a man who raped two women, whose husbands then conspired to murder him, whereupon both couples were shipped back to their countries as criminals. Under American law, they had had no right to take the vengeance they did.

The entire camp was abuzz, after that happened. "Barbarians," Aliniana said, weeping. "We have arrived in a world of barbarians!" Zamatryna didn't know if she meant that the man was a barbarian for raping the women, or that the husbands were barbarians for murdering him, or that the Americans were barbarians for sending the couples back to their countries. One couple was from Nicaragua, the other from Lebanon. Grandfather Timbor said quietly that this itself was a form of murder, because the couples would probably die of famine or war when they went back home.

Maybe Aliniana meant all three kinds of barbarity. She had nothing good to say about their new world. But Zamatryna was afraid to ask, because Uncle Darroti, who had never become normal again, didn't eat for three days after the couples were deported. He spoke only once, in a whisper, to Erolorit, who reported the conversation to the rest of the family.

"He is afraid that if the Americans learn that he is a murderer, we will be cast out of this place."

Macsofo snorted. "What are they going to do? Send us back home? How?"

"No one will find out," Timbor said mildly. "We will not tell them."

Harani shook her head. "The question isn't whether we'll get to stay here. It's whether we'll ever get to leave the camp."

For Zamatryna's family, who had arrived without papers, were a great mystery to the Americans, who kept asking them questions. The Americans thought that Timbor's family had gotten off one of the refugee trucks from the East (for in the press of the crowd, apparently, no one had seen them simply appear). Their names were not on the master list kept by the soldier on duty, the list Zamatryna had mistaken for a poem, on which every name had already been checked off. They spoke no known language, and there was no record of them anywhere in the computer, which tracked the transportation of refugees from across the country here, to Nevada. And yet they must have been processed at one of the airports, the Americans said, must have had papers at some point, or they never would have gotten this far.

That was why Zamatryna's family had spent their first night in a quarantine tent, why their blood had been drawn to check for diseases. The Americans knew that this must have already happened, if the family was here—for no one could get onto the trucks without a health check—but they did it again, to be safe. And the fact that Zamatryna's family so obviously had never seen needles before puzzled and worried them, although when all the tests came back negative the next morning, the family was still allowed into the main camp.

Because Zamatryna was the oldest child, and more fluent in English than her parents, the Americans asked her a great number of questions, which she relayed to her grandfather. Timbor answered the questions as succinctly and truthfully as he could. The Americans didn't find these conversations very satisfying.

"Where are you from?"

"Home."

"Yes, but what is the name of your home?"

"In our language it means the Glorious City."

"What language is that?"

"It is our language."

"Would you say the name of the city in your language, please?"

"Lémabantunk."

"We have never heard of Lémabantunk. Where is it?"

"It is home."

"Sir, what country is Lémabantunk in?"

"Gandiffri."

"We have never heard of any country called Gandiffri."

"Well no, not in your language, of course not."

"But no one speaks your language! No one here has ever heard your language."

"Of course people speak our language. We speak it."

"How did you get here?"

"We walked."

"You *walked*? To the United States? That is impossible. That would mean you were from South or Central America, and you speak no language known in those places. You could have walked from Canada, but there are no refugees from Canada. And you were in the trucks from New York. You could not have walked from South or Central America to New York. If you were from South or Central America, you would have been in a convoy from Los Angeles or Texas."

"We walked from our city to this desert."

"Sir, that is impossible."

"I am sorry that you think it is impossible. We are here, whether it is impossible or not."

"Why do you have no papers?"

"We had to leave so much behind."

"But you must have had papers with you, to get into the country! The borders are guarded very carefully, and the trucks are guarded even more carefully."

"I am sorry. If you give us papers now, we will guard them very carefully."

"But we can't give you papers unless we know where you are from. Do you understand?"

"I have told you where we are from."

"Can you show us on a map? If we bring you a globe, can you show us your country?"

"I cannot read your maps. We do not have globes, in our country."

"What direction did you walk in, when you walked to the United States? Did you walk north? If you walked, you must have walked north. Otherwise you would have had to walk across an ocean, which is impossible."

"We walked forward."

"Sir, please understand that we are not trying to be difficult. We want to help your family. But if we cannot get fuller information from you, you will be deported. You will have to go back home."

"We cannot go back home."

"Why not? Why did you leave home? Why did you come here? Was there a war, or a famine, or a plague? Were people persecuting you?"

Here, at last, Timbor lost some of his composure. Zamatryna knew that he wanted at all costs to keep from the Americans the fact that Darroti had committed a crime, since criminals were not allowed to stay here. In her pocket, she could feel Mim-Bim tracing its constant X, and she wondered if silence about the cause of their exile was what the beetle was commanding so urgently. "We came here to begin again! It is painful to us to think about why we had to leave. Do you understand that?"

"Yes, sir. Sir, we are very sorry, but we still need to ask you these questions. There are laws here."

"Go away, please. We are grateful for the shelter and the food you have given us, and for teaching us your language, but I think you have asked enough questions for today."

They went away. They came back. They brought with them a woman, an immigration lawyer, who explained patiently that to remain in the United States without papers, the family would need to fulfill certain conditions. If they were not already sponsored by relatives, or by an employer, or by a church, they could request asylum in the United States. But that was a complicated legal process, which would involve proving that they had left their own country out of justified fear of persecution based on race, religion, political views, social affiliation, or nationality.

"And who," Timbor asked, "decides if the fear is justified?"

"We do," the lawyer said gently. "The court does, based on its knowledge of the region from which you came."

Zamatryna saw her grandfather squeeze his eyes shut in pain. "The court will have no knowledge of the region from which we came. To you, it never existed. To us, it no longer exists."

The lawyer shook her head. "I don't understand. Your village has been destroyed? But we keep track of such destruction; if you're from a war-torn region, there will be records—"

"No," Timbor said bleakly, "there are no records. Just as we have no papers."

The lawyer sighed. "Mr. Timbor, you're here. You must have come from somewhere."

"Yes. But it is not a somewhere about which Americans have records."

"Ask her," came a strange voice from the back of the tent, "ask her what will happen to the family if we cannot justify ourselves."

Zamatryna turned. It was Darroti who had spoken, Darroti who always hid in shadows now, who had said nothing in weeks. His voice sounded like wind blown through a hollow reed. "Ask her, Zamatryna. If we cannot justify ourselves and we cannot go home, what will happen to us?"

Zamatryna asked. The lawyer frowned and said, "If your request for asylum were denied, you would be deported."

"And if we cannot be deported, because our home no longer exists, because there is no way for us to get back there? Ask her, Zamatryna."

Zamatryna asked. The lawyer shook her head, and said, "If that were really true, I suppose you would have to stay in the camp indefinitely. But it can't be true. You came from somewhere, and you can go back, even if you don't want to. I understand that you don't want to. We'll do whatever we can to help you, but to do that, we need to know where you came from."

"Tell her," Darroti said, "that we do want to go home and cannot," but Timbor frowned and made the slashing X for silence. Mim-Bim echoed it in Zamatryna's pocket. This was what the Americans must not be allowed to learn.

No one spoke for a few moments after the lawyer left, and then the adults began talking all at once in low, guarded voices, even though they were speaking their own language, which no one else understood.

"So we are stuck here," Erolorit said. "In limbo. We cannot go back home and we cannot leave the camp."

"It is my fault," Darroti said.

"We could invent a history," Harani said. "Zamatryna and the cousins have heard enough stories by now of where other people are from. We can tell a story."

"But we do not speak the languages of those countries," Macsofo said. "We do not know the names of their cities. The deception would be discovered."

"It is my fault," Darroti said. "I am the reason you are all in limbo."

"Darroti," Timbor said, "do not speak nonsense. Our home, of which these people have never heard, is the reason we are all in limbo."

"If I were not here, you could tell the truth and you could leave the camp. You could say you were being persecuted because of me. I am the criminal. I am the reason you could not stay in Léma—"

"No," Aliniana said. "Darroti, did you listen to nothing that woman said? We would still need to be from a place whose history they already knew." But Darroti had begun to weep, and gave no sign of having heard her.

Macsofo and Erolorit went to comfort him, and Zamatryna saw their weariness, and their fear. They were guarding him again. Perhaps they had never stopped. Mim-Bim traced its pattern in her pocket, and a great hopelessness descended on her. They would never get out of this camp, with its dessicating heat in summer and its brutal wind in winter, its stench and its deprivation. They would never see flowers again, never be able to bathe whenever they wished, never be able to go outside the wire fences. A great longing for home rose in her, and she crept to her mother's side.

Harani held her and rocked her. "Sleep, Zamatryna. Everything will be all right. I don't know how, but I promise you it will be. Sleep, child. We have made you do all that work of talking, too much work, and you are tired."

She slept. She woke to find herself in her own bed, still in her clothing, Mim–Bim still pacing in her pocket. She propped herself up on an elbow and peered around the tent in the dim light from the lanterns, which they never turned off completely because Poliniana was afraid of the dark. Everyone else was asleep too, Timbor and Aliniana snoring. Erolorit and Macsofo had moved their cots to either side of Darroti's. She lay back down, too tired even to unbutton her pocket so that Mim–Bim could roam beneath the covers, and slept.

She awoke again near dawn, pulled into consciousness by an unfamiliar sensation. Her pocket—there was a buzzing from her pocket. Mim–Bim was frantically vibrating its wings, trying to get out, trying to fly through the cloth. The beetle had never done that before. Zamatryna stuck her head under the covers and unbuttoned her pocket; Mim–Bim shot out and tried to fly out from beneath the sheets, which it had never done before either. "No," Zamatryna whispered, catching it in her hands and stuffing it back into her pocket. "No, no one can know you're here, or the Americans will kill you." As often as she had wished to be rid of the insect, she couldn't let that happen. Back in her pocket, Mim–Bim began tracing the X again, but jerkily, more quickly than usual. Dread filled Zamatryna. Something had happened.

She pulled the covers back and sat up, scanning the room.

Timbor and Aliniana had stopped snoring; Erolorit and Macsofo had both started. Everyone else was—no, wait. The cot between Erolorit and Macsofo was empty. Darroti was gone.

Bile filled her throat. She got up, ran over to her father's cot, and began to shake him. "Papa! Papa! Uncle Darroti is gone. Papa—"

"What, what?" He woke up groggily. "Zamatryna, what is it? Did you have a nightmare?"

"Uncle Darroti is gone! He isn't in his bed!"

She saw her father's face tighten, saw him glance at Darroti's empty cot. But he spoke cheerfully. "He probably just got up to relieve himself. I'm sure he's fine, Zamatryna."

Mim-Bim was buzzing again. Zamatryna wondered how her father didn't hear the vibrating wings. She began to cry. "I'm afraid."

Macsofo was awake now, blinking, and soon Timbor woke up as well, and not long after that, everyone was awake. Zamatryna couldn't stop crying, although she knew she was being a baby.

"Erolorit's right," Timbor said. "I'm sure Darroti went to the Porto-San. But I will go look for him, to reassure Zamatryna. Macsofo—"

"I'll come with you too, Father."

"I'm coming," Zamatryna said.

Timbor shook his head. "No, child. Stay here."

"I'm coming with you!"

Harani had gone to examine Darroti's bed. "One of his sheets is missing," she said, her voice curiously even.

"I'm coming with you," Zamatryna said, and at last they let her; everyone went except Aliniana and the cousins. The family stayed very close together, moving through the chill darkness, and Zamatryna thought fleetingly of how they had huddled together after they came through the door from Lémabantunk.

Darroti wasn't at the Porto-Sans, which were empty. He wasn't in the food tent or the shower tent. They wandered about the camp in the first glimmers of dawn, calling him. "Darroti! Where are you!" They were answered only by grumbles from people who had been asleep. But then there was a shout from the nearest edge of the camp, and all of them began to run. Erolorit swung Zamatryna up into his arms, for she wouldn't have been able to keep up with the adults.

They ran toward the perimeter, where they found a group of Americans, even paler than usual, gathered around something hanging from the fence.

"No no no no no no," Harani said. "No. Oh, no." Erolorit tried to cover Zamatryna's eyes, but she pushed his hands away. She knew what she would see. She had known since she woke up to Mim-Bim's buzzing.

It was Darroti. He had twisted his sheet into a rope and hanged himself from the fence.

3

Darroti

He's out of his body now, bobbing in the air like a feathered seed-pod, watching the scene in front of the fence. Dying hurt less than he expected: a few awful moments and then it was over, blessed relief. Since that terrible night with the knife, living has hurt far more than his death just did.

He knows he should have done this in Lémabantunk, before the family went into exile. If he had been able to summon the courage to do it there, they would not have had to leave. But he was a coward. If the dead cannot speak to the living, still some of his people believe that the dead can speak to the dead, that the dead commune in their own world.

That is what Gallicina believed. "We will not always be apart, dearest. You will conquer this demon of drink and then it will be fitting for us to tell our families that we love one another. When you have won the battle with the demon, we will be together for the rest of our lives, and after our lives, too. Not even death will separate us."

Not even death. That promise, the prophecy she intended as a blessing, became a curse; Darroti himself made it a curse, that terrible evening. And afterwards in Lémabantunk he did not dare to kill himself, even to spare his family from exile, because he could not face the possibility of meeting Gallicina. The very thought of her is an agony, even now.

Even now. Death has not released him from his crime; it will be his burden forever. He knows that. But now he has done what he needed to do. He has freed his family to leave the camp, freed them from the burden of his presence. He killed himself out of love for them, love that finally gave him the courage to put the twisted sheet around his neck. Surely they will be happy, as soon as they realize this.

They are not happy yet. The limp sack of his body leans against the woven metal fence; the Americans gesture in consternation, and his family howls and keens in rage and grief. Somehow, although he hangs above them, he sees them as if they are in front of him, too, sees all sides of them at once. Macsofo has collapsed onto the ground, beating at the dust with his fists. Erolorit, shoulders shaking, kneels next to Macsofo. Harani clings to the girl-child Zamatryna. Of all of them, only Zamatryna seems calm. He can tell that she was crying before the family found him, but she is not crying now.

Timbor stands apart from everyone, ashen, until the little girl breaks free of Harani and goes to comfort him, putting her arms around his waist and patting his stomach. He says nothing. His face is tracked with tears.

They should be happy. They will be happy, soon, once they have had a chance to think. If they cannot return to Lémabantunk, because Darroti's fear kept him tethered to them for too long, at least now they will not be stuck in the refugee camp because he is a criminal. He wrote them a note to tell them this. The note, written in their own beloved language, is in the pocket of his tunic. They will find it soon, and then they will know why he has done this. Because he loves them.

They find it; an American soldier finds it, and gently hands it to Timbor, putting a hand on the old man's shoulder. Timbor reads it. Now he will smile and be relieved.

He doesn't smile or look relieved. He puts a hand to his face, over his eyes; he weeps and staggers and holds out the note in a clenched fist to Erolorit, who takes it and reads, who hurls the paper with an oath to the ground, and Harani bends and picks it up and reads, tight-lipped, and hands it to Macsofo, who is sitting up now, his face and front smeared with dirt. Zamatryna stands with her arms around her grandfather, watching wide-eyed as the paper passes from hand to hand.

Darroti's note has not helped them, as he intended. It has all gone wrong. Everything he does goes wrong. That is his curse.

It is full morning now; a crowd has gathered to gape. The soldiers keep them back. Some people in white come, and Darroti watches as his empty body is cut down from the fence and gently laid on a stretcher, where it is covered with a sheet. One of the doctors closes Darroti's eyes, which will never see anything again. Darroti finds it oddly touching, this quiet reverence from someone who does not even know him.

The doctor who closed Darroti's eyes speaks now to Zamatryna, who speaks to Timbor and the others, who nod. Darroti's body is taken away. Darroti's spirit remains, bobbing above his family, and when they turn at last from the fence and, leaning heavily upon one another, make their way haltingly back to their tent, he is pulled along behind them, like a child's toy on a string.

They are back inside the tent now, and so is he, watching as they tell Aliniana and the cousins what has happened. Aliniana becomes a wailing, crumpled heap of cloth upon her bed, and the children, lower lips trembling, rush to their grandfather, who collapses now too, wracked with grief. Harani rocks Zamatryna. Erolorit and Macsofo curse and rage and shout, and their fury buffets him where he hangs beneath the ceiling.

They hate him. He loves them, did what he did only out of love for them, and they hate him. He turns all love for him into scorn and rage. He wonders helplessly how anyone could ever have loved him: his family or Gallicina, the daughter of the third cousin of the second wife of the Prime Minister, who was far too good for the drunken youngest son of a carpet merchant.

Beautiful, brave Gallicina, who fought for the right to be a Mendicant, that she might have equal standing in the Temple. How she must hate him now, for his clumsiness and stupidity! How he hates himself! He cannot bear to think of it. He cannot bear to watch his family, whose pain skewers him. Impaled, he twists and tries to flee, tries to escape through the roof of the tent, but he is trapped here by their tears.

Americans have come now, to counsel and comfort: someone in green, someone in white, someone in black wearing a pendant of crossed sticks, the symbol for silence. The person with the pendant, oddly, talks most of all. Little Zamatryna looks bewildered as she translates for the others, who stare stonily at the speaker.

He wishes that he could hear what they are saying. All he can perceive is the family's emotions, an oceanic expanse of loss. How can they grieve to lose him, who was only a burden to them? How can they hate him and so desperately mourn him at the same time?

It is unendurable; the feelings are unendurable. If he were still alive he would kill himself again, to be away from these feelings, but of course he would not be away from them, for he is not away from them now. He wonders what he would have done if he had known that, before he twisted the sheet. Is there no escape? He cannot leave the tent. Where can he go?

He goes into his memories; he goes into the past. He remembers the beauty of Lémabantunk, but it is only a pain to him, for he has lost that beauty and caused his family to lose it. He remembers the day he met Gallicina in the market, a day forever scented with cinnamon, but that, too, brings him no joy, for he must perforce remember also their terrible parting.

He remembers his mother, dead of fever. It is a comfort to remember Frella, for she died of fever before anything else happened, before she could know what a shameful son he was, before he had disgraced the family. When she died, he had not yet met Gallicina. When she died, he sometimes came home drunk with wine, but as yet it seemed nothing more than the foolishness of youth. She died loving her youngest child, believing him worthy of that love. How glad he is that she never realized she was wrong!

Delighted to have found solace, he wraps himself in his earliest memory of his mother; indeed, it is his earliest memory of anything. They are in the garden, at home. The air is rich with thyme and jasmine, and the soil is luxuriously warm under his bare feet; he delights in curling his toes into the earth, like little worms. Lizards run across his feet, tickling him, and he laughs, and laughs also at the butterflies, who are his friends. He has been toddling after Frella as she weeds and tends the vegetables; she has just picked some tender baby peas for him to eat, and now she is explaining to him why she must bless the peas before she pops them into his mouth.

"They might contain the spirits of the dead, Darroti."

He peers in wonder at the peas, pale and shining, which look only like peas to him, precious green pearls. He knows they will taste wonderful when he eats them; he can taste them already. "How could they?"

"Anything could."

"Anything at all?"

"Yes. That is why we lead lives of blessing."

"But how do you know if the peas have dead people in them?"

"We cannot know; no one knows for sure. Once, very long ago, the spirits of the dead could speak to us to let us know exactly where they were, but that is no longer true."

"Why not, Mama?"

And so she sits herself cross-legged in the dirt, pulls him onto her lap, and tells him the Tale of the Great Breaking, as the sun shines down on them and the butterflies frolic above the blossoms. "Once, at the beginning of time, there were four worlds. One was all earth, one all water, one all wind, and one all flame, and they were the only things in the cosmos, so far apart that none of them knew of any of the other three."

Darroti frowns. "But fire needs air." Even as a baby, he knows this. "To put the fire out, you put things on it to keep the air away. How could there be fire without air?"

Frella laughs and kisses him. "How smart you are, Darroti! You will hear the answer, if you listen. For indeed these worlds did not work like ours: for the Judges of each world decreed that everything on that world should be all alike, and that nothing should ever change, and the elemental creatures thought themselves content. But on each world one creature grew restless and desired change, desired to meet entities unlike itself. And the Judge of each world accounted this terrible rebellion, an infection that would make all the elemental spirits unhappy, and so the four were sent into exile.

"Each Element wandered for a long time through the Void, weeping in great loneliness, but finally all four of them met, and they rejoiced, for they had found what they were seeking in the very punishment imposed on them for having sought it. And then they stopped cursing their Judges and blessed the Judges' wisdom instead, and they formed a village, and that village became our world. And they loved one another so much that soon there were many children in the village. Fire and Air gave birth to the sun, to flames that need both their parents to survive; Fire and Earth gave birth to the moon; Fire and Water gave birth to oceans and rivers and streams. Earth and Water gave birth to the lands, to meadows and mountains; Air and Water gave birth to storms and rainbows. Fire and Air gave birth to Mind, to thoughts and fancies; Fire and Water gave birth to Sensation, to feelings.

"Now these last two things were the most troublesome of the elemental children, for they were unruly and sought to marry everything they saw, and the mountains did not want the burden of thought, and the rivers did not want the burden of pain. And so the

Elements, all four together, created new homes for Mind and Sensation, homes to which they would be bound: little simple plants and animals in which thought and feeling could dwell. Only living things are made of all four Elements, you see. But as change was the law of this world, the thing the Elements had come here seeking and therefore the one thing they could never banish—both their treasure and their curse—the plants and animals began to change, to become larger and more varied and more numerous, until there were more of them than their parents could count. All had different portions of Mind and Sensation, and people—who came last in the chain of changes—believed that they had more than anyone else.

"Now the world was getting crowded with all these creatures, for they kept loving and marrying each other and having children. The Elements were loath to banish love and could not banish change, and so—to make room for more love in the world—they decreed that each creature's body would die to make way for new ones, but that each creature's Mind and Sensation, combined to form that creature's Spirit, would float free above the earth, to inspire and protect all things still in their bodies. Thus it is that the spirits of trees maintain us in the hope of spring, even in the depths of winter; thus it is that the spirits of worms give us endurance to burrow in the darkness of our lives, seeking sustenance; thus it is that the spirits of birds allow us to soar even while we are still earthbound.

"But the spirits of people were restless, ever ambitious, ever proud, always wanting to be something in themselves rather than merely to comfort or inspire others. Too often they caused dissension and disharmony, creating nightmares and regrets in those they had left behind. And so the Elements conferred with the other creatures, and it was decided that human spirits would be allowed to share bodies with simpler creatures, whose spirits could teach the human spirits simplicity, and give them peace. The more complex and troubled the person, the simpler the creature chosen for that person's spirit. Thus the spirit of someone who had died while very young or very old, someone whose mind was easy and smooth, might share a body with a monkey or a dolphin or a dog, a complicated beast; but the spirit of a scheming prince would find itself in the body of an acorn or a grub, for only there could the prince's plotting soul be taught to cherish basic things, rain and wind and food.

"Now this system worked well, because spirits and bodies could still speak to one another, and the prince who learned simplicity could teach it to whomever among his former court sought the same lessons. And thus the friends and family of simple folk had wondrous converse with monkeys and dolphins and dogs, and the friends and family of the great learned to appreciate the gentle counsel of seedlings and slugs, starfish and salamanders.

"But it came to pass that a very powerful prince lost his wife and son in childbirth, and was inconsolable. His son would have been his heir, and his wife had been his chief advisor. She understood the ways of the court better than he did, and knew whom to flatter and whom to avoid, which courtiers would respond to threats and which to gifts, and which tradespeople would manufacture gifts— if gifts were required—most quickly and cheaply. And she had been young when she died, and very beautiful.

"The baby boy's spirit became enclosed within a gray stallion, that he might learn power and movement who had died dependent and confined. But the mother's spirit was housed in a reed, for her mind had shaped itself to the mazelike ways of the court, and she needed to learn the wisdom of straight lines, and of being part of an equal multitude rather than standing above and alone, and of valuing sunlight and water rather than gems and costly gowns.

"Now the prince still loved them both, as much as he could truly love anything, and every day he rode on the stallion to visit his wife among the reeds. But whenever the stallion spoke joyously of the glories of freedom, of galloping under the sky, the father grew more angry and bitter that his son had not lived to run in human form. And whenever his wife spoke of the contentment of drawing nutrients from the earth, the prince despaired that he had lost his advisor, who had so cunningly guided him through the bogs of politics. And, just as fathers sometimes begrudge the bond between mothers and babies, which excludes them, the prince began to grow jealous of the growing love between the stallion and the reed, for both of them relished the wind, which meant nothing to him, and rhapsodized about the flavor of rain, which to the prince was only an annoyance which forced him to cover his head.

"One day he rode to the reeds in a great quandary, for dark rumors were swirling in the court that his youngest brother and several courtiers were plotting against him. Yet he had no proof, and if he accused them or acted against them without cause, he would hurt his own cause with his father, the king, who already thought him unbalanced with grief. And so he urgently sought his wife's counsel, for once she would have known just what to do.

"He told the entire story to the reed, but his wife's spirit said only, 'How tiresome the court is! If you lived here by the river, you would know the magic of the dawn.'

"'But I do not live by the river. I live in the court, and must continue to live there. Help me as you used to do!'

"'This is truer help than any I ever gave you, husband. Learn to love the sunlight and the soil, and scheming courtiers will lose their power.'

"And then the stallion said, 'Oh, Mother, how true that is! How clear the sunlight is today, and how moist and fertile the earth!'

"But nothing in his life but loss and rage were clear to the prince, and he understand now that he had lost not only his moist and fertile wife, but her counsel, and thus his own hopes of survival in the court. And bitterly he said, 'Wife, are you happier now as a stupid reed than you were in my arms, when we loved one another and plotted the increase of our power?'

" 'Oh, yes! I have learned happiness you never could have taught me, for the truest love is love of life, and the truest power lies in being part of many, as reeds are by the riverbank.'

"And the prince, who no longer loved his life, and who thought he would be nothing if he were not first among men, flew into a rage: and he reached down and tore his wife's reed from the soil, and broke it into two pieces, and cast them on the ground. And the stallion, in horror and terror at what the prince had done, reared up and struck him with its hooves, and the prince died in great pain.

"And the Elements saw then, in grief, that the living and the dead could not be permitted to speak to one another, for the living who most needed the wisdom of the dead would ever be the greatest danger to the peace and comfort of the dead. And so the Elements decreed that henceforth, there should be silence between spirits still in human bodies and spirits who dwelt elsewhere in the world; and the broken reed, which the prince had cast onto the ground in the form of an X, became the symbol of that silence, the Great Breaking."

Little Darroti, listening to his mother tell the story in the warm garden, leans sleepily against her breast. He has not understood most of the tale; it has washed over him in soothing waves, and he has caught only parts of it. He touches one of the pearly peas in his hand and says, "Then there might be a prince in this pea?"

"Yes indeed, Darroti. And you would not know, because the spirit could not speak to tell you. And so you must bless everything you eat, lest some spirit go unthanked for helping your body grow."

Little Darroti says, "Thank you for feeding me, peas," and puts them in his mouth. They taste like water and sunshine and love; their flavor fills him, the most wonderful thing he has ever known, and he laughs in joy.

But dead Darroti, cocooning himself in that memory, finds he cannot remain there: for now he must remember everything else, too, all of the rest of his life, both the happiness and the pain, the memories coming faster, faster, until they reach the present, the now, the tent in the refugee camp in America, in exile, where his family is still grieving, where their grief is still like knives in flesh he no longer possesses.

He understands then that he cannot escape into the past, for every moment of the past contains everything that has happened to him, and all memories will lead him back here. But he understands something else, too. For his spirit is not contained in a reed or a stallion or a pea. It floats unmoored in his family's tent. And if that means that he cannot learn the wisdom of leaves or lizards, it also means that the history of spirits is different in this world. Perhaps there has been no Great Breaking here; perhaps the living and the dead still can speak to one another.

He must pray that it is so, for his family's pain is unendurable. Timbor staggers out of the tent now, to use the Porto-Sans; one of the Americans goes with him, and Darroti is pulled helplessly after them. It is his father to whom he is tethered, then, for his father's pain is greatest.

How can Darroti speak? How can he comfort Timbor? He tries to form words, but nothing happens. He tries to sing, but the melody goes nowhere.

He weeps, in rage and confusion; he weeps, and watches as his father, stumbling through the dust of the camp, wipes his own cheek. The American looks up for a moment, frowning, and pulls off his hat. There on the brim is a dark circle, a raindrop, a miracle of water in the cloudless desert.

4

ROOMS

The weeks after Darroti died were terrible. It was August, and a life-sucking heat had settled over the desert. The sun beat mercilessly on the tents, and everyone yearned for rain that showed no sign of coming. What came was smoke: for there were brushfires all across the state, and even though the closest was miles away, the smell of ashes pervaded everything, making the air nearly unbreathable. In the drought, showers were rationed even more strictly than usual, and everything, including drinking water, tasted of burning. Two old people and a baby in the camp died of lung problems. Every day the Army people reassured the refugees that the fires were coming no closer. No one wanted to think about what would happen if they did, if the refugees had to be evacuated.

"Let the fires come," Erolorit said grimly. "If we had to be evacuated, perhaps we could escape, and get away from this terrible place."

"We would be recaptured if we tried to escape," Macsofo said. "Either we would be recaptured or we would die of thirst."

Harani shook her head. "Hush, both of you. You're scaring the children! Little ones, the Army will keep the fire away. No one else will die. Everything will be all right."

But everything wasn't all right, couldn't possibly be all right, for Darroti's death loomed above all else. The adults were frantic with grief, and the children were bewildered with fear and confusion, and the family was beset by a seemingly endless stream of Americans. Many of their fellow refugees, even the few other children Zamatryna and her cousins had become friendly with at school, avoided them, for suicide was a shameful thing in many of their countries, a thing that brought bad luck to anyone associated with it. But Americans, determined to be helpful, flocked to the family's tent. The family quickly discerned that helping, in America, meant fixing or erasing: an impossible proposition, since Darroti's death could not be repaired or undone.

The Army had initiated an investigation into how Darroti could have killed himself on the fence without any of the guards noticing and stopping him. They learned that one soldier guarding that section of the fence had fallen asleep at his post, and the other had gone to the Porto-Sans. An officer wearing a jacket decorated with a great many gew-gaws, an outfit entirely inappropriate for the brutal heat, came and stood stiffly in their tent, holding his hat in his hand. He told them that the Army apologized for its carelessness. He promised that both of the soldiers would be punished. "I really am so terribly sorry," he said at the end, and his voice cracked, although it had been strong before.

"Tell him," Timbor told Zamatryna irritably, "that punishing these men will not bring Darroti back. Darroti would have found a way to do what he did anyway. It is not their fault. I cannot blame them unless I also blame Darroti's own brothers, who also fell asleep. I do not want to blame anyone. What kind of land is this, where people are punished for doing what their bodies need to do? Tell him, Zamatryna. I cannot say it properly in English, and I am weary of wrestling with their words!"

But the officer, when Zamatryna had told him, shook his head. "Those soldiers had a job to do, sir, and they didn't do it, and now your son's dead. And I just hope you'll let us know what we can do to help you now."

"Nothing," Timbor said in English. "Nothing, unless you let us leave the camp!"

The officer looked pained. "There are laws, sir. We're doing the best we can, but you have to give us better information."

And so they were visited by the same social workers and lawyers who had talked to them before, who asked them the same questions; but now there were new people, too, therapists and ministers and a puzzling procession of ladies bringing casseroles. Evidently this was an American funerary custom.

"I know it's a little silly," the first casserole lady told Zamatryna. She had puffy hair of a yellow Zamatryna had never seen before, and she wore a shirt picturing animals with impossibly large eyes. But she smelled like flowers, and she was kind. She was the wife of the man who had worn the crossed sticks and yammered at them about Heaven and Hell, both places the family was now determined to avoid. "You get your food at the cafeteria tent, I know, and you don't have anywhere to keep this. But it's home-cooked, and food's a real comfort when you're hurting. This is what my sister-in-law brought to my house when my mama died, and it made me feel better, and I got the recipe from her, and now it's what I bring folks who've lost someone they love. I hope you like it, even though it's not anything you'd eat wherever you came from."

She'd brought paper plates and plastic forks. She insisted that the family sit on their cots while she served them the meal, and she listened respectfully while Timbor blessed it, instead of trying to force her husband's blessing on them. It was very strange food, little bits of chicken and broccoli and raisins suspended in orange jello, but they were grateful for it, because it meant that they wouldn't have to go to the crowded cafeteria tent, which was even hotter, if possible, than every other place in the camp. They ate all of the strange dish, so that the kind woman who had brought it to them wouldn't have to take it back home, and they could tell that she was pleased.

She must have told her friends, because after that there was a different casserole every night. None of the others featured jello: most included vast quantities of cheese. If many were nearly inedible, some were very good, and some of the people brought dessert, too, cookies and brownies and pies. One evening someone brought Rocky Road ice cream, packed in a cooler, and the cold sweet stuff was such a startling, improbable wonder in the charred heat that Zamatryna never ate ice cream after that without remembering the first time she had tasted it. For the rest of her life, Rocky Road ice cream would be the flavor of hope; for if there was ice cream in this horrible place, maybe there were other good things waiting to be discovered, too.

Most of the casserole people only visited them once, but the first lady, the one who had brought them the chicken in orange jello, came back many times. They learned that her name was Lisa, and that her husband, Stan, was the pastor of the Living Waters Bible Church. They were afraid that he would come back, too, but he never did. Lisa told Zamatryna that he was too busy building houses, which was the work he did to make money, because his church was so small. "It's only ten people right now. Everybody comes to our house for Bible study on Tuesdays and worship on Sundays. They sit on folding chairs in our living room. Stan so wants a real church, but I tell him a real church is wherever two or three people are gathered together, just like the Bible says. When Mama died she left me her big old house, and just as soon as Stan gets enough money, he'll fix that up into a fine church building. But first we have to clean out all of Mama's stuff, and that's slow work, because it makes me so sad. I sure do feel for your loss, honey."

Zamatryna didn't understand much of this, but she liked Lisa, who praised her English and brought her and her cousins crayons and coloring books of their very own, so they wouldn't have to share the torn, grubby ones in the school tent. Lisa brought books, too, and read to them, holding Poliniana in her lap while Zamatryna and the twins sat in front of her. She read them Dr. Seuss books, which made all of them giggle, and fairy tales which were frightening but had happy endings, and Bible stories, scarcely distinguishable from the fairy tales in their implausibility. The adults were wary of Lisa, but grateful to her for entertaining the children; whenever she came, they sat quietly and talked among themselves.

One evening she came and said glumly, "I can't read to you tonight, kids. I'm sorry. I thought I'd be driving Stan's van, see, so I put the books in that, but Stan and I got our wires crossed, and he took the van and left me the Ford. I sure am sorry. We can play word games, or color."

"I want *The Cat in the Hat*," Poliniana said, pouting.

"I know you do, sweetie. You like that funny story, huh? I sure am sorry I don't have the books with me."

"I can say it," Zamatryna offered shyly. "There won't be any pictures, but I can say the words."

Lisa laughed. "Well, good for you, honey! You tell us as much of the story as you remember, and you other kids can step in when she forgets something, eh? That's good. That's better than reading."

"But I remember all of it," Zamatryna said, puzzled. "It's not very long." And she proceeded to recite *The Cat in the Hat* in its entirety, for she'd known it all for weeks now. Her cousins listened happily, but Lisa looked more and more astonished.

When Zamatryna was done, Lisa gave her a big hug and said, "Listen to that! What a memory you have!"

"Well, it wasn't very hard to learn," Zamatryna said. "I used to learn longer poems than that, at home."

"You did? Really? That's wonderful. Can you tell me some?"

"I don't know," said Zamatryna, suddenly shy. She put her hand over her pocket, where Mim-Bim buzzed angrily, forever trying to escape: Zamatryna had used three safety pins, a gift from one of the

American nurses, to close off the places where the beetle could have crawled out. She didn't understand how the insect could both demand silence—for it still traced its perpetual X—and attempt to flee into the world where everyone would see it, and probably kill it. Unsure what to do, she fed it and kept it captive, hoping that something would become clearer soon.

X. She felt the beetle crawling in her pocket, under her hand. Did that mean she wasn't supposed to speak the language of Léma-bantunk to this nice woman? Zamatryna looked across the tent at the grown-ups, who were sitting together on their cots, whispering; her father had his arms around Timbor, who was weeping into a towel. Timbor carried that towel everywhere with him now. It was perpetually damp, even in the drought.

There was no one she could ask what to do. "You wouldn't understand it," she told Lisa. "It's not in English."

"Well, of course not. But you could tell me what it meant, couldn't you? And I'd like to hear some of it, to hear what the language sounds like."

"It doesn't sound like anything," Zamatryna said, her head down. "That's what the people say who keep making us talk to them. They say they've never heard it before."

"Well then," Lisa said kindly, "you're teaching them something new. But you don't have to if you don't want to, honey. I didn't mean to make you sad. I just think it's great how smart you are, that's all. Not many little girls could learn entire books."

"Your children don't do that?" Zamatryna said.

Lisa shook her head. "The good Lord hasn't seen fit to give me children of my own. Me and Stan, we were talking about adopting an orphan baby, maybe from China or Russia or Africa, but it's awfully expensive. We can't afford it yet, not even with the inheritance from Mama. So when the government decided to put the refugees here, we figured it was God's way of letting us help other people's families."

Zamatryna blushed. "I didn't mean—I meant children here. Children in this country. I meant—"

"That's all right, honey. I think I've got it. When you said 'your children' you meant 'children in your country,' not 'Lisa and Stan's children,' is that it?"

"Yes. I'm sorry."

"Why are you sorry? You don't have to be sorry about anything. But this is your country now too, sweetie. You're one of our children, too, you and Poliniana here and Rikko and Jamfret. You're all American children."

"No we're not. We're not! Because they won't let us out!" And to her horror, Zamatryna began to cry: because she was tired of being so hot and breathing ashes and never seeing flowers; because she didn't know if her grandfather would ever smile again; because she didn't know what to do about Mim-Bim and couldn't ask anyone; because she couldn't fall asleep without seeing her uncle's body on the fence; because she had already begun to forget parts of the poems she had memorized at home, and her wooden doll would never have eyes or hair again, and her stomach hurt from too much of that evening's casserole. "We'll never be Americans! We'll never be anything here!"

"Oh, sweetheart." Lisa was crying too. "Oh, sweetheart, of course you're something. Of course you are. You all are! Who told you—"

"What are you doing to her?" Erolorit had risen from his cot and made his way through the crowded tent to their corner. "Why is my child crying?"

"She's not doing anything," Zamatryna said in their own language, wiping snot off her face. "She's being nice, Papa. Don't be angry at her. I was crying because I miss Uncle Darroti, that's all."

She didn't, not really. She missed the old mirthful Darroti, but not the gloomy one who'd wound up on the fence. But she knew that all the adults missed Darroti, and she wanted to distract her father from his anger against Lisa, who had done nothing wrong.

"She's filling you with her husband's stories, isn't she, saying you'll go to their hell—"

"No," Zamatryna said. "No, that wasn't what she said, Papa, she didn't say that—"

"Why can't you leave?" Lisa said. The other adults had roused themselves now; Macsofo pulled Poliniana and the twins, who looked bewildered, to the other side of the tent. "Why won't they let you leave the camp? Please tell me. I want to help you. Zamatryna, will you ask him?"

She didn't have to ask him. She already knew. "They won't let us leave because we can't tell them where we came from. We don't have papers and they don't know our language and we can't—we can't prove our city was ever real. So we can't leave and we can't go home. We have to stay here."

"This woman has to go away," Erolorit told Zamatryna in their own language, and then said in English, "I am sorry, but you must leave our tent. My daughter is upset. You cannot come back here."

"I'll sponsor you," Lisa said. "My husband and I can sponsor you to stay here. We're a church. We can do that. We can help you get out."

Erolorit shook his head. "I am sorry, but no one can help us get out. We are trapped here. You cannot sponsor us unless we can convince the Army that we cannot go home, or unless we can show them where we came from. It is too complicated. I am sorry: you have to leave now. Please do not come back here. My daughter is too upset."

"No!" Zamatryna said. "Don't make her go away! She's nice! She's my friend! I like her!"

"Hush," Harani said, putting her hands on Zamatryna's shoulders. "You are trying to be kind," she told Lisa, "we know that, my husband knows that, but it would be better if—"

"I'll go," Lisa said. "Of course I will, if you don't want me here. I'm sorry I've upset you." She stood up, gathering her books of word games and putting them back into her tote bag, which showed a cartoon child kneeling in front of an X. Zamatryna saw that her hands were shaking, and when she spoke again, her voice was shaking too. "Good-bye, kids. Good luck. I hope I'll see you again sometime."

Then she was gone, and Zamatryna, angry and bewildered, looked up at Erolorit. "Why did you do that? She was our friend!"

"No, I don't think she was. Her husband said—"

"He wasn't even here, Papa! And she never said anything mean about burning forever, even if he did! Why did you send her away?"

"Because you are my child, not hers," Erolorit snapped, and Harani murmured something Zamatryna couldn't make out.

"Peace," Timbor said. He stood clutching his damp towel. "Peace, all of you! Zamatryna, come here. Come sit on my bed. I want to talk to you. The rest of you will listen too, but Zamatryna will sit with me, eh?"

And so she sat on his lap, and Timbor hugged her and said, "Little one, we have grown distracted by our grief, we grown-ups; we have yearned so after Darroti, who is no longer with us, that we have not paid enough attention to you and to your cousins, who are right in front of our eyes. And so it has been easy to let the American woman talk to you for hours and tell you her stories, and perhaps, yes, certainly she was kind to do so. But all good parents want to be with their children when their children are upset, and so I think that when you began to weep and you were with her, and not with us, Erolorit blamed himself for not being the person to whom you had voiced your pain. And if there is fault there, it lies with us, not with her, but Erolorit grew angry with her as a way of being angry with himself. Zamatryna, do you understand?"

"No." She felt as if she understood nothing here. She had understood things at home. Had the door into exile done something to her brain?

Timbor sighed. "Never mind. I suppose I should not have expected that you would, for you are still very small, for all that you have a big mind and a big heart. You will understand one day. Erolorit, am I right?"

Erolorit stared at his hands, clenched in his lap, and didn't answer. Harani touched his shoulder and said, "Timbor, even if you are right, it is more complicated than that. We have lost our home and we have lost our brother, and if now we lose our children to this new place and these people, what will we have left?"

"That is exactly right," Timbor said quietly. "And yet we have no choice. For this is our home now, and theirs, and we must hope that they do well here. It is the only home they will ever have, for we cannot go back. And we must all learn to live in it."

"Even if we never get out of the camp?" Macsofo's voice was bitter.

"Even then. If we never leave the camp, then the camp must be our home, and we must live in it fully. And so from now on we will do what everyone does. We will send the casseroles away and eat in the cafeteria tent. We will no longer remain by ourselves, for if we do that, how will we ever find anything to replace what we no longer have?"

"There is nothing here to find," Erolorit said. "We have been here long enough to know that."

"And yet we must keep looking," said Timbor with a shrug. He picked up his towel, folded it, and handed it to Harani. "This is partly my fault. I have wept too much."

Zamatryna's mother shook her head. "No, Timbor! How can you say that? No one could blame you—"

"Perhaps not. But it is time for all of us to learn to live with our loss, rather than dying of it. I am your elder, and I have spoken. Tomorrow morning we will have breakfast with everyone, in the cafeteria tent."

And so they did: breakfast and lunch and dinner, and school as usual, although smoke now hung so thickly over the camp that everyone's eyes watered and grew red. Even though the actual fires were no closer, the smoke was so bad that the Army had begun to make plans to evacuate the refugees after all, to another place farther out in the desert. There was more truck traffic in and out of the gates than usual; the refugees were told to pack their things, although no one was sure when the move would take place. The transfer kept being delayed because the Nuts were making trouble at the new site. Several of them had disguised themselves as Army people and torn down a stretch of fence. And so the refugees waited, while everyone coughed and choked, while infants and the elderly wheezed. The hospital tent was full to overflowing, although it provided no shelter from the smoke.

Even though Timbor claimed to have done with weeping, his damp towel somehow never dried. The family took to passing it from hand to hand, wiping their faces with it, covering noses and mouths. The sun, when they could see it at all, shone as a small, bright red disk overhead. There were no stories, no casseroles, no ice cream: only smoke, and confusion, and fatigue. It was such a strange, dreamlike time for all of them, a time out of time, that the wonder of the towel that refused to dry went by without comment. Wonder would have taken energy, and they had none left to spare.

They packed their things as they had been told to do, although there was little enough to pack. They had been told that their section of tents would be evacuated on a Thursday morning in late August, although areas of the camp had prepared to move before and then been postponed. But on that Thursday morning they were ready, standing in line in the murk with many others, trucks towering in the gloom ahead of them. Around them moved other vehicles driven by trusted volunteers, collecting tents and supplies to take to the new camp.

Step by step the line moved closer to the trucks. Zamatryna, one hand held by her mother and one by her father, Mim–Bim crawling ceaselessly in her pocket, could make out the olive-green canvas now, the ugly metal tailpipe jutting out from behind the truck bed, the deep pattern of the tire-treads. She wondered if they would have a bigger tent in the new camp, if the air would really be any better. Her chest hurt.

Step. Step. And then suddenly there was a great boom and a rushing wind, and screaming, a great outcry of voices, people running and cursing, someone nearby yelling in English, "What's happening, what's happening?" And the smell of new smoke. Flames: Zamatryna could see flames, could hear sirens now. What was happening? Her parents clutched her hands as people around them ran; the soldier supervising their truck had fled, and people were getting out of the truck now, running off into the smoke and the howling, and Timbor was saying, "Is everyone here? Are we all here? What happened?"

"Bomb," someone running by them shouted. "Someone set off a bomb." And the howling got louder and so did the sirens, and vehicles were driving very fast in every direction, raising yet more dust, and suddenly Lisa was next to them, her eyes wild and her face smudged with dirt.

"Zamatryna. Are you all here? Is everyone here?" It was the same question Timbor had asked. Zamatryna stared at her stupidly, saw Lisa counting them, her lips moving. "All right. Get into my van, come on, get in, all of you—"

She pushed them toward the van. Erolorit resisted and Lisa said to Zamatryna, "This is your chance to get out of here, do you understand? Tell your father that! Get into the van. There are blankets in the back, I was ferrying blankets to the new place, get under them. Hurry!"

"Do as she says," Timbor said, and they did: clambered into the van and under the blankets, which smelled like smoke and wool and other things: spoiled milk, peanut butter, soap. The floor of the van was very hard. Zamatryna lay cradled against her mother's stomach, and then the van door slammed shut and the engine started and they were being driven away, very quickly, too quickly, the van jouncing their spines as it hit every pothole, while Lisa wept and railed in the front seat. "Oh Lord, Lord, sweet Jesus, help me, forgive me Lord, you know I'm doing this to help this poor family who doesn't have a place to call their own, keep us safe Lord and don't let us get caught and help me figure out what to tell Stan, oh Jesus help all the poor burned people, how could they do it, who did it, it must have been a Nut who snuck in a bomb oh Lord save your fallen people and protect them, protect all of us and please dear God don't let the Army catch me smuggling these people out or I'll be shit on toast, Lord, and I don't want to go to jail again but this might be their only chance, dear Jesus who has mercy on sinners have mercy on me and all of us and protect these poor people, God, help me protect them because that's what your Son would have done, Jesus, that's what You'd do and I'm just trying to follow You even if it means breaking the law, oh God, how am I going to explain this to Stan?"

The prayer went on and on, rising and falling, until finally the road smoothed out and the jouncing grew less and Lisa stopped praying and said, "The radio, there will be news, why didn't I think of that," and there was a click and voices filled the van, people talking about an apparent terrorist attack on the refugee camp outside Gerlach. A truck bomb had sparked fires which were now sweeping the compound. At least fifty people were dead.

"Oh God, oh dear Lord," said Lisa, her voice thick with tears. She turned the radio off again. "Oh, all those poor people! I'm sorry. I can't stand to listen to it. You back there, are you okay? Are you all okay? Please tell me you're okay."

"I want to sit up," Poliniana said.

"No, sweetie, I'm sorry, you'd better stay down. Stay hidden. Stay under the blankets, all right? And if we get stopped, don't talk, whatever you do, okay?"

"Where are you taking us?" Timbor asked.

Zamatryna heard Lisa take a deep breath. "I'm taking you to Mama's house. You can stay there while we figure out what to do next. It's a bit away from town, by the river, and it's on a chunk of property so there aren't any neighbors right there; that will help. It's filled with old-lady stuff, but it's better than the camp. There are a bunch of rooms and two bathrooms and a kitchen. Oh sweet Jesus, I'd better call Stan. He'll be worried sick about me. Where's my cell? Okay, here it is . . . Stan? Yes, it's me, I'm all right. Honey, I'm fine. I'm fine. I got out. No, I'm not coming home. I have to go to Mama's house. Would you meet me there? Just meet me there, please. Go over there now and turn on the AC, all right? Stock the fridge with sandwich stuff, and make some lemonade. No, I can't come home first. No, I can't tell you why. I'll explain when I see you. I'm fine. No, I'm not hurt, I promise. No, I'm not in shock, or maybe I am, I guess I must be, but I know what I'm doing, really. I'm fine. I love you too. I'll see you in a little while, sweetheart."

It seemed like more than a little while; they lay on the hard floor of the van for what felt like days. Toward the end Zamatryna, exhausted with fear and bewilderment, managed to doze. When the van stopped, she woke up and poked her head out of the blankets.

Trees. That was the first thing she saw through the windows of the van. There were trees here! Her heart gave a great leap, for if there were trees, perhaps there would be grass and flowers too. "Trees!" she told her mother, and Harani nodded, looking dazed.

"He doesn't like this," Macsofo said grimly. They were all sitting up now. "I don't think he'll let us stay."

Zamatryna blinked, wondering what her uncle meant, and then saw that Lisa was outside the van, talking to her husband, who kept shaking his head. He was wearing blue jeans and a shirt with a picture of a frog on it; he looked a lot less scary without his black clothing and the symbol for silence, but Macsofo was right: Stan clearly wasn't happy. He and Lisa were standing a few feet away, but they moved closer to the van now, until Zamatryna could hear them.

"Stan, they were trapped in the camp! They don't have papers, and I don't know why but it's not fair that they couldn't leave, and this was my chance to get them out of there. Wherever they came from, they've suffered enough. I only did what the Spirit guided me to do."

Stan shook his head again. "But if the police—"

"If the police figure it out, I'll go to jail." Lisa started to cry again. "Stan, it's a mess back there, it's horrible, a lot more people are going to be dead, the good Lord rest their souls, and I don't think these folks will be missed. Everybody will think they died in the fire, that's all. Nobody's going to look for them here. We can hide them here until we figure out what to do."

He put his arm around her, but then he shook his head. "And how long do you think that will be?"

Lisa wiped her face. "I don't know. Stan, they need to come inside now; they've been lying on the floor of that van for two hours, all the way from Gerlach, and they need water and they probably need to use the bathroom."

"Lisa, this house is my church—"

"No," she said, and pushed him away. Her voice had grown quieter, but she was facing the van, and Zamatryna could see that her face was resolute, the tears gone. "This is my mama's house. It's mine, Stan."

He coughed. "It's *ours*. That's the law, Lisa. Nevada's a community property state and in Christian marriage two people become one, and either way the house is mine too—"

"No, sweetheart. I'm sorry, but Mama left this house to me, and I don't *care* if the State says it's half yours, and how dare you even think about something like that when I just escaped from that fire! I could have been killed! I grew up in this house and it's mine and that's the right of it, State or not, and you know it, and these people are coming inside!"

"The Law of Hearts," Timbor murmured. Zamatryna saw that he was holding his towel, which dripped silently onto the blankets.

Stan said something Zamatryna couldn't hear; Lisa answered in a bellow. "No, Stan, it is *not* your church, not yet! Someday it will be your church, when *I* say it can be, but it isn't yet, because we don't have the money to turn it into a church yet. And even if it were a church, we couldn't put it to any better use than using it to help these folks! They need to come inside now. They're coming inside. Into my house. Are you going to welcome them and show them Christian hospitality, Stan Buttle, or are you going to stand in the way? Do I have to ask you what Jesus would do, Reverend Buttle?"

He seemed to shrink, then. He blushed and stammered and came to the door of the van and said, "Please come in. Please come in, all of you. I'm sorry. I—I was so worried about Lisa and then—"

"Never mind," Lisa said tartly behind him. "They don't want to hear your apologies. Stop blocking the door, honey, and let them get out."

They were all stiff from the long ride; Timbor stumbled climbing out of the van, and Stan caught his arm and said, "Are you okay, old man? Be careful, now. Please come in. Bring your family inside, where it's cooler."

It was already cooler here than it had been at the camp, and the air was less smoky, although a gray pall still hung over everything. Zamatryna stared at the trees, and saw, beyond them, a glimpse of water. And there was a little patch of grass and some flowers, yes, beautiful purple flowers she'd never seen before, growing on a bush almost as tall as she was. They smelled wonderful, even in the smoke, and she buried her head in them.

"What are they?" she asked Lisa.

"That's lavender," Lisa said. "Don't you have lavender at home, honey?"

"We have other flowers," Zamatryna said, and Harani tugged gently at her shoulder.

"There will be time for the flowers later, Zamatryna. Come inside."

It was dark and cool inside the house, amazingly cool; the air didn't smell like smoke. "Thank goodness the AC's working," Lisa said with a sigh. She led them to a room with great puffy furniture which cradled them when they sat on it, and brought them glasses of a drink that was sweet and tart at the same time. They sat in the semi-darkness, sipping and blinking. Zamatryna thought that perhaps this was all a dream, and feared that she would wake up soon and find herself back in the burning camp.

"I'll turn on the TV," Stan said. "There will be news—"

"No," Lisa said. "We've seen enough for one day. I don't want to look at any of it. I just want to be here and be peaceful and thank the Lord for my deliverance and not think about what happened back there, Stan, all right? Now, who wants a sandwich?"

Lisa's sandwiches were nothing like the ones at the camp, which had always been limp and stale. These were wonders: the bread nutty and firm, the lettuce watery and crisp, the cheese and meat more flavorful than anything the family had yet eaten in America. "I'm sorry it's not fancier," Lisa said, but Timbor shook his head.

"It is wonderful food. Thank you." And Zamatryna, remembering the chicken in orange jello, was glad that Lisa hadn't made anything more fancy.

When she had eaten two sandwiches, Zamatryna clambered out of her puffy chair to explore the room. It was filled with little tables, and on every table were pictures and statues of very strange men wearing baggy clothing. Their shoes were far too large for their feet, and their eyes were too large for their faces; they had giant red lips and giant red noses, and tufts of bright orange hair sticking out on either side of their heads. Many of them were weeping.

Zamatryna touched one of the statues, gingerly; it was hard and glassy, cool to her touch. "Are these holy people?" she said. Perhaps this was what Mendicants looked like, in America.

Lisa laughed. "Bless you, child, they're clowns! Mama loved clowns. She went to a circus when she was a little girl, and a clown gave her a balloon, and she's collected clowns ever since. I have to pack them all up and sell them or something, because we don't have room for them at our house, but Mama loved them so much that I can't bear to put them in boxes. Whenever we went on a trip and asked her what she wanted, she told us to bring her another clown, and if there was a clown in a store or a catalog, you could bet she'd find it. I have to find a clown museum someplace; Mama would want them to go somewhere special. I wrote to Ringling Brothers, but they never answered. Bless you, sweetheart, you aren't understanding a word I'm saying, are you?"

Zamatryna shook her head. "Why are they crying?"

"Well, that's a, you know, that's the way people paint clowns a lot. Clowns make people laugh; that's their job, but the tears are because they're unhappy on the inside. They have a cheerful front, but they've got pain in them they'd never let you know about, and that's why people love them, because we all feel like that sometimes. And Mama, well, she had some hard times in her life, but she never let it show. So I guess she could relate to clowns. Come on: if everybody's done eating, I'll show you the rest of the house."

The rest of the house was filled with more clowns, and also filled with marvels: a giant metal box that held food and light and coldness, a box on top of that one that spit out chunks of frozen water if you touched a button, shiny metal mouths that gave water if you turned a lever. There were no Porto-Sans here. The toilets were inside, in impossibly clean rooms that smelled like flowers instead of shit. The carpets were so soft that Zamatryna didn't understand why Lisa kept fretting that there weren't enough beds. "We can sleep on the floor," she said, and Lisa laughed.

"Bless you, Zamatryna! We'll do better than that, I promise. But maybe not tonight. Tonight some of you may have to sleep on the floor; I'm so sorry. I've got pillows and blankets, anyway. We'll work the rest of it out tomorrow, when we can all think better. You're out of that camp. You're all alive and safe. That's what's important."

Zamatryna saw a spasm of pain cross her grandfather's face, because Darroti wasn't alive. But Lisa hadn't meant to say anything hurtful, and Zamatryna knew it, and she knew that Timbor knew it, too. And so he smiled and said, "Thank you."

Dinner was more sandwiches and more lemonade. Lisa insisted on washing the extra clothing they'd brought with them in another wonder, a box that did laundry with a cheerful thumping and gurgling. "I'll do it on gentle, I promise. I don't want to ruin your nice things, but we need to get the smoke out." Everyone in the family got to take fragrant, steaming showers and put on clean clothing, and walk barefoot on the impossibly thick carpets.

"Now," Lisa said when they were all clean and back in the living room, "Stan and I need to go home and get some sleep. I'm tuckered out, and I know all of you are, too. You can sleep anywhere in the house you want—I put clean sheets on the beds, and I'll show you the linen closet so you can get whatever else you need. You just settle down wherever you're comfortable. But I have to ask you, at least for tonight, not to go outside, okay? Not that anyone's around here, but I don't want to take chances. And if the phone rings, screen the call and make sure it's us before you pick up, okay? I don't think anyone else will be calling here, but you never know."

Timbor shook his head, and Zamatryna said, "We don't understand that. What is a phone, please, and where is the screen for it?"

"Oh," Lisa said, and laughed. "You don't have phones at home, huh? Okay, let me show you. I'll call the house phone here on my cell."

She took a tiny box out of her purse and pushed buttons, and after a moment there was a ringing in the house. "The answering machine's in the kitchen," Lisa said. "It picks up after four rings. Come on, I'll show you." So they followed her into the kitchen, and listened in amazement as she spoke into her box and the box on the kitchen table magnified her voice. She showed them how to pick up the handset if they heard her voice, how to talk into it. "Don't pick up if it's anybody but me or Stan," she said. "Okay? Okay, good. Goodnight, everybody. I'll be back for breakfast tomorrow. I'll make you all pancakes. You never had those at the camp, did you?"

After she and Stan had left, the family found its way into the room with the big bed, the room where Lisa's mother had slept. The bed held Macsofo and Aliniana and their children; everyone else slept on the floor. Zamatryna snuggled into her blanket, grateful for the AC which made blankets bearable, and thought about clowns and lavender and phones until her thoughts turned into dreams of screaming and burning. In her dream she saw Darroti, weeping so loudly that his tears hammered on the roof of the house and woke her.

It hadn't been a dream, the sound of water on the roof. She got up silently and stepped over her family's sleeping bodies to peer out the window, where the trees were blowing in a wind laced with rain, rain, sweet blessed water. The sound of the water made her need to make her own, so she found her way to the bathroom and turned on the light. The light dispelled her nightmare, and she sat happily on the beautifully clean toilet, with the roll of scented paper next to it. A clown looked down at her from the opposite wall. This clown was smiling, and she smiled back. They were out of the camp, truly in America at last. Now everything would be all right.

But then she felt Mim-Bim in her pocket, Mim-Bim from home, who should have died months ago, who demanded secrecy but had no way of telling Zamatryna what it was she couldn't say. She looked up at the clown again, and wondered what his smile was hiding. Did he have an angry beetle in his pocket?

And yet she still could not help but be glad to be out of the camp. She made her way joyfully back to bed, went joyfully to sleep, awoke joyfully to find sunlight streaming in the windows. The world had been washed clean by the rain. Lisa and Stan came and made pancakes, delicious fluffy things with fruit on top, and there was orange juice and several kinds of tea, and after breakfast Lisa let them all go outside for a little while, and the air didn't smell like smoke anymore, but like sagebrush and lavender, and the mint and thyme and roses that Lisa's mother also had in her garden. Zamatryna and her mother and auntie spent a long time exclaiming over the garden, and then they went down to the banks of the river, where the cousins were already happily playing, splashing in the water under the willow trees. "Mama," Jamfret cried, and pointed, "look, on that rock, a lizard! It's like home!" And the lizard cocked its head at them and scurried away, and overhead was blue sky and puffy white clouds, and the mountains were blue and white in the distance, glowing in the sunshine.

Some funny birds ran by, a mother and ten tiny babies; they had topknots which bobbed up and down in time to their gait. "Quail," Lisa said happily, when Zamatryna asked what they were. "I love those birds. They're such a hoot: they look like wind-up toys. Sometimes at dawn I've seen deer out here too, and sometimes coyotes. Mama even saw a bobcat once. She didn't tell anybody but me, because she was afraid the cops would come and shoot it. There's a school about two miles away, and people panic whenever there are big cats around. They're afraid their kids will get eaten. But the bobcat didn't hurt nobody. It was just trying to live, like we all are. Look, honey, look up there, where I'm pointing: see that bird? That's a redtail hawk. We get owls too, and I've seen eagles sometimes."

"Everything's so pretty," Zamatryna said. After the bleakness of the camp, she felt as if she could taste every color here.

Lisa nodded. "Yes, it sure is, isn't it? This is a beautiful part of the world, and I thank the Lord every day that I live here. It eases the hurt in your heart, to come outside and look at those mountains."

Finally they went inside, to have sandwiches for lunch. Timbor blessed the food in their own language, and Stan blessed it a bit more loudly than necessary in his, and then they ate. Halfway through the first sandwich, Stan said, "What does that mean in English, that grace you say, old man?"

Timbor smiled. "I don't know how to translate it into your language."

"Could your daughter tell me? Zamanina, can you say it in English?"

"Her name's Zamatryna, honey." Lisa passed Timbor a plate of cookies. "And she's had too much work to do translating things. She's only a little girl. Let her be, Stan, all right?"

"I just—"

"These folks have had too many people yammering at them with questions, Stan. They need a rest. They only got out of that camp with their lives yesterday, remember?"

"Thank you for bringing us here," Harani said quietly. "Thank you for everything you've done for us. Both of you."

"You're welcome," Lisa said. Stan mumbled something and looked away, his jaw set. Lisa gave him an unreadable look and said, "We watched the news last night. When we went home. It's bad, what happened at the camp. They still didn't have the fire out this morning; they didn't get rain there last night, like we did." Her voice was thick with tears now. "A lot of people died, refugees and Americans both, over a hundred. And now they're trying to find out who snuck in the truck bomb. It looks like somebody in the Army who was working with the Nuts."

Erolorit shook his head. "Why would anyone do that? Why do those people hate refugees so much?"

"Lots of reasons." Lisa wiped her eyes. "Some folks just don't like anybody who doesn't look like them, or anybody from somewhere else, especially after what happened in 2001: the big attack, and all the scares after that, anthrax and smallpox and those crazies who got caught smuggling a bomb into Cleveland. Never mind that everybody here is from someplace different, unless they're Indian. Some folks are scared of disease, since a lot of the refugees are from Africa and places like that where so many folks have died of

HIV. A lot of people who can't find jobs think the refugees will take all the work if they stay here, and some people are just upset that anything the rest of the country doesn't want gets dumped in Nevada. There are folks who think the refugee camp is as bad as Yucca Mountain, where all that radioactive waste is. I don't think it's anything like that, because I don't think people are poison. But we've still got more open room than any other state in the country, except Alaska, and some folks just don't want to share it."

Stan looked back at them now. "People are just full of evil," he said quietly, but he sounded sad, not angry. "It's hard to withstand Satan, yes it is, and a lot of people just never hear Jesus knocking at their hearts. Or they hear him and slam the door in his face, give in to the Tempter instead. I'm sorry if I've been unkind to you. I'm a fallen man, and I have my own struggles, and I just pray to the good Lord to set my feet on the right path."

Timbor and the rest of the family just stared; Macsofo raised his eyebrows at Zamatryna, who had no idea how to translate any of what Stan had just said. But Lisa looked happy. She wiped her face again, and leaned over to give Stan a hug, and said, "Bless you, honey. You surely are a comfort. Now, listen, it's getting on toward two. Do you think you could run those errands we talked about, while I stay here and get these folks settled more comfortably?"

"Sure," Stan said with a sigh. "I'll be back in a few hours with more food and some clothing for all of you. Lisa, I still think you'd be better at the clothing than I'd be."

"Never mind, honey, get a few things, whatever you can, at Kmart and Costco and the Salvation. We'll do it bit by bit. These folks can't go downtown until they have American things to wear, that's all. It would draw too much attention. You need money?"

"I have money."

"We'll pay for it out of Mama's—"

"Never mind that," he said gently, and bent and kissed the top of her head, and waved to the rest of them, and was gone.

When the door had shut behind him, Lisa rubbed her eyes and said, "All right. I need to talk to you. Macsofo, Aliniana, can your little ones play outside by themselves, without folks watching them? No, of course not, it's too dangerous with the river—can they play in the other room by themselves, nicely?"

"Yes," Macsofo said, his voice chilly. "But why can't they stay here?"

"They're little, that's all. I have to talk about grown-up things. Children shouldn't be burdened—"

"We share everything as a family," Macsofo said tonelessly, and Lisa bent her head.

"Of course. You're their daddy. Zamatryna, sweetheart, I may need you to translate again if I say things your folks can't understand. I'm sorry."

"It's all right," Zamatryna said.

"Good," Lisa said, and took a deep breath. "Thank you. All right, now, there are things I haven't told Stan about you. He knows you don't have papers, but he doesn't know that nobody knows where you came from. I didn't tell him that part. Stan likes things set and settled, you know; he doesn't do well with anything that doesn't fit into what he already knows. And he has this way of thinking the worst about anything he doesn't understand: if there's a hole in something, you know, he plugs the Devil right in there. And you folks don't need to deal with that. You've had enough trouble already."

Timbor shook his head. "Who is the Devil, please?"

"The Tempter, the one who makes evil in the world. The opposite of God and Jesus, who make everything good in the world. The Devil's where all the bad things come from."

"Is the Devil a Nut?" Jamfret asked, and Lisa laughed.

"Oh, sweetie, yes, the Devil's a Nut! The first Nut, the one who gives all the others their nasty ideas. That's very good. Stan would like that, but we're not going to tell him we had this conversation, all right? Stan's a good man, but there are things he doesn't need to know. And he doesn't need to know that you know what I'm about to tell you." She took another deep breath, and said, "Stan met me when I was in jail. I ran with a bad crowd when I was young; I went wild after Daddy died, and Mama couldn't do anything with me, though the good Lord knows she tried. I fell in with a motorcycle gang, and I drank too much and got into drugs, and for ten years, from sixteen to twenty-six, I had nothing in my heart but hate and despair. I don't know why I didn't die: that's a miracle, I'll tell you the truth, that I didn't OD or get HIV from a needle or ride with somebody who drove his bike into an embankment somewhere, because believe me, I knew people who died from all of those things. And some of them were bad people and some of them were just, well, lost, you know: they wanted to be better and didn't know how, and I still pray for all of them every day, even though it's been twenty years since then." She sniffled and took a drink of juice, and said to Zamatryna, "Do you understand that, honey? Do I need to say it differently?"

"We understand enough," Harani said kindly, and reached out to pat Lisa's arm. Zamatryna didn't understand anything, except that Lisa was upset, but her mother would explain it to her later.

"Thank you," Lisa said. She squeezed Harani's hand, and went on. "So I wound up in jail on a drug possession charge. Now I can say that it was the best thing that ever happened to me, because I got off drugs in there, and I met Stan when he came in to do prison ministry, and that's how I found the Lord. But at the time, all I knew was that I was cramped up and wouldn't see the sun again for years, and I'd never valued fresh air until I didn't have it anymore, and I missed my mama and hated how I'd hurt her, though I'd spit in her face often enough when I was free. I didn't think anybody could love me, and I was amazed when Stan did, and when he asked me to be his wife when I got out I said yes in two seconds, although he was the kind of man I'd laughed at before. Stan didn't mind how many men I'd been with before that: he just cared that my heart was washed clean in the Lord, and that I accepted Jesus as my Savior." She stopped for a minute, and swallowed. "Stan's an awfully good man, really he is. He's better than he knows, I think. All he sees is his own evil, which everybody's got, and he thinks he has to fight it to the death, that he can't ever relax. And that's why he's so scared about breaking anybody's rules, God's or the government's. He talks about God's grace and forgiveness, but I don't think he believes it. He believes it for me and for everybody else, but not for himself, not really."

"And that's why you didn't tell him more about us," Harani said. "Because we don't fit the rules."

Lisa bobbed her head up and down vigorously. "Yes, that's right. Thank you for putting that so clearly. And because I—well, I'm going to break some more rules. To help you. I don't see any way around it. You folks need papers, and if you don't have them, we'll have to buy them. And if you're not from someplace the government knows about, we'll just have to say you are, that's all. We'll just make up a place you're from, because you're here now, and that's more important than wherever you came from."

"And how," Erolorit asked, "will we do this?"

"Illegally," Lisa said, and made a face. "When I was who I used to be, twenty years ago, I knew people who sold fake papers. I can find them again, if I have to, or people like them."

"We have no money to buy these papers," Timbor said.

"No, of course you don't. I have money: the money Mama left me."

Timbor raised an eyebrow. "Stan would not like this. The money is for his church, is it not?"

"Some of it," Lisa said crisply. "But it's my money, like it's my house. We were saving some of it to adopt an orphan baby: well, I'm adopting all of you instead. And no, he surely wouldn't like it, not the illegal part. But he isn't going to know, is he? Because none of us will tell him, right? Right, Zamatryna? Right, Jamfret and Rikko and Poliniana?"

The children just stared at her. Zamatryna, her hand over the pocket where Mim–Bim traced its constant pattern, hunched her shoulders, all happiness fled. She felt oppressed by pleas for silence; the burden of the beetle, combined with Lisa's secrets, was more than she could stand. Knowing nothing that was safe to say, she said nothing.

Harani frowned. "Lisa, if we get these papers after having none, will Stan not know what has happened?"

"I don't think he'll look into it. I don't think he'll want to know. He just wants everything to be all right; he doesn't want trouble. He wants everything to be normal. So we just won't tell him about anything that isn't normal, will we? We won't show him any holes he can plug the Devil into."

Macsofo shook his head. "I do not understand. Why are you doing this? It is dangerous for you, and hurtful to your marriage. A little while ago you did not even know us, and now you are lying to your husband and being illegal. You could go to jail again, yes?"

Lisa sighed. "It sounds bad when you put it that way, I have to admit. I wouldn't lie to Stan if he asked me something straight out, but I'm not going to say anything until he does. It's what lawyers call a technicality. You know that word, Zamatryna? No, sweetie? Well, now you do. Technicality. It's a white lie, which is better anyway than a black one. And as for why I'm doing this—well, I've been praying on this for a long time, ever since I found out that you all couldn't leave the camp. Everybody deserves a second chance. That's what grace and forgiveness mean: that's what Jesus came to teach us. I got my second chance in jail, when the good Lord and Stan Buttle handed me a fresh start on a platter, and now God's given me a chance to do the same for you. So it's my way of saying thank you."

"You are very kind," Timbor said, but then he shook his head. "Stan will want us to worship this Jesus, yes? And if we do not, he will plug in the Devil?"

"Well now," Lisa said, "I hope you'll find your way to the Lord, of course I do. Stan does too. But nobody can force that, and Stan knows it, even if sometimes he acts like he doesn't, and I'd do what I'm doing anyway. I think what matters is what's in your heart, not the words you use." She laughed suddenly and said, "That's another thing I don't talk to Stan about. So listen, is everybody with the program here? What Stan doesn't know won't hurt him, right?" They nodded, not knowing what else to do, and Lisa said cheerfully, "Well then, if we've got all that settled, let's talk about rooms. You'll have to stay here for a while, until you can all start working and get your own place, and I want you to be comfy. So we need to talk about who wants which rooms. Have you thought about that?"

They hadn't thought about it. Lisa, it turned out, had thought about it a great deal, and had firm ideas on the subject. There were four bedrooms and a sunroom; she thought that the two biggest bedrooms should go to the married couples, and that Timbor should take the third bedroom, and that Poliniana and Zamatryna should take the fourth, "because they're girls and they can share. And Jamfret and Rikko can share the sunroom. It's not a real bedroom, but it will feel like camping out, and little boys like that."

"Timbor is the head of our family," Erolorit said. "He must have the biggest room. Harani and I can take one of the smaller ones."

"Nonsense," Timbor said in their own language. "I am one person: everyone else is two. I will take whichever room is smallest."

"I want my own room," Zamatryna said. "I don't want to share." She couldn't do it anymore, keep Mim-Bim a secret while she was sharing a room with other people. She was tired of sneaking the beetle from one pocket into another, tired of having to pretend that she wasn't worried about what the insect meant, tired of the constant yearning to speak, to ask for help and advice. If she had a room to herself she could cry and whisper to Mim-Bim without everyone hearing her, and perhaps she'd be able to find out what the insect wanted. And surely, sometime, Mim-Bim would end its improbably long life, and then she would be free and she could share a room.

The others stared at her. "Zamatryna," Harani said, "don't you love your cousin?"

"Yes, I love Poliniana—Poliniana, I love you—but I want my own room! You can give me the littlest one and put Grandfather in a bigger one! I don't care! I want my own!"

"But even if you share one with your cousin, it will be more space than either of you had in the camp, Zamatryna." Erolorit came and knelt next to her. "And you were happy sleeping with everyone last night, weren't you? You seemed happy."

She couldn't explain it to them. Oh, how she wanted to, but she couldn't! It was against Mim-Bim's rules, which were as incomprehensible as Stan's or the government's. Rage and impotence filled her until her voice came out in a screech. "I—want—my—own—room!"

Harani shook her head. "Daughter, little one, this is selfish and unkind—"

"Hush," Timbor said sharply. "Harani, do not scold her. Zamatryna, come here."

She went, sniffling, and he held her on his lap, as he had done in the camp after Erolorit sent Lisa away. "Lisa is right. You have had too much to do, translating, and too much to see, because you were with us when we—when we found Darroti. And so you want a place to be away from everyone, eh? It is not because you do not love us, or because you are bad. You need space to be sad in without worrying that you will make others sad, is that right?" She nodded, miserably, and put her head against his chest, where his heart went boom-boom-boom reassuringly. "All right," Timbor said, stroking her hair. "All right, little one. That is all right. But we do not blame you for being sad. No one would blame you."

She couldn't explain it to him. "I want my own room," she said in a very small voice.

"Then you shall have it," Timbor said, and hugged her.

"How?" Erolorit held up five fingers. "Four bedrooms and a sunroom. If you have one and she has one and Poliniana has one—for if Zamatryna demands her own, Poliniana must have one too—and the twins have the sunroom, there is only one room left, and two couples. Where will everyone go?"

"This is stupid," Harani said. "Stupid! We have more room in this house than we ever did in our tent in the camp, and only now are we fighting over it!"

"I do not need a bedroom," Timbor said. "I will sleep in some other room, on the floor."

"You are the head of our family!" Macsofo said. "You must not—"

"I am the head of our family, and I have spoken! I will sleep wherever I wish, and what I wish is to give up a bedroom so that Zamatryna may have one! And I will not have you deny me!"

"Don't yell," Zamatryna said into her grandfather's tunic. "Please don't yell. I'm sorry I was bad—"

"You are not bad, Zamatryna." Timbor's voice was gentler now. "You have been hurt. We have all been hurt. We all have different ways of healing from hurt. It is a gift to know what you need to heal, Granddaughter, and a gift to be able to ask for it. And what I need to heal is to give you what you need to heal, eh? And I am glad I can do it. Harani, Erolorit, comfort your child, who is not unkind."

"I would rather she were unkind than in pain," Erolorit said grimly.

"Then allow her to have what will salve her pain, and do not scold her for it!"

"Please don't yell," Zamatryna said, shaking. How she wanted to squash Mim-Bim! But she knew that would be wrong, truly unkind.

"What's the matter?" Lisa said in English. She'd been watching the argument, frowning. "Why is everyone upset? Is there anything I can do?"

"Nothing," Timbor told her crisply. "It is family business. We have settled the matter of the rooms, Lisa, and we thank you."

And so Zamatryna, heartsick, got her own room, the smallest one. It had a wonderful view of the garden, and she asked Poliniana if she wanted the bigger of the small rooms—which had no view—or wanted the one where she could see the flowers. "You can have the flowers because you're sad," Poliniana said, but Zamatryna could tell that the littler girl was trying not to cry, and her heart twisted. She hugged her cousin, vowing to be as nice to her in every other way as she could, and Harani put a hand on both their heads.

"Everyone can see the flowers when we go outside. Poliniana, we will teach you about the garden, eh? Your cousin will help you learn to make things grow."

They heard the front door open, and Lisa called cheerfully, "Stan's back! So how'd you do with the clothing, honey? Let's see what you found."

He had found great piles of socks and underwear, of which he was very proud. He had overalls for Timbor and the uncles, skirts for the women, little pants for the twins. And for Poliniana and Zamatryna he had bought t-shirts and sun-dresses.

"I hope they'll fit," he said happily. "I thought they were real pretty, see, they have flowers on them, you girls like flowers, and this one here has ladybugs. Aren't they cute?"

Lisa beamed. "You did real well, honey. I couldn't have done any better myself."

"Poliniana can have the one with the beetles," Zamatryna said. The ladybugs reminded her too much of Mim-Bim. And looking at the sun-dresses, she was more grateful than ever that she had demanded her own room, for the dresses had no pockets. She would have to find some other place to hide her fellow exile.

5

Timbor

I would have preferred my own bedroom, because I had my own hurts to hide. But whenever I looked at Zamatryna I saw Darroti at the same age—for both were bright and headstrong, and both had Frella's almond-shaped green eyes—and my heart twisted. Darroti had begun his life as just such a responsible, curious child, and I had missed some wound in him, with what results you know. And if his fate on the fence was not my fault, what father would not feel it was? And so I was loath to deny Zamatryna whatever she might need to mend, especially when she began to scream and cry; for she had never acted so before. And my feeling then was that we had all had too much to bear, and that she merely voiced what all of us carried inside.

And so Zamatryna took the little room overlooking the garden, and I claimed a corner of the family room. I was most comfortable sleeping on the floor, for I found American beds too soft, but the woman Lisa found a screen for me, to make the spot more private, and cleared some clowns out of a bookcase, so I could keep my few things there. I still had my old clothes to wear in the house, because I could not bear to discard them, although I only wore American ones outside. I had my prayer carpet. I had an ivory box, a courting gift from Frella, the one treasure I had brought into exile. Inside the box was a lock of her hair. I had a box the Americans had given me, with Darroti's ashes inside, for they had burned his body as we would have done at home. Of course his spirit was not in them, could not be, but the ashes would be fine fertilizer if we ever gained a garden of our own. I kept Darroti's prayer carpet rolled next to mine; he had seldom used it—rarely before the Mendicant's death, and never after—so it brought back no memories of him, but I could not bear to discard the pattern of his soul.

I had something else, too: a silk cord Darroti had worn around his neck and kept hidden under his clothing, and which the Americans had given back to me before they burned his body. On it hung a silver pendant, two circles touching at a point: what Americans would call a figure-eight. I had never seen such a symbol before, and it puzzled me, and Darroti's brothers—who had been with me when the Americans brought the thing, with Darroti's clothing, to our tent—knew no more about it than I did. "A bauble he bought in the market," Macsofo said with a shrug.

"He wore few ornaments," Erolorit answered. "It must have been precious to him, for him to have brought it here."

"Whatever the mystery is, we will never unravel it." Macsofo's voice was harsh, hoarsened by the smoke we all breathed then. "Father, put that thing away. I do not want to look at it. I do not want to think about Darroti! Darroti brought this doom upon us all!"

And so I put it away, and kept it away, to spare my surviving sons. Our story might have gone very differently if I had shown it to the others, but I believed then what I had said in the camp, after Erolorit sent Lisa away: that we must all become Americans as far as possible, and cease to dwell in the past. Our job now was to help the children adapt fully to this new place, even if we never could ourselves. So I kept my little store of old things in the bookcase, and hung a blanket over the front of it, and tried to train myself not to reach behind the blanket, although at least once a week I did, despite myself. Something would remind me of Lémabantunk—the smell of roses in sunlight or the sound of the river flowing over rocks—and a great hunger for home would come over me, and I would find myself cradling in my arms the box my wife had given me. I understood then, for the first time, what Darroti's thirst for liquor must have been, the force that drives your hands to reach for something your mind believes you should not have.

And so each night, having either reached for the bookcase or successfully resisted, I lay behind my screen and talked to the clown on the wall. He was a large clown in clashing shades of pink and yellow and purple; he was one of the weeping clowns, and his tears were palest blue. Lisa had offered to take him down when she removed the smaller clowns from the bookcase, but I told her that I welcomed him, that he would keep me company. And so he did.

I spoke to him partly as a way of delaying sleep, for every night I dreamed of the burning camp, of screaming and the smell of smoke; and every night Darroti came into my dreams, urgently trying to tell me something I could not understand, and every night I was overjoyed to have found Darroti again, although he could not speak to me. And every morning I awoke and Darroti was gone again, still dead, and the people who had died in the fire were still dead, and sorrow crushed my chest as if an ox were standing on me. Mornings were terrible.

And so at night I talked to the clown to keep the dreams at bay, although I always entered them at last. "Clown," I would say to him, but not aloud, "this is hard work, this being merry when all you want to do is weep. Clown, this feels like death. Tell me how you smile for the crowds, Clown, for I must become like you. I must put on my floppy shoes and my rubber nose, and cheer the children. Clown, why do you weep? Do you miss your home? Do you have a child dead by his own hand, a child whose hands dealt death to someone else? Clown, are you like me, enmeshed in lies and riddles, in things you cannot say?"

For there was also the puzzle of the towel which would not dry. I had ceased to cry, outwardly at least, but the towel remained damp, no matter if I put it in the sun or in Lisa's dryer. The water I squeezed from it was salt; the towel was wet with tears. "Clown, are they your tears that wet the towel?" But they could not have been, because the towel had come with us from the camp. And so I kept the damp towel folded in the bookcase, behind the blanket, and did not speak of it. It was too strange. It was a hole into which Stan, I feared, would plug his Devil.

And thus I felt myself swallowed by a maw of many silences. For outside the house, of course, we could no longer speak of the camp, any more than we could speak of Lémabantunk. The Army must believe that we had died in the fire. And yet the fire, and the people dead in it, haunted me almost as much as Darroti did. We had known many of those people. The family in the tent next to ours, from Pakistan, had died: a mother and a father and three children. One of the social workers had died who so often asked us questions. And the Army man with the buttons and ribbons on his shirt, the one who had stood in our tent with his hat in his hand, the one who had tried to comfort me when Darroti died—he too was dead, burned. His name was Neil Glenrock, I learned from the television. I had not paid attention to it when he came to our tent. I had been rude to him when he tried to be kind, and I had no way to make amends. I could not go to his widow and his children and tell them I was sorry. I could not tell them the story of how he had been decent to a fellow man in pain, who was churlish in return. I could not do that, because the Timbor who had been there was not supposed to be alive.

"I'll do it," Lisa said. I broke down when we saw the man's face on the television—Aliniana was outside with the children, and Stan was off building houses, but the rest of us adults were watching the morning news—and she made me tell her why I wept. "Timbor, you just tell me anything you want to say about that man, and I'll tell his family. I can say I was there. I'll make it sound like I was in your tent when he did that, or like you told me about it. All of you: you just tell me anything you want anybody to know about all those poor souls, and I'll be your voice. I'm the reason you can't talk about it, so I'll talk for you. That's the least I can do."

And so she did. I told her the story, and she went to see Neil Glenrock's wife and grown sons and told it to them. They were very grateful, she said. There were Nuts in their family—the kind who wrote letters, not the kind who built bombs—who did not approve of the camp and had not approved of the work Neil Glenrock did there. It comforted them to know that other people thought he had been of value.

She stopped for a moment, then, and went on carefully. "They'd heard about you and your family, Timbor. Neil, he'd told them about Darroti and how bad he felt about what happened, how you'd lost your son and all. It ate at him, that his men were the ones who weren't paying attention when Darroti died. So it meant a lot to his family when I showed up and said how nice he'd been. He'd felt like he hadn't done any good. He'd told his wife that, and I was able to tell her that he'd been wrong, that he had so done good. I was able to comfort her."

"And now she thinks we are all dead," I said, seeing nothing but gloom.

Lisa looked unhappy. "I know. Timbor, I'm sorry. I don't know how else to handle it. We'll turn this all to good yet, I promise. You'll all learn English and get jobs and earn money, and the kids will go to school and do real well, and someday you'll look back on everything you're going through now and it will have been worth it, just like being in jail was worth it for me. You just have to be patient. It's hard now. I know it is. It's hard for me too. We all just have to do the best we can. If I hadn't gotten you out of there, you might really be dead."

She was a good woman, Lisa. But her secrets worried me, for I did not see how she could keep them from her husband for long, and I foresaw nothing but trouble when he learned that she had been lying to him. She was treating him like a fool, although she loved him. The love would make the lies sting more, when they emerged. And Stan Buttle was no fool, although I had thought he was at first; I felt for him even as I feared him. For he was determined that my family become the followers of his god. That, I knew, was why he allowed us to stay in the house he wanted for his church. He would not tolerate us long if we refused, whatever Lisa said.

And I could not follow his god, Jesus who had risen from the dead, and who was useless to me. The forgiveness I recognized and valued, for Jesus did what the Necessary Beggar does in Gandiffri: blesses people and releases them from the past, that they may venture into the future unburdened, free and able to do good again. But Stan insisted that the dead would rise again in their bodies at the Judgment, and my dead—Darroti and the people in the camps—had no bodies left but ashes. And Stan insisted that the only path to heaven was through Jesus, and how could I accept that, who had come from a world where Jesus had never existed, and where no one knew his name? And Stan insisted, when I was bold enough to ask him, that Jesus had forgiven everyone once and for all, everywhere and in all times. But I could not accept that either, for it made a mockery of crime. How could Jesus already have forgiven Darroti for murder, which had caused such pain to Gallicina's family? And if Darroti had already been forgiven, then our exile meant nothing, and I needed to believe—indeed, I did believe—that it was just. I clung to that belief in justice, lest all that we had suffered be a waste.

Stan Buttle's god would have turned my sorrows into nonsense. And Stan Buttle's heaven seemed a bleak, cold place, for as he told it, the spirits of the dead were plucked forever from the world, rather than remaining in fruit and flowers, in leaves and lizards.

And I needed to believe that my dead were in sight, even if I could not speak to them. I needed to believe that they were growing and learning and alive.

And so I used the blessings we had brought with us from home. I allowed Stan to say his grace, but I always said my own. *Souls of the dead, thank you for succoring us, that we may remain among the living.* I could wear American clothing, eat American food, speak American words, but I could not forego the grace of Gandiffri, for Darroti could be in anything I blessed. And when Stan insisted that I tell him what the words meant, and frowned and called them Satanic superstition, and said that he feared greatly for my soul, I answered only, "I am fifty-nine years old, Stan, and I have been saying this prayer my entire life, and it is a piece of my homeland. I have lost more than you will ever understand. You cannot expect me to give this up so quickly."

I did not intend ever to give it up, but I could not tell him that. I had to let him believe that he might convert us, in time. I had to let him have that hope, lest he cast us out of this new, precarious home, as he had told us that his god cast unrepentant sinners into the outer darkness, where there was much wailing and gnashing of teeth. And yet he called his god a god of love. I could not fathom it, unless the outer darkness be like exile. Certainly we had wailed and gnashed our teeth, in this new world. And yet there was hope here, too, and beauty, and kindness, and wonders like toilets and ice cream. There were flowers here and rainbows. It was not all the endless, dreary misery of Stanley Buttle's hell.

And so, for my sake and my family's, I worked at being friends with Stan. I wanted there to be some bond between us, so that he would continue to help us for our own sake, not simply for his god's. Before he learned of Lisa's lies, as I knew he someday must, I wanted him also to have learned to care for us as people in ourselves, apart from her.

So I asked Stan questions about many things other than his god:

about his work, and the machine he used to cut the grass, and the things we saw on television. I let Stan teach me about wristwatches and peanut butter and jogging shoes. I learned that he missed his father, who had died when he was small, and who had loved old cars and old movies, as Stanley loved them now.

I spent many hours sitting in the dark with Stanley, watching Chaplin and the Marx Brothers and fifties comedies, in which people who spoke entirely too quickly blundered through endless errors, always emerging into marriage and money. "Now, those were movies," Stan said happily. "None of this stuff with half-naked teenagers being chased by psychos with chainsaws. Good movies don't need blood and cussing: there's too much of that in the world already. Give me Groucho and Harpo any day." And indeed, the movies made me laugh and eased my heart, and the children loved them too, and in that way Stanley grew to love the children. Poliniana learned to walk like Charlie Chaplin, and Rikko and Jamfret memorized the lines from "A Night at the Opera," and Stanley laughed until his cheeks grew red, and praised them.

And the cars were wonderful, although I could not at first imagine how they could be. We had only ever seen ugly cars here, like the trucks in the camp, raising dust and belching smoke. Other cars, like Lisa's van, were quieter, and did not belch smoke, but they were still ungainly boxes. I could not fathom how anyone could like cars. "They are hideous," I told Stan.

"Aw, Timbor, you only think so because you've never seen the old ones. New cars are butt-ugly, that's right, just like new movies are. But vintage cars . . ." He shook his head and smiled. "You just have to see them. I'll take you to the Auto Museum tomorrow."

And so he did. It was one of my first trips downtown, wearing American clothing; at the beginning the family only went out a few at a time, lest we attract attention. I wore my new American clothes, a pair of short pants and a Coca-Cola shirt, and sat in Stan's ugly car, the Ford, and looked out the window, as I had not been able to do when we were in the van coming from the camp. The speed made me dizzy, and I braced myself against the roof.

"Just relax, Timbor, and put your arms down. If you're sick to your stomach, look at a point on the horizon, something fixed and far away. I learned that when I was in the Navy. You okay?"

I nodded. I did not want to talk; I feared that if I opened my mouth, I would vomit. I put my arms down and tried to relax, and looked at a mountain on the other side of the valley. We were driving east, toward downtown, where there were more buildings, and taller ones, than I could ever have imagined. It was bewildering even from a distance, and when we got there it was more so, because the buildings rose on all sides so that one could not see the tops of them. "Don't crane your head like that," Stan told me, laughing, when we had gotten out of the car. "You have to learn not to look like a tourist, old man."

"But I am one," I said; and so I was, except, of course, that tourists can go home again, and I could not. But Stan was very pleased when I acted like a tourist in the Auto Museum, when my eyes got big at the sheer size of the building, with its huge rooms and its rows and rows of cars.

Stan was right. They were beautiful, intricate things, gleaming and graceful, made of wood and polished brass and other metals; one was even made of burnished gold. The older ones had lanterns, and baskets in the back for food, and fluid curves that comforted the eye. The cars were still and silent. I suppose they had belched in their day, but now they rested, inviting admiration. "They'd never look that good if people were still using them," Stan said with a sigh. "They'd be full of dust, you know; it takes a ton of work to keep them spiffed up like this. But anybody who could afford a car like this back then had servants, too. I bet the servants didn't like these cars one bit. Too much work. Look at that, Timbor: this car cost sixteen thousand dollars in 1921! That was a fortune, back then. You could have bought five houses for that, probably."

We were in front of a Rolls-Royce Silver Ghost, all gleaming copper and sweeping running boards. Against a wall were cases of the clothing people would have worn then, like the costumes in the movies Stanley loved.

"Nineteen twenty-one," he said. "Eighty-nine years ago. This car is almost twice as old as I am, and it looks brand new."

"And much more ele—ele—what is that word, Stanley? Elegy? The one that means beautiful?"

"Elegant," he said. "Elegy is a noun, not an adjective. It's a kind of poem. A mourning poem."

"A morning poem? To greet the sunrise?"

"No, the other mourning, mourning with a 'u'—a funeral poem. A poem you say when someone's dead, to talk about how good the person was."

"Oh," I said, and shivered. "Then this museum is an elegy, is it not? An elegy for the elegant?"

Stan looked at me. "Yes," he said quietly. "Yes, I suppose it is. That's exactly what it is." He shook his head. "You're amazing, Timbor. I've spoken English my whole life, and I wouldn't have thought of that. An elegy for elegance. That's—that's perfect."

He sounded as if he might cry, and I realized then how much alike we were. Both of us looked backwards to a beloved time that was lost to us, a time where everything had been beautiful. Both of us looked forward to some time and place that would be better. And both of us were here, now, in a grim, unhappy time where little was as we wanted it to be. We lived in our memories and in our hopes, enduring the present because we had no other choice, and because we loved the people who lived here with us.

"You should wear a tux like this," Stanley said more cheerfully, and pulled me to the case of clothing. "Darn, but you'd look good in that. Tails and a top hat, Timbor. You'd look elegant. You'd look like Fred Astaire. You'd look right at home in one of those cars."

"Yes," I said. "A tux is more elegant than a Coca-Cola shirt. But hotter, too. And it costs money, yes?"

He nodded. "A lot of money. Nothing like that at Kmart, I can tell you. But you need one anyway. A tux and a top hat, and maybe a cane."

"And the car," I said. "I need the car, too. How much would it cost now, the one from 1921?"

"More money than we'll ever see," he said with a laugh. "Much more than the tux and top hat, that's for sure. But it's a nice dream, isn't it?"

"Yes," I said, and looked at the clothing in the case; and suddenly I saw my face reflected in the glass, and saw Darroti's mouth and chin, Darroti as he would have looked had he grown old. And I remembered then, in a rush, a morning in the garden in Lémabantunk, long ago when Darroti was very young, and a toy wagon he had pulled behind him on a string. The wagon was wood. I had made it for him, a pretty thing with curves and sturdy wheels. How Darroti had loved his wagon! How he would have loved these cars!

"Timbor," Stan said. His hand was on my shoulder. "Timbor, old man, are you all right? What is it?"

"Nothing," I said. "Nothing. Just—just an elegy. I am fine now. I think I am hungry. Is there food here?"

"Not here," he said. "But there are restaurants real close. I'll buy you a hot dog. Your favorite American food."

"Yes," I said. I enjoyed hot dogs a great deal, with mustard. "I eat American food, and now I want an American tux. What will be next, Stanley?"

6

NAMES

"New names," said Lisa. The family was gathered in the kitchen on a glorious October morning, two months after their arrival at the house. Sunlight pooled on the kitchen table; outside, the Truckee chattered along its bed, carrying fallen leaves. Stan was working at a construction site north of town, and Lisa had called a family conference. "Listen, we really lucked out in the documents department. There's a clerk in the camp who's willing to sell me the papers of some of the folks who didn't make it through the fire, God rest their souls. A couple with two kids from Palestine and a couple with three kids from some little mountain village in Afghanistan that got wiped out by an earthquake. That's nine people: that's all of you. That way you'll be in the INS computers as having entered the country legally, if anyone checks. And this guy can get us fake green cards and Social Security cards, too. But it means you have to take new names."

"No," Macsofo said. They all looked at him. "We have lost enough. Now you want us to lose our names, too?"

Timbor held Poliniana on his lap; she was playing with some brilliant red and yellow leaves she'd found outside. "Macsofo, be reasonable. We need these papers to survive here. Why does it matter what people call us?"

"It matters because it is who we are!"

"Who we are is not contained in a few syllables," Timbor said mildly.

Zamatryna remembered walking through the door into exile, repeating her name to herself. My name is Zamatryna-Harani Erolorit. Harani is my mommy, and Erolorit is my daddy. My name is Zamatryna-Harani Erolorit. She had been afraid then that she would forget her name, or lose it. Now she was going to lose it after all. She pressed herself unhappily against her mother's side. "I want to keep my name, too," she said.

Lisa sighed. "This guy might be willing to change the names and country of origin for more money. Make you all from Afghanistan, say. But he'll charge a fortune. He's already charging a fortune. There are nine of you. That's a lot of people. This is going to wipe me out, guys. It will take all of Mama's money, and when Stan finds out—"

"When we have the green cards, we can work?" Macsofo said.

"Sure. But you need skills to work, and getting skills takes a while."

"We will work. We will pay you back. We will repay our debt. But I cannot give up my name, Lisa. Perhaps you think it foolish."

She shook her head. "No, I don't think it's silly. I'm not sure I could give up my name, either, and that's the truth."

"I think it is silly," Timbor snapped. "You have done enough for us, Lisa. We cannot expect you to spend all your money on this. Macsofo—"

"We will pay it back. I will pay it back by myself, if I have to! I will spend the rest of my life paying it back! Father, I came here out of loyalty to my family. And then Darroti did what, if it had happened at home, would have kept us from having to come here at all. We came here for nothing, following a coward and a weakling—"

"No," Erolorit said. "Macsofo, you must not say that. We loved Darroti, although he had done wrong. We do not know why he did what he did, and we must not judge. You must not speak evil—"

"I speak the truth!" Macsofo said in Gandiffran. "We know that he killed a Mendicant; how can we not judge that? He exiled all of us for nothing! We cannot go back. We have lost too much, too much, and I cannot also give up my name!"

Aliniana was crying. Poliniana, on Timbor's lap, ripped the beautiful leaves into small shreds. Zamatryna sat at the table, her limbs like lead. She wanted to be happy. When would everyone be happy again?

Harani coughed and said in English, "There is another problem, no? Lisa, the families you listed had four adults and five children. We have five adults and four children."

"That's minor," Lisa said. "If this guy changes names, he can change ages, too. Okay, look, in for a penny, in for a pound. We'll do the names too. That's probably best, in the long run. But you're all going to need the same last name, okay, because that's how it works here. It will just be too complicated otherwise."

"Our last name is the father's name," Timbor said. "So my last name is Banto, who was my father, and Erolorit and Macsofo's last name is Timbor, for I am their father, and their own children—"

"Nope," Lisa said. "That's a real pretty way of doing things, but it's too complicated. It won't work here. Now listen, I have to run get some groceries. You talk about it and figure out what you want the last name to be. You can keep your own first names, that's less important—people have all kinds of crazy first names—or make them more American, too. All of you could have American names pretty easily." She laughed and pointed at each of them. "Tim, Max, Alice, Erroll, hmmmm, Harani—well, that one can stay the way it is—Rick, James, Polly, Trina."

"Trina?" Zamatryna wrinkled her nose. "That's ugly. It sounds like latrine."

"Latrine." Lisa turned around, shaking her head. "You know the word 'latrine'? Where'd you learn that word?"

"From your dictionary, Lisa. It means toilet." Zamatryna's cousins shrieked and giggled, and she said, "I don't want a name that sounds like a Porto-San."

"Honey, you are a wonder. Well, then, call yourself something else. Call yourself Zama; that's fine. Or you can keep calling yourself Zamatryna, but it's too long, and people will get tangled up in it. Okay, we need bread and milk and eggs, toilet paper, cereal, light bulbs. Anything else?"

They made the grocery list, and Lisa left, and the family was left sitting around the kitchen table. "Well," Macsofo said bitterly, "what shall our new last name be?" Aliniana was still sniffling.

"We could all call ourselves Timbor, because he is the head of our family," Erolorit said.

Timbor waved a hand in dismissal. "No, I cannot be Timbor Timbor. We must think of something else. If we are going to use all of Lisa's money, at least we need to think of something that works for all of us."

"We should call ourselves Darroti, because he is the reason we are here," Macsofo said tonelessly, and Timbor's face went pale.

"No, Macsofo. I could not bear that. It would be cruel, both to him and to us."

"Our fate is cruel. I think it fitting."

Harani shook her head. "You must learn to forgive, Macsofo. If our fate is cruel, it cannot now be undone, and your bitterness is poisoning you. Timbor, could we call ourselves Lémabantunk, to remind ourselves of home?"

"The Americans will not be able to say that," Timbor said. "But the idea is fine, Harani. We can call ourselves Gandiffri. That is most fitting, for we are all of Gandiffri that exists here."

Macsofo stared moodily out the window at the falling leaves. "And every time we say it, we will remember how much we miss our country."

"As if we could forget that, whatever we called ourselves,"

Aliniana said through her tears. "I like Gandiffri. In English it means Land of Gifts, and I suppose we must try to see this place as a land of gifts too."

The grown-ups stared, for Aliniana rarely voiced any opinions, let alone in opposition to her husband. Harani put her hand on Aliniana's shoulder, and Zamatryna squinted up at her aunt. "I like Gandiffri too. It's pretty."

"Well then," Timbor said, and smiled. "Well then, we have our name. We shall see what Lisa thinks of it."

Lisa thought well of it, to the family's relief. "Gandiffri," she said, pulling a carton of eggs out of a grocery bag. "That's good. It sounds foreign, but not too foreign. It'll work just fine. Okay, Harani, here's that waffle mix you wanted, and Zamatryna and Poliniana, you girls, I got you some more little hairbands. These have pretty plastic stars on them, see? They'll match your new sandals, the pink ones from Payless."

"Oooooh," Poliniana said. "Can I put them on now? Please?"

"You're already wearing five barrettes," Aliniana said with a small smile. It was the first time she'd smiled in days. Poliniana adored American hair things, and would have worn so many that no one could have seen her actual hair, had her mother permitted it. "Thank Lisa for the gift, child."

"Thank you, Lisa."

"I'll go put mine away now, please," Zamatryna said. She felt a little sick that Lisa was giving her all these things, and that she had nothing to give in return.

"Yes, honey. And I got you some new socks since you lost those others. I'll never understand how dryers eat socks and only ever eat just one, but anyway, here you go. You can put them away, too."

"Thank you," Zamatryna said, and took the things and went to her room. She loved her room, with its view of flowers and its wallpaper covered with butterflies, although she still felt a pang of guilt about the tantrum she'd thrown to get it. But Poliniana liked her room, too, and Grandfather Timbor seemed to be fine sleeping in the family room, so maybe it was all right.

And she needed her own room, because of Mim-Bim. She opened the closet door to put her socks away, and there was the peanut butter jar with holes in the top, Mim-Bim tracing its X inside. It was a relief to have the insect in a jar, not to have to worry about keeping it in her pocket anymore, but the beetle was still a burden. Every morning Zamatryna opened the closet door, hoping that Mim-Bim had died during the night, but its improbably stubborn existence continued. If anyone else had lived in the room, the insect would have quickly been discovered; as it was, Zamatryna had gone to great lengths to convince Lisa and her mother and auntie that she was an extraordinarily neat child, so that they wouldn't feel the urge to come into her room to straighten up. The boy-cousins helped her without meaning to, for Jamfret and Rikko's sunroom was a constant obstacle course of toys, rocks, books, piles of clothing, and small mounds of decomposing food the twins had brought to bed and then forgotten. They had only been in Lisa's house two months, and already they had amassed so many belongings that sometimes it was impossible to see the floor around their beds.

So Zamatryna went out of her way to be tidy with her own things. On the shelf next to the peanut butter jar was the wooden doll Darroti had given her so long ago. It was still blind and bald, as it had been ever since the Americans washed it in the camp. Zamatryna no longer wished to repair it. It was ugly, infinitely less alluring than the sleek, jointed Barbie dolls Lisa had given Zamatryna and Poliniana. Barbie could not have been less like Darroti's doll; in all of her manifestations—homemaker Barbie, cheerleader Barbie, astronaut Barbie—she had eyes that filled half her face, and hair half as long as her body. Zamatryna loved the Barbies and hated the wooden doll, but she was afraid to throw it away, just as she was afraid to do anything to actively shorten Mim-Bim's monotonous life. And so they sat together, two dimly understood reproaches.

"If you never say anything new, I'll never know what you want," Zamatryna whispered to Mim-Bim. "And it will be your own fault. So there." More than once she had been tempted to let Mim-Bim out of its jar, but Stan killed insects when he found them in the house. He said they had no souls: he said that was devilish superstition. He said that they were just vermin.

And yet he delighted in the butterflies in the garden, which were also insects. Zamatryna did not understand Stan at all.

She very deliberately turned her back on the beetle and put her new socks next to a small collection of underwear on another shelf in the closet. Her leggings and tunics from Lémabantunk were there, too, but Zamatryna rarely wore them anymore, and indeed, would soon outgrow them. She preferred the brightly colored American sun-dresses and shorts, which made her feel like a flower, especially when she also got to wear Lisa's perfume.

When they got the new papers, she would be able to go to school. That was what Lisa had told her. Lisa said that going to school was very important, and the people in the camp had said the same thing. Doing well in school was the secret to doing well in America, they said. Lisa said it would be easy for Zamatryna, because she was smart and learned things quickly. "Just look how fast you picked up English, honey. Your English is better than anybody else's, although all of you are pretty good at it. And the memory on you, child! I never will forget how you said the whole *Cat in the Hat* that time. I wish we had those church camps Stan said he went to when he was a little boy, the ones where you had to memorize the names of all the books of the Bible. They gave a prize to the kid who could say them all right and do it fastest: they timed it with a stopwatch, Stan said. And every year he tried, every single year, and he always got something wrong: forgot a book, or got it out of order, or said it just a little slower than some other kid. But you'd win that prize with no trouble at all, Zamatryna, wouldn't you?"

Zamatryna had already started memorizing things from the

home-school materials Lisa borrowed from a friend. She'd memorized the alphabet and all the times tables and the periodic table and the first half of the *Webster's New Collegiate Dictionary,* which was how she'd learned the word latrine. She'd memorized the names of all the states and all their capitals, because Lisa said that was something she'd had to do in third grade. She'd memorized *Green Eggs and Ham* and *And to Think That I Saw It on Mulberry Street.* Lisa had begun to bring her other books, books for older children; now Zamatryna was working on memorizing *The Lion, the Witch and the Wardrobe,* a story she loved because the children in it had walked through a door into another world, as she had.

Every day she worked on memorizing something new, so that she wouldn't forget how, and so she'd do well in school. That way, maybe everyone would be happier. Stan would decide that he'd done the right thing by helping her family, and Uncle Macsofo would know that being in America wasn't such a terrible thing after all, and Auntie Aliniana would stop crying all the time.

Keeping Stan happy was especially important: all the adults said so, although Zamatryna didn't completely understand why. She had heard her parents talking about it many times, worrying that Stan would make them leave the house unless they accepted his god. "His faith is monstrous," Erolorit had said once, when he thought Zamatryna had fallen asleep on the couch. "His god handed his own son, who is also himself, to the executioners. This is a god of murder and suicide, and furthermore this god has too many souls inside, like a seed or a flower crammed with too many dead."

"He says it is a god of forgiveness," Harani had murmured. "Lisa says so also, and even Timbor—he says Stan's god is like the Necessary Beggar, who erases past wrongs."

"And yet Stan says that Darroti is burning in hellfire forever for having taken his own life. Where is the forgiveness there?"

"I do not understand it," Harani had admitted with a sigh. "It is very confusing."

"We must not let him convince the children of these things."

"We cannot reject his ideas too openly, beloved. We depend on his goodwill for everything, until we can get our papers and get jobs and get our own house. And Lisa says that houses are expensive."

The grown-ups talked a lot about what jobs they would try to get when they had their papers. They talked about jobs the way Zamatryna talked about school, although it seemed to her that they did not welcome the idea of working the way she welcomed the idea of learning; they did not think that jobs would make them happy.

"For really good jobs you need to go to school," Lisa told them one morning over breakfast. "It's hard to get a nice clean job if you haven't been to college, or at least to high school. The kids will have it easier. But you folks, well, maybe you guys, Erolorit and Macsofo, can get into some kind of construction work, if you're good with your hands: Stan has connections, although you have to worry about union stuff on those jobs. You can do things like selling newspapers, I guess. You see guys standing by Kmart all the time, waving the *Gazette-Journal* at people who don't even nod at them or say hello, let alone slow down to dig change out of their pockets. I swear I've never seen someone buy a paper from one of those folks: don't ask me how they make any money from it."

"Are they Mendicants?" Zamatryna asked.

"Are they what, honey?"

"Mendicants. Holy beggars."

"Holy beggars? They have those in your country? Holy like sacred, you mean? Our beggars are just holey because all their clothing is full of holes. Oh, Lord, no, the newspaper sellers aren't begging: they're working. The beggars are downtown, heaven help them, sleeping in the park by the river, under the bridges and whatnot. The cops sweep 'em out every few weeks. We don't have nearly enough shelters here. No, you don't want to wind up homeless, believe me. We're not going to let that happen."

"This is a job?" Erolorit asked, frowning. "Sleeping in parks?"

"Oh no, no, that's what happens to people who can't get jobs, or can't keep them. Or some people who can, for that matter. I was almost there a couple times myself, before I went to jail. If it hadn't been for Mama—"

Lisa wiped her face with her napkin, and Harani said gently, "You were telling us about jobs."

"Jobs. Right. Thank you, sweetie. So anyway, you can flip burgers, plenty of high-school kids do that, but it doesn't pay enough to keep you in toilet paper." The cousins shrieked again, as they had at the word latrine, and Lisa chuckled. "Kids. They always love potty humor: doesn't matter what country they come from, does it? So yeah, you can flip burgers. Or, um, well, sometimes you see ads for people to stuff envelopes at home, housewife type work: I don't have a clue what that pays. Not much, probably. If you can count and make change you can clerk at convenience stores like 7-Eleven, although that can be dangerous. They get robbed."

"Robbed?" Erolorit asked. "What is that?"

"Well, you know, people stealing things. Criminals. They come into the store and put a gun to your head and ask for all your money."

Poliniana cocked her head. "Are they Mendicants?"

"What? Your holy beggars?" Lisa laughed. "Lord, no! You have a choice about whether to give your money to a beggar: crooks make you do it, or they'll kill you."

Poliniana squinted up at Lisa. "Why would they have to do that? Why wouldn't people just give them the money?"

"Bless you, honey, people do give them money if they want to stay alive. Sometimes the crooks kill them anyway, though. But if you gave your money away all the time you wouldn't have anything left, now would you?"

"Not if you only gave them what they needed to live."

"Now, how would you know that? Crooks would tell you they needed all of it, even if they didn't."

"Why would they do that?" Rikko asked. "What would they do with money they didn't need?"

"Buy things they wanted. Drugs or booze, most likely."

"What are drugs and booze, please?"

"Oh, Rikko. You kids are so innocent. They're—they're pills you take, or things you drink, to make you happier. To get you drunk or stoned."

"Like Uncle Darroti," Poliniana said. "He used to get drunk. You remember, Rikko. He walked funny and couldn't talk right, and sometimes he peed on himself." Jamfret shrieked, but Rikko nodded.

"Was Uncle Darroti a crook? Is that why he—"

"Rikko," Macsofo said sharply, making the X for silence, "hush. It is not proper to speak of this!"

"Are we crooks, Lisa?" Jamfret said. "Because you gave us your money?"

"What? No, sweetheart! You didn't ask me for it, did you? I did it of my own free will."

"But we're taking all of your money," Zamatryna pointed out. "For the papers."

"I'm *giving* you all of my money, and your mommy and daddy and aunt and uncle and grandpa will work to pay me back, and you too, when you're a smart grown-up lady and can get any job you want. That's different."

"The man at the camp who is selling the papers," Macsofo said. "He is a crook, yes? Because he is taking all your money?"

Lisa took a deep breath. "Well now. Well, that's tricky. Yes, he is, but that's because he's falsifying information. The papers would cost money anyway; they just wouldn't cost as much. And at least we're getting something for the money. So yes, he's a crook, just like people who sell drugs are crooks, but—well, he's not saying we have to give him our money or he'll kill us. So it's different. He's a—a cleaner crook."

Jamfret tugged at Macsofo's hand. "Papa, is that why Uncle Darroti killed the Mendicant? To get her money?"

There was a short, appalled silence. "I just told your brother," Macsofo said, his voice dangerously quiet, "that we do not speak of that."

"Uncle Darroti gave money to Mendicants!" Zamatryna said. "He always did, just like everyone always did! He wouldn't have—"

Harani pulled Zamatryna up onto her lap. "Hush, child. Hush. It is all in the past, and we are here in America now, and Darroti is dead. No good will come of talking about this."

"I begin to think," Erolorit said drily, "that Lisa is right, and that the children should not listen to every conversation."

Lisa shook her head. "It's okay. Everything's okay. Whatever that poor man did, it was good of you to keep loving him, just like it was good of Mama to keep loving me when I was a bad person. I don't think any less of any of you for standing by him. You did the right thing. Everybody needs love, even if they've done wrong."

"Of course we stood by him," Erolorit said, frowning. "He was our brother. Would people in your country have deserted him?"

"Some would. Sure they would. There's no law that says you have to love your family, after all."

"There isn't?" Jamfret asked. "Why not? That's the law in our country. The Law of Hearts. That's why we came here."

Lisa shook her head again. "Then your country's better than this one, sweetheart, and I hope you can teach us some things!"

"I think I prefer the laws in America," Macsofo muttered, and Erolorit shot him a glance that could have charred wood.

Timbor cleared his throat. "We were talking about jobs."

"Jobs," Lisa said. "Right. Time to get back on the subject."

"I do not think any of us want jobs where we may meet these crooks, Lisa. Can you tell us about jobs where there are no crooks?"

"Oh, Timbor! You really do come from a different place, don't you? I don't think there's any job in the world where there aren't any crooks. Not all of them have guns, that's all."

Later that day, after she had memorized all the words beginning with Q in the dictionary and the list of preservatives on the back of the Cheerios box, Zamatryna pondered this conversation. She thought about Uncle Darroti, who had made her the wooden doll, and who had wept so ceaselessly before he died. He had always been kind to her. How could he have been kind and still have been a crook?

Before Zamatryna went to sleep, Harani came into her room for an hour of reading. Lisa said it was good to read before bedtime. Usually parents read to their children, she said, but Zamatryna knew more English than her mother did, so she read to Harani, explaining the words. It was good practice for school. But tonight she didn't feel like reading.

"Mama, why did Uncle Darroti kill the Mendicant?"

"We don't know, child. We will never know. Both Darroti and the Mendicant are dead."

"But surely he didn't do it for money?"

"I can't imagine that he did it for money, no. But I can't imagine any other reason he would have done it, either. It is unimaginable, and yet it happened. He never denied that he had done it—our poor Darroti!—but he could not explain it, either."

"Did he know the lady?"

"Everyone knew her; she was famous, because she was one of the first female Mendicants. I do not think he knew her better than anyone else did. We had no converse with her family, which was nobler than ours. We sent messages afterwards, of course, each family offering condolences to the other. They were kind in their grief. They sent us a fine blanket to take into exile, although we wound up leaving it at home for lack of room, and because it caused us pain. But they never said that she had known him."

"Mama, where do you think Darroti's spirit is now? In a simple thing, or a complicated one?"

Harani sighed. "I do not know, child. He seemed simple enough, but he was evidently more complicated than we knew. He might be in a bird, for instance, if he were really simple, but I think that he was not. I think he must be in a flower or a berry."

"And that is why we bless everything we eat. Because it might be Darroti."

"Yes."

"Stan thinks the dead live in the sky."

"Stan believes many things we do not, Zamatryna."

"I wish the dead could speak to us. Then Darroti could tell us what happened, and Macsofo would not be so unhappy."

"I wish the dead could speak too, child. Everyone does. The Great Breaking is a great sorrow. But I do not think Darroti would tell us what happened even could he still speak, for he never told us when he was alive. And I do not know if Macsofo would be happy even if we knew the story."

"He wants to go back to Lémabantunk."

"And yet he complained even there," Harani said, "although we never noticed it so much. I begin to think Macsofo was born to be unhappy, and maybe Darroti, too."

"What of Papa, then? He is their brother."

"Your father looks for reasons to be happy," Harani said, kissing Zamatryna. "And you are the biggest reason of all. It heals our heart to see you thriving in this place, as Lisa says you are. Goodnight, child."

Harani left the room, and Zamatryna snuggled into her pillow, thinking about Darroti. Was he in the hamburger she had eaten for lunch, or the apple she had eaten yesterday? Was he in her now, feeding her? Or was he back at the camp where he had died, in the sagebrush blackened by the fire?

Poor Darroti, who had summoned such shame! And that was

why she must work very hard to be a good American, to make her parents happy and proud.

And indeed, she liked many things about America, although some of it was confusing. Lisa took her shopping sometimes, to the grocery store or to the mall. Zamatryna was enchanted by the rows and rows of food, or shoes, or books, or clothing in each store; she was even more enchanted by the lights of the casinos, but Lisa would not let her go inside.

"They're pretty from the outside, sweetie, but they're wicked. You don't want to go in there. That's where people throw away their money."

"They throw it away?" Zamatryna was confused. "Why? So other people can pick it up who need it?"

"No. They throw it away because they think they'll get more that way."

Zamatryna frowned. "You mean, because if they show they don't need it, more will come to them? That is why we give money to Mendicants. Do they throw their money at Mendicants?"

Lisa looked at her. "No, they throw it at machines, but yes, they hope they'll get more that way. Don't worry about understanding it. You can't."

"Why do machines need money? They aren't alive."

Lisa laughed. "You're right. The machines don't need money."

"But what do the machines do with the money they don't need?"

"They eat it. Except sometimes, when they spit out a lot of it at once, and then whoever's there can take it home. And everyone who goes in there thinks they'll be the person who'll get the money, if they stand there long enough. It's foolishness."

"The machines spit it up? They vomit it?"

Lisa laughed again, a hearty laugh from her belly. "Yeah, they vomit it. That's a good way of putting it."

Zamatryna wrinkled her nose. "That sounds disgusting."

"Yes, it is, and that's why we're not going in there. Now, where do you want to go for lunch, sweetie? McDonald's, or Taco Bell?"

Zamatryna chose McDonald's. They were giving away small toy aardvarks in improbable shades of orange and purple and pink, characters in a cartoon Poliniana liked. Zamatryna did nice things for Poliniana whenever she could, to make up for having been mean to her about sharing a bedroom, and she knew that Poliniana would be happy to have more aardvarks.

Outside the McDonald's stood a very dirty woman in a tattered sweatshirt and blue jeans. She wore no shoes. Her hair was matted and stringy, and she smelled sour. She held up a cardboard sign that said, in heavy, crooked letters, "I need gas $$$ to get to California. Pls help."

Zamatryna tugged on Lisa's hand—an American Mendicant!—and they stopped. The woman smiled at them; several of her teeth were missing. Lisa took a step backwards, pulling Zamatryna with her, and said quietly, "I saw you last month at the Salvation. You're running a scam."

The woman's smile vanished. "Am not. I am not! I've been trying to get to my brother's family in Sacramento—"

"So why doesn't your brother help you, then? I'll buy you a meal, but I'm not giving you cash."

The woman scowled. "I'm not hungry. I ate this morning. I need—"

"You need food, because everybody does." Lisa slipped something into Zamatryna's hand and said, "Here, honey, go buy her a Happy Meal, okay? Make sure you get the right change."

Zamatryna glanced at what Lisa had given her—a folded $10 bill—and ran inside. Behind her, Lisa and the Mendicant woman had begun to argue.

They were still arguing when Zamatryna came out, with the Happy Meal and a bright pink plastic aardvark. "What are you going to do?" the woman said to Lisa, jeering. "What are you going to do? Call the cops on me because I need gas money—"

"Plenty of agencies in town would help with gas money if that's really what you needed! You'd better watch yourself. I'm not going to call the police, but other people might. Zamatryna, give her the food and let's get out of here."

"Here," Zamatryna said, holding the Happy Meal and the aardvark out to the Mendicant woman. Mendicants in Lémabantunk didn't argue with people, but then, everything was different here.

The woman, glaring, snatched the bag of food out of Zamatryna's hand. "Don't want that stupid toy. You keep that to play with, eh? Bet you have a lot of toys at home. Bet she buys you plenty of toys. Aren't from around here, are you? You aren't really her kid, are you? Skin's too dark. People coming over here taking American jobs—"

"You could at least say thank you," Lisa snapped, and hurried Zamatryna back into the car. She was shaking. "We'll go to another McDonald's, honey. I'm sorry. You try to help people and they just spit in your face, I swear, I know it's my Christian duty to do the best I can by folks whether they're nice or not, but that woman gives people who are really down on their luck a bad name, and it's just a shame. I wish we hadn't given her the food."

Zamatryna looked down at the pink aardvark. "Everyone has to eat. You said that."

"Yeah, I did, and it's true. Bad people have to eat too, I know that, or they'll never get the chance to be better. But it sure is easier to feed people who have some manners, I swear! Well, the police will pick her up soon, if she keeps acting that way."

"What will they do to her?"

"Put her in jail." Lisa, maneuvering deftly in the traffic of South Virginia Street, looked over at Zamatryna and said, "She'll get meals in jail. And maybe she'll get her head on straight, like I did. We have to hope so. I'll pray for her."

"Lisa, are there any Mendicants here who aren't crooks?"

"Sure. Sure there are, sweetie. Most poor people aren't crooks, whatever rich people think. It's the rich people who are more likely to be crooks, with all that money they don't need. Most homeless people did the best they could before something came along and whomped them: they lost a job, or they got sick or got divorced—that's hard on women, especially with kids—and then they just couldn't save enough for an apartment. Rents around here are murder. You can't get a closet for under eight hundred a month."

Zamatryna studied the aardvark, which was missing an ear. Poor thing! "Divorce is when married people get unmarried? Stan says that is a sin."

Lisa sighed. "Honey, I love Stan a lot, but he's never been married to somebody who beat him black and blue every two days, or who took up with somebody younger and kicked him out the door. There's a whole lot of sin in the world, and sometimes it means you can't live with people anymore. To my mind that means it wasn't a real marriage in the first place, not a marriage God would want to last. People make mistakes. It's not easy to find the right person. And God has to know that, since God knows everything. God wants us to be happy, not miserable."

"But your god burns people. That is what Stan says. If this god does not want people to be miserable, why roast them like chickens?"

Roasting them like chickens was a phrase Macsofo had used once. Lisa gave one of her belly laughs, and said, "Well now, that's a good question. You sure are smart, Zamatryna. And the answer is that God doesn't want them to be miserable. They choose to do things that will make them miserable, and God's as sad about it as anybody else who loves them would be. And God just keeps giving all of us second chances, but some people throw them away. That woman back there isn't ready to pick hers up. She may not be ready for a while. She may never be ready."

"Lisa, do you believe that my uncle is roasting like a chicken?"

Lisa didn't answer. She turned left onto McCarran and pulled the car over to the side of the road, on the right-hand shoulder near the Albertson's. She sat there for a moment, looking at Zamatryna. "Sweetheart, I can't say. I wouldn't presume to pass judgment. I don't know what was in Darroti's heart, or if he repented when he was dying. I just don't know."

"Then how can Stan know?"

Lisa was quiet for a long time, while traffic drove by them, and then she said, "He can't. But don't you ever tell him I said so. It would just hurt him. Stan has to find his way, like everybody else."

More commands for silence. Zamatryna sat oppressed, her head bowed, until Lisa said gently, "Zamatryna, where do you think Darroti is now? What do you think happened to him?"

"At home we believe that the spirits of the dead go into other living things, simpler things like flowers or animals. And the other living things teach them what they didn't learn when they were alive. But we can't talk to them, and it makes us sad."

"Yes," Lisa said. "Yes, that makes everybody sad." She started the car up again. "I talk to Mama in my head all the time. And sometimes I think she answers, but I know it's only my imagination. Well, I hope your uncle Darroti is someplace where he can learn things. That's a nice idea. And some Christians believe that too: that there's not just Heaven or Hell but Purgatory, where you wait until you've learned enough to go on."

"Purgatory," Zamatryna said happily. " 'An intermediate state after death for expiatory purification.' I should have remembered that, from the dictionary, except I don't know what all the words mean. But the dictionary says it is a place of punishment. Listen: 'a place or state of punishment wherein according to Roman Catholic doctrine the souls of those who die in God's grace may expiate venial sins or satisfy divine justice for the temporal punishment still due to remitted mortal sin.' Lisa, what does that mean?"

Lisa laughed and shook her head. "It means that people are of two minds about what happens in that place, if they even believe in it. It's just like jail, you know. Some people think jail is a place for crooks to be miserable in, to punish them, and some think it's a place where they can learn new things, so they won't be crooks anymore when they get out. I've seen it work both ways. But I bet on the learning way whenever I can, because that's what happened to me. Now listen, do you still want to go to McDonald's, or are you tired out from all this talk? We could just go home and have sandwiches."

"Sandwiches, please." Zamatryna had the aardvark for her cousin, even if it had lost an ear, and she was afraid of meeting another Mendicant like the one they had seen before, who had been rude and had upset Lisa so much. "Lisa, are all the Mendicants here, the ones who choose to be Mendicants instead of having to be Mendicants because they lost their jobs or got divorced—are they all bad people? Because at home, many people choose to be Mendicants for a little while, and it is an honor. Do people here"—she stopped and thought, struggling with the words—"do people ever ask other people for things so that—so the other people can show that they are good people by giving them the things? And then the Mendicants can go back to not asking for things afterwards, and no one thinks they are bad?"

"Whoa," Lisa said. "That's kind of complicated, isn't it?"

"I'm sorry. I didn't say it well. I meant—"

"No, sweetie, you said it fine. Well, there are folks whose job is to ask people for money to help other people, you know, but they get paid for doing it. That's a job. I guess the closest to what you mean is Halloween."

"What is Halloween, please?"

"It's in two weeks, actually. It's a holiday for kids. You know those displays we've been seeing in stores, the scary masks and the piles of candy, and the pumpkins? Those are Halloween things."

"Oh. Those things are not always there? I thought the masks were for children to wear during their games. But why are they scary? They are only pieces of plastic."

"You're right," Lisa said with a chuckle. "They aren't scary. They're supposed to look scary, though; they're pretend-scary."

"Why do people pretend to be scary? And what do the pumpkins have to do with it? I thought the pumpkins were a symbol of harvest, even though here you have the harvest in your supermarkets all year long."

"Well, I guess Halloween's a kind of harvest festival, or was once. The way we do it now, kids dress up in costumes and knock on people's doors, and the people give them candy, except these days you can only go to the houses of people you know, and you have to go through the candy really carefully, because there are some sick people out there, and it's sad. But anyway, Halloween's a game more than an honor, like you said your Mendicants are. I'll take you kids trick-or-treating in our neighborhood, Stan's and mine. You'll like it. You get to dress up and ask for candy for one night, and then the next day you get to go back to being your normal self, if you aren't sick from all the candy. The costumes are the best part, if you ask me. You get to dress up as anything you want. But carving pumpkins is fun too."

Stan, it turned out, did not think that carving pumpkins was fun, and he did not approve of wearing costumes to ask for candy. He stood in the kitchen the Saturday before Halloween, watching Lisa lug a huge pumpkin in from the car. The children followed her; they had helped her pick the largest pumpkin from the supermarket. "Lisa, what are you doing? Is that for pie?"

"I'll buy another one for pie," she said, easing it gently onto the table. "I'll make you some pumpkin pie, Stan. I know how much you like it. With vanilla ice cream and whipped cream. But first we're making a jack-o'-lantern."

Stan grew pale. "Lisa, we're Christians."

"Yes, we surely are." Her voice was calm. "Okay, so which of you kids wants to take a pencil and draw the face?"

"Lisa! This is Satanic supersti—"

"Stan Buttle, it's no such thing! It's fun, that's all! Now look here, every single year kids come to our door on Halloween, and you never said I couldn't give them candy. You think some of those costumes are cute. You know you do. Remember that itty bitty girl dressed up as a ladybug last year? You liked that costume as much as I did."

"She was a ladybug, not a devil! And we give out candy with Scripture verses on the wrappers!"

"And how many of those kids read them, do you think? Stan, be reasonable. You went trick-or-treating when you were a kid and so did I, and neither of us got struck down by God. Come on, now. Jesus has more important things to worry about than jack-o'-lanterns."

"Since we have taken in this family," Stan said stiffly, "it is our responsibility to make sure that they learn Godly ways—"

"And it's our responsibility to make sure they learn American ways, too, and if Halloween's ungodly, I'll eat my hat. Sure, some people use it as an excuse to do bad things. Some people do bad things with Christmas. Is that ungodly too, Stan?"

"I want to dress up as an aardvark," Poliniana said happily.

"I want to draw the face on the pumpkin," said Jamfret.

"No," Rikko said, "Zamatryna should draw the face, because she's the oldest, and anyway she's the best drawer." Zamatryna flushed with pride.

Stan cleared his throat. "I'm sorry, Lisa. I can't permit—"

"Stan." Timbor stood in the doorway. "Stan, friend, how can the children do this so you will be happy with it? If they dress as ladybugs instead of devils, will that be all right? Or if you bless the pumpkin?"

Stan blinked. Lisa grinned. "Okay, there you go. No monster costumes. Princesses and butterflies and, oh, knights or football players or something for the boys. How's that, Stan?"

"I know," Rikko said, hopping on one foot, "I know! We can be the Marx Brothers! There are four of us!"

"I can be Charlie Chaplin," Poliniana said. "But I want to be an aardvark, too! Lisa—"

"Honey, Halloween comes around every year. You can be an aardvark this year and Charlie Chaplin next year. Okay?"

"Charlie Chaplin and the Marx Brothers are actors," Timbor said. "You explained that to me, Stan. So the children will be actors too. And that is not evil, is it? You do not think the movies with those actors are ungodly."

"And aardvarks aren't evil, because they're animals, and they were on the ark, and that means God loves them," Poliniana said, looking winsomely up at Stan. He had told them the story of the Flood the previous Sunday, and all the children had been enchanted by the tale of brave Noah rescuing two of every kind of animal. They had talked about it later, among themselves, wondering if there had been enough animals to hold the souls of all the poor drowned people.

Stan looked very unhappy. "The Devil wears a fair face."

"And cannot withstand prayers, or so you have said," Timbor answered smoothly. "If you pray over the pumpkin, and over the children before they go out in their costumes, will that be all right?"

Stan looked at him, because Timbor had never invited him to say prayers before. Timbor looked back, and smiled. Zamatryna, watching both of them, knew that Stan was afraid, and that Timbor was trying to comfort him. But Macsofo and Erolorit, who had just come into the kitchen, both looked worried.

"Father," Erolorit said in their own tongue, "what of our own blessings?"

"We will have both," Timbor answered, and then in English, "We will offer our own prayers that these things be done well and with love and kindness, and you will offer yours, and that way our children will be doubly protected, Stan, yes?"

Stan had stiffened. "Yours might—your incantations might— yours might just invite the De—"

"Stan," Lisa said. "Stan. Baby steps, Stan. Mysterious ways, Stan."

She looked at Timbor and said, "I think that's a fabulous idea. You do your prayers first, and then Stan will do ours. Two blessings."

Zamatryna gasped. They all looked at her. "Hallow!" she said, squirming with pleasure at the connection she'd just made. "Hallow in the dictionary means 'to make holy or set apart for holy use'! And that's what blessings do! And that word's the first part of Halloween! Lisa, am I right?" She knew that English was deceptive sometimes, and that words that sounded alike sometimes were not, like horse, which was an animal, and hoarse, which meant unable to speak, and hearse, which was a carriage for dead bodies, and whores, which was such a very bad word that Lisa refused to tell her what it meant. She would find out when she got to that part of the dictionary.

"Yes," Lisa said. "Yes, that's exactly right. Very good, Zamatryna. Very good. Timbor, would you bless the pumpkin, please?"

Timbor held up his hands, and the family said in their own language, *Spirits of the dead, thank you for succoring us, that we may remain among the living.* Repeating the familiar words, Zamatryna wondered whose spirit was in the pumpkin, and what that spirit was learning, and how it would feel about having a face carved into it.

"Thank you," Lisa said. "Now, Reverend Stan, would you favor us with a prayer?"

She and Stan bent their heads and clasped their hands in front of them. "Dear Lord God Almighty," Stan said, his voice rough, "protect these innocent little children from all the evils of the world. Keep them safe from the Devil, Lord, and from heresy and unbelief and idolatry. As they carve this here jack-o'-lantern, let it be a window for them into your own eternal truth, not into the falsehoods of Satan, and when we put the candle in the pumpkin, may that flame be for them your own glorious light of revelation in the Spirit, not the scathing and unquenchable fires of Hell, which burn forever where no balm or comfort is. This we ask in the name of your only son, Our Lord Jesus Christ, who harrowed the righteous

souls from the miseries of Hell and brought them into the blessed-
ness of Heaven. Amen."

"Amen," Lisa said cheerfully, although to Zamatryna, Stan's
prayer was far scarier than the pumpkin itself could ever be. "All
right, kids. We've got ourselves one holy pumpkin here. And now
we have to carve some holes in it." Zamatryna giggled: more fun
with English. "I'll go get a pencil, and you kids decide who's going
to draw the face."

The cousins unanimously elected Zamatryna. She sat at the
kitchen table, clutching her pencil and studying the pumpkin. What
kind of face should she give it? A happy face, to make Stan happy, but
whose?

Darroti's. It should be Darroti's face, because she wanted him to
be happy wherever he was now; not miserable and roasting like a
chicken. She would draw Darroti as he used to be, before he became a crook and began crying all the time. Darroti laughing, jug-
gling pieces of fruit while he hopped on one foot. Darroti giving
her a doll.

So she began drawing Darroti's funny lop-sided eyebrows, his
sideways grin, the mole on his cheek that was shaped like a starfish.
She drew Darroti happier than he had ever looked at his happiest
when he was alive. She concentrated very hard as she drew, and the
adults watched her quietly. When she was done, Lisa said, "That's
sure a happy face, Zamatryna. It looks a little like one of Mama's
clowns. Is that a clown?"

"Yes," Timbor said quietly. "A clown. Happy outside and sad inside."

Zamatryna looked up. "Grandfather, was it the wrong face to
draw?"

"It is a wonderful face," he said, his voice thick. He bent and
kissed her. "Thank you, child."

Lisa did the carving, and then they put the candle inside, and

Darroti's grin flickered and leapt with the flame; the cousins clapped their hands, and even Stan smiled.

"Now that the pumpkin's done," Lisa said briskly, "we need to start thinking about costumes. Poliniana, you want to be an aardvark, right? I'm not sure how I'm going to make that costume, honey, but I'll do my best."

Lisa and Aliniana wound up making the aardvark costume out of paper plates and bags. Zamatryna thought it looked like a shapeless mess, but it was purple, and Poliniana loved it. Zamatryna herself had thought of being a ladybug, since Lisa had said that Stan had liked that costume, but a ladybug was a kind of beetle, and pretending to be a beetle made her too uneasy, as if somehow it would be breaking Mim-Bim's silence. So she decided to be a princess instead, because that meant she got to wear her prettiest dress—a frilly thing with sequins and bows that Lisa had found in a thrift store—and lots of perfume. Jamfret, stealing Poliniana's idea, decided to be Charlie Chaplin, and Rikko chose to be Harpo Marx; Lisa made him a cardboard harp.

On Halloween, they put on their costumes and got into the van for the trip to Lisa and Stan's neighborhood. "I told the neighbors we had some friends visiting," Lisa said. "It's not even a lie. Just, if they ask you questions, stay in character, okay? Here, kids. I've got bags for you."

Zamatryna liked Halloween, the candy and the admiring ooohs and aaahs of the grown-ups who handed it out. Everyone told her how pretty she was, and they laughed at Jamfret and Rikko. Poliniana's aardvark was less successful; the more tactful adults asked her what she was, but some of the others hurt her feelings without meaning to. "My, what's this, the Incredible Purple Blob? Ooooh, I'm scared!"

"I'm not scary!" Poliniana said indignantly. "I don't want to be scary! I'm an aardvark!"

"Ooooh, an aardvark," the grown-ups said, scratching their heads. "Well here you go, aardvark. Here's some candy for you."

They encountered other children wearing other costumes. Some had green makeup and fake pegs sticking out of their necks; some had capes and very long teeth; some were furry and growled. A number of children were wearing white sheets. "What are you?" Zamatryna asked one of these draped figures, when they had arrived at someone's door at the same time.

"I'm a ghost! Boo!"

"What is a ghost, please?"

The other child, who was very small, only giggled and said "Boo!" again; its mother looked at Zamatryna and said, "Not from around here, are you?"

When that family had gone away and Lisa was leading Zamatryna and her cousins to the next house, Zamatryna said, "Lisa, what is a ghost, please?"

"The spirit of a dead person, honey, but that's just a story. Ghosts aren't real."

"Dead people live in sheets here?" Zamatryna asked doubtfully. "I thought they lived in the sky, and had wings."

"That's right. They live in Heaven. Some folks believe in ghosts, but that's just a scare story. You don't have to be scared of any ghosts."

"What do ghosts do that is scary, Lisa?"

"Nothing, honey. They don't do anything, because they aren't real."

This wasn't a very satisfying answer, but Zamatryna soon forgot about it in the excitement of making herself sick on Halloween candy. Quickly after that there was the excitement of making herself sick on turkey and stuffing and cranberry sauce, and then the delirium of Christmas—a holiday of which even Stan seemed to approve, for a change—with its beautiful trees and ornaments and piles of presents, its stories about angels and sheep and Baby Jesus. When Zamatryna heard the story about the angel who came to say that Baby Jesus had been born, and who told the shepherds not to be afraid, she asked Lisa, "Was that angel a ghost? Is that why it said not to be afraid? Because ghosts are scary?"

Lisa paused in her task of pressing red-hot buttons into gingerbread dough, and said, "The angel was a messenger of God, honey, not a dead person. And ghosts aren't real. I don't want you to be scared of ghosts. Angels are real, and ghosts aren't."

"But why did it say not to be afraid?"

"Because people are always scared by what's bigger than they are, and God's plan for us is bigger than anything."

"Oh," said Zamatryna, and ate a red-hot.

Lisa smiled and handed her another one. "So how do you feel about starting school, eh? Now that you all have your papers? Are you excited?"

"Oh, yes," Zamatryna said, and indeed she was. Stan and Lisa had debated the wisdom of having her and the cousins start school mid-year, when all the other children would already know each other, but finally they had decided that it was more important for the children to get established as quickly as they could. Zamatryna and the cousins had taken a number of very easy tests; Zamatryna would begin fourth grade, where the other students would be a year older than she was. Lisa seemed a little worried about this; Zamatryna didn't know why. She was older than her cousins, but they still all loved each other. And she had gone to school in the camp and done very well.

So on January 3, wearing her best new jumper and clutching ethnic Barbie, the one who looked most like her, and wearing a backpack filled with new pencils and notebooks, Zamatryna found herself in the fourth-grade homeroom of Sarah Winnemucca Elementary School. Lisa had told her that Sarah Winnemucca was an Indian lady, a Paiute. "She's ethnic too, honey. It's a good omen." But there didn't seem to be a lot of other ethnic children in this room, and Zamatryna suddenly felt acutely out of place, far more than she ever had in the camp, where everyone else looked more or less like her. At the camp school there had been children of all different sizes. Here she was the smallest person in the room.

The teacher, Mrs. Checkham, smiled at her. Mrs. Checkham had very red hair and very blue eyelids. "Children, we have a new student. This is Zama Gan—Gandiffri. Did I say that right, Zama?" When Zamatryna nodded, Mrs. Checkham beamed and said, "Oh, good. Welcome to our class. Can you tell the other children where you're from?"

Lisa had coached her on this part. "I am from—from Afghanistan," she said, the lie sticking in her throat. At least it sounded a little like Gandiffri. "But I do not remember it. I am very happy to be in America."

"Excellent!" said Mrs. Checkham, although some of the other children were staring at Zamatryna in a way she sensed to be less than friendly. "And who's your friend, there?"

Zamatryna held up her doll. "Barbie," she said. Surely all the other children knew Barbie.

"Refugee Barbie," came a boy's voice from the back of the room.

The other children giggled. "Wrigley!" said Mrs. Checkham. "That wasn't nice! Tell Zama you're sorry."

Zamatryna turned. If she was the smallest person in the room, Wrigley was the tallest. He had hair so pale it was almost white; his eyebrows looked invisible against his pale face. He wore a shirt with a monster on it, one of the monsters with the green face and the pegs in its neck. "Will not. It's true, isn't it?" He looked at Zamatryna. "You're a refugee, aren't you?"

"I was a refugee. Someday I will be a citizen," Zama said, as Lisa had taught her.

"That's exactly right," Mrs. Checkham said. "That's excellent,

Susan Palwick

Zamatryna. Children, the Constitution offers protection for everyone here."

"Oh yes," Zamatryna said eagerly, back on solid ground. Lisa had taught her about that, too. "This is a wonderful country. Would you like me to recite the Declaration of Independence for you?" Surely the other children would accept her, if she recited the creed of their country.

But instead they laughed. "Nerd," someone said, and someone else said, "Freak," and Mrs. Checkham frowned.

"Er, well, no, Zama, we don't have time to hear that. But you can tell us what your favorite thing about America is."

She swallowed. Everything she had said so far had been wrong. And then she remembered the monster on Wrigley's shirt. "Halloween," she said. "I was a princess for Halloween." Zamatryna turned to look at Wrigley. "What were you for Halloween? Were you that monster on your shirt?"

She meant to be kind, but the other children laughed, and Wrigley turned red. "I was a ghost. I dragged a chain and I was dripping blood and I went Wooo-hooo-hooo!" He waved his hands in the air. "I was scary!"

"My friend says ghosts are just a story," said Zamatryna, and Mrs. Checkham made approving noises.

"Are not," said another little girl a few rows away. She had brown braids and freckles. "My mother saw one once. We used to live in a house where a lady had been murdered, and her ghost came oozing out of the wall and touched my mommy with its icy hands, and we moved away the very next week!"

"I'm sure she was dreaming," Mrs. Checkham said firmly.

"Was not! The lady was murdered fifty years ago and they never caught who done it and she can't rest in peace 'cause of that. Has to haunt people and try to get them to find the murderer. That's what Mommy says."

"But the dead can't speak to the living," Zamatryna said.

"Can so! Ghosts come to tell people things like who murdered 'em. They want revenge, ghosts. Don't you know anything in Afghanistan?"

"Alicia!" Mrs. Checkham said. "I think that's enough. Children, time to start our spelling lesson. Open your books, please."

Zamatryna pretended to pay attention to her spelling—although she already knew all the words—but instead she thought furiously about what she had just learned. The dead could speak, here. There was no Great Breaking in America. The dead could give messages to the living, and they would keep trying for fifty years, if they had to. They weren't confined to flowers or birds, which would teach them wisdom. The dead floated by themselves, oozing out of walls, seeking revenge with their icy hands.

Stan would call that Satanic; perhaps it was why Lisa had told her so little about ghosts. Lisa would call it a story. But what if it were true?

As soon as she got home that afternoon, she went into her room. She told Lisa and her parents that she was tired, that school had been fine, thank you, and she would tell them all about it later, but now she wanted to take a nap. She went into her room and shut the door, and then she opened her closet and took out the peanut butter jar with Mim-Bim in it, and put it on her desk.

"You," she said in the language of Lémabantunk, very quietly lest anyone overhear. "You came with me from Gandiffri, where beetles can hold the spirits of the dead but cannot speak. You came here, where the dead can speak, and when we got here you began making your X. Are you giving me a message, Spirit? How can silence be a message?"

X.

"Are you Darroti, beetle? You grew upset when Darroti died, I remember that. But you had made your X even before that. Whatever spirit is in you was there first, before the fence. Who are you, beetle?"

X.

Zamatryna shivered. What spirit would have wanted to come with the family into exile? What spirit would want revenge? "You are the Mendicant woman, beetle, aren't you? You contain the spirit of Gallicina, and you are trying to give me a message. But your message says nothing, and I do not know how to help you. Gallicina, Darroti is dead. If you want revenge, you already have it. We are in exile, and he is dead. I cannot help you."

She was sure now that she was right, as sure as she was of the desk under the beetle's jar, or the sunlight outside, or of her own skin. The beetle who refused to die was Gallicina's ghost. But the beetle answered only as it had always answered, with its slow, stubborn sign for secrecy.

7

Darroti

He spends most of his time in the bookcase now, the one in the living room next to his father's sleeping pallet. He huddles there and weeps into Timbor's towel, a small sodden spot of misery. When the family left the camp he was yanked after them; he rode along helplessly in the air above the van, looking back at the devastation of the fire. At any moment, surely, he would be joined by hundreds of other spirits, the souls of the slaughtered: but if indeed that happened, he was unable to perceive it. Perhaps the van pulled him away from them too quickly, or perhaps here the dead are forbidden to speak to one another, as at home they are forbidden to speak to the living.

He has not met any other souls here. There is no one to speak to. He has tried to communicate with his family; he has entered their dreams and seen them wake, screaming or weeping. He no longer tries to speak to the children at all, because it sickens him to frighten them so, and because they cannot know or remember enough of Gandiffri to understand the tale he needs to tell. But his brothers and their wives, who do remember, will not hear. His dream-visits bring them only horror, not comfort; and their sleeping minds have, in defense, begun to push him utterly away. Only Timbor still lets him in.

Always Darroti tries to bring relief; always he tries to tell the story he now—too late—wants his family to know. But Timbor's sleeping mind, while it permits him as a guest, will not listen to the tale, which is long and winding. Timbor's thought flits off among the events of the day, pondering cars and pumpkins and small men with canes wearing bowler hats and mustaches; it recalls Darroti's mother Frella; it remembers the old man's years of selling fine carpets in the Great Market of Lémabantunk, the warp and woof of jewel-like wool. Into these things it mixes fragments of Darroti's tale, but it will not heed the whole. Why should it? It does not think the dead tell tales at all; it thinks these fragments only dreams.

It was, in fact, in the carpet stalls of the Great Market of Lémabantunk that the tale began, two years before the family's exile, two years before that dreadful dawn when the City Guard found Darroti, clutching a bloody knife, sobbing over the body of the woman he loves.

For he loves her still. He has never stopped loving her, never will: never can, for then he would cease to be himself.

He does not love her yet, on that hot summer morning in the Great Market, for he has not yet met her. He is twenty-two, foolish and careless; he spends his days helping his father sell carpets in the market, and his evenings drinking wine with his friends, and his nights, quite often, coupling with whores purchased with his share of the carpet sales. He is kind to the whores, and fair: he rotates among them to share his endowments—which are considerable, and always skillfully employed—and his money, and often he shares his wine, too. They are fond of him.

He is fond of them. He is fond of his father, fond of his brothers and their wives, fond of his little nieces and nephews, for whom he makes toys and plays the jester. He is, perhaps, fondest of his dead mother, whom he truly misses; but all his love is dutiful, not fiery. Darroti knows much about affection, lust, and carpets, but he has not yet discovered passion. To his married brothers' queries about when he will take a bride, he simply laughs. Marriage seems a dull and dreary thing, a thing for older brothers.

This morning in the Market, he is unpacking a new shipment of carpets from Barrina, the great sheep-herding region to the south. These are fine goods, the wool dense and finely woven, the colors true. They will fetch high prices; he will be able to purchase many whores. He is by himself today. His father has taken some of their best wares to the home of a wealthy and querulous widow, who demands a private showing because the press of the Market overwhelms her. The spice merchant across the way is unloading new goods of his own, and the air smells of cinnamon; it tickles Darroti's nose. He whistles as he deftly sorts the carpets into piles, first by use and then by size and color: carpets to sleep on (thickest, and woven with soothing spiral designs to inspire sleep), carpets to walk on (of two types: tough outdoor ones and softer indoor ones), carpets to pray on (both lightest and thinnest, that they may be carried easily to Temple, and that they not remove the worshipper from knowledge of the good hard ground).

The prayer carpets are the most intricately patterned, for they are used in meditation. In the Temple, those who have served their year as Mendicants—who have learned to depend on generosity and abundance, and not upon their own skill—gather to contemplate the Elements and their ever-changing dance, in which the same four steps lead always to new and renewed life. The Elements are the warp and woof of the cosmos, and creation is the carpet they weave, and prayer carpets are the symbol of that great joy and mystery. They are woven in the colors of the Elements: creams and whites for air, blues and purples for water, blacks and browns for earth, reds and oranges for fire. No two are alike. In some, the colors are evenly distributed; in others, one color predominates, although all prayer carpets contain all four groups. The weaving of prayer carpets is a high and holy calling in Gandiffri.

For the custom in Gandiffri, as long as there have been Temples—and no one remembers a time when there were not—has been this: the person who wishes to enter the Temple, preparing to spend the necessary year as a Mendicant, meditates upon the Elements of which all people are made, and seeks to discern his own mixture. Is he mostly earth or air, fire or water, or are they balanced evenly in him? How are they combined? What is his pattern?

When he thinks he has glimpsed the answer, he goes to find a prayer carpet that will match his vision of himself. He must seek one ready-made, rather than paying weavers to produce the pattern he thinks that he has seen; for people can be wrong about themselves, and sometimes, browsing through the piles of woven wool, the seeker sees a pattern utterly unlike what he expected, but that nonetheless sends his heart leaping and his soul thrumming within him. Sometimes such a carpet represents what he already is. Some-times it represents what he must seek to become, to grow a balanced soul. The ecstasy of beauty will lead him truly, for all prayer carpets are beautiful—as all people are—but each is lovely in a different way.

The seeker buys the carpet that has spoken to him. He meditates upon it for a day, a week, a month; he memorizes it. And then he rolls it up and puts it aside and dons the plain homespun robe and sandals of the Mendicant, and spends his year begging in the streets: a year when he must live by generosity and grace, when he cannot work. As he begs he keeps the pattern of his carpet before him, and prays that what he receives from strangers will help the pattern grow and deepen in him. And when his year is done, he goes home, and puts his normal clothing on again, and takes the prayer carpet to Temple, and unrolls it. And always, when he does this, he sees things in it he did not see before, for always his year as a Mendi-cant has made him more sensitive to the richness of the universe.

The cosmos showers humankind with bounty as beautiful as dia-
monds in a humble begging bowl.

Men are Mendicants, and go to Temple; women, who themselves weave—both in wool and their wombs—and who maintain
the pattern of the home, have less need of such discipline. Or so
say men, who wish to come from Temple home to soup and bread
and mended clothing. Some women have begun to claim that they,
too, deserve more time for meditation in the company of those
outside their families. They say that Temple is not a discipline for
minds that need it, but a luxury, a privilege they wish to share.

"Aye," Darroti's father Timbor has said, when the family has discussed the matter. "If Temple is a discipline, then so is cleaning. Let
men and women trade places for a while. Should not disciplines be
balanced, like the Elements themselves?"

"And if I go begging as a Mendicant, you will cook?" Harani
asks tartly, and everyone laughs.

"If we lose you as a cook, we will all go begging," Macsofo says,
"for I would rather eat anything but father's burned eggs and meat."

"I would practice," Timbor says, looking pained. "I would im-
prove."

"And the children would starve in the meantime," Harani says.
"You notice that the women who want this are all wealthy, from
households with cooks and other servants. It takes leisure to demand
the luxury of Temple. No, I will seek the patterns in my roasts and
salads, and feed my family."

Darroti himself has little opinion on the matter. If women wish
to beg, let them; whom will it hurt? He has already dutifully served
his own year as a Mendicant, after picking out an earthy, airy prayer
carpet in browns and whites, with hints of other colors around the
edges. The carpet suited him, for he is grounded and dreamy at the
same time, fond both of the things of the senses and of the reveries
into which they sometimes lead him. So he served his year as a

Mendicant, holding out his hands for bread and wine and coins; it was pleasant enough, but he found it difficult to think about the pattern of his carpet, the pattern of himself. He preferred to think about the whores who gave him favors without payment, that year, or the wine he needed no coins to buy. He would cheerfully have been a Mendicant forever. When he returned home, sorry only that he had not been chosen as a Necessary Beggar—an honor all Mendicants desire—he had nearly forgotten what his carpet looked like, save that it was mostly brown and white.

And so he took it to Temple and unrolled it, curious to see it again: and indeed it was mostly brown and white, but now he saw, encircling those colors, a ring of flame and water, passion and mutability; and it seemed to him that this ring would devour or strangle him, and he was afraid, and knelt trembling on the carpet, praying for strength and balance. But soon that fear and vision faded, and Darroti felt the same as he always had, both solid and slight, a kind and ordinary man who would never be remarkable.

And so now, on this fine morning in the Great Market of Lémabantunk, he sorts the prayer carpets, wondering what kinds of people will come to buy them. Here is a gorgeous one, flaming in reds and purples and oranges and blues, shot throughout with white and brown, slender threads of air and earth containing the brillant pattern of fire, which is cooled only slightly by branching waters. Ah, that is a noble carpet, thinks Darroti, arrested now by admiration. Never has he seen one so alien to his own nature, and yet so beautiful. He could wish to be more like that, or to meet such a one. He carefully covers the carpet with others, to protect its colors from the sun, and turns to the sturdier pile of tough, muted outdoor mats.

Here is a customer, asking for an indoor carpet in white and rose. Here is another, who haggles over the price of a sleeping mat already marked down almost to nothing; one corner is slightly frayed, gnawed by moths before it reached the Market. It is nothing an artfully tossed pillow will not hide. Darroti bargains, annoyed and wishing that the fool would take his business somewhere else, and at last the fool tosses a few coins onto the table, sweeps up the sleeping mat as if he is doing Darroti a favor, rather than the other way around, and leaves.

Another customer approaches the booth, now: a slight figure in a plain hooded robe. Darroti automatically assesses the quality of the fabric. It is heavy silk, silver-gray, worth as much as all the carpets in the booth combined. Darroti feels his eyebrows rising. Only the nobility wear such, and the nobility do not come to the Great Market. They send their servants.

"May I help you?" he asks, and looks at the face beneath the hood. A woman's face, delicate, with high cheekbones and large eyes, but the nose is straight and proud, the mouth a resolute line. A woman? Say rather a girl. She cannot be out of her teens, and she has come alone to the Market in a robe worth as much as a house. No servants are with her. Something in Darroti's chest tightens. He wants to tell her to wear coarse linen, if she is going to venture out by herself, but he holds his tongue. It would not do for a common merchant to say such things to someone wearing silk.

She stares at him now, her face fierce and desperate. She swallows. Her hands are clasped in front of her; she looks like someone who is struggling for her life, not like someone who wishes to buy a piece of cloth to put on the floor. "Lady," Darroti asks her gently, "are you well?"

He should not have said that. He has been impertinent, and will lose her business. But she relaxes slightly, the lines in her forehead smoothing, and says, in a voice like music, all piping flutes and throaty violins, "I wish to buy a prayer carpet."

And then she glares at him, as if daring contradiction.

"Of course," Darroti says quietly. "We have a new shipment from Barrina, just in this morning." He gestures at the covered pile and says, "May you find the pattern of your soul here." It is the standard blessing, but she gives him a glance of such gratitude that he feels as if he has invented the phrase for the first time.

It is standard also to give the seeker privacy, but Darroti watches her out of the corner of his eye as she works her way neatly through the pile. A very young woman, very noble, who wishes to be a Mendicant: her family must not approve, or she would not have come here alone. And she is afraid. Her people have been harsh with her. And yet still she has come. She must be brave, although it may be that she is also foolish.

He bends to tally some accounts on a piece of paper, acutely aware of her concentration a few feet away. She flips past some of the carpets with hardly a second glance, frowns at others, pondering, her lips pursed; goes back to study one, goes on, goes back again. She stands there, her fingers drumming against the wool.

"When you find it, you will know it at once," Darroti says conversationally, as if to his ledger sheet. "If you hesitate, it is not the one. Move on, lady."

She acknowledges this with a quick nod, flips through the carpets quickly and then more slowly and deliberately—and then, turning back the corner of one to see the one beneath it, gives a muffled gasp. "Oh," she says. She tugs at the corner to free the carpet. "Oh, look, this—"

"Let me help you," Darroti says, and abandons the pretense of accounts to hurry to her side. The carpet she has chosen is the one that stopped him this morning—hours ago, it seems now—the flaming, noble pattern, all fire and water. His heart thumps in his chest. He pulls the carpet free of the pile above it. "You have a beautiful soul," he tells her, and at once could bite his tongue. But she only looks up at him in wonder.

"I did not really believe it, that I would find one to match my self. I thought it was like picking out a—a dress, or a cooking pot, some merely useful thing. But it is not like that at all."

"No," he says, his mouth dry.

"I did not think I would know my fate so quickly, all at once," she says, and he thinks, *Nor did I.* He has had no wine since last night, and yet he feels drunk: the good drunk, light and floating, before sickness sets in.

And now she will give him money, and go away, and he will never see her again. He begins to feel sick after all. But she sighs, looking down at the carpet again, running her hands wistfully over it. "It is very fine."

"The best in this shipment," he says. "Indeed, the finest I have ever seen." *The finest in the world,* he wants to say, but prudence stops him.

"Very fine," she says bitterly. "And I cannot afford it."

From anyone else this would be prelude to a round of bargaining, the mandatory protests of poverty from buyer and seller alike, who can never possibly name a price higher or lower than the one they have just offered, and yet always do, until at last they meet in the middle. She expects him to name a price now, this child who could buy half the market with one corner of her silken hood. She expects him to be a merchant, not a man.

He shakes his head. He does not name a price. "Lady?" he asks.

"They will not give me money of my own."

"Merchant!" Someone is calling him from the pile of sleeping mats. He turns in annoyance, putting out a hand to keep the girl from fleeing, and sees a heavy man, all jowls and glistening sweat, with gold rings on his fingers. "Merchant! I seek a sleeping mat in green and amber! Have you any such?"

"None," Darroti says, feigning disappointment, although in fact there are three or four such in the pile. He should tell the man to come back tomorrow, that there will be another shipment— but no, for the man might come back when Timbor was here, and speak to him, instead of Darroti, and thus Timbor might learn of the lie. So instead, wanting only to be rid of this irritation, Darroti says, "Have you tried the carpet booth across the Market? I think I saw some there."

The fat man leaves, grumbling at how far he has to walk. Darroti sends up thanks that Timbor is not here, to see that he has thrown away a sale. He turns back to the girl. "Lady. They will—"

"Not give me money of my own," she finishes quickly. "My father buys me anything I want, but he will not buy me a prayer carpet. He says it is not seemly for women to be Mendicants. He says I am too young. He wants to keep me at home, caged like a bird; he claims I have no need of Temple. How can he know my needs? He does not know my soul; he does not wish to look at it."

I do, Darroti thinks. "Lady."

"And so for three years, since I was fifteen and first dreamed of going to Temple, I have saved up bits of change: spare coins from buying sweets or trinkets, the coins my parents give at holidays. I have collected fifty alaris that way, and it was slow work. I thought that fifty might purchase what I needed. But this is worth far more than that."

Worth the world, he thinks. The carpet is, in fact, worth at least four times that much.

She is still speaking, as if to herself, her head down. There is no guile in her, no will to bargain. "My father says that I cannot be a Mendicant because men will only want to take from me, not give. He says I will be hounded and harassed. My mother and older sister say they find their souls at home, and so can I, and thus—"

"None may tell where any of us will find our souls," Darroti says. He is thinking furiously. He could hold the carpet for her, but Timbor would be suspicious when he came back, and would want to see a down payment; if it has taken three years for her to collect fifty alaris, there is little chance of her gathering the full price. If the carpet stays in the pile, there is the danger that someone else will buy it, for it is a gorgeous thing, and others might fool themselves into believing it the pattern of their own souls.

He glances at the sun. Mid-morning: Timbor will soon be back from his meeting with the widow. He must act quickly.

And so he does, heart pounding. He takes the prayer carpet, swiftly rolls it into a neat tube, and offers it to her with both hands. *And with my heart.* "Tell your father that he is wrong. Tell him that men will give you what you need, just as the cosmos does, for now I give you this."

Her eyes widen. She shakes her head. "No, merchant! I cannot deprive you of your livelihood—"

"I cannot deprive you of your soul, lady."

Her face tightens. "I am not a Mendicant yet. What then would you have for this?" She is suspicious now. She fears that he seeks some advantage over her, that he will ask for favors of the flesh; that he is only what indeed her father has told her all men are.

Pained, he shakes his head. "Nothing, lady. Unless you grant me knowledge of your name. I am Darroti-Frella Timbor, of honest kin although not noble, and I salute your courage, and wish you fair fortune."

Still she does not trust him. She holds out a small cloth bag. "You must take my fifty alaris."

Something has occurred to him. "I will take your fifty alaris, and for them I will give you a sleeping mat to wrap about that other one, so your family will not see it when you take it home."

"Ah! That is good thinking, merchant. That one, on top: the green and purple. I will take that one."

He relaxes, allows himself to grin at her as he rolls the sleeping mat around the other. "And now, what will you say when your people ask you why you went alone to the Great Market to buy a sleeping mat?"

"They will not ask me. I left my maid Adda in the healer's house. I took her there so she could lean upon me; she is old, forty at least, and her back is sore. She did not know I was coming to the Market. I will say—I will tell her and the others that I bought the new sleeping mat for her, to ease her aching back. She favors green and purple."

"Well done," Darroti says, approving. "But she and your family will not be angry that you came to Market alone, even so?"

"Nay," the girl says, and smiles for the first time. Darroti finds himself trembling, as he did once on a winter day when the sun shone from behind a cloud; blinded by the glory of light where a moment before there had been only gloom, he was transported by wonder. He was very small then. This is the first time in all the years since that he has felt that way, as if he is larger than the boundaries of his body. "They know I am impetuous. They will scold me for it, but Adda will love me, and my parents will be pleased. They wish me to be generous, but not to ask for generosity from others."

Her smile fades a little as she says that last. "I give to you because life has given to me," Darroti says, very quietly. It is what people say when they make offerings to Mendicants. The girl looks him full in the face, now, and he sees her tremble, as he did when she smiled.

"I take from you with thanks, as I take from the cosmos," she whispers. It is the other half of the formula. She has grown pale. She swallows and says, "I am Gallicina-Malinafa Odarettari, good merchant."

"Darroti," he says.

"Darroti." She inclines her head.

He bows, very low. When he has risen again, she is gone, making her way through the crowded Market with her precious bundle. He wants to cry after her, wants to implore her to return, that he may feel the sun again. He wants to tell her that only her magnificent soul can elevate his paltry one. But that would not do, and so instead he turns to his ledger sheet, to the dull columns of marching numbers.

Timbor returns a little while later, pleased because he did good business with the widow, who bought new carpets for every room in her large and garish house. "There are so many knick-knacks there," Timbor says, laughing, "that you cannot move without knocking something over. Ivory fans on wooden stands, alabaster jars, glass statues of animals. I feared that I would break some treasure and have to discount its price from the sale; indeed, I wondered if she had put out the things especially for that purpose, if she had some store-room full of hideous miniatures she only pretended to cherish, that she might use them as a bargaining tool when they were smashed. But I was deft, both with my limbs and with my speech, and all is well."

Although Darroti is fond of his father, and would normally enjoy the tale, he can barely bring himself to grunt in response. Gallicina, Gallicina. All is dross but that. He forces himself to act interested, and indeed he is grateful that Timbor's expedition went so well, since the sale will help make up for Darroti's extravagance.

Timbor, humming, is looking through the new shipment now. "These are lovely work."

"Aye."

"Made you any sales this morning?"

"A sleeping mat, marked down for a frayed corner," Darroti answers, making a comic face. "Another, whole, for fifty alaris. A room carpet."

"It was slow, then."

"Aye," he says, the lie sticking in his throat. The shape of the universe has changed, and he must feign talk of common commerce.

Timbor flips through the piles, still humming. Darroti realizes that his father, of long habit, is counting the new goods to check them against the bills of lading. The pile of prayer carpets will be one short, and he cannot account for it by a sale. "The prayer carpets were not all there," he says. "We purchased ten and received only nine."

Timbor looks at him in surprise. "Aye? The Barrina weavers are not usually so careless."

"Perhaps one was stolen along the route," Darroti says. He does not wish to get the weavers in any trouble: he must be careful here. "The packaging looked torn, although I saw no damage to the nine." There have been such thefts before, although they are infrequent; he prays that his father will accept the explanation.

"A pity," Timbor says with a shrug, and turns away, whistling. The widow has put him in an excellent mood, and Darroti sends up thanks. "Well, little matter, if it does not happen more often. May whoever took it have found the pattern of his soul."

Or hers. "Aye," Darroti says quietly. "That is a good wish."

Timbor looks at him now, frowning, alerted by some new note in Darroti's voice. "Are you well, son? You look pale."

"I am fine, Father."

"Were you out drinking again last night?"

"I was with friends. I am fine, Father. I am not ill."

Timbor shrugs and smiles, and reaches out to squeeze Darroti's shoulder, and then turns to speak to a customer. Business is brisk for the rest of the day, and Darroti forces himself to concentrate on work. He bargains well, seeking by small increments to make up the price of the gift he gave this morning, and by the time the Great Market closes at sundown, he and his father have done very well indeed.

As they lock up the booth, Timbor says, "Will you come home with me for supper, Darroti?"

Always Timbor asks this, but usually Darroti declines. He goes off to have supper with his friends, to eat greasy sausages and drink wine and then seek out whichever whore is next on his list. But tonight Darroti wishes to do none of that: he only wants to be alone, to dream of Gallicina. "Aye, I will," he tells his father, and Timbor gives him a startled glance.

"You are sure you are not ill, Darroti?"

"Only tired from a day of bargaining," Darroti says, summoning a smile, and Timbor chuckles and looks pleased.

And so Darroti goes home for supper. The family is delighted to see him, if surprised. His brothers smile, and their wives fuss, and the children clamber on Darroti's lap. They treat him like a king, and he realizes, with a kind of wonder, how much they love him.

After supper—Harani's excellent bread, and stew, and cool clear juice to drink—Darroti tells them he is sleepy and goes to his small room. His sleeping carpet is slightly dusty, and he realizes that he cannot remember when last he actually slept here. He lies down, staring at the ceiling; at last, after this long day, he can allow himself to drift completely in reveries of Gallicina. He replays each delicious moment of their meeting, each word she spoke, the tone of her voice, the planes of her face in the shadows of her hood, the play of sunlight on the costly gray silk of her robe. He wonders if she thinks of him at all. He finds himself hoping that she has made a hero of him, for his gift, and then he is ashamed: he gave the carpet freely, and not to buy her love. And yet how he hopes that she will recall him, remember his name, come back to thank him!

And if she did, Darroti? If she came back to thank you with Timbor there, how then would you explain yourself, eh? And how should the daughter of a noble family love a merchant, who is a merchant's son? Know simply that there is such beauty in the world, and be content.

How be content, without tasting more of it? I could marry such a one.

Marry! You, marry, who have never thought to marry? And marry that one? How would her family allow it? You overreach yourself, Darroti.

And yet I love her. And indeed, all desire for whores has been removed from his limbs, although, with a kind of superstitious dread, he does not yet allow himself to imagine the curves under Gallicina's robes.

She cannot love you, fool. She will forget you before the week is out.

So he torments himself, arguing back and forth, painfully conscious for the first time of how much less he is than he could wish to be. He tells himself that for Gallicina's sake he will be better, nobler, even if he never sees her again; her memory will be his shrine. And then, despairing, he answers himself that if he never sees her again—as is most certain—all his life will be a waste, for the universe cannot contain two such women.

He falls asleep in this feverish debate, and wakes, near dawn, befuddled and ill, seized with a great thirst. Wine. He must have wine. He has never felt such a craving before, and under its impetus he sneaks, trembling and unthinking, into the kitchen, and finds a bottle and drinks, until his shaking hands have steadied and his head is clear again.

Fine work you have made of ennobling yourself, Darroti.

He blinks, standing there, holding the half-empty bottle in the gray light of dawn, and remembers his thoughts of the night before, and is ashamed. Now he must hope that Gallicina does not remember him, if he is so weak.

Nay, nay! You were thirsty, that is all. You awoke surprised out of sleep. Perhaps you are ill, as Timbor thought, and your body needs the wine as medicine; you will be better soon, and governed by your waking mind.

More cheerful now, he puts the bottle away and goes back to bed, and sleeps for another hour, until it is time to get up and go back to Market. Again business is brisk, but today he bargains badly; he is distracted, constantly scanning the crowds for a slight figure in gray silk.

He does not see her. She does not come. Wretched, he once more follows his father home at the end of the day, and allows himself to be pulled into a game with the children in the garden, until Harani calls them to supper.

There are potatoes on the table, and a roast fowl, tossed greens, and a pitcher of juice. Next to the pitcher sits the half-empty bottle of wine Darroti drank that morning.

He stops, stares, feels himself growing ridiculously red. "If you must drink it," Harani tells him quietly, "have it at the table, in the open. Drink it with us, Darroti, with your family."

"I'm sorry. I'll pay you for it. I'll—"

"What nonsense!" Her voice is sharper now, and she is frowning. "Pay for refreshment from your own kin? What are you saying? This is your home, Darroti, not a bawdy house."

Stung, he sits and eats, but finds none of the comfort he found the night before. All the food tastes flat; the voices of his family buzz around him like gnats; even the sweet children do nothing but annoy him. The walls of the house are closing in on him. He cannot stay here.

And so he excuses himself after supper and goes out, trying to ignore Harani's frown, Macsofo's knowing and disgusted look, Timbor's quiet disappointment. He goes to his favorite wine hall and sits with his friends for a while, but although he drinks, he cannot become happy, cannot attend to his fellows' cheerful chatter about dice and women.

There is only one woman. There is only Gallicina.

You will never see her again, fool. Forget her.

It has only been one day. She may still return. I cannot forget her.

"Darroti, attend your betters!" one of his friends says, laughing, and smacks him lightly in the head. A throbbing ache begins inside Darroti's skull, and he finds himself unreasonably angry.

"Nay," he says, "I am not in the mood for this talk tonight," and excuses himself from his friends as he did from his family. They jeer and jest, careless and callow, but he escapes out onto the street, cool now in the darkness, where he can breathe.

He can breathe, yes, but where will he go? To the whorehouse? Nay: the thought turns his stomach, for none of those women is

Gallicina. Nor does he wish to go home, to face his family's questions.

Temple: of course. He has not been to Temple in too long, and prayer will help settle his mind. And so he sneaks home, climbing unseen through the window of his room, and grabs his prayer carpet where it lies, neatly rolled and dusty, by the wall, and flees again, going to the Temple in the center of the city. It is always open, lit now by candles. The most devout, who come here every day, pay for niches in which they keep their carpets, so they will not have to carry them from home. Because it is an unusual hour and not a feast day, only the most devout are here now: a few dim figures, rocking on their prayer carpets, their lips moving silently.

Darroti unrolls his carpet and places it on the floor. He kneels and dutifully studies it, the dull brown and white surrounded by a ring of fire. He does not really expect anything to happen, but something does: vertigo seizes him, the same dizziness he felt when he first beheld the carpet after his year as a Mendicant, when it seemed to him that his little life was surrounded by a doom. Now he knows that doom's name. It is Gallicina.

Gallicina, Gallicina. He closes his eyes and tries to pray, but all he can see is the pattern of her carpet, not his own. He opens his eyes again to fix them upon his own carpet, and there is the ring of fire, which is her soul, and he imagines her surrounding him, embracing him, containing him. And so his meditation becomes a prayer of fervent and lustful thanks to the Elements, for creating Gallicina.

This is not proper practice. Prayer is meant to remind the supplicant of his proper place in the dance of all things; prayer is meant to bring perspective, not obsession. Darroti knows that.

And so he tries to meditate on his own pattern. He tries very hard, but always he finds himself remembering Gallicina's instead, and praying that her desire may be granted, that her family may allow her to be a Mendicant. That part of his prayer, at least, is noble.

At last, exhausted, he sneaks back home, through the window again, and goes to sleep. The rest of the family is long abed. Perhaps he will see her tomorrow. There is still hope; it has only been two days.

But she does not come to the Market the next day, either, and Darroti finds himself descending into a black pit. He bargains well enough, for his brain seems detached from the rest of him, but he takes no joy in the sales, or in the beauty of the day, or in the hearty lentil salad, usually his favorite, that Harani has packed as his lunch. By the end of the day, all of his limbs feel weighted with rocks. She is gone. Gallicina is gone. He will never see her again.

That evening he does not go home at all. He goes to the wine hall, makes small talk with his friends, gets drunk. He does what he used to do, what used to give him pleasure, but he feels no pleasure now. When he leaves the wine hall he goes to the brothel, where the women greet him cheerfully and tease him about his absence. The whore it is his turn to see tonight is his favorite, the oldest and most skilled, but tonight even buxom, supple Stini cannot rouse him.

"Darroti," she says, frowning, after half an hour of dextrous manipulation which has done no good; he lies as limp as a dead fish. She rocks back on her heels and looks at him soberly. "Darroti, dear, what ails you? Are you ill?"

"I am sorry, Stini. I am weary—"

"Your mind is elsewhere," she says. "Your body is here, but your spirit is somewhere else, and so even your body is distant. Where are you, Darroti?"

"In the Great Market," he says dully. "Three days ago."

Stini frowns again. "I have never heard you speak of business."

"Not business," he says. "I—I met someone—a woman—she is far above me, Stini, and—"

"Do not tell me her name, then." Whores are expert at discretion, which is their honor, but something tells Darroti that Stini is right, that he must not speak Gallicina's name here. "You may be able to win her love; these things are not unheard of. But then you should not come here, Darroti."

"I will never see her again. I despair of the thing. That is why I came here. I thought—I thought I must forget—"

"But you cannot," she says briskly. "Your flesh remembers very well, and knows that I am not your beloved, and so for all your youth and vigor"—she grins, and trails a finger over his normally sprightly member—"your body will have none of it. And three days is not so very long. Go, Darroti. I will only charge you half the fee tonight. Go, and do not despair."

He goes, despairing. His old ways are closed to him, and the new way, the way of love and hope, has been withdrawn. He goes home and once again recalls each word of his encounter with Gallicina. He weeps. He has played the fool for a girl who tricked from him the best thing in his stall; she is in her mansion or her palace now, laughing, if she remembers him at all. He has cheated his father and dishonored himself, and all his life will be a waste from this day on.

But the next day at noon, bargaining with a customer over a green and yellow room carpet, he glimpses over the old woman's shoulder a flash of a slender figure in gray silk. He freezes, feels his heart leap, loses the sense of his sentence. There: standing five stalls away, pretending to examine a display of pots. It is Gallicina. She is gesturing to him! He nods at her as imperceptibly as he can, and turns back to the old woman, who suddenly finds herself with a new carpet for a far lower price than she expected. She waddles off, gloating. Darroti turns back to the pots. Gallicina is still there: his heart, his soul. She is coming toward him now, pretending to look at the wares in the other stalls.

Where is Timbor? There, by the pile of sleeping mats, haggling with a man and wife. Darroti moves to the other end of the stall, towards Gallicina, and begins neatening a set of outdoor mats. She stops a few feet away from him, idly flipping through a pile of mats in rust-colored reed. He can smell the clean scent of her hair. He fears he will faint from joy.

"Lady," he whispers.

"Good merchant, Darroti—I need your help." Her voice is very low, and troubled; he thrills to it, even as his pulse races with horror at the thought that she is in any kind of danger. "I would not ask, and yet you have been kind—more than kind—and there is no one—"

"Lady," he says, "Gallicina, I would do anything for you."

And so he would; he would cut off his right hand, if it would spare her any trouble. But he should not have said so, should not have used her name. He has overstepped himself; she will think him an impertinent fool, and flee in disgust. He stands trembling, his head down, for the three beats of silence before she answers, even softer than before, "You have already given me my soul. How could you do more than that?"

He takes courage, then, and looks up at her face, and finds it tracked with tears. The sight slays him: he cannot move. What pain is she in, to weep in public? "Lady! What—"

"Can you speak freely here?"

"No." He gestures at Timbor, still arguing amiably with the couple; they are all grinning broadly, their protests of poverty becoming increasingly more florid. They are enjoying themselves. "My father, he must not know—he must not find out—"

"About the carpet you gave me. Because you did not sell it as you should have."

He nods, too grateful to speak. In the midst of her own troubles, she has thought about him, has entered the world of the carpet merchant, so far below her own, enough to grasp his situation. How quick she is, how compassionate! His hopes soar. "Yes," he says hoarsely. "It is delicate—"

"Indeed. Darroti, can you meet me after the Market closes?"

"Anywhere. Where?"

She names a quiet public square at the edge of the city, near the district where the wealthy live. She names a time. Darroti agrees at once, although the place is distant; he would meet her on the surface of the sun, if she commanded it. He spends the rest of the day in a delirium, scarcely aware of where he is or of what he is doing. He feels himself shining, transformed, transmuted by the alchemy of love. He has been lit by Gallicina's flame, all his grossness purified and precious now.

The hours are an agony until their meeting, but at last the time comes and he hurries there; he wears his best clothing, fine costly linen, having told his family that he is going to a feast in honor of a friend. He navigates the unfamiliar streets near the square Gallicina has named, ecstasy alternating with terror. What if she is not there? What if her cruel father has kept her at home? What if—

But here he is, in the square, and there she is, sitting quietly on a bench with a book. Several other people are in the square, and this is Gallicina's neighborhood: they may know her. He forces his steps into a stately walk, trying to look as if he belongs here, and goes to sit beside her, but not too close. "Lady," he breathes.

"You were good to come," she says quietly, and he trembles.

"You are in trouble—"

"My mother found the carpet," she says bitterly. "I hid it behind my summer robes, and she—well, no matter how she found it. She did, and she told my father, and he is furious. He thinks I have shamed myself." She looks down, blushing. "He demands that I return it. And he demands that I demand back the money I paid for it." She looks up again, smiling grimly. "You see my difficulty."

"Where is it now, lady?"

She bends her head. "I hid it in an alley, not far from here. This morning. I told my father I would take it back to the Market, for he stormed and raged and threatened to disown me." She has begun to cry; it is all Darroti can do not to reach out and wipe the tears from her cheeks. Instead he pulls a cloth from his pocket and passes it to her; their hands touch as she takes it, and Darroti's flesh thrills. Dare he hope that hers does also? "My father threatened to disown me," Gallicina goes on, her voice thick, "and then he went to meet with the other men who own land east of the city, to talk rents and tithes. He will be back tonight, with money on his mind. He will demand the price of the carpet, as if I am a farmer who owes him bushels of corn."

Darroti reaches back into his pocket. He always carries quite a bit of money, and he has more than usual now, because Stini remitted half her fee last night. "Here, lady. Here are two hundred alaris. Will—"

"No! I did not come here to take your money!" She is clutching the cloth he gave her, her knuckles white. "This is wrong! You are a merchant and I steal your livelihood—"

"Hush," he tells her, for the other people in the square have glanced over at them. "Lower your voice, lady. You steal nothing from me. I give it to you. Lady—Gallicina—I am not a good man. I give you what in a week, or less than that, I would spend on wine and whores." He takes a deep breath; there. She cannot think him better than he is, now. "And now I will not have that money to spend on those things, and so you see, you make me better. You help me. It is an honor for me to give you this."

She stares at him. Those eyes! She shakes her head. "You are a good man. I know you are a good man. You—"

"Take the money," he says quietly, and dares to take her hand to press the alaris into it. Her hand is very warm. He folds her slender fingers over the gift, holds her hand in both of his own for a moment, and then releases her, his skin burning from her touch. Her free hand still holds his cloth. "The money is the least of it. There are larger problems than that to solve. You cannot keep your soul in an alley, lady."

"No." She looks away. Is that a flush on her cheeks, in the dim light of dusk? "I cannot. But where then shall I keep it?"

The answer comes to him at once, but he hesitates. "I—I want to help you. I have a way to help you. But I do not wish you to believe yourself beholden. I do not wish to place you under any obligation. Gallicina, do you understand? I would not poison your soul. I would help you keep it."

"How?" Her voice is taut.

"I can rent an alcove in the Temple for my own prayer carpet. And I can buy a bag with straps, which many people use, and put yours in it, and tell my family it is mine. They will not look. And then—"

"And then," she says, "and then we will have to meet, for me to study my carpet." Her voice has a new, odd note in it, which he cannot read. Is she happy, or reluctant? "But where, Darroti? I cannot go to Temple."

"Do you have friends you can take into your confidence? You could go to someone's house, perhaps? You would—you would never have to see me, if you did not wish to. I could meet your friend, or your friend's servant, and give that person the bag—or meet you only for a moment to give it to you, or—"

"I have no friends whom I would willingly expose to my father's wrath," she says. "Most servants gossip. No, that way is not safe, Darroti."

He understands at once. She can expose Darroti to her father's wrath because he is a merchant. "Very well, then," he says. "There are inns—"

She shudders. "No. That involves more money, and I cannot pay and do not wish you to pay—"

"I have friends," he says. "I will find some other way. We will find a way. But Gallicina, tell me this, now: if it took you two years to save fifty alaris, how will you tell your father you saved two hundred? Especially if he thinks that you, that you—"

"Sold myself," she finishes flatly. She puts her chin in her hand and ponders. "I will tell him I sold some jewelry, some trinkets an aunt gave me. He dislikes that aunt. He would not be angry that I sold her gifts."

"Very good. And how will you explain that you did not tell him that before?"

"Ah. You have a quick mind; thank you. I will tell him that I was too hurt by his accusations even to answer them, which is only the truth."

Darroti nods. "And where does your family think you are now, while you speak to me?"

She smiles. "They think I am napping in my room before dinner, as I have done every day since I was small."

He shakes his head. "If they looked in on you—"

"I would be undone. But they will not; they never have. And I think I will take Adda into my confidence, for I would trust her with my life, although she is a servant."

He shakes his head again. "If your father is as cruel as you say, would she not forfeit her own life, if the ruse were discovered?"

She laughs now. "No, he would not kill her! She might lose her job, but she would get another, and my mother would fight to keep her. Adda runs the house while my mother plays at cards. No, the punishment would fall on me. And that is how it should be. And I promise you that even so, I will not tell her your name, lest my father learn it. You will meet me here tomorrow, Darroti, at the same time, and tell me what is to be done?"

"Of course," he says. He is both delighted, delirious with joy, and afraid: they are weaving a complicated pattern indeed, and it may trap them. "But should we pick another place? If we are seen here too often—"

"Very good," she says, smiling, and names another square, not too far away. "Farewell, good Darroti, until tomorrow. And thank you." She gives him back his cloth; it is all he can do not to press it to his face, to inhale any lingering aroma she has left there.

"Bring the carpet tomorrow," he tells her. "And I will bring the bag for it."

By the next evening, he has arranged everything, having gone straight from his meeting with Gallicina to the whorehouse, where Stini has agreed—for a fee—to grant him the use of her private apartment for two hours every early evening, when she is at work. Her apartment is in a quiet, respectable part of the city, neither too wealthy nor too poor, and not so far from where Gallicina lives that all the time will be taken up in travel. He will not tell Gallicina it is a whore's apartment; she knows now that he has been with women he had to pay, but he does not wish her to know that he is paying for the space. He remembers what she said when he suggested an inn. He will tell her that he is borrowing the place from a friend, which is also true enough.

"I have let others use it for lovers' assignations," Stini tells him in satisfaction, "and most of them are married now. It is a place of good omen. I wish you luck and joy, Darroti. Here are two keys."

"It will be used for prayer."

"Oh, indeed!" Stini says, and laughs until her belly shakes.

"Truly," Darroti says, patient. He cannot blame Stini for not believing him. "May she keep her prayer bag there?"

"She may keep there anything she wishes," Stini says, grinning, "as long as it fits neatly upon the wall. Prayer carpets are fine for making love, Darroti, although sleeping mats are thicker. I have done so myself, many times."

And so he meets Gallicina; she has the carpet, which he puts into the bag, and then he leads her to Stini's apartment, a small, neat place, surprisingly spare, looking out onto a courtyard with a pomegranate tree. He takes Gallicina into the apartment, and hands her the prayer bag, and hands her a key. "Lady, you may keep the prayer bag here; my friend agrees. Now you have what you need, and you can come here every day if you so choose, to learn the pattern of your soul."

"Where is your friend?"

"Working. Will you pray now, Gallicina?"

"In a moment." Gallicina wanders restlessly around the room; she has thrown back her hood, for the first time since Darroti has known her, and he can see the silky mass of her hair, drawn back into a bun, the clean line of her neck below it. "Darroti, how can I come here if you are not here too? It is your friend who has given me the place. It would feel too strange."

How he yearns to accept that invitation! But he must not; it would be dishonorable. "The place is for your use this little time each day, Gallicina. I have other things to do. I will be glad to see you sometimes, but I do not—"

"Ah!" She has stopped in front of a mirror and removed something that is hanging on it. "A hairband. And here are earrings. Now I understand. This is a woman's apartment. You have a—a lover, it must be, if she is not your wife, you—"

"No," he says, and quickly spins a lie. "She is an old family friend, old enough to be my mother." That part, at least, is true. "She has been fond of me since I was a child; she wishes to help me."

"Why?"

The question startles him. "Because I asked her to."

"Why?" She turns from the mirror, comes now to stand in front of him, her small fists clenched. "She knows who I am, and wishes to further your suit with a noble's daughter?"

"No," he says, stung. "No, Gallicina! I have no dishonorable intentions, I swear to you, and she does not know your name. I have not told her that!" He makes the slashing X, the symbol for silence and secrecy, but before he can complete the gesture, Gallicina has put both of her hands on his, to keep it still.

"Kind friend," she says softly, "I did not speak of dishonor." And then she raises his hand and kisses it.

They are both trembling. Darroti's veins are full of fire. He forces himself to be calm, to be rational. "Gallicina—lady, I have only known you a handful of days. I have spent less than three hours with you. I have helped you because you raise me above myself, but I would not presume—"

"To give me my soul? To help me hide it? To help me keep secrets from my father? All that you have presumed, Darroti." She kisses his hand again, more fervently this time; again he forces himself to remain still, although it is an agony. He must be very careful here. He reminds himself that he does not really know this girl: if she claimed rape, she could ruin him and his family. But then she says, "Darroti, tell the truth: do you love me?"

He closes his eyes. Why is she tormenting him? "Gallicina-Malinafa Odarettari, you are a noble's daughter, and I am a merchant and a merchant's son. I will tell you the truth: I have loved you since the moment I saw you. But I am not helping you because I ask for your love in return. You are too far above me. I love you as the reed loves the river and the sunlight: he depends on both for his very existence, but he knows that were he to draw too close to either, he would be consumed. He must love them from a distance."

"Because you are Earth and Air, and I am Fire and Water," she murmurs.

He swallows and opens his eyes. Her face is radiant, luminous, only inches from his. "Yes. That is exactly right."

"Do not say consumed, then. Say completed. For it takes four Elements to make a soul."

And then her mouth is on his and he succumbs, gives way, puts his arms around her and crushes her to him, and her mouth is open now and he can taste her, and his hands are in her hair and her hands are tugging at his tunic and their clothing falls away and they are on the prayer mat, and Stini is right, it is a fine place for coupling, and she is poised above him now, and his head clears just long enough for him to gasp and roll away.

"Gallicina! We must take care, we must take care. You must not conceive a child. Not until you marry." He dares not say, *Until we marry*.

"Clever Darroti," she says, her voice thick, and kisses him again. "You are right. Show me what to do, then, to avoid that fate."

And so he does. He uses all his skill, everything he has learned from his hours with the whores, to please her with hand and tongue; he teaches her to please him. She is an apt and ready pupil. They devour one another. All too soon the time has fled; he longs to hold her in his arms for hours more, but instead he hands her her clothing, and dons his own.

"You did not pray," he says ruefully, pulling on his tunic.

She laughs. "Was what we did not prayer?"

"Not of a type that is accepted in the Temple, beloved."

"I will pray tomorrow. Will you be here?"

"I think that if I am here, you will not pray."

"I think that if you are not here, I will not pray: I will only dream of you."

He shakes his head. "Gallicina, did you come to Market to find a prayer carpet, or a lover?"

"I came to find the first, and found them both," she says. "Darroti, please be here tomorrow."

How can he refuse? "I will. Of course I will."

"Then why do you look so troubled?"

"Do I look troubled?" He is silent a moment. "I am sated, and overjoyed, and I love you, Gallicina. But I fear this burden of secrecy. I fear it will poison us." He makes the slashing X for silence, and says, "It breaks things. It is a symbol of breaking."

"Ah." She reaches out to hold his hand in both of hers, as she did before. "Remake it, then. Reshape it." She turns his hand palm up, and on that palm, with a slender fingertip, she traces an X, but without ever lifting her finger; the entire figure is one flowing line. "See, look: it is a joining now, not a breaking. Two souls touching at one point, and flowing each into the other." She leans forward and kisses him gently on the mouth. "It is a kiss, Darroti. If your lips are sealed, they are sealed by my lips. Nothing is broken. We will let nothing break us."

"Dear love," he says, feeling his soul transformed. "Tomorrow, then."

There are many tomorrows; they meet every day for weeks, making passionate and ever more inventive love. Always at parting Gallicina traces their private symbol, the one that means a kiss, on Darroti's palm; when they lie in one another's arms, she often traces it dreamily on his back or chest or stomach. Before a month is out, she has vowed that she will marry him, after she has served her year as a Mendicant and entered the Temple; and Darroti, feeling as if all the universe cannot contain his joy, has wept and returned the vow, awash in relief. For when they are married, they will no longer need to keep their love a secret.

But when will that be? Their fornication, delicious as it is, does nothing to further their marriage, since Gallicina insists upon being a Mendicant first. "You must forego me for several nights a week," Darroti tells her firmly, stroking her hair. "You must pray upon your carpet, dearest, and learn its pattern. And you must find a way to convince your father to allow you to be a Mendicant. You must do all this for me, that I may become your husband."

And so they agree that several nights a week, they will not meet: Gallicina will go alone to Stini's apartment. For a while, all is well, and absence makes them more fiery, more ecstatic, on the nights they are together. But soon Darroti discovers that the burden of dissembling, which at first he hardly even noticed, has become a heavy weight. With his family and friends, he must continue to play the careless, thoughtless youngest son. He and Gallicina have agreed that once she has been a Mendicant, she will say she met him in the streets near the Market, that they met and talked every day, and so fell in love. Her family will still be enraged, but she and Darroti will handle that somehow; a way will present itself.

But he cannot admit he knows her now, not yet; he cannot speak of her, cannot share his joy or his pain. And this pulls him from his family and makes him impatient with his friends, and the strain begins to disturb his sleep and wreak havoc with his bowels. It distracts him from his work. It shortens his temper and lengthens his thirst.

For wine helps him: it keeps him calm, helps him play his role. A year after meeting Gallicina, he is drinking every day; where once he drank only in the evening, with friends, now he drinks at noon, from a flask he has smuggled into his lunch basket. His thirst for wine begins to outstrip his budget, especially since Stini, every three months, has raised the price she charges for her apartment. "Motivation to marry," she tells him crisply. "It is still a bargain, Darroti, and I have been very good. I have never sought to learn your lover's name, and so you need not fear blackmail."

It is blackmail enough, the price she charges, but he cannot refuse to pay it, or she will change the locks. And he cannot tell Gallicina of his plight, not without admitting that he lied to her at the beginning. So he pays, and worries, and dulls his worry with ever cheaper wine, and tries to play the unworried fool.

His family notices the wine, and worries for him. His friends berate him that he will not join them at their own wine, now too dear for him. And worst of all, Gallicina begins to guess how much he drinks.

"Your breath smells of herbs when you come to me, as if hiding something else," she says, holding his head between her hands. "Your eyes are often bloodshot. Darroti, look at me! I love you. You know I love you. But dearest, if I marry a merchant, he cannot also be a drunk. My family will never permit that; it will take enough persuasion for them to consent to the other. You cannot persuade them with liquor-addled wits."

"I will stop," he tells her, stung. "I promise I will stop."

And so he tries to do; and succeeds, for a week or two at a time. But always, and always on the nights he does not see Gallicina, his thirst overtakes him, a galloping fever, and on those nights he gorges himself with wine and wakes, sometimes, with no memory of the night before. And his terror grows, for he wants to stop; he truly means to stop. Yet somehow he cannot.

"You have succumbed again," Gallicina says, her face tight, whenever they meet again after one of these nightmares. She can always tell. And Darroti, desperate, begins to blame her, to deflect blame from himself.

"It is the strain of secrecy, Gallicina. When are you going to convince your father to let you be a Mendicant? It has been almost two years now. Why do you delay? Why—"

"Do not scold me about things you do not know! You have never met my father! I will tell him on my twentieth birthday, for then I will be of legal age and he will not be able to prevent me, even if he disowns me. Darroti, if he disowns me, will you still marry me?"

"If you will be a carpet merchant's wife," he says, and kisses her, all his anger dissolved in love. For their love is vivid as it ever was, made only deeper by their intervals of strife. He still delights in her silky hair and firm thighs, her small breasts and large labia, her clever mouth and graceful fingers, which still, always, trace the pattern of a kiss upon his skin. No other woman has tempted him since he met her; he does not even think about the whores, except to worry about his payments to Stini.

And then there comes a week when sales have been slow in the Market; and Darroti, fresh off a binge, cannot pay Stini's fee. He begs her for more time, tells her he will get the money somehow, but when he goes to meet Gallicina the next evening, she is standing outside Stini's apartment, fuming. "The key will not work. The locks have been changed. Darroti, what is this?"

He swallows, opens his mouth to speak, finds he cannot. "I—Gallicina, I don't—I—"

"Darroti, my soul is in there!"

"I know, dearest."

"Why are we locked out?" She comes to him, glowing with beauty even in the dimness of the landing; she puts her hand on his face and traces kisses on his cheeks and chin and forehead, but with her other hand she holds him at a distance, so that he cannot truly kiss her. "Darroti, tell me the truth."

And so, sickened, he does. He expects her to yell at him, but she does not yell; instead she grows silent, distant, terrible, her eyes full of tears. "Are you still having sex with this whore? Do you love her?"

"No! I have had sex with no one but you since we met! I love no one but you! I have never loved anyone but you, Gallicina! Anything I did before that was merely moving bodies, scratching itches."

She does not thaw. "Does the whore love you?"

"Of course not! Gallicina, be reasonable. She loves only my money. That is what this is about."

"And you do not have the money for her because you spent it on wine. You love wine more than you love being with me."

"No," he says, heated, "I do not! I want to be with you forever! I want to marry you! You are the one who insists on waiting, who insists on secrecy—"

"Who kept the secret about paying the whore, Darroti?" Her voice is taunting now.

"I did not want to wound your pride! And I never thought this deception would go on so long!"

She frowns, shifts her weight, grows thoughtful. "You are right. It should not have gone on so long. It must end."

Terror seizes him. She is leaving him. She does not love him anymore. He finds himself kneeling on the landing outside Stini's apartment, weeping, his arms around Gallicina's knees. "No, no, you must not say that, it must not be over, you must not—I cannot—Gallicina, I will never love anyone but you, do not leave me, Gallicina, dearest—you must not leave me—"

"Darroti!" Her hands are in his hair; she kneels now also, so that she is facing him. "That is not what I meant! Be calm. Love, dear generous foolish love, I am sorry. Compose yourself. Darroti—"

"You do not love me anymore. You—"

"I love you now, and I will love you always. Darroti, listen to me. I did not mean that I was leaving you. What I meant is that you are right: the deceptions must end—at least some of them. I must tell my father that I am determined to be a Mendicant."

He swallows. "And then you will marry me?"

"And then I will marry you, joyfully. But first we must retrieve my prayer carpet."

She goes home and asks Adda for the money; Darroti gives it to Stini, who lets him in one last time so he can collect the carpet. He carries it to the square where he and Gallicina had their first clandestine meeting, an age ago; he gives it to her. They cannot kiss here, in public, but they sit and talk. "Darroti, dearest, I go now to confront my father. I will tell him I have been sneaking away each evening to pray upon my carpet. I will not tell him where, or with whom. I will tell him that the risk of being a Mendicant is no greater than the risks he has already forced me to take. And I hope that he will listen to my pleas, and let me take to the streets. But he may not. He may lock me in the house instead: forever, or for a while. I do not know when I will see you again."

Darroti takes a determined breath. "He cannot separate our souls."

"No. He cannot. But you must have faith that if you do not see me, I still love you. Always remember that I love you, Darroti. It will always be true."

"And I will always love you, Gallicina. You know that. Tell me this: if he allows you to become a Mendicant, where will you go to beg? I must know so that I can look for you there, every day."

She smiles, and names a corner near the Market. And then she reaches out and presses into his hand something in a small bag. He thinks fleetingly of those fifty alaris, so long ago. "What is this, Gallicina?"

"A kiss, for you to keep."

He opens the bag. Inside is a silver figure, the pattern of their kiss, on a black silken cord. He flushes, overcome with love. "I will wear it always. But I have nothing to give you—dearest—"

"I could take nothing with me, as a Mendicant, save the clothing on my back and a begging bowl. But Darroti—Darroti, who has given me my soul—how can you say you have given me nothing?" And then she presses his hand, and is gone, and he puts on the necklace, which for all he knows may be their last kiss.

Time becomes an agony. Every day he looks for Gallicina on the corner she has named; he seeks her there even before the time when she could possibly be free to come, for Mendicants must purify themselves for two weeks before they begin to beg. He looks for her there every day, and every day he fails to find her. And because he cannot speak to anyone, he drinks instead. He sneaks wine at breakfast now. He shakes if he cannot get it, and sees monsters in the shadows. He is always at his father's booth in the Market; he bargains well enough, but with only a quarter of his mind. He thinks Timbor does not notice his misery. He cannot tell. He cannot sleep, cannot pray, some days cannot eat. He still plays with the children at home, still joins his friends for conversation. But he is in chaos.

And every day, when he does not see Gallicina on the corner by the Market, his despair grows. The monsters in the shadows, the ones quieted only by wine, whisper to him that she never loved him, that she was only using him, that she has gotten her prayer carpet and taken her pleasure with a merchant's son, and now he is discarded.

He will never see her again. Only the silver kiss on its silken cord gives him strength at these times, for it is proof that he is not mad, that he and Gallicina truly loved. It is her promise. And so when he is most afraid, he clutches it, and praises her foresight in giving it to him—for surely she knew that he would be tried this way—and remembers what she told him. *Always remember that I love you.*

And then one day, three months after their parting, he goes by the corner in the evening, on his way home—as he always does—and she is there. Gallicina is there, wearing the burlap robe of the Mendicant, holding a blue begging bowl.

It is all he can do not to cry out, for that would attract attention from the other people on the street. He stops, digs in his pockets for all the money he has, approaches her. She has seen him. Their eyes lock. They are both trembling, as they were that first time in Stini's apartment. But then, as he draws closer, she begins to frown.

Why is she frowning? He cannot ask. He puts the money in her bowl with shaking hands, says hoarsely, "I give to you because life has given to me." And under his breath, so quietly that his lips barely move, he adds, *Beloved.*

"I take from you with thanks, as I take from the cosmos," Gallicina says clearly, with a graceful bow, and he feels her finger tracing a kiss on the underside of his wrist. His heart bounds. But then she murmurs, "Meet me tonight, in the alley by the square where you gave me the prayer carpet. Ten o'clock."

And she is frowning again, and someone else is approaching her to put a pomegranate and some coins in her bowl, and he cannot ask her anything. He nods, bows, retreats, walks home in a daze. He tells the family he is sick and cannot eat; he hides in his room, and spends the time until ten rocking on his bed, praying that Gallicina has not wearied of him. If she no longer loves him, why the kiss? But if she does still love him, why the frown? He cannot make it out; his brain is all awhirl.

Her father has relented, at least, and let her be a Mendicant. That is a great gift. Darroti tells himself that even if she no longer loves him, he has done her good, has helped her reach her goal. And yet the prospect of a life without her fells him utterly. That cannot be the meaning of the frown. He could not bear it.

He meets her at ten, as he promised; she is just inside the alley, alone, her face anxious, and he calls out—"Gallicina!"—for no one else is near, and she turns and they are embracing, kissing, their hands moving over one another's robes, and all is as it should be, all is well, she loves him; she will always love him, just as she promised, and nothing can ever hurt him again. The cosmos has given him its greatest gift.

But then she gently pushes him away, and holds his face between her hands, as she has done before, and says very softly, "Darroti. Love. I am happier than I can say to see you. But Darroti—you were drunk this afternoon. And you have been drunk before this. Your face is puffy. You look ill. In just three months—dearest love, the change is shocking. I hardly knew you."

He shakes his head wildly. How can she speak to him like this, now of all times? "I have not seen you for three months! I have been beside myself! I will be better now. Gallicina—tell me you love me, tell me you still want to marry me, Gallicina—"

"I love you, Darroti. I just told you I did. I will love you forever; I have told you that, too. But now I will tell you again what I have told you once before. If I am to marry a merchant's son, he cannot also be a drunk."

"It was because I could not see you! It was—"

"It was because of me? And before that, it was because I would not speak to my father about becoming a Mendicant. But I have done that, successfully, and still you were drunk this afternoon. Will I always be the reason, Darroti?"

"Gallicina, I am sober now." And indeed he is clear-headed, for he has had no wine since five, when he sneaked a flask behind the booth, and the shaking has not yet overtaken him to tell him it is time for more. He moves to kiss her again, and she lets him, for a while—he can taste her hunger as clearly as he tastes his own—but then she pushes him away once more.

"Yes, you are sober now. But that is a matter of hours, and hours are not enough. Darroti, I have been through sore trials these past three months. I know that you have, too. But I must set you another one."

"Name it," he says, desperate for another kiss, frantic to keep her. "Anything. Name anything, and I will do it, Gallicina!"

"Do not drink at all for thirty days. And do not seek me out. If you can stay away from wine that long, then meet me one month from now in this same alley, at this same hour. But if you cannot, do not come."

"Another month?" He is stunned. How can she ask this of him? "Another month, after the three that have just passed? Gallicina—"

"You said you would do anything." Her voice is bitter.

"And so I shall." He strokes her hair and kisses her again; she lets him. "I shall, I promise you."

"Good. If you cannot—Darroti, if your love of wine is stronger than your love for me, then stay away. Let me go; do not torment me. And Darroti, dear Darroti—do not think to drink during the month, and then come and tell me you have not. I will know if you are lying."

He pulls away, stung. "You will set spies on me? You do not trust me?"

She pulls him back. "I will not have to set spies. I will know. I have always known. Are you not the other half of my soul?"

Their kiss then is the deepest they have ever had, the longest and most passionate. Darroti wishes it to last a lifetime. But it ends, and Gallicina gently pushes him away. "Tell me I will see you in a month, Darroti."

"I promise it," he says. "I swear it by the Elements."

She smiles at him at last. "Good, beloved. Go."

He goes. He goes home and tells his family that he is going on a trip, a jaunt of a week or so, to the ocean with some friends. He tells them it is a last-minute expedition on which he has just been invited; he packs his things, whistling, and asks his father if he can borrow some money. Because he so seldom asks such a thing, Timbor gives him three hundred alaris, and his blessing; Darroti promises to bring home presents for the children.

He goes whistling out the door, carrying his luggage. He is no longer whistling when he reaches the whorehouse; he is already afraid, for already the galloping demons are after him, making him shake. Stini is with a customer, and he must wait to see her, but when she emerges, when he explains to her what he needs, she understands at once.

"Aye, Darroti. This is a good thing you are doing, a fine and brave thing. Everyone who loves you will thank you."

"Then you will lock me in your apartment for a week, with food and water, but no drink?"

"And I will not give you wine no matter how much you beg. Darroti, have you ever grown dangerous with drink?"

"No." The question startles him. "At least, not that I recall. No one has ever said so; surely they would have told me. And Stini, I will not be drinking."

"That is what will be dangerous. You may destroy things, fighting your demons. If you break anything in my place, you must pay for it."

"I understand."

She puts a hand on his arm. "And you may die, Darroti. People die, sometimes, coming off drink. Even if you do not die, the beginning will be terrible. You understand that?"

He closes his eyes. Fear grips him. "Yes. I understand. But if I cannot stop—if she leaves me—oh, Stini, I will die then, too!"

"Brave Darroti. Come now. Come with me. For you are already beginning to shake, yes?"

He goes with her, allows himself to be locked into the apartment where he spent so many hours with Gallicina, which Stini now strips of anything fragile or capable of cutting. It is as she has said; the beginning is terrible. For three days he rages, screaming. All the monsters come out of the shadows, and with them spiders and centipedes, every insect that has frightened him since he was small, and mocking images of Gallicina with other men. He would do anything for wine: he would kill his family, kill Gallicina, kill Stini, who stays outside the door and does not heed his threats and wheedling. For three days he endures a wilderness of rage and horror; he convulses, the shaking uncontrollable, and emerges from unconsciousness certain that he is about to die; he becomes so ill that he cannot keep down food or water.

But somehow he survives. He is young and strong, for all his dissipation, and he clings to his love, to his hope for marriage, to his yearning to be good enough for his bride. And so one day he wakes clear-headed, and the demons are gone. He can see things for what they are again. He has no thirst for wine, but only for the cool clear water that Stini gives him as she praises him. And although he is terribly weak, he is jubilant. For the monsters are gone for good. He can feel it. And in only three more weeks, he can be with Gallicina again, can kiss her; and although the rest of her year as a Mendicant, the time before they can marry, will be torment, it will be nothing compared to what he has just undergone.

So he gets up and pays Stini the remainder of her fee; he paid her only half at first. With the little cash left to him, he buys sweets and seashells from the market, careful to let no one he knows see him. He goes home and gives the gifts to the children, and tells his family he was taken ill on holiday, and allows kind Harani to nurse him. They can sense the change in him. They are wary and puzzled, but pleased.

He goes to sleep every night dreaming of his wedding, and grows every day more joyous. He drives better bargains in the Market than he ever has before. And by the time the month is up, he has conceived a merry plan. He will go to meet Gallicina in the alley, but he will disguise himself, will ask her to be his Necessary Beggar; and then, when she asks what wedding it is, he will say, "Your own!" and sweep her into his arms. And then his entire life will be bliss, and nothing will be able to hurt him, ever again.

And so on the night he is to meet Gallicina, he wears a new robe, one she will not recognize, and brings with him a fine loaf of bread to give her, and hurries to the alley, just at ten. She is sitting there—dear heart!—sitting on the ground, carving a pineapple with a knife someone has given her. Is she weeping? Why does she look so sad? Dear Gallicina!

"I seek a Necessary Beggar," he whispers to her, laughing, having crept silently into the alley—she did not even look up, why was she not looking for him?—and suddenly she drops the knife and flies at him, weeping and screaming, hammering at him with her fists.

"Darroti, Darroti, you are marrying your whore, I know you are, I saw you with her in the streets the very night we spoke a month ago, Darroti! You were always with her, the entire time you were with me, weren't you?"

"No, Gallicina! I can explain—"

"Tell the truth, Darroti! How can you ask this of me, Darroti, how can you come here, you never loved me—"

"No! Gallicina, I love you, I always have, I was not—she was taking me to a place where I could give up drink, so I could keep my promise to you!"

She rages at him, her face streaked with tears and spittle. "Yes, you are sober, I see that. I smell it! You have made yourself sober for her, not for me! Haven't you, Darroti? You never cared for me. You used my body—"

"Gallicina, no! Gallicina, how can you believe this of me?" But even as he asks, he knows the answer: she saw him with Stini a month ago, and she has had a month to weave a tale explaining what she saw. She has brooded on it; it is fixed in her mind. He finds himself, in a vertiginous rush, imagining what that month must have been like for her. Mendicants have ample time to think: that is their task. Every moment must have been a torment for her, as it would have been for him if he had thought she loved another. "Gallicina, dearest—"

"You mock me with your cruel request, Darroti! I could not stand to officiate at your marriage to—"

"To you," he says, desperate, pushing away images of her huddled against walls, clutching her begging bowl as nightmares of Stini overcame her. "Oh, Gallicina! To you. I only wish to marry you."

But she is talking at the same time, talking over him, not listening. "You made love to your whore in the same spot where we made love, Darroti, didn't you? In that same apartment! You laughed and gloated together—"

"No! Gallicina, listen to me!" He tries to embrace her, but she bends and snatches up the knife, and he backs away, afraid that she will threaten him. Does no one hear their argument? Why does no one come?

"I hope you will be very happy with her," she says, and reaches up with one quick movement, and cuts her own throat with the pineapple knife.

"Gallicina!" Darroti cries. He catches her in his arms, forced to watch as her life blood leaves her, gushing; he is too stunned at first even to be horrified. He knows better than to try to seek a healer. He has seen people with such wounds in the Market, after brawls. People with such wounds do not survive.

And so, bewildered and bereft of hope, he spends the last moments of Gallicina's life trying to make her understand, as her blood runs bright and hot over his hands onto the cold, dark stone of the alley. He tells her how he paid Stini to lock him in, that he might battle with the demons. He curses the stupid joke that has gone so fatally wrong. "It was our own wedding I spoke of, Gallicina, I swear to you. It was my wedding with you, dearest love, I will never love another, Gallicina, my own heart—"

He cannot tell if she hears a thing he says. He thinks that perhaps, just as she is dying, she begins to trace a kiss upon his arm, but her hand falls limp before she can complete it, and perhaps it was only his own wild fancy. All night he holds her body. He rocks and weeps; he thinks of cutting his own throat with the pineapple knife, but fear of meeting her furious spirit stops him. For he has killed her, as surely as if he made the wound himself. He knows that. He has killed her with his drinking and even with his struggle not to drink; he has killed her by not telling her the truth quickly enough; he has killed her with his stupid, stupid jest.

And so when the City Guard finds him, he does not try to defend himself. He does not tell them that she cut her own throat, or why. He accepts the sentence of murder and exile. For to tell the entire story now, he would have to further shame her family, and his own. Her people could only be disgusted that she had been with him; his people could only be disgusted, and betrayed, by all his lies. So he maintains the lie by silence, and adds another. To his family's distraught demands to know what happened, he tells them he was drunk, that he succumbed again to wine that terrible night, and killed the Mendicant woman without knowing what he did. It is close enough to truth.

And now his spirit is here, in America, weeping into the towel in Timbor's bookcase. And now, at last, he wishes them to know the truth, to know what really happened, for if he cannot make known the story of his love, that love will truly die, as if it never were. Telling the story is his only way to bring Gallicina to life again; to bring himself to life, as he was in the first days of their love, when he was brave and generous and happy.

There has been no Great Breaking here. Timbor could know the story if he would only listen. But always, after Darroti has tried

Susan Palwick

to speak in Timbor's dreams, the old man wakes frowning, shaking off the fragments of the tale. Sometimes, when no one else is there, Timbor takes out the pendant, the silver kiss Darroti brought with him into exile—both piercing joy and terrible reproach, but nothing he could ever leave behind—and ponders it. But the fragments do not form a whole, for him. Timbor stays bewildered.

And so Darroti weeps. He would do anything to ease his family's pain, anything to change the past. He would give anything to hold his love again, to feel her fingers tracing on his skin the pattern of their kiss.

8

HONORS

Zamatryna kept Gallicina in her closet for years. She didn't know what else to do; the command for silence never changed. She wondered what Gallicina was learning from being in the beetle, if she was learning anything. Gallicina must have been a very complicated person. Clearly the force of her will was sustaining her beetle body, which should have died after one summer.

The girl concocted theories. She read ghost stories—careful not to let Stan know that she was doing so, since he wouldn't have approved—and watched soap operas with Lisa. The plots of soap operas also went on for years, every bit as improbable as the beetle's survival. Soap operas were always about love and money, and so Zamatryna found herself spinning stories about Gallicina and Darroti. They must have known each other, for Gallicina to have followed the family into exile, and for her spirit to be so stubborn now. They must have either loved or hated each other, or maybe both, and there had probably been money involved too, since Gallicina's family had been rich. But whenever Zamatryna thought about her uncle, she could only summon increasingly blurry snapshots of a laughing clown, often drunk, but never hurtful. It was hard to fit the Darroti she remembered into a soap opera.

The ghost stories all agreed that the living needed to take action on behalf of the dead, to release them, to free them from having to haunt. Here in America, spirits needed to be freed from the world, whereas in Gandiffri, they lived within it. And so perhaps Gallicina, for whom the beetle's body would have been a blessing back home, found it a prison here, in this new world. But Zamatryna had no idea how to free her. She knew only that she was not allowed to speak of the beetle to anyone else, and that she dared not release it from its jar, lest Stan find and kill it.

She did not think about the beetle all the time, of course. She had too much else to do. Although the subjects she studied in school were very easy, she quickly learned that there were other challenges. Her family, and Stan and Lisa, wanted her to be successful, to get good grades. But success also meant being accepted as an American, being seen as normal, and being very smart was not considered normal. Part of success was popularity. The smartest students were rarely also popular. They were excluded and called names, "nerd" and "freak," the things that Zamatryna had been called her first day in school. Some were put in special classes for gifted and talented children; the grown-ups said this made you special, but special was also what they called children whose brains had been damaged at birth. Special children of either type weren't popular, and therefore weren't successful, and therefore weren't the best Americans.

The trick, then, was to be as much like other, normal children as you could, while being smart enough to please the adults. So Zamatryna worked very hard at making friends. She studied commercials and magazines to learn what to wear, what to watch, what songs to sing. She learned to get top grades without seeming so interested or special that she would be put in the gifted and talented classes. She dutifully studied sports, although they baffled her. She spent hours at the mall with other girls. She concocted crushes on singers and movie stars, on everyone but the actual boys in her classes, whom she and her friends pretended to despise until the second half of middle school, when they began to date. You could date in middle school, but you couldn't really fall in love: that had to wait until high school, where it was also safer to be smart.

In high school, students in Advanced Placement classes weren't automatically called freaks. They could be popular, too, if only among themselves, but that was all right, because belonging to a clique, any clique, meant you were successful, although it was better to belong to several cliques. High school was a big relief.

While Zamatryna and her cousins were working at all this, the adults were working, too. They had all gotten jobs. Timbor had learned to operate a car, and now drove a taxicab. Harani was a cook in a casino restaurant. Erolorit had started out as a bagger at Albertson's, and now managed the meat department. Aliniana painted women's nails in a hair salon. Macsofo, who had been a bricklayer in Lémabantunk, did the same thing here, and made more money than any of the others.

None of them made a lot of money, though: not enough for their own house. So they paid Lisa rent—which was really repayment for their documents—and continued to live among the clowns, in the lovely old house by the river. Stan and Lisa must have reached some sort of agreement, because he continued holding his little church in their own house. He seemed more tired to Zamatryna every year, grayer, his prayers less fervent. He had stopped trying so hard to convert the family, although they were still careful to avoid anything that might actively offend him. He and Timbor were fast friends now: they had adopted one of the cars at the Automobile Museum, a 1936 De Soto Airstream taxicab, cream with orange and white trim and orange plastic sunbursts on top. They had picked the taxi in honor of Timbor's job, and Zama thought it looked like a creamsicle. Stan and her grandfather went to the museum every Saturday, and spent ten hours a year polishing and maintaining the De Soto; their names were on the display card next to it. Stan looked happy whenever he came back from spending time with the car, and happiest after the quarterly parties the Auto Museum gave for the cars' adoptive parents. "He acts like that thing's an actual child," Lisa said once, shaking her head, "and your grandpa isn't much better."

"Lisa," Zamatryna said, "is Stan all right? He seems—old."

"Well, he's older than he used to be. We all are. Mainly, I think he's having a real long midlife crisis. He started out with high hopes for our church, you know, and it's just the same little group of people it was at the beginning, and folks are starting to wander away. Stan feels like the Spirit's meandered off someplace, like the fire in his belly's gone. He's never spoken in tongues, you know, or had a vision of Jesus, even. He feels like he's just an ordinary man. And I tell him that's all he has to be, an ordinary man who's following the Lord and doing good, but I don't think he believes it. I don't think he sees that he is doing good, just by being himself. He thinks good has to be dramatic, you know. He has trouble seeing the quiet stuff, like the way your mom does good just by cooking for people."

If cooking was a way of doing good, though, it wasn't good enough. The children understood that their job was to make more money than their parents did, to go to college and acquire careers. Jamfret and Rikko already knew that they wanted to be engineers; Jamfret wanted to build bridges, while Rikko wanted to design computers. Poliniana wanted to be the kind of doctor who sucked the fat from women's bodies and injected poison into their faces. The family agreed that this would be perfect for her; Polly loved to make people look pretty, and this kind of work was very profitable.

Zamatryna couldn't decide what she wanted to do. She was interested in several lucrative careers, but she was most drawn to the non-lucrative versions of them. Even as she studied how to look like the models in *Seventeen* magazine, she found herself unable to forget the refugees, who still lived in camps north of town and were still vulnerable to attacks from Nuts. The Nuts responsible for the bombing, the disaster that had freed Zamatryna's family, had been caught; they were on death row. Zamatryna was very confused by the idea of killing someone as punishment for having killed someone. Exile seemed far kinder and more sensible. But Timbor, who had watched the televised trials and read all the stories in the paper, shrugged and said, "America has no doorways to other dimensions. And after the criminals die, their spirits will go into simple things, and learn love and compassion."

"But that's not why the State's doing it," Zamatryna said. "That's not what the Americans believe, Grandfather. They believe you can only learn things while you're still alive. They believe these people will go to hell when they die."

"And roast like chickens," Timbor said with a sigh.

"Like the people who died in the camps," Macsofo said grimly. "It is fitting, is it not? Zamatryna, do you feel sorrier for the criminals than you do for the victims?"

She shook her head. "I feel sorry for all of them. If I feel sorry for the bombing victims who were killed, shouldn't I also feel sorry for the criminals who will be killed? It's the same thing."

"The criminals deserve death. The victims didn't."

"Ah," Timbor said gently, "you hate America, Macsofo. And yet you have become more American than any of us. More than the children, even."

Zamatryna thought about that conversation for a long time. Gallicina hadn't deserved death, surely, but neither had Darroti. It seemed to her that someone somewhere must love the criminals who were going to be put to death, as people had loved the victims who died, as her family had loved her hapless uncle. What good could come of making more families suffer, of sending more people into the voicelessness of death?

And so, when she pictured being a lawyer, she always saw herself defending people who could not speak, or could not make themselves heard: immigrants, or poor people, or people on death row, or animals, or trees. When she pictured herself as a doctor, she imagined healing people in the camps, or homeless people living by the river, or babies in orphanages. But while one could be popular—at least with some people—and do all this, one could not be rich. Half of the ingredients for success would still be missing.

Left entirely free to choose, she would probably have been a social worker, but that was out of the question. Her family approved of her warm heart, she knew. Timbor and Aliniana did, especially; in their own jobs, they heard many sad stories about failed marriages and estranged children, about illnesses and deaths, about lost dreams and crushing debts. Their most successful customers never told them anything important; such people merely sat, in their expensive clothing and fine accessories, impatient to get what they were paying for, and then to leave. But unsuccessful people liked cabs and manicures, even though the least successful people couldn't afford such things. The middling-unsuccessful—often rich enough, but unhappy—would talk to Timbor and Aliniana for hours, if they were permitted.

Zamatryna loved the stories her grandfather and her aunt brought home, loved sitting around the kitchen table, discussing what advice to give these customers if they returned. Lisa often sat with them; she said that Timbor and Aliniana were practicing a kind of ministry. Lisa and Zamatryna both found themselves doing research on all kinds of odd problems: Gamblers Anonymous meetings for swing-shift workers, therapists who specialized in underwear phobias, sources of free dentures. And sometimes the customers came back, and Timbor and Aliniana got to pass along what they had learned, and the customers were grateful, and tipped well when they could.

Zamatryna would have been glad to do such work for a living. But she was also the oldest child, the one who would enter the workforce soonest, the first one who would be able to help the family acquire real independence. And so she tried to be practical. Medical school was six years at least, law school only three. She would go to law school, then, and work eighty-hour weeks for a firm until her family had their own house, and then follow her heart, and help poor people and trees.

In the meantime, community service was important for getting into college, and also law school and medical school. So while she took her AP classes and edited the yearbook and did cheerleading splits—a combination which made her guidance counselor scratch his head and say, "We don't get many like you"—she also collected canned beans for the food pantry, and volunteered at the library, and started a club called "Growing Girls," consisting of young women who helped old people do their gardening.

"*When* do you sleep?" asked the guidance counselor. His name was Ronnie Hilliard, and he was known as Rumpled Ron around the school; he was a short man, pale and heavy, his clothing perpetually wrinkled. There were always sweat stains under his arms, even in winter. Zamatryna had gone to his office to discuss college applications.

"At night," she said. "Like everyone else."

"That wasn't what I meant." He nudged her file warily, as if it might bite him. "You're fifteen. And you're planning on graduating next year, right? You're doing high school in three years?"

"Yes. Is there something wrong with that?"

"No," Ron said, but he sounded unhappy. "It's just—it's awfully fast. You were already accelerated a year. You're only young once, Zama. You should enjoy it."

"I'll enjoy it in college," she said impatiently. "Why should I stay here longer, when I can already do all the schoolwork? It's boring."

"Boring? You're taking AP Bio, AP English, AP Calculus, AP History, and AP Art. And you're fifteen. If you're bored by that stuff, you're going to be bored by college, too."

"If I'm bored by college, I'll do college in three years. And then I'll go to law school and then I'll get a job. That's what I want to do, to help my family. I want to make money. I need a college degree for that."

Susan Palwick

"Right," Ron said, and sighed. "No wonder so many people around here feel threatened by immigrants. Okay, so where are you planning to apply?"

"UNR."

"*UNR? The University of Nevada, Reno?* You act like a kid who's aiming for Harvard or Stanford. You don't need to do all this stuff to get into UNR, Zama. Go someplace better."

"I can't leave my family," she said. "It's a good school! There's an honors program—"

"Any school's good if you use what's there, but UNR won't look as good on a résumé as Harvard or Stanford would. Not for someone as ambitious as you are. Don't you want to see someplace else, see another part of the country, instead of going to college two miles from where your family lives?"

"No," she said. "Why should I want that? I already had to leave one place I loved. Why would I leave another one if I didn't have to?"

He gave her a long look, then, and said quietly, "Okay, I'm sorry. I can see that. Your family came here from someplace else, and you got knocked around and you want to stay put for a while. Or they want you to stay put. Sure, I can see that. But if you're thinking career, you should look into scholarships to other schools—you're ethnic, you've got the SAT scores, they eat that stuff up. You want to go to law school? Harvard and Stanford have the best. You do one of them undergrad, you'll have a much better chance of getting into a top law school. UNR won't get you into Harvard Law, kid."

"That depends on my LSATs."

"Jesus." He laughed. "You've got it all figured out, don't you?"

"Yes. I do."

Ron gave her a half-smile. "Modest, too. No, you don't, not actually. Look, I don't just exist to push paper around. I'm a counselor, Zama. I know something about people. It's my job. And I've seen a lot of kids—and not just from immigrant families, either—working their hearts out to please their parents, and I've seen a lot of them crash and burn because all that stuff wasn't what they wanted to do, not really. It was what they were told they had to do, or what they thought they had to do. Your family must be proud as hell of you. I would be, if you were my daughter. But I'm sure they want you to be happy, too. And at some point you're going to need to slow down and figure out who you are apart from them, and it's better to do that now than when you're fifty and have spent half your life slaving away at something you suddenly realize bores the living crap out of you."

"I'm happy," Zamatryna said. Rumpled Ron bewildered and frightened her. What was he talking about? Of course she wanted to help her family; that couldn't be wrong. "What makes you think I'm not happy?"

"Well, you just told me you're bored by all your classes, for one thing. Do you have friends, Zama?"

"Yes," she said, back on safe ground. "I have a lot of friends! I'm on the yearbook and the cheerleading squad and—"

"Zama," he said gently, and leaned forward. "I know all that. I've got the list here." He tapped the file. "I didn't ask you if you had activities. I asked you if you had friends."

"The other people who do the activities are my friends!"

"*Good* friends? The kind of friends you could tell anything to?" She just stared at him. There was no one like that, not even in her family: no one to whom she could tell anything, because of Gallicina's ghost, the tiny creature who bore the great burden of voice-lessness, and had imposed it on Zamatryna.

She couldn't think of a safe answer to the question, so she just nodded. Ron's eyebrows rose. "Yeah? Really? So why do you seem so lonely to me, and why do you look like you're about to cry?"

"I have plenty of friends," she said, but she heard how small her own voice sounded, and knew she didn't sound very convincing. He was accusing her of being a clown, someone who was happy on the outside but sad inside. Someone like Darroti had been. She didn't want to be like Darroti, but Darroti's secret, which she didn't even know and had no way of learning, had become hers. She squirmed in her seat and said, "I'm happy. I like the yearbook. I like cheerleading and gardening. Gardening's fun!"

He leaned back in his chair again, steepling his fingers. "Sure it is. But all your fun stuff has to be a line on your résumé, too. Even the gardening. And that makes it work. Is there anything you do just because you want to, even though it won't impress anybody else?"

"I spend time with my family," she said. She'd gotten her voice under control again. "I talk to my grandfather and my auntie and my cousins. This is none of your business, you know."

"You're right. It isn't."

"I came here for help with my application."

"Zama, you don't need help with your application. But since you asked, here's a piece of advice: the name 'Growing Girls' is just a little sexist, and I'd change it, if I were you. Boys should be able to join that club."

She rolled her eyes. "They don't want to! We didn't have a name for our first three meetings, but only girls came, so then we picked the name. We'd have picked something else if boys had come. It wouldn't be good for boys to join. The other boys wouldn't like them. They wouldn't be popular."

Rumpled Ron laughed. "Well, they certainly won't join with a name like that. Unless they think it's a dating service, and let's not even go there."

"If a guy wants to join, we'll change the name. The football team is all boys, isn't it? Why is this worse than that?"

He shrugged. "It's not. You came here for advice, so I'm giving you advice. Change the name."

"But Growing Girls alliterates. It's a pun. It's cute!"

"Yes, it's cute. But you can find something else that's cute and alliterates. You're very clever, Zama. With a verbal SAT like that, I know you can solve this particular problem. And if you aren't going to listen to anything I have to say, why did you come here in the first place?"

"For help with my application!" She glared at him and said, "I have to go to class now."

He nodded. "I know you do. Get going. And think about what I said."

She told herself she wouldn't think about it, told herself it was nonsense, that he had no right to tell her who she was or how she felt. He only existed to push papers around. But the conversation nagged at her for the rest of the day, making her irritable and snappish. She found herself unable to concentrate on photosynthesis or the history of perspective drawing or Dostoyevsky. She gave cheerleading practice and the after-school yearbook meeting only half her attention, and was relieved when she could go home.

She found her grandfather sitting at the kitchen table and staring into space. She stood outside, looking through the screen door; he hadn't yet realized she was there. How sad he looked, and how tired! He was playing with something on the table, something shiny on a black cord; he ran the cord back and forth through his fingers, the shiny thing glittering in the light. Zamatryna squinted, but couldn't make out what it was.

He had begun to sing now, an old song from Gandiffri, a lullaby; Zamatryna remembered Harani singing it to her when they were still in Lémabantunk:

> Little baby, you are woven of the Elements;
> Little baby, you are my most precious possession.
> Little baby, drink your mama's milk
> And grow like a persimmon;
> Sleep in the sunlight, child,
> And grow like a snapdragon.

The song ended. Timbor wiped his eyes. Zamatryna, watching, realized that he must have sung the lullaby most recently to Darroti, who had been his youngest son. She carefully backed up ten paces, until she had turned the corner to the garage, and then came back up the walk, slapping her hand on the side of the house and singing "My Best Boyfriend," the latest hit by the Gabbing Girls:

> Sky's the limit
> On his credit limit.
> He's buying a Ferrari
> And I'll be sitting in it.

And so when she walked into the kitchen, Timbor wasn't crying anymore. He was smiling, and his face was dry, and he must have put the shiny thing on its black cord in his pocket, because Zamatryna didn't see it. "Hello, Zama. You are singing that terrible music again."

"It's what my friends listen to, Grandfather."

"It sounds like an off-key raccoon who has broken into the aluminum recycling bin and is foraging for crumbs in the cans."

"Thanks," she said, hugging him. "I love you too. How was your day?"

"Ah," he said, and shook his head, making a face. "It was fine until my last customer. I had a bad customer, a very nasty man. Railing against immigrants, you know, because they take jobs real Americans should have."

"The old story," Zamatryna said. She felt her stomach knotting, although she tried to keep her voice light. "He sounds tactful."

"Yes, terribly tactful. I told him I was an immigrant and that the company was hiring drivers if he wanted to do my job and drive a cab."

Zamatryna laughed, pulling up one of the kitchen chairs and

plunking her books down on the table. "Good for you. And what did he say?"

"He didn't say anything, then." Timbor sighed. "But then we passed a homeless woman on a bench by the river, and I felt sorry for her and I still had half my sandwich from lunch, so I said, 'Sir, do you mind if I stop for just a moment to give this food to that woman?' And he said no, he said that wasn't what he was paying me for and he was in a hurry, and I could go back later and tell her to drive a cab so she could earn money to buy food. And a block after that there was a red light, you know, and he got nasty and said that if I hadn't slowed down to look at the woman it would still have been green and he wouldn't have been delayed. I hadn't slowed down very much at all; I do not think it would have made a difference. And I was angry, and I said that if I had stopped to give her the food, the light might have been green again by the time we got there, and we still would have stopped, but we would have stopped to do something useful instead of just sitting at a light."

"Ooooh," Zamatryna said. "You were in a feisty mood today! I bet he didn't like that."

"Not at all," Timbor said, making a face. "Not one bit. I need to learn to keep my mouth shut."

"So let me guess. No tip from that fare."

Timbor laughed now, finally. "Right! I was afraid he would not even agree to pay the full fare, because he was so mad I'd slowed down to see the woman. But he did. I hope he doesn't complain about me to the company."

"I wouldn't worry. He won't want to spend the time. Did you go back to give that woman the sandwich?"

"Yes, but she was gone by then." He shook his head. "I shouldn't have tried to stop. I know it would not have been company policy, and I should have known that customer would not agree. Others might have. But I do not understand how people can be so mean to beggars here. Especially to women. She was about your mother's age, I think, and she had five big plastic bags." He hugged himself and looked down at the table, and Zamatryna knew he was thinking about Gallicina.

"Maybe you'll see her again tomorrow. You can bring her food then. But there are places she can go for food, Grandfather. She'll be all right."

"It is not the same," he said quietly. "Standing on a line at a soup kitchen, that is not the same. It would be better if one person stopped to give you food. It would make you feel like someone cared, like you were honored. Even in Lémabantunk, when I was a Mendicant, it made a difference how people said the blessing when they put coins or food in your bowl. Some of them muttered it like an annoyance, and did not even stay to hear your response, and you knew they were in a rush to get somewhere else. Some of them smiled and looked you in the eyes. Those were the best people."

Zamatryna blinked. She knew that there had been Mendicants in Lémabantunk; she knew that her grandfather, who still knelt on his prayer carpet every morning and evening, had gone to the Temple at home. But not until now had she realized that, of course, this meant that Timbor had served his year as a Mendicant, too. He'd never talked about it before. She had a sudden dizzying sense of how much of Gandiffri she would never know, how much she and her family had lost.

But she was an American now. That was her job, to be an American. Mourning for Lémabantunk was like mourning for Atlantis, a lost place that might as well never have existed at all.

She heard footsteps on the walkway outside, and turned around to see Aliniana coming home with several bags of groceries. "Hello, hello, Zama, will you help me put these things away? Timbor, why do you look so sad? Where are the other children?"

"Rikko and Jamfret have wrestling practice," Zamatryna said, getting up to carry a carton of eggs to the fridge. "Polly went to the mall with friends, I think. I thought you were working until six today?"

"No, Veronica didn't show this morning so they called me to come in early, so I'm home early, too. Ai, what a day! I do not know why it was so busy on a Wednesday. Non-stop customers, many mothers with babies, and the babies howled so much you would have thought they were having their heads cut off, not their hair, and I had to listen to this while I painted nails. It was very unpleasant."

"I guess everybody had a bad day," Zamatryna said. She was going to tell Aliniana about Timbor's customer, but her aunt and grandfather both looked at her, their eyebrows raised, and she realized that she'd given herself away. Maybe she'd meant to.

"You had a bad day?" Timbor asked quietly. "What happened, dear one?"

"Oh, nothing, really. My guidance counselor hassled me about some stupid stuff. He wants me to change the name of the gardening club. He thinks 'Growing Girls' is sexist and will keep boys away. I told him boys didn't want to join anyhow."

Timbor chuckled. "You could call it Planting Persons."

"Or Horticulture Helpers," Aliniana said.

"Or Fertilizing Folks," said Zamatryna, and they all laughed.

"Get some boys to join with the name you have now," said Aliniana. She put the last grocery item, a bag of rice, in the pantry and sat down at the table. "Then the counselor will not complain. What about your boyfriends? How many do you have this week? Three? Get them to join."

Zamatryna wrinkled her nose. "They aren't really boyfriends, Auntie. They're just people I do things with. Bill from cheerleading, he's gay, so we just hang out, and Donald from the yearbook is funny but we're just friends, and Enrico's just my math study partner, that's all. They're nice guys, but I'm not in *love* with any of them. I'm too young for that."

"Oh, oh," Aliniana said, rolling her eyes and throwing her hands in the air, "excuse me, I forgot how grown-up you are, so grown-up that you know you aren't grown-up enough to be in love, well excuse me, Miss Zama, but that's very silly. When you fall in love you won't sit down and weigh it all out like meat, so many pounds of this and that, and what's the best thing for dinner. It will just happen. It is your soul matching someone else's. When I met Macsofo"—she gave a huge sigh, and Timbor and Zamatryna smiled at each other, knowing they were in for a familiar tale—"oh, I looked at him and I knew at once that I would be with him forever. It was in the court-yard of my parents' house, where he had come to fix a brick wall. The first day I just watched him, and the second day I spoke to him about the weather and the garden, and the third day I gave him a cup of water and our hands touched, and I knew then that he knew, too." She sighed; her eyes had begun to grow moist, as they always did when she remembered Lémabantunk.

"Some souls match at once," Timbor said mildly, "but some souls only join over time." Zamatryna knew he thought that Alini-ana and Macsofo were growing apart; she had heard him discussing it with her father. Macsofo often came home from work later than he should have, and he was often moody. He had never gotten over his bitterness at their exile; Zamatryna thought he didn't want to. "And this is America, Aliniana. Zama must do as people do here."

"Other American girls have boyfriends," Aliniana said.

"If you're with only one guy, he wants to have sex," Zamatryna said. "I don't want to do that yet. I want to wait." One of her more persistent theories about Darroti's tragedy, based on careful study of soap operas, was that Gallicina had been pregnant, and had pursued the family in rage that her child had also been killed, also been broken and silenced. "Lisa says that's really smart."

"Smart," Aliniana scoffed. "Certainly it is smart. But when you meet the man you love, smart will fly out the door. Certain things you cannot plan, Miss Zama. Certain things are gifts you could not have imagined. That is why, at home, people getting married gave gifts, instead of receiving them: to repay what they received in each other. People here act like the man and the woman getting married are poor!"

Zamatryna shrugged. "Sometimes they are."

"Not if they love each other!"

"People who love each other still need furniture and cooking pots," Timbor said. "I think it the same thing, Alini: a way of using humans to represent the graciousness of the Elements. And some people getting married here ask their guests to give to the poor. A passenger of mine said her daughter was doing that."

"Ellie Etiquette says that's bad form," Zamatryna said. "She had a column about it in the paper last week. You aren't supposed to ask your guests to do that, because you aren't supposed to act like you're assuming they're going to give you anything at all."

"Aaaaah." Aliniana waved a hand in disgust. "That is stupid. People here are selfish."

"Some people in Gandiffri were stupid and selfish, too," Timbor said. "Lémabantunk was not paradise, even if it was home."

"Aaaah, listen, last week I did manicures for a young woman getting married, and her mother, and very fussy they were too, and all they could talk about was the gifts she was getting, where she was registered and who had bought her which piece of fancy china and why hadn't uncle so-and-so been willing to spend more than thirty-five dollars, and didn't I think that was a shame? I never even learned the husband's name! Does this sound to you like someone in love, or someone generous?"

"Did they tip?" Zamatryna asked.

"Yes, but only ten percent." Aliniana sniffed, and Zamatryna and her grandfather shared another smile. "Listen, Miss Zama, when you get married, you give gifts to your guests. You be generous."

"She is already generous," Timbor said.

"Well, I'll try to remember my husband's name, anyway."

Zamatryna looked at Timbor and said, "Are you going to try to find that woman tomorrow? The homeless woman?"

"I will look for her, yes, if I can. If my routes permit it."

"Take her a jar of peanut butter. We have two now. Peanut butter and some crackers. She doesn't need a place to cook, to eat that."

Timbor patted her hand. "You are a good child, Zamatryna."

And then the phone rang and it was her friend Suki from Growing Girls, calling with a request from a woman who needed her rose bushes trimmed, and of course Zamatryna had to tell her about the conversation with Rumpled Ron, and then the twins came home from wrestling practice and Macsofo and Erolorit came home from their jobs and it was time for dinner, and then Zamatryna had homework to do, with half her brain, while she talked on the phone with Jenny from cheerleading and Ross from the yearbook; and then Bill and Donald and Enrico all called, one after the other, so she talked to them too; and by the time she went to sleep, she was feeling much better. She had *lots* of friends, and her grades were good, and that meant she was successful; and if she was successful, she had to be happy.

But putting her clothing away—for she had maintained her habits of neatness from childhood—she saw the beetle in its jar, and felt a pang of guilt. She only fed it once a day now, and she saw that this morning's lettuce had begun to rot. That couldn't be very nice for the beetle. So she unscrewed the lid of the jar and held the insect gently between her fingers, so it couldn't fly away, and dumped the lettuce into a tissue with her free hand. She'd flush the tissue down the toilet. "You'll get more food tomorrow," she told the beetle. "I don't have any more right now. I didn't bring you anything from dinner, you stupid thing. I'm sorry."

X.

Zamatryna shook her head. "Gallicina, I hope you weren't this boring when you were a person." Then, with a sigh, she dumped the beetle back in the jar and replaced the lid. What a dull life the creature led! No flowers, no sunshine, just bits of lettuce and radish, and drops of water, and the slick sides of a glass jar. Such an existence had to be as bad as Stan's hell, as painful and dreary as roasting like a chicken would have been. "I'm tired just looking at you," Zamatryna said, her compassion mingled with disgust. "I'm going to bed now. Goodnight, Gallicina."

She was tired the next day, too: tired and irritable, sick of classes. She sat with the yearbook staff during lunch—she tried to rotate between the yearbook, the cheerleaders, and the gardeners—but couldn't interest herself in gossip about whether the school nurse's picture looked so much better this year than last because she'd been giving herself Botox injections. Zamatryna picked listlessly at her fruit and cottage-cheese salad, which was only food here, which didn't contain anyone's soul. She found herself wondering what her life would have been like if the family had been able to stay in Lémabantunk. Would she have been bored there, too, learning to cook and clean house, keeping the garden, maybe helping out in the Market? Had Gallicina been bored? Was that why she had fought so hard to be a Mendicant?

She sighed and excused herself from the table, getting up to bus her tray. When she turned around she saw Jerry Zanger, the senior quarterback of the football team, coming toward her. He was Jenny's boyfriend. He was going to UNR next year to study accounting, and he was the most boring person Zamatryna had ever met. All the air seemed to drain out of the room whenever he opened his mouth.

He stopped a foot away from her, and blinked. "Hey, Zama."

"Hey, Jerry." She stood waiting to hear what he'd say next, and trying to be patient. Jerry's synapses fired very slowly; she always pictured them trying to turn over, like a car engine, and failing. Jerry's brain needed a new starter.

He scratched his ear, and blinked again. "So, Zama, Suki told Jenny you talked to Rumpled Ron yesterday. And Jenny told me."

"Yes, Jerry," Zamatryna said, trying not to gasp for oxygen like a beached fish, "I did talk to Rumpled Ron yesterday." Behind her, she heard someone in the yearbook clique snicker, and immediately felt a visceral surge of indignation. Jerry was pathetic, but they still shouldn't laugh at him. "But I can't imagine why you'd find that interesting."

Jerry coughed. "Well, Suki told Jenny that Rumpled Ron says you need guys in that, uh, gardening club. And that you need a new name."

"Ron says it would be a good idea to add guys," Zamatryna agreed politely. "If we add guys, I guess we need another name. Do you know any guys who want to be added?"

"Well," Jerry said, shifting from one foot to the other, "Coach is saying the football team should do community service. To show people we aren't just dumb jocks." Someone at the table began making choking sounds; Zama turned around and saw Ross doing a Heimlich maneuver on Christabel, the Layout Goddess.

"Oh, cut it *out*," she snapped, and Christabel hawked up a piece of chicken, and Ross gave a thumbs-up sign, and everybody else at the table made vomiting noises. "Go back to kindergarten," Zamatryna said, and turned back to Jerry. She wondered if he had any idea that they were making fun of him.

"It's okay," he said. "Football people and yearbook people never get along. It's an ancient rivalry. Like the Middle East, without car bombs."

Zamatryna felt her eyebrows rising. "He knows the word *rivalry*," Christabel said in a stage whisper.

"He's studying for the SATs," someone else whispered back—not Ross, or Zamatryna would have hit him over the head with her cafeteria tray—and Jerry actually laughed.

"I already took them, dumbass. I didn't do so badly, either. Zama, do you need help with that tray?"

"No," she said. "But I need to bus it. Come on, tag along, and tell me whatever you were going to say before they started their little comedy routine."

"Well," he said, standing next to her as she dumped her uneaten salad into the trash, "the football team needs community service, like I said. And a bunch of us do lawnwork anyway. Pruning bushes, mowing grass, you know, that kind of stuff."

"Stuff with power tools," Zama said, tossing her silverware into a tray of soapy water.

"Yeah," Jerry said, falling into step beside her as she left the cafeteria, "stuff with power tools: that's right. So I thought we could team up with you. It would make sense. But then you need a new name."

"You mean the football team doesn't want to be known as Growing Girls?" Zamatryna asked, and Jerry laughed again.

"No, I don't think so. But then I thought we should help you with the name."

"Ah," Zamatryna said. "That's very nice of you. Well, I'd like to keep it as a pun, and something that alliterates."

"Oh," Jerry said. She wondered if he'd ask what "alliterate" meant if he didn't know. There was a long pause—she was walking to her locker now, and he was still beside her—before he said, "Well, I'd thought of Seeds of Hope. That's a pun, isn't it?"

"No. It's a cliché. That's not the same thing."

"Oh. Okay." Zama started spinning her locker combination, making a list of the books she needed for her afternoon classes. Calc, bio—lab book, not textbook—English. They were reading *Crime and Punishment*, which she found so mind-numbingly dull that being trapped in a glass jar and fed moldy lettuce would have been preferable. "What about Seeds of Kindness?"

"What?" She turned, vaguely startled that Jerry was still there.

"Seeds of Kindness," he said. "That's not a cliché, is it?"

"No. But it's not a pun, either. And it's mushy."

"Oh. Well, I guess we can't have that." She turned back to her locker to collect her books, and Jerry said, "Vegetable Love?"

"What?"

"Vegetable Love. You know, the name of that punk band. But it was from a poem first, I think. By somebody named Marvel? Some comics guy?"

Zamatryna shook her head, kicking her locker closed because she needed both hands for the stack of books. "That sounds perverted, which is worse than mushy. Look, it would be nice to keep a verb in there somewhere. Like 'growing,' you know? An action word."

"Oh. Okay. You need help carrying those books?"

"No," she said. Jerry had used up all his synapses remembering the word rivalry, and he was becoming a serious annoyance. "I carry my books every day. I do it all by myself. But thank you."

"You're welcome. Where are you going now?"

"Math," Zamatryna said. "Where we're studying the Fundamental Theorem of the Calculus." She hoped this information might dissolve Jerry's synapses entirely, but it didn't work.

"Hmmm," he said. "Hey, what about Pruning Pals?"

"What?"

"Pruning Pals. As the name of the gardening club. You know: pals who prune. You know, bushes."

She was almost at her math classroom, and glad of it. "Er, no. That sounds like we're chopping away at our friends with shears. Because it could mean that we were pruning the pals, not just that we were pals who were pruning." A teacher walking by gave her a mystified glance, and Zamatryna realized how inane this conversation must sound. Well, it was inane. "And we do more than prune, anyway, so it isn't even accurate. Jerry, this is my class. I have to go inside. See you later."

"Yeah, okay. Thanks for explaining that. I'll keep thinking about it."

"Great. You do that. Thanks for the suggestions." She escaped gratefully inside, wondering how Jenny put up with this bonehead. Jenny said he was really sweet, but surely she could have done better. What in the world did they talk about? She probably just went out with him because he was the quarterback, a trophy guy. Jenny was very insecure.

Calc was easy. The bio lab was easy. English was beyond boring. When Zamatryna got home that afternoon, feeling as if her brain had been turned into a howling wasteland, she found Timbor sitting at the kitchen table again. He wasn't singing or weeping this time: he was arguing with Macsofo, who was still in his gritty work clothing, gulping hot tea.

"Why are you giving our things away to a crazy woman? Father, it isn't right!"

Zamatryna knocked on the screen door to let them know she was there, and then let herself in. "Uncle Max, what are you doing home so early?"

"I'm sick," Macsofo snapped. He sounded as if he'd swallowed a collection of nail files. "They made me come home because I'm sick, but that means I may lose some pay, and now I find that Father wants to bring food to some crazy lady! We worked for that food. We are trying to buy our way out of this wretched house, and you go and give—"

"Peanut butter and crackers," Timbor said mildly. "It was Zama's idea. It is a very good idea. Betty can fix herself peanut butter and crackers even if she has no place to cook."

"Let her go to the soup kitchen!" Macsofo started coughing, and swigged some more tea. "That is what the free food is there for! This is not Lémabantunk, Father. This Betty is no holy Mendicant!"

"She is a person. My duty is the same."

"Who's Betty?" Zamatryna asked, sitting cautiously at the table.

"The woman from yesterday, the one I saw when the nasty man was in the taxi. I told you about her. I found her today. I found her on my lunch break and talked to her. She was afraid of me at first, because many people have hurt her, but then she told me all about herself. Oh, Zama, she has suffered terrible things!"

"She was probably lying," Macsofo said.

"I do not think she is capable of lying. She is not quite, how do the Americans say, right in the head."

"You see?" Macosofo said triumphantly. "Crazy! I told you. Let her go to the hospital, if she is crazy."

"I do not think it is something a hospital can fix. And I do not think she is crazy. She is simple; she was a child who did not get enough air at birth, I think. Zama, I am going now to bring her the peanut butter. Would you come with me? I think she would like to meet you. She has a daughter of her own; she gave the child to a foster family who could care for it better than she can, but she misses the little girl terribly. It would help her if you were kind to her."

"Sure I'll go," Zamatryna said, getting up. She had a lot of questions, but she knew better than to ask them in front of Macsofo, who looked like he was about to combust. "Which car are we taking? Can I drive?" The family had acquired three ancient vehicles, including Stan and Lisa's old van; they kept all three keys on hooks in the kitchen, and anyone who needed a car took whichever was available. Stan and Timbor and Erolorit spent hours working on the cars, patiently keeping them running, coaxing extra miles out of them.

"The Honda, I think," Timbor said, and Zamatryna's heart sank. The Honda was the most ancient and crotchety of all the cars; on the other hand, it was also the least valuable, and therefore the best practice vehicle. Her father said that if she could learn to drive the Honda, she could drive anything, which would make passing her driving test much easier.

So she drove the Honda, lurching and scraping the curbs going around corners, while Timbor briefed her on Betty's life. "She is forty-two. Her daughter is twelve, and her parents are dead. Her older brother—Zama, slow down now, here's a stop sign, stop, good girl—her brother, who raised her after their parents died, is also her daughter's father. Now start again: you've stopped long enough. Betty and her daughter are both simple in the brain, yes, but Betty wants the best for her child. Five years ago she married a man who was kind to her, patient with her daughter, and who would stand up to her brother. Slow down, child: you are five miles over the limit. But Betty's husband is one of the gambling addicts, and so he spent all their money, his own pay and Betty's disability check, and also money her brother had given her for the daughter. Zama, remember your turn signals, we are taking a right up here, turn the wheel now, yes, very good. So she left her husband and moved in with an aunt and uncle in Winnemucca, but then they told her she had to leave, because they needed the space for a child of their own who was coming home. So she came back to Reno, but her husband had gone, she does not know where. Zama, now you are going too slowly: speed up just a little bit. And so Betty went to the State and told them to take her daughter because she wanted the daughter to have a home. She told the State she wanted to learn to read and to count, so that people would stop taking advantage of her. But it is not clear that she is able to learn to read or to count, and they have not found a place for her to live yet, and she is afraid to go to the shelters. And so she is thinking of moving back in with her brother, who at least will never turn her away. Left up here; mind the child on the bicycle! Why do parents let their children ride bicycles in the street? Without helmets? I do not understand it."

"That's horrible," Zamatryna said. The story had washed over her in nauseating waves as she concentrated on navigating; her hands ached from clutching the steering wheel. "I mean Betty. Not the kid on the bike. Why isn't her brother in jail? Why isn't her husband in jail? Why can't the State find somewhere for her to live?"

"I do not know about the State. I think she does not want to send the men to jail. She does not seem able to be angry at them, although she has acted to protect her daughter. She feels sorry for them; she thinks they cannot help themselves from doing wrong. Look, there she is. Here, Zama. Stop the car."

Zamatryna pulled over to the curb and stopped the car, and they got out. Betty was sitting on a bench, surrounded by huge black garbage bags. Her face was as black as the plastic and as round as a full moon, and when she saw them and smiled, it was as if that moon had come out from behind clouds. She smelled of sweat and rot; the scent rolled out from her in waves. "Tim. You came back. I didn't think you would. Where's your cab?"

"It is at the company lot, Betty. This is my car. And this is my granddaughter, Zama."

"You're pretty," Betty said, nodding. "Zama?"

"Yes, Zama."

"That's a pretty name. How old are you?"

"Fifteen."

"My girl's twelve. She's with a family now, so she doesn't have to live out here. Someday I'll get her back, when I have a place again. Her name's Theresa."

"We brought you some peanut butter," Zama said, holding out the bag. "And bottled water, and crackers. The crackers will keep a long time, if they don't get wet."

"Thank you, sweetheart. Did you bring a knife for the peanut butter?"

"Oh—oh, no, how stupid, we didn't—I didn't think—"

"That's all right, darling. I can use my fingers. Or the crackers, but sometimes they break."

"I'm sorry," Zamatryna said, feeling wretched. But at the same time she wanted to get away, because Betty's smell was making her sick. "Do you get cold at night? We could bring you a blanket."

"No, sweetheart, I have blankets." Betty patted one of her plastic bags with the hand that had been hidden in her lap, and Zamatryna saw that the hand was moving in a constant, spasmodic flutter, although the rest of Betty was as still as the mountains on the horizon. She thought immediately of Gallicina, of the beetle's obsessive X, and her chest tightened.

"Betty," Timbor said gently, "What is wrong with your hand? Are you sick?"

"No, my hand always does that. It always has."

Zamatryna swallowed. "Even when you sleep?"

"I guess so."

"Does your arm get tired?"

"I don't know. It hurts sometimes. Do you want some peanut butter?"

"No," Timbor said. "The peanut butter is for you, Betty. I will come see you again, eh? I will look for you and find out how you are doing."

"Thank you, Tim. Thank you, Zama. Good-bye, darling." And as they were getting back into the Honda, she called after them, "God bless you."

Zamatryna, her own hands shaky, started the car, but after a few blocks she pulled over and said, "Grandfather, would you drive home?"

"Yes. You are very quiet. Are you all right, Zama?"

"I'm sad."

"I'm sad, too."

"Can't we do something for her? Can't we, I don't know, bring her home with us and—"

"Like a puppy from the pound? She is a person, Zama. And where would she sleep? And how would we convince your uncle?"

"It's not fair."

"No. It is not. Many things are not."

They drove the rest of the way home in silence, and arrived to find that Aliniana and Erolorit were home, also. Aliniana was cooking, since Harani was working a late shift at the casino; Erolorit sat at the kitchen table, playing solitaire, while Macsofo nursed the same mug of tea, or another one.

"Uncle Max," Zamatryna said, "you should go to bed, if you aren't feeling well."

"I don't want to go to bed. Did you find that woman?"

"Yes, we did. We gave her the peanut butter." Something in his voice warned her to change the subject. "Where are my cousins?"

"At friends' houses, where other people will feed them, which is excellent, since you are giving our food to bums."

There was a short silence. Aliniana turned from the stove, and Erolorit looked up from his cards, frowning. "Yes," Timbor said calmly, "that is how it works. We feed people, and people feed us. Did you take aspirin, Macsofo? It will make you feel better."

"Do not treat me like a child, Father."

"Do not act like one, then."

Erolorit cleared his throat. "I think—"

"Do not try to think, Brother. You are not very good at it."

Erolorit shook his head. "Macsofo, we are in this house because of charity. We have been given—"

"Do not remind me what we have been given! We have been given a debt we can never repay! I hate this house! I hate this country! Taking charity is no honor here, do you understand? It means we are weak! And giving our hard-earned wages to bums makes us fools!"

"Macsofo," Aliniana said. She had turned the stove burners off; she turned now and put her hands in his hair, stroking. "Dear husband, you are not weak, and your father is not a fool, and—"

"Get off," Macsofo said, and reached up to fling her hands roughly from his head. "You disgust me." Zamatryna, watching, remembered Aliniana's story of the first time their hands had touched, the moment when she had known she loved him. She had been giving him water, then. He had been taking charity. She remembered Macsofo supporting Aliniana as they entered the refugee camp, Macsofo saying, "It is a city of Mendicants." He had been unhappy then, but he had not been cruel. When had he changed?

He had changed when Darroti died, when the entire world had changed.

"This is no way to treat your wife," Timbor said sharply. Macsofo made a dismissive motion and got up from his chair; Aliniana tried to embrace him, but he pushed her aside, his lip curling. Again she reached out to him; this time he made a spitting noise like a cat. "I told you, get away from me! You are nothing but a spineless slug, and I wish I had never seen you!"

Aliniana tried to smile, and said in a wavering voice, "Macsofo, dearest, surely you do not mean that—"

"Do not tell me what I mean!" He raised his hand as if to strike her, and Zamatryna, standing frozen, saw her father shake himself and move quickly between them.

"Enough, Macsofo. You are not yourself. Go to bed!"

"I will not," Macsofo said, and pushed past Erolorit out the door, snatching one of the car keys as he went. The door banged shut; they heard an engine starting, and a squeal of rubber as he pulled out of the driveway.

"He is going out to drink," Aliniana said, her voice curiously even. "That is what he has been doing, when he stays away from home. He is becoming Darroti, whom he hates. Will he kill me, I wonder, as Darroti killed that woman? He has not hit me yet. He will soon; I can feel it. How is it that I still love him? I followed him here. I have been a good wife. I—"

"Auntie," Zamatryna said, and moved to embrace her. "Auntie, he—he did not mean it. We will not let him hurt you. I think he hates himself, and so he hates us who love him, and—"

"You are a wise child," Aliniana said, but Zamatryna could feel her shaking. "I must cook now. We must eat."

"I will cook," Timbor said quietly. "Zama, comfort your aunt."

"Come," Zamatryna said. "Auntie, come into the living room. Sit down, here on the couch. It is all right to cry." It frightened her that Aliniana, who always wept so easily, was not weeping now. "I am glad you are here, Auntie. I am glad you came with us."

"You will do well here," Aliniana said. "My children will do well here. You will be excellent Americans. We have not lost everything."

"No," Zamatryna said, and hugged her. "And you will do well too, Auntie, you are already doing well, you are helping people."

She felt Aliniana shudder. "And my husband hates me for it."

"No, no, Auntie, he—he is confused, he—"

"He was so happy at our wedding, Zama. I know he was." Aliniana put her head back against the couch, her voice grown dreamy. "So happy. He was so proud of how much we were giving our Necessary Beggar, and when the Beggar married us and spoke the blessing, Macsofo's face shone."

Good. Let her remember, if it would make her happy. Zamatryna held her aunt's cold hand, and said, "What was the blessing, Auntie?"

"Oh, the same blessing the Necessary Beggar always gives, the wedding blessing. 'For what you have given me, your errors and those of all your kin are forgiven. For charity heals shortcoming, and kindness heals carelessness, and hearts heal hurt.' It is very beautiful. It made Macsofo very happy. He told me he would never do anything unkind again."

"I never heard it before," Zamatryna said. She had known that the Beggar gave a blessing at weddings, and that this had something to do with forgiveness, but she had never heard the words. "It's wonderful."

"It was wonderful then." Aliniana's voice was listless, the dreams drained out of it. "What good is it here? It has run out, that blessing, or it cannot work in this new place. We need a new blessing for all the hurts that have happened since then, but we will not get one. That is not how weddings work here. You and your cousins will have American weddings. You will eat cake and get lots of presents, and the guests will get drunk, and no one will be forgiven for anything. And then you will probably get divorced."

Zamatryna, frightened, chafed her aunt's icy fingers. Aliniana, often sad, was never bitter. "Do not say that, Auntie! You—"

"Ah, Zama, I am sorry. You are right. I did not mean to curse you, child. You will have a lovely life. You are a good American. You will be prosperous and happy. Here, child, give me a hug. There, there. Everything is all right. Come now: let us go back into the kitchen and eat our dinner."

Timbor had burned the roast. Aliniana and Erolorit teased him, and Zamatryna sensed the current of some old story, once joyous but now laden with regret. She was afraid to ask what it was. There was already too much ancient pain in the room.

After dinner she went to her room to do homework. She had hidden a piece of green bean in her pocket for Gallicina, and as she put it into the jar, she remembered Betty's hand moving in tremulous flutters.

She couldn't concentrate on math. She finally closed the book and curled up on her bed, pulling the comforter over her. She still felt chilled from Aliniana's hand. She thought about Darroti and Gallicina, about Macsofo and Aliniana, about Betty and the men who had hurt her so. She thought about the words of the wedding blessing, and it came to her, then, what she must do.

She must be a good American. She must do well here, and earn money. But since she was the oldest, she would be the first to marry, and when she got married, she would have a Necessary Beggar: Betty, or someone else, someone who needed gifts, someone who needed to feel honored. And the Necessary Beggar would pronounce the wedding blessing, and her family would be forgiven for everything they had done since Macsofo's wedding. Macsofo would be forgiven, and Darroti's spirit would be forgiven, and Gallicina would leave off her vengeance and be at peace, and everyone would be happy again. She would have helped all of them, would have mended all the broken places in their lives. And then she could be happy herself.

She fell asleep, spinning that story, and awoke still within it. It was a good plan. It would take years to achieve, of course, because her family would not let her marry until she was at least eighteen, and because it would not be easy to find a husband. But it would allow her to begin helping everyone even before she went to law school.

She put the plan aside. She went to school thinking about calculus and Raskolnikov. To her surprise, she found Jerry waiting for her at her locker, smiling. "I think I've got it," he said. "I think I found a name for the club. Planting Pals. Does that work, Zama?"

She looked at him. "Yes," she said. "Planting Pals. Yes, that works."

9

Timbor

Oh, the things we kept from one another! All those hours sitting at the kitchen table in Lisa's house, talking and talking about other people: about Betty, and Aliniana's customers, and Zamatryna's friends. If Zamatryna or I had once told the entire truth about ourselves, our story would have been very different. But we did not, and who is to say that it was not for the best? We kept our silences out of love, and we found our way at last.

There was a psychiatrist who rode in my cab every morning and every afternoon. His name was Richard Farthingale, and he had to take my taxi because he was not allowed to drive. He had been a drunk, and he had lost his license for DUI; and now he was in AA and sober, but still he was not allowed to drive for three years. He had already been sober a year when he became my customer. And so every day for two years—Zamatryna's last year of high school and her first year at UNR—I took him to his office and back again. His wife had left him, and he did not want to ask his friends for rides. He worked in downtown Reno and lived in Galena Forest, at the base of Mount Rose. It was a very long drive, very expensive for him; very good for me, because he tipped well, and because the drive toward the mountain was beautiful, and comforted my soul. And because it was a long drive, it gave me time to talk.

I told Richard all the things I could not tell anyone else. I told him about my dreams, for every night I dreamed about Darroti and about the woman he had killed. Often I dreamed about the silver pendant, the symbol Darroti had worn. And most nights I dreamed about the camp, about the bombing. I did not tell Richard this, because no one was supposed to know that we had been in the camps. I told him that I dreamt about people dying where we had come from. I told him about Darroti, how he had been a drunk, how he had killed a woman and then killed himself; I told him about Macsofo, who was drinking now also and being cruel to his wife, unkind in ways Darroti had never been. I was terrified for Macsofo, who would not listen to me, and sick for Aliniana, who had to endure his insults. She loved Macsofo still; and if she had not, where could she have gone? We were all her kin in this place, and all her country.

Richard listened. That was his work, and he did it very well. He listened and he talked. He told me that drinking and suicide run in families, and that they run together; he said it was good that I did not drink myself, and he told me to caution the children to beware of alcohol. He told me that Macsofo would stop drinking only when he was ready; he told me about treatment programs we could not afford. He suggested that Aliniana and I attend Al-Anon, which was free, but he also warned us that cultural differences might make it too foreign to us. "The Twelve-Step model hasn't worked nearly as well for minorities as for whites. It's a real problem in ethnic communities, especially Native American ones. Are there other people from your country here? Can you talk to them, form some kind of support group?"

"We have not found any," I said bleakly. I was driving Richard home at the end of the day, in a blazing January sunset. There was fresh snow on the mountains, which glowed against the sky. We were still on the freeway, but soon we would exit onto local roads, and then turn onto Mount Rose Highway.

"Where are you from, again?"

I could not say Afghanistan. There were Afghan immigrants in Reno, quite a number of them, and Richard probably knew that. "It is—a very small country, very far away, very isolated. In Central Asia. You will not have heard of it, Richard."

In the rear-view mirror, I saw him raise an eyebrow. "Well, all right. But how does your culture handle this problem? What would you have done at home, to cope with an alcoholic son?"

What had I done at home, to cope with an alcoholic son? I had been as loving as I could. I had hoped that he would stop. I had told myself that he would be all right, that he was young, that he would settle down, that surely everything was fine because he still came to the Great Market every day and still drove good bargains on carpets. I had been blind, and a fool, but there had been no way to know that then.

"In our culture," I told Richard, "families help each other, always. And we help others. But problems stay within the family, and the family solves them. Not because the problems are shameful, but because that is what families are for, and so the person having the problem will always know that he is loved. But my son Max, the one who is drinking now, he has stopped listening to the family. He thinks our love is weakness; he thinks it is weakness to ask for help, or to give it, although where we come from, help is a blessing." I was silent for a few minutes, while I negotiated the traffic getting off the freeway; Richard did not speak. When I was safely in the proper lane, I went on. "Max has rejected the old ways, and he claims to reject America, also, but it seems to me as if he has embraced the worst of American ways. And yet perhaps that is not fair. He works hard at his job. He brings home his pay to help us. And yet he uses that to insult us, to prove that we are weak; he says that he is better than we are. And he has begun to bring home less of his money, now. He says that if we are not working as hard as we might to help ourselves, there is no reason for him to help us. He says that he should be able to use some of his money as he pleases, and what pleases him is drinking. And he is cruel to his wife, as I have said. And yet he loves his three children, and he is proud of them, of how well they do in school, of how smart they are. He is gentle with them as he is with no one else. He is glad that they will make more money than he does, when it comes time for them to have jobs of their own."

Richard listened, and then he spoke. "You know, in America, we say that alcoholism is a disease. That isn't a shameful thing."

"But he enjoys it. He enjoys drinking. No one enjoys being sick."

Richard sighed. "He'll stop enjoying it, at some point. Tim, how would your society explain what's wrong with Max? What metaphor do you use? Some cultures believe that addiction is caused by spirits, for instance."

"No," I said, turning onto Mount Rose Highway. The highway is straight for perhaps ten miles, and then it becomes very twisty, very narrow and dangerous. I was always glad that Richard did not live farther up the mountain, because people die on that road every year, especially in the winter. "We do not believe that the dead can speak to the living; that is a grief to us. I wish more than anything to speak to Darroti."

"Yes, of course you do."

"Every night I dream about him. And sometimes I dream he is trying to tell me something, but he is always so sad, and I cannot bear to listen. And everything gets mixed up in his story: people dying, and the carpets we used to sell in the Great Market of our city, and the necklace he brought from home. I have never had such dreams before."

"Post-traumatic stress syndrome," Richard said quietly. "People who've been through terrible things often dream about them. It will help you if you can find somewhere to tell your story, Tim. If you can tell it in the world, it may stop dominating your dreams."

"I am telling it to you, Richard. My family already knows it, and what they do not know would be too big a burden for them."

"I'm honored," he said. "Thank you for telling me. I'm sorry you've gone through so much. But if you don't believe that drinking is an illness, or a form of possession, then how do you explain it?"

I scratched my ear. "I do not know. I am not sure I ever heard anyone talk about that before. I suppose we would say that the Elements were not in balance in that person. Darroti was mostly earth and water, aye, and so perhaps liquor kindled fire in him. I do not know."

"Medieval humors," Richard said. I did not know what he meant. "That's a very ancient model, but it's not really so far from how we think about some things now. Your son probably has some sort of biochemical imbalance, triggered by trauma. Medication might help him, along with therapy."

"That would mean asking for help," I said. "He would not do that."

In the rear-view mirror, I saw Richard make a face. "Well, he's become a good American that way, at any rate. Or a good Nevadan. Self-reliance."

Yes, I thought. Self-reliance. Like paying seventy dollars a day for a taxi because you will not ask your friends for rides. What Richard spent on cab fare was incomprehensible to me. What he was paying the taxi company, I should have been paying him, for listening to me talk.

We were in the trees now, the thick pines at the base of the mountain, the very end of the place where the highway was still straight. Richard lived among these trees, in a huge house that made me shiver whenever I imagined living in it without any family to warm the rooms. Richard had no children. I dropped him at his house and told him I would see him in the morning, and then I turned the taxi around and began the lonely drive back home. It was less pretty in this direction, driving away from the mountain, and it was not always good for me to have so much time to think. I worried about many things, many people. I worried about Max and Aliniana, of course. I worried about Betty, who still did not have a permanent place to live, who had been in and out of shelters and group homes, and who more than once had been robbed and beaten on the street. Betty looked older and more frightened every time I brought her peanut butter. And I worried about Stan.

I talked to Richard; Stan talked to me. He talked to me while we were working on the three cranky cars my family owned, and he talked to me every Saturday when we went to the Automobile Museum to visit our beautiful vintage taxicab, so much more elegant than the ordinary yellow one I drove. The shining De Soto, with its happy plastic suns on top, never failed to cheer me, but as much as Stan loved it, it seemed to make him sad. He wanted there to be cars like that still on the streets, and there were not, except during Hot August Nights, the antique car festival in Reno. But too many people got drunk during Hot August Nights, and there was too much loud music. I did not enjoy it, and neither did Stan. He wanted the cars at the museum to be everyday cars, not party cars.

Stan was sad about many things, not just about cars. When we first came to America, he had told us endlessly about Jesus. But now, so many years later, he talked to me not to convince me that his faith was the only correct one, but to complain that he himself had lost his way. "I don't know, old man. I always thought that if I followed Jesus and did what was right, I'd be rewarded, you know, and people would flock to me because I could give them the Word of God. But I don't feel like I have anything to give anybody anymore. I see people lying and robbing and stealing and they don't get struck down; they're doing better than I am. How can God allow that? How can I talk to my flock about God's righteousness when I can't see it in the world myself?"

I thought about all the people who had died when the camp was bombed, and wondered just when Stan had begun to notice that bad things happened to good people. But he was glad that the bombers would be put to death, I knew, and he probably thought that the people they had killed were in Heaven, standing on clouds and playing harps. Whenever I tried to picture angels, I saw Harpo Marx, with wings. "What is it exactly," I asked him, "that you want your God to do?"

"Punish evildoers," Stan said. "Reward the faithful. There's this guy at work, now, his name's Harry, he's a total sumbitch. Gambles and drinks and cheats on his wife, and he's making out like Flynn. He went to Hawaii for two weeks on his last vacation. Hell, Tim, I can barely afford the thirty-five dollars a year to come here and look at these cars, you know? And I know you and the family are working real hard and paying Lisa rent, and I don't meddle in her mama's property, because we decided a long time ago that that was her business. And I guess it's okay that we're still meeting for worship in our own house; there are fewer people now anyway, so there are enough chairs for everybody. But it seems to me like, with what her mama left her and with what you folks are paying, we should be doing better."

We were paying her back what her mother had left her, and we had paid only a fraction of it. I could not tell him that. Lisa had been a bad person before she became a good one; maybe he would think that she was still a bad person, if he knew what had happened to her mother's money.

"Maybe your God is waiting," I said. "To see if these people learn. Maybe Harry will be better someday." Maybe Macsofo would, too. "Does your holy book not say that the last will be first? That seems a kind and good saying, to me."

I had read Stan's New Testament as soon as I knew enough

Susan Palwick

English, because I wanted to understand his beliefs better; but I had never been able to make the God he talked about, the God of punishment, fit with the God of forgiveness described in those pages. The Jesus of the New Testament would have loved Macsofo, and probably Harry too. Lisa worshiped the Jesus of the New Testament. Stan worshiped some other Jesus. I could not worship either of them. I was a father myself, and I could not conceive of any loving father who would require his child to die in agony. Jesus' father had not saved him from the cross, not even after Jesus begged him to do so in the garden. I would have done anything to save Darroti from the fence. I would have died myself, gladly. And so now I said, "It must have seemed to the people who watched Jesus die that God was not acting then, either. And yet you believe that good came of that, Stan."

"That was only three days," he said. "How long will I have to wait?" We were standing in front of the De Soto, then; Stan reached out as if to touch it, and then withdrew his hand, for it was forbidden to touch the cars at the museum, unless we were cleaning them. And I thought then that he was like a child, reaching for a toy. He wanted his God to be a father who gave him toys and lollipops, and also he wanted his God to heel like a puppy and come at his command.

In Gandiffri we knew that we could not command the Elements. We could try to discern their patterns, and to work within them rather than destroying them, but we did not make those patterns. Our own weavings, our own stories, were only tiny pieces of the whole, for the Elements and all their shapes had existed long before us, and would exist long after. And so when something seemed to destroy the pattern, as Darroti had when he killed the Mendicant, we tried to act kindly and carefully to repair it, as one would mend a beloved carpet. But I could not say this to Stan, because although he no longer quite held to his own faith, he would still reject mine.

He no longer believed in God, but he believed very firmly in the Devil.

"It isn't right," he said, still staring at the De Soto. "Your family has suffered so. You lost one son, and now Max is wandering, too. And that poor woman, Betty! How can anybody make sense of what's happened to her?"

"I do not know," I said. "We make sense of it by trying to help, yes?"

"Yes," he said, and reached out and gripped my shoulder. "We're Christ's army in the world, old man, battling the forces of Satan. Thank you. You strengthen my faith when nothing else does."

I wondered how I could strengthen a faith I did not share. I wondered how Stan could feel sorry for Betty and Max, and not feel sorry for Harry. I wondered how he could say that giving someone peanut butter was part of a battle. I thought that I would never be a real American, and I thought that I was glad of it.

But also I was glad that the children were such excellent Americans. Richard went to AA for comfort, and Stan went to me for comfort, and I went to Zamatryna for comfort. She had graduated as valedictorian of her high-school class, and had won a number of awards for math and science and service, and now she was in the honors program at UNR. She had a double major in political science and environmental science, and planned to go to law school. She had so many friends that I could not keep their names straight. She managed the food bank at UNR to help poor people, and she still ran Planting Pals, but also she worked in a law office. She bought her clothing and books with her own money now, to help the family, and her endless chatter about classes and roses and football games was one of the few things that could make Alini-ana laugh. Zamatryna bought very garish outfits in the strangest colors she could find—peach and purple and bright green, yellow and blue and black—and challenged Aliniana to paint her nails to match them, and the two of them giggled like children. And Zamatryna's cousins adored her, and wanted to be just like her, and indeed they were also very smart and good, although they were still in high school. And even Macsofo admired her. "She will become President," he said, blinking at her through bloodshot eyes.

That is why we were all so surprised when she began to date Jerry. He was a fine football player, but he was not good enough to be professional, and he received B's in his accounting classes. Aliniana, who had followed Zamatryna's social life as carefully as she followed soap operas—which, indeed, it sometimes resembled—shook her head and sighed. "Ah, he has loved her forever. That is very clear. He loved her when he was still dating Jenny, and then when Jenny dumped him and Zamatryna was dating Howard the math genius, he watched and waited until she should be free again. And when Zamatryna dumped Howard because he criticized the food bank, there was Jerry with bags of rice to give her, and tickets to a movie. He is a sweet boy, and when I tell her to be careful of his feelings, she laughs at me. She says they are just friends. I do not think Jerry thinks so. He worships her. But what does she see in him, other than kindness?"

It seemed to me that kindness was enough. And also, he did not drink. But it was true that I could not imagine what they talked about. "The other girls in her sorority are jealous," I said. "Because he is the top football player. So maybe she dates him to impress them."

Aliniana made a sniffing noise. "They are silly girls. She belongs to that sorority only so she can ask them to garden for the old people."

"They are her friends, Aliniana."

"Yes, but she is better than they are. She needs to find friends at her own level."

"Howard the math genius was at her own level, but she dumped him because he was not kind."

"Her own level in all ways," Aliniana said. "Which will be difficult."

Richard, when I told him this news—for sometimes I told him of the good things in the family, too—said that Zamatryna might be weary of her level. "She and her cousins have been working very hard to make up for everything else that's gone wrong in the family, Tim. That's a huge burden. Dating an ordinary kid is probably a relief for her."

It was a mild May day, the spring of Zamatryna's freshman year; in a few more weeks, Richard would have his license back, and I would no longer get to talk to him. "Why a burden?" I said. "She is successful, and she is happy."

"Would she tell you if she weren't?"

"Oh, she tells us everything. You should hear her chatter to her auntie!" How little I knew, then! But Richard made me angry, for I could not bear to think that Zamatryna was not truly happy; and now I can see that there were times when she tried to tell us that, and we would not listen. "I will miss you when you can drive again," I told Richard, to change the subject. "I will miss talking to you."

"I'll miss you too, Tim. I wish you could find other people to talk to. You're still having those dreams, aren't you?"

"Yes. Every night, always the same."

Richard was quiet for a little while, and then said, "You could write about it. Write down what you'd tell Darroti, if he were still alive. That might help. Write him letters."

"That is a fine idea, Richard. I will tell him that his nieces and nephews are doing well here, and that coming to this country has not been so terrible for us."

Richard sighed. "No, Tim, you have to tell him the bad stuff too. The painful stuff. The stuff you aren't talking about. That's the whole point."

But how could I burden Darroti with more pain? How could I want him to know that we still suffered, in our exile? And so, when I no longer saw Richard, I indeed began to write letters to Darroti, but only happy ones: about the garden, and about the cars at the museum, and about Zamatryna.

10

CUSTOMS

She went out with Jerry because he was there. Howard the math genius had exhausted her; his flights of inspiration had alternated with fits of despairing self-doubt, and so when he suggested that her work for the food bank was taking up time she should have been devoting to her classes, she'd happily used the issue to pick a fight and dump him. She was already getting straight A's in a double major in the Honors Program: why on earth would she have wanted to spend more time on schoolwork? If Howard wanted to be a neurotic workaholic dweeb, that was his privilege, but he'd have to do it by himself. And her sorority sisters had never been able to talk to him, anyway, although several of them had made heroic efforts. Howard wasn't someone who could help Zamatryna reconcile the complications of her life.

She didn't think Jerry was, either, but she knew him, and he had never been anything but helpful to her, and she couldn't imagine anyone less like Howard. Jerry was steady, dependable, forthright. And if he was also boring, well, there were worse things than boring, especially after six months of Howard's 2 A.M. phone calls about his grade-point obsessions. Jerry never would have dreamed of calling her at 2 A.M., or of suggesting that she spend more time on coursework. Jerry was in awe of her accomplishments, which he very properly recognized to be far above his. Jerry knew his place.

And so when he invited her to his fraternity's Spring Fling dance at the end of her freshman year, she accepted. It would be fun; it would be relaxing to go to the dance with someone who was more of an old friend than a boyfriend. She had exams to study for, and she didn't need first-date jitters on top of them. Jerry would be perfect.

Her sorority sisters acted like she'd landed a date with the President, and Zamatryna, rolling her eyes, tried to discourage their gossip. "I know him from *high school,* okay? I've known the guy for years. He went out with one of my best friends. Just chill. This isn't a big romance."

"Right," said Sarah-Bee. There were five girls named Sarah in the sorority; all five had blond hair and blue eyes, so they'd picked ways to distinguish their names. Sarah-Bee and Sarah-Cee used the first initials of their last names; Sarah-Lee and Sarah-Sue used middle names; Sarah-Harrah used her status as the niece of the current owner of Harrah's Casino. Sometimes they called her Sharrah, but that made whomever was speaking sound drunk, which they tried to avoid on principle, since so many people thought sorority girls were always drunk. "Come on, Zama, I've seen how Jerry acts around you. He always looks at you like you're the only person in the room."

"Well, he probably looks at whatever's in his range of vision that way. I don't think he can absorb very much information at once."

"That's mean," Sarah-Bee said, although she was laughing. "You shouldn't go out with the guy if you're going to make fun of him."

"You're right," Zamatryna said with a shrug. "I shouldn't. I'm sorry. But I doubt I'll be seeing him very long. It's probably just for this dance."

"Not if he has anything to say about it."

"What, he's talked to you about this?"

"Of course not. He's very honorable."

Zamatryna rolled her eyes. "How old-fashioned."

Sarah-Bee laughed again. "Well, he's got to be better than Howard."

"Yeah. At least he knows how to tie his own shoelaces. I think Howard would have had to be institutionalized if he'd been born before the invention of Velcro."

"Damn, Zama! Why are you so bitchy today?"

"Dunno," Zamatryna said with a shrug. "PMS, maybe. Or chocolate withdrawal." But in fact, she knew very well why she was in such a sour mood: because her college classes, true to Rumpled Ron's prediction, were almost as boring as her high-school ones, and because Betty, picked up by the cops for vagrancy, had just had to spend a night in jail again, and because Macsofo had been beastly again last night. He'd come home raging about his job, about how stupid his boss was, about how he wanted to quit and do something else, anything else. He'd heard that the railways were hiring freight handlers for the trains to Yucca Mountain. The pay was supposed to be very good. He planned to apply for one of those jobs.

"The pay's good because the work's so dangerous," Erolorit had said sharply. "Max, those trains are full of plutonium. That's poison. You don't need to do that."

"Ah, the fear of plutonium is a bunch of tree-hugger propaganda. There has never been an accident."

"There have been close calls," Timbor said, his voice grim. "I do not want you doing that, Macsofo."

"And who are you to tell me what I can do? Am I a child?"

"You are my child. I have already lost one child; I do not want to lose another. Whatever extra money you would earn, we do not need. You liked being a bricklayer, when we were in Lémabantunk."

"Yes, but we are no longer in Lémabantunk. We are in Reno,

where I must earn extra money because no one else seems capable of doing so. Especially my wife, who in all these years has learned to do nothing more useful than paint smiley-faces on other women's fingernails."

"What then would you have me do?" Aliniana asked quietly.

"Oh, you could always be a prostitute. That way you could make a lot of money doing for other men what you will not do for me."

Once this comment would have had Aliniana weeping for days. Now she did not even blink. "How then should I do for you, husband, when you are always wilted with whiskey? Do you think they will hire a drunk to work on the plutonium trains? Oh, that makes me feel very safe!"

"They will hire anyone who will do the work," Macsofo said, and spat at her. His spit landed on the side of her head and dripped onto the table; Zamatryna and the others sat, frozen, while he stormed out of the room. When he was gone, Aliniana got up and cleaned herself off, and then ran a new sponge under very hot water and wiped the table.

"I am sorry you heard that, Zama. I am sorry for everyone, but you most of all. Would he have spoken that way in front of his own daughter, I wonder? I am glad she and her brothers were not here!" Indeed, Rikko and Jamfret and Polly spent more and more time away from home, and Zama thought they were probably seeking to escape their father.

"He hates himself," Harani said, her voice strained, "and so he is trying to make us hate him, too." Zamatryna had said something very similar, once; it was what everyone in the family thought.

"He succeeds," Aliniana said drily, giving the table a final scrubbing, and Zamatryna felt her stomach knotting. Kind, simple, loving Aliniana, who had always been so devoted to her husband: hearing her say such things was worse than listening to all of Macsofo's hatefulness.

Zamatryna needed to remember that there were still people in the world who were kind and simple, and she could think of no better proof than Jerry, a considerate and consistently untaxing companion. And so she went happily with him to the dance, where the loud music spared them the necessity of conversation; she was pleased to note that he drank only one beer. He drove her carefully home at the end of the evening, and shyly kissed her cheek—a gesture she found almost comically straightforward, after Howard's baroque agonizing over all things sexual—and shyly asked her if she was free for dinner the following week. And because he was kind and simple, she said yes. "Great," he said, beaming. "I'll make you spaghetti with my grandma's sauce. She's from Sicily. It's awesome."

"Zanger's Italian?" Zamatryna asked, intrigued.

"No, no, Zanger's German. My mom's side of the family is Italian. Are you okay with anchovies?"

"Um, sure. I mean, I guess so. I haven't eaten them much."

Jerry frowned. "I'll leave them out, then, if you aren't sure. Anchovies are one of those things you have to be sure about."

"He's *cooking* for you?" Sarah-Bee said the next day at lunch. Sarah-Cee and Sarah-Harrah were also at the table. "After one date? Are you serious?"

"Spaghetti's cheap," Zamatryna said. "He may not be able to afford a meal out, you know?"

"Fuck, Zama, he's on a football scholarship. He can afford whatever he wants. You don't seriously think his feelings are still platonic, do you?"

"He's gonna put the make on you," Sarah-Cee interjected. "Cooking. In apartment. Bedroom also in apartment. It's transparent. There'll be mood lighting over the couch, mark my words."

"There'll be mood lighting over the stove," Sarah-Harrah said with a snort.

"No," Zamatryna said, annoyed now. "That's not—he's not the type. One of my best friends went out with him for two years, okay?" She actually wasn't best friends with Jenny anymore; they hadn't even talked to each other for six months. But it would weaken her argument to point that out.

"He's not what type?" Sarah-Bee asked. "You mean he's not straight?"

"No, of course he's straight! I meant he's not a seducing creep. You were the one who told me he's honorable."

"Well, he is honorable. He's not going to *rape* you. But honorable guys can still be horny."

"Bring your own condoms," Sarah-Cee said. "In case he's run out. Guys can be dopes about that stuff."

"So," Zamatryna said firmly, "how about that latest anti-plutonium demonstration, huh?" But they'd spooked her enough that she did bring condoms with her to Jerry's apartment, along with the salad he'd asked her to bring. The way the Sarahs had gone on about it, she almost regretted having accepted his invitation.

She needn't have worried. Jerry was a perfect gentleman, and there was no mood lighting anywhere in the apartment; there weren't even candles. It was a spartan studio, the single bed made with military corners, Jerry's accounting books arranged neatly in the one bookcase, spices racked alphabetically in the kitchen. Jerry, it turned out, liked to cook. He had a file box of German and Italian recipes from his family, and his kitchen table—oak inlaid with blue and white tile, the only piece of furniture with any personality in the apartment—had been built by a great-uncle who was a cabinet-maker. Jerry had already made the sphaghetti sauce, but while the pasta was cooking, he told Zama how this great-uncle had made him toys when he was a little boy. "He made me go-carts, you know, and wooden puppets. He died of cancer about ten years ago, and my cousins' kids have the toys now, so when I came to college I asked if I could take the table."

Zamatryna thought of Darroti's doll, and shivered. She knew that Timbor had made wooden wagons for his sons when they were children; she could just barely remember Rikko and Jamfret playing with them, back in Lémabantunk.

She'd come here so she wouldn't have to think about any of that. "So how were your classes this semester?" she asked. Jerry gave her an odd look.

"They were fine," he said. "How were yours?"

Boring. "Fine. Do you want me to set the table?"

"Sure," he said, and showed her where plates and silverware and napkins were. "I should have done it before you got here."

"It's okay," she said. "I like to help." And indeed, setting the table made her feel useful. "These are pretty plates." They had flowers and birds on them, which seemed incongruous for a football player.

"They were my parents' first everyday set, when they were married. They have better ones now. What kind of dressing do you want on your salad?"

He had a collection of salad dressings; he had salad forks, and laughed at Zamatryna when she didn't put them out. "It's not like washing two more forks is so much work." They ate salad and the spaghetti, which was indeed very good, and she helped him do the dishes, and then—just as Zamatryna was wondering when he'd suggest moving to the couch—he said, "I thought we could go out for ice cream for dessert, and maybe walk by the river."

"Sure," she said, relieved. "That sounds great."

It was a beautiful night, with a full moon shining on the Truckee. They strolled along the well-lighted paths by the river; Zamatryna deliberately held her ice-cream cone with her right hand, since Jerry was walking on her right. That way he couldn't try to hold her hand, at least until the ice cream was eaten. She ate it very slowly, and racked her brain thinking of things to talk about. Movies. Movies were always safe. "So have you seen *The Excellent Adventures of the Mummy's Chiropractor* yet?"

"Naw. That stuff's stupid. Where's your family from?"

"What?"

"Your family," he said patiently. "Where are you from? You know, like I'm German and Italian. What are you?"

"I—well, we're from very far away. You won't have heard of it."

"Zama. I'm not that stupid."

"What?" She stopped, ice cream dripping onto her hand, and stared at him in dismay. Now she'd hurt his feelings. She hadn't meant to do that.

"I'm not that stupid. I know everybody thinks I'm a dumb jock because I don't talk a million miles a minute, but I've heard of other countries. I've looked at maps. I know the United States isn't the entire world, you know? So if you tell me where your family's from, I'll probably recognize the name."

No. You won't. Feeling miserable, she looked down at her feet and said, "Well, we're from a tiny village in central Afghanistan that was destroyed by an earthquake."

"Afghanistan," he said, shaking his head. "Did you really think I wouldn't have heard of *Afghanistan?* Zama, everybody's heard of Afghanistan!"

"I meant you wouldn't have heard of the village."

"Okay, so try me. What's the name of the village?"

"Lémabantunk." What had made her say that? But it couldn't do any harm, could it?

He smiled. "Well, you're right. I haven't heard of that. So do you miss it?"

"No. I don't remember it well enough to miss it."

"Does your family miss it?"

"Yes."

He looked at her. "Did a lot of people die, in the earthquake?"

"Yes," Zamatryna said, remembering the bomb. "A lot of people died. Jerry, I'm an American now. I don't—I don't like talking about—"

"Okay," he said. "Okay, I'm sorry, Zama. I was trying to learn more about you, that's all. Because I want to know more about you. Because I like you. You're smart and you're pretty and you're a nice person."

And I'm too good for you, Zamatryna thought. And I shouldn't have agreed to let you cook dinner for me. But at the same time, she felt a certain wonder at the serene, uncomplicated way in which Jerry had stated his feelings for her; it had taken Howard seven weeks of dodging and feinting even to say hello to her in class, and nothing at home seemed simple anymore either, if it ever had been. "Thank you," she said. "I—"

"It's okay if you don't like me," he said. "I mean, if you don't like me the same way."

"Sure I like you," she said weakly.

He laughed. "You do not. Not that way. Not yet, anyway. But can we be friends, and maybe you will, sometime?"

"Sure," she said, feeling herself redden. "We're already friends."

"Great," he said happily. "So how about dinner again next week?"

"Sure," she said, wondering what she was doing. "But it's on me, this time, and I don't cook, so we have to go out." She couldn't invite him to the house, not with the possibility of a scene between Macsofo and Aliniana.

So she told the Sarahs that Jerry had behaved impeccably, and the following week she took him out for Thai and a movie. Four days after that, he took her out for lunch, at which point she suggested they should do everything Dutch. And so, for the rest of the semester and most of the summer, they saw each other once or twice a week, sometimes at his apartment, sometimes other places. It was perfectly pleasant. He was a gentleman. He never tried to kiss her, even, although she could tell he wanted to. They made decorous small talk and maintained their status as friends, despite the Sarahs' skepticism. Zamatryna knew that she was using him, knew that she should look for someone with whom she had more in common, but he was restful. Being with him was a welcome break from the tension at home: from the fights between Max and Alini, and the arguments about Max's new job, and the utter dullness of working afternoons in a law office. Jerry was just a summer fling, and not even that. She'd find someone else when school started again.

A few weeks before the beginning of the semester, she met him for dinner at Blue Moon Pizza, one of their favorite spots. As usual, she had come armed with carefully prepared conversational topics—music, TV shows, even football—but this time, Jerry didn't seem interested. He wanted to ask her advice about his mother's garden, which had been suffering from pests all summer. So they talked about roses and slugs for twenty minutes, and then he said, "How do you spell the name of the village you're from?"

"Lémabantunk?" she asked, instantly wary. Jerry hadn't said a word about her origins since that second date. "Why?"

"Well, I did an Internet search a while ago. For Afghanistan and earthquakes. Because I wanted to learn more. And I didn't see anything that sounded like that, but I kept forgetting to ask you about it."

He wasn't a very good liar. She could tell from his voice that he hadn't forgotten to ask her: he'd been waiting for what he thought was a good time. She wondered why he'd picked tonight. "It's Lémabantunk in our language," she said, her mouth dry, "but I don't know what people call it in English." How long had he been doing research on her, anyway?

"Oh, okay. I guess that explains it."

"Do you want hot pepper flakes on your pizza?"

"No thanks. So are your folks friends with other Afghan immigrants?"

"No," she said, heart pounding. "We're Americans now. I told you that a long time ago. Jerry, why are you asking me all these questions?"

"Because I like to learn things," he said gently. "Especially about other places. My family would be a lot poorer if we didn't have my grandmother's recipes from Sicily. My dad's family still does Oktoberfest. Customs like that are important, but all you ever want to talk about is stuff that doesn't matter. I think you still think I'm dumb, Zama. And I'm not. I can talk about things that don't involve television or touchdowns. Really. And I want—I want to get closer to you. If I can. If you'll let me. People like to be with people who understand where they came from, right?"

No one understands where we came from, Zamatryna thought bitterly. "So you're being a cultural anthropologist, is that it? You're collecting the quaint folkways of my people? Why can't I just be from Reno?"

Jerry frowned. "Well, you can. But if you were from Reno you'd have stories about lambing, or gaming, or divorce ranches or something. Everybody's got something like that, even if they take it for granted. In my family it's food and woodworking. You must have something like that, too." Yes, we have drunks and murderers and suicides. And possessed beetles. "Zama, why are you holding me at arm's length? I know you aren't in love with me. It's okay. I'm not going to bite you. I promise."

She had to tell him something, or he'd get more suspicious. "Okay," Zamatryna said, "we have this custom about carpets. My grandfather and father and uncle brought their prayer carpets with them when we came here. They're woven of colors representing the four Elements. They pray on them every morning. Fascinating, huh? Do you feel edified now?"

"Yes, I do. That's interesting. It sounds kind of Native American. Except the prayer carpet thing sounds kind of, what, Muslim?"

"Well, we aren't Native Americans or Muslims. We're ourselves. But that's our quaint custom. Their quaint custom. And my grandfather still blesses every bit of food he eats, because it might contain the soul of a dead person." Why was she telling him all this? "And we like epic poems. We memorize them. Little kids do. I did, before we came here."

"Before the earthquake."

"Before the earthquake."

"The prayer carpets weren't buried in the earthquake?"

"Our house was less damaged than others," Zamatryna said.

"What are the epic poems about?"

"All kinds of things. Gardening. Geometry." Zama, shut up. Why are you telling him this?

"You memorized epic poems about *geometry*? When you were a kid?"

"Yes. But I don't remember them anymore. But that's one reason I'm good at school, because I'm good at memorizing things. I—I memorized *The Cat in the Hat* once, right after we got here. The American lady who gave us the book, our friend Lisa, she was amazed."

"I'll bet," Jerry said, and laughed. "But why are you ashamed of all this stuff? It's neat."

"I'm not ashamed of it."

"Then why do you hate talking about it?"

"I don't hate talking about it! I've been talking about it for the past five minutes, haven't I? But what good will it do me to talk about it? It's all gone. Our home—our home was destroyed and we can't go back and—"

"Zama," he said. "Zama, people rebuild after earthquakes. Why can't you go back? Zama, are you crying?"

"No," she said, and sniffled furiously, and pulled her hand back, because it had been perilously close to his on the table. "I can't—I can't explain. It's too complicated. But I'll never live there again and I can barely even remember it. I'm an American now. That's my job. I don't know why I told you all that stuff, anyway."

"Because I asked."

"Because you asked," she said, and realized that no one had ever asked before. She had a sudden clear and unwanted memory of Rumpled Ron telling her that a friend was someone you could talk to about anything. Well, then, friends were for people who didn't have criminal uncles. Or possessed beetles in their closets.

The pizza came, and she was spared further conversation by the necessity of eating. She ate with total concentration, as if she would never see another pizza again. She chewed the garlic especially carefully, hoping that it would keep Jerry at arm's length.

She ate four pieces of pizza; Jerry only ate two. When she finally looked up from her plate, Jerry said, "Would you like the other two, Zama? You seem awfully hungry."

"No," she said, blushing. "No, thanks, that's okay. You're the football player. You need the calories more than I do. I'm sorry I made such a pig of myself."

"You didn't. You're skinny: the calories aren't going to hurt you. But I'm not hungry, honest. Do you want to take them home?"

"No," she said. "I'll take them to my friend Betty. She'll eat them."

Jerry cocked his head. "You never mentioned her before."

"No," Zama said drily. "You're learning all about me, aren't you?"

Jerry smiled. "Where does she live?"

"Down by the river, mostly. On benches and behind bushes. Sometimes in shelters."

She watched Jerry to see if he'd look disgusted, but he only looked worried. "That's dangerous. All of those places are dangerous."

"Yeah. She's gotten hurt a bunch of times."

"How'd you meet her? Through the food bank?"

"No. I met her two years ago, when we were still in high school. My grandfather saw her when he was driving his cab one day, and we went to bring her some food, and we—well, we've kind of adopted her, I guess. Except she can't live with us because there isn't room."

Jerry looked even more worried. "She's been homeless for two years?"

"Yeah. Longer than that, actually. She can't work because—well, she's a little retarded—"

"She could work a simple job. I have a cousin like that. There are training programs and group homes, you know."

"She's been in those places. She never likes them or stays long. I'm not sure why. She wants her daughter back: she gave her daughter to a foster home, but she always planned on getting her back, but now she never will, I think. Because she can't stay in the programs and homes."

"She couldn't take care of a kid," Jerry said.

"No. She couldn't. So anyway, I bring her canned stuff she won't have to cook, but it's always nice to bring her hot food, too. And she likes pizza. So I'll bring her these two slices."

"We can order her a whole one. Why don't we do that?"

"I—Jerry, that's really sweet, but I may not even be able to find her. Sometimes I can't. If she's not in her usual places."

"If we can't find her, we'll split the pizza and each take half of it home." He smiled at her and said, "I know you keep saying 'I,' but there's a reason I keep saying 'we.' All of those places are dangerous. So I'm going with you, to look. Especially if you're going tonight. Which you'll have to do, if you still want the pizza to be hot."

She should have been annoyed. Somehow she couldn't make herself be annoyed. She looked down at her hands and said, "We came here in separate cars. You want to follow me? This could take a while."

"Let me think about that while I order the other pizza. That will take a while, too. What's her favorite topping?"

"Ummm, just cheese and sausage, I think."

"Okay." He went up to the counter to give the order, and when he came back he said, "Will she get scared if she sees my car behind yours?"

Zamatryna never would have thought of that. "I have no idea."

"Okay, well, then we should just take yours. If you don't mind driving me. You can drop me off here later, or if it's too late and you don't want to do that, you can drop me at the frat house and I'll get somebody to give me a lift up here tomorrow."

"Are you sure?"

"Sure," he said, and smiled. "Is this a custom where you come from, too? Bringing food to people?"

She noted that he'd said "where you come from," not "Afghanistan." Paranoid much, Zama? "Yeah. As a matter of fact, it is."

"Cool. Should we bring her something to drink?"

"Just water. I always worry about whether she gets enough clean water."

"Well, we'll bring her bottled water, then. We can bring her a whole case, if you want to."

"No. She wouldn't have anywhere to put it, Jerry. It would just get stolen. A bottle or two, or three. That will be fine."

So Zama found herself driving down to the river with Jerry in a car that smelled like pizza. She parked on Riverside near the Keystone Avenue Bridge and got out, holding her flashlight and scanning the line of benches along the river. She didn't see Betty, or any other homeless people, for that matter; Betty avoided this area when there were a lot of other transients here, but she liked it when there weren't. Which meant she might very well be here now. Zama walked ahead a few feet, peering, and caught sight of a large black Hefty bag near a bush. There. That could be one of Betty's. She was down to two now, because so much of her stuff had been stolen. But then, of course, all Hefty bags tended to look alike.

"Do you see her?" Jerry said. "Should I bring the pizza?"

"I'm not sure. Leave the pizza in the car for a sec, okay?"

He followed her to the Hefty bag. She risked turning the flashlight on—sometimes flashlights freaked Betty out, because flashlights belonged to cops—and saw that the bag was ripped, with a blue and white sweater poking out. Definitely Betty's: the sweater was an old one of Timbor's he'd given her last winter. "Betty?" Zama called, and then caught a whiff of Betty's signature stench. She was here somewhere, then. But where?

And then she saw a leg sticking out from behind the bush, and said, "Betty!" and pushed aside undergrowth to find Betty lying on her side, clutching her arm. She turned her face away when Zamatryna shone the flashlight on it: her face looked gray, sweaty.

"I feel funny." Her voice was hoarse, strained.

"Betty, what happened?" Zamatryna ran the flashlight up and down her body, but saw no injuries. "Did someone attack you again?"

"No. Feel funny. Hid here. Who—"

"I'm Jerry," Jerry said, kneeling down on the grass. "I'm a friend of Zama's. Betty, are you having trouble breathing?" Nod. "And your arm hurts? Your left arm, where you're holding it there? Does it feel heavy?" Nod. "Okay. We have to take you to a doctor, then—"

"No doctors!"

Jerry reached out and patted her on the shoulder, and then turned to Zama. "Where's your phone?"

"What?"

"Your cell phone. Call 911, Zama."

911? "Call the *police?* But—"

"Hey, Zama, didn't anybody ever teach you the symptoms of a heart attack? Call 911. Now. Do it!"

She ran back to the car, feeling useless and incredibly stupid, and dug her cell phone out of her purse and called an ambulance. Then she went back to Betty and Jerry. He was holding her hand and talking to her. "Zama called an ambulance, okay? Don't be scared when you see the flashing lights. It won't be the police. It will be medics, to help you. No, Betty, don't try to get up. Just sit there, okay? Stay quiet."

"They'll throw out my things," Betty said plaintively. "People always throw out my things."

"We won't let them," Jerry said. "Zama, can you put Betty's bags in your car, please, so no one throws them out? Betty, is it okay with you if Zama puts the bags in her car?" He gave Zama an unreadable glance and said, "And then Zama should probably stay near the street, so she can show the ambulance crew where you are."

Betty nodded, and Zama picked up the two bags and carried them to her car. She was glad that Jerry was thinking so clearly, because she certainly wasn't. Maybe it was easier to think clearly when you didn't know the person having the heart attack. She might just as well have been having a heart attack herself, for all the oxygen that seemed to be reaching her brain.

Sirens. The ambulance was here already: good. She showed the medics where Betty was and then stood back while they talked to her, examined her, lifted her swiftly onto a stretcher. There was an oxygen mask over Betty's nose and mouth now, and they were wheeling her toward the ambulance, and someone was saying something incomprehensible into a radio.

"Okay," Jerry said next to her. "Now we follow the ambulance to the ER. Zama, you okay?"

"I—is she going to—"

"I don't know anything. I don't think they do. Zama, you're shaking. Let me drive, okay? Can you walk to the car?"

"Of course I can walk to the car." She took a step on rubbery legs, and stumbled, and Jerry put his arm around her. The ambulance had just driven away, sirens blaring, and suddenly the place where they were standing seemed very dark and deserted. "Oopsy-daisy. Lean on me to the car, okay? And then you need to drink some of that water."

"I didn't know what to do. I didn't even know—I had no idea—if you hadn't been here—"

"If I hadn't been here you probably would have handled it fine," Jerry said, guiding her into the car. "If you'd been alone, you'd have done what you needed to do. That's how these things work. But you weren't, so you went into shock because she's a friend of yours. And I was here, so your body knew it was okay for you to go into shock. That's how it works, sometimes."

"How do you know all of this?"

"I've had a lot of first-aid training. Seatbelt on? You want to call your family?"

"What?"

"Your family," he said patiently, pulling away from the curb. "They're Betty's friends too, right? And it's getting late now and they're going to wonder why you aren't home, and we'll probably be a while, at the ER."

"Oh. Okay."

She was still clutching the cell phone. She dialed the number for home; after two rings she heard Timbor say "Hello?" in a voice as strained as Betty's had been. In the background she heard screaming, Aliniana and Macsofo, screaming, and a crash, something breaking. "Hello?" Timbor said again, and Zamatryna hung up, terrified. Whatever was happening there, it wasn't the time to tell Timbor about Betty.

"No one's home," she told Jerry.

"You can try again later. Let me know if you see a space, okay?"

Zamatryna blinked; they were in the parking lot of St. Mary's. "Shouldn't they have taken her to Washoe Med? That's the county hospital, isn't it?"

"This is closer."

"Jerry, she doesn't have insurance!"

He shook his head. "Hospitals can't turn away people in life-or-death situations. They're required to treat them. That's the law."

Zamatryna shivered. "You saved her life."

"Well, you saved her life, I hope. We never would have been there in the first place if you hadn't thought of bringing her the pizza."

Betty was already in a treatment room when they got to the ER. "She had a cardiac arrest," a nurse told them. "I can't let you go back there; she's got too many people working on her. They'll admit her and she'll probably wind up in the cardiac care unit, CCU, if there's a bed. You, uh, are you two her family?"

"We're friends," Zama said.

"We're the people who called the ambulance," Jerry said.

"Yeah, well, okay, legally I'm not supposed to give out information about her condition to anyone except family. Privacy laws. Do you have contact information for her family?"

"No," Zama said, her mouth dry. "She has a daughter in foster care, her daughter's—slow too, like she is—"

"Okay, so Sierra Regional Center will probably have a file on both of them. I'll tell the social worker that and they'll get on it tomorrow. What's her last name?"

"What?"

"Her last name. She doesn't have any ID on her, and she's not very coherent at this point."

"I don't know," Zama said, ashamed. She'd never known Betty's last name. Betty had always just been Betty, like a doll or a pet. "My grandfather might know. I can call him and ask."

The nurse sighed. "Well, you do that. Call your grandpa, go get some coffee from the cafeteria, sit out in the waiting room. I'll come out again when I know something else."

"Even though you aren't supposed to," Jerry said with a smile.

"Right," the nurse said, and smiled back. "Good thing this happened to her now, before the resettlement."

"What?" Zamatryna said. Nothing was making any sense tonight. Resettlement was something that happened to refugees. Betty lived here.

"The resettlement," the nurse said, as if Zama was the one who was slow. "You know, because of that Public Nuisance Law? It's the latest get-rid-of-the-homeless scheme. In a few weeks, before the cold weather sets in again, the cops will start doing sweeps and bussing them all to the refugee camps."

"*What?* How can they do that? That's, that's—"

"The police are saying it's a kindness," the nurse said drily, "because they'll have tents and meals and blankets. And there are doctors out there. And I guess they're right. But those camps are crowded enough already. The real issue is that the county doesn't want to build more shelters: it's a NIMBY thing. Listen, I have to get back to work now. Go get coffee."

"NIMBY," Zama said blankly to the nurse's retreating back.

"Not in My Back Yard," Jerry said.

"Oh. Right. I knew that." She let him take her elbow, let him guide her to the cafeteria and buy her a cup of coffee. "Jerry, people die in those camps." *My uncle died there. I can't tell you that. A friend's someone you can tell anything. But I can't tell you that, because I'm not supposed to have ever been in the camps in the first place.*

"People die on the streets, too."

"Yeah," she said, looking down at her white styrofoam coffee cup. "I guess they do." *Just like Gallicina died on the streets, because Darroti killed her. I can't tell you that.*

"Let's go back to the waiting room," he said, "and then you can try your grandfather again, okay?"

"Okay," she said numbly. *Manners. Manners, Zama.* "I—Jerry, you don't have to stay here with me, it's awfully good of you to have come—oh, but you don't have your car—Jerry, I'll drive you back to your car and then I'll come back here—"

He started laughing. "Zama, right now I wouldn't trust you to drive around the block. Drink your coffee, okay? And call your grandpa?"

She sat. She drank coffee and tried not to look at or listen to the other people in the waiting room: a thin man holding to his head a towel drenched in blood, a woman, moaning in pain, lying across three chairs, a heavy boy vomiting methodically into a bowl his weary mother held for him. Zama drank her coffee, grateful that Jerry wasn't trying to talk to her, and then looked unhappily at her cell phone, still clutched in her hand. She was going to have to call again. She didn't want to call. She didn't want to hear Macsofo and Aliniana screaming.

She called. Timbor answered. "Grandfather, it's Zama. I need to ask you a question. What's Betty's last name?"

There was a pause. "Hello?" Zamatryna said. "Are you there?"

"I am here, Zamatryna. Where are you, and what is wrong with Betty?"

Zama closed her eyes. "She had a heart attack. I'm at St. Mary's. I can't see her, but a nurse is going to tell me when—when they know something. But they need to know her last name, so they can contact her family."

"Her last name is Pierre. Are you all right?"

"Yes, of course. I'm fine. I'm just shaken up."

"You called before," Timbor said. "You called and you heard your auntie and uncle yelling, and then you hung up. That was you, wasn't it?"

"Yes," she said, ashamed without knowing why. "Are they—it sounded like something broke. Are they—all right?"

"A clown broke," Timbor said. "The large clown on the hutch in the dining room. I will tell you the rest when you get home. Do not worry. Do you need me to pick you up?"

"No. I have my car, and Jerry's here. I'll be home as soon as I can." She hung up, wondering numbly what the broken clown would add to the amount they owed Lisa, wondering how it had broken. She thought she probably didn't want to know. The clown on the hutch in the dining room had been one of the best clowns in the house, one of the most expensive: Lisa's mother had brought it back all the way from Florence, Italy. It was made of fine china painted with real gold leaf and inlaid with actual gemstones. It was hideously ugly, and it had cost a fortune.

"Is everything all right?" Jerry said.

"I don't know." A friend's someone you can tell anything. Of all her secrets, this one was the least dangerous. She looked away from him and said, "My aunt and uncle have been fighting a lot. It sounds like it got pretty bad tonight."

"I'm sorry."

"Yeah."

"You're really having a rotten night, Zama."

"Yeah."

"Hey." He put an arm around her shoulders and squeezed; she felt herself relaxing into the warmth despite herself. Then she pulled away from it, because the nurse was coming back.

"Pierre," Zamatryna said, looking up at the faded scrubs and the tired face above them. "That's her last name. Betty Pierre."

"Great. Thank you." The nurse made a note on her clipboard and said, "Okay, listen, she's in CCU. She seems stable at the moment. They'll start doing tests tomorrow. You shouldn't try to see her to-night; she needs to rest. Come back tomorrow, okay? Go home and get some rest yourselves."

"Thank you," Jerry said, and Zamatryna tried to say thank you too, but her voice wouldn't work, and then Jerry had her on her feet again and was walking her to the car. "I'll drive you home, Zama."

"We have to get your car."

"I still don't think it's a great idea for you to drive. I'll drive you home, and then I can call a cab to get to the frat house. I'll call a cab on your cell phone, okay?"

"I should invite you in," she said miserably. "For tea or some-thing."

"Not if your folks are fighting. They wouldn't want me there."

"Well, then my grandfather should drive you to the frat house. Or to your car."

"No," Jerry said. "He's upset too, right? Your aunt and uncle are his relatives, and Betty's his friend. Look, Zama, why don't you stop worrying so much about what you think you *should* do? Worry about what you need to do. Or want to do. Isn't that better?"

He sounded like Rumpled Ron. She felt anger flaring in her gut, but that was all right: anger steadied her. "Okay, I've got a better idea. You drive to the frat house. Take the pizza with you. And I'll drive home from there. It's not far."

"But—"

"Jerry, please. It's easier on me this way. This is what I *want* to do. Okay? I need a few minutes to myself before I go home."

"Okay," he said unhappily. When he got out of the car he squeezed her shoulder again, but to her relief, he didn't try to kiss her. "Call me tomorrow and tell me how everything's going, okay?"

"Sure," she said. She got out and moved to the driver's side. When she was buckled into her seat she said, "You like being depressed, huh?"

He was still standing next to the car. He bent, ducked inside, and kissed her on the cheek again, as he had after the dance. He smelled very clean, like soap and aftershave. "Don't say that. Everything may be fine."

"Right," she said, staring out through the windshield. She hadn't turned when he kissed her. "I have to go home now."

"I know you do. Call me."

When she got home, everyone was asleep but Timbor, who was sitting in the living room, waiting up for her. "How is Betty?"

"Stable," Zamatryna said. Timbor's face looked like Betty's: gray and sweaty. "Grandfather, are you all right? You look terrible."

"Ah. It was not a good night. Sit down, child. You need to know what happened."

She sat, numbly. "Did Macsofo throw the clown at Auntie Alini?"

Timbor gave a small crooked smile. "No. She threw it at him."

Zamatryna swallowed, feeling sick. "Was anyone hurt?"

"Not injured, no. No blood." He was silent for a moment and then said, "They are getting a divorce."

Zamatryna found herself shaking her head. "But—but we don't—"

"Well, it seems we do, now. We have become true Americans." He put his face in his hands and began to weep, and Zamatryna went to kneel next to him, stroking his arm. She didn't know what to say. Families stayed together. Families always stayed together, in Gandiffri. That was why they were all here, in America.

She had to say something. "We—we're here now, Grandfather. We have to live the way people live here. There must have been unhappy marriages in Lémabantunk, too. Isn't this better? They've been miserable. We've all been miserable. And if Macsofo leaves then maybe, then maybe he'll realize what he's been doing and—"

"He isn't leaving," Timbor said, his voice fiercer than Zamatryna had ever heard it. "That was what Aliniana wanted. She wanted me to kick him out. She told me I had to choose between my no-good drunken son and her, and I told her I could not possibly do that, that I would as soon cut off my own arm as cast off any member of my family. And she said I was defending someone who had been hateful to her and to all of us, and I said that I was talking about both of them, that I was talking about her, too, that I could not possibly willingly part either with my left arm or my right, and that throwing the clown had been hateful. And she said, well then, she was leaving."

"That's crazy," Zamatryna said. "Where will she go? She doesn't make enough money to pay for her own place."

"Yes, Macsofo told her that, and she accused him of throwing it in her face and said she would do just fine, and her children would help her, she had talked about it with them already and they wanted to live with her, not their lout of a father."

Zamatryna shook her head again. "But—he loves them. And they're in *high school.* They can't help her pay for an apartment by working at McDonald's. And if Max is decent to anybody, it's them. Oh, Grandfather, this won't last. She doesn't mean it. She's just trying to scare him."

"I do not think so. Because she told us that she has been having an affair with the man who owns the beauty parlor—"

"She *what?*"

"You heard me. She has been having an affair with this man and she is going to stay with him. She is there now. She left tonight. Macsofo is alone in their room. And this man will help her pay for an apartment, too."

Zamatryna fought the urge to laugh. "Do you *believe* that? Alini, sleeping with someone else? It's a story she's telling. She's been watching too many soap operas. Grandfather—"

"What else can I believe? Has she ever lied to us? She told Macsofo that it was his fault, that he had driven her to it by being drunk and cruel and impotent, and that he had only himself to blame."

"Ooooh." Zamatryna rolled her eyes. "She's been watching daytime talk shows, too. Alini the drama queen. And just how long has this supposed affair been going on?"

"Six months, she said."

"Is the guy married?"

"I do not know."

"He must be married. If he weren't, he'd be offering to marry her, not to help her pay for her own place. He's married and shacked up in a motel with Alini while his wife thinks he's at a beauty-parlor convention. If he even exists."

"Is this supposed to make me feel better, Zamatryna?"

She gave him a hug. "Grandfather, this is all craziness. It's going to blow over. She'll come back. This has soap written all over it; it's not real. Alini's probably staying with a girlfriend, plotting more stuff she can say to make Max feel horrible so he'll apologize for being shitty to her."

"And the idea of Macsofo feeling more horrible, is that supposed to make me feel better?"

"If it makes him get his act together, yes." She kissed the top of Timbor's head, feeling more cheerful than she had in weeks, and said, "Don't worry. Everything's going to be fine."

"I do not think you would say that if you had been here."

She grimaced. "Well, maybe I wouldn't. But it's a good thing I wasn't, or Betty might not have gotten to the hospital in time."

"Ah. Poor Betty! You must tell me how that all happened."

"Tomorrow. We're both exhausted tonight. I'm going to bed, okay?"

She fully expected, the next morning, to find Aliniana in her usual spot at the kitchen table, the crisis forgotten, just a bad dream. But she didn't. Instead she found her parents, looking grim, and Timbor, looking drawn, and Macsofo, alternately weeping and raging in nearly incoherent Gandiffran. Zamatryna, standing in the kitchen doorway, raised her eyebrows at her father, who jerked his head toward the back door.

When they were out in the yard, Zama said, "Were you there last night?"

"Yes. I was already asleep when you came in. Father said he told you about it. He said you do not believe that Aliniana is actually having an affair."

"Do you believe it?"

"I don't know if I believe it or not. But Macsofo believes it, and he terrifies me. Darroti was a quiet, sad drunk who killed himself. Macsofo is likely to kill someone else."

"Dad, Darroti killed someone else, too. A woman, no less."

"Aye." Erolorit made a face. "And I would never have believed it of him, and I still cannot. Of Macsofo, I would believe it."

"Has he actually threatened her? Or this presumed lover? I mean, if you really think he's dangerous, we should call the cops and get a restraining order. Shouldn't we?"

"No. Or yes. I do not know. I do not want to involve the law." Zamatryna shook her head. "Well, look. Tell him that if he threatens anybody, we'll have to do that. Right? And tell him that if he wants Aliniana back, wants to live with his kids again—"

"You tell him."

She stared at him. "What?"

"Zamatryna, he will not listen to me, or to Timbor." Her father looked desperate. "He may listen to you. I think you are the only person he respects in the entire family. And he has not hurt you the way he has hurt everyone else, even his own children, so it will be less complicated if you talk to him. With everyone else, there is too much anger and guilt. He cannot hear what we are saying. He does not even wish to look at us."

She shook her head again. "Dad, I'm not at all sure—"

"I know I am asking a lot of you. You do not have to do it if you do not wish to. And I know it may not work. But then I do not know what else we can do."

"I'll try," she said unhappily. "But if it doesn't work, don't blame me, okay?"

They went back into the kitchen. Macsofo was in one of his weeping phases; he had his head down on the table. There was a bottle of beer next to him. Zamatryna cleared her throat. "Uncle Max. Uncle Max, look at me, please."

He looked up, his eyes bleary. "What do you want?"

"I want to talk to you."

He took a swig of the beer and propped his elbows on the table. "And what do you have to say to me, little Zama? What everyone else is saying? That everything is my fault?"

"Not everything," she said, trying to keep her voice steady, "but a lot. You've been rotten to Alini. You know that. You've been rotten to nearly everybody else. You've been especially rotten to yourself."

"And so I deserve this. That she has run off and is sleeping—"

"By herself, probably. Uncle Max, I don't think she's having an affair. I think that's a story she's telling to make you crazy." She saw a flicker of hope in his eyes, and said, "I may be wrong. But she never talked to me about anything like that, and Alini's not very good at keeping secrets. If she were in love with somebody else, I think I would have picked up on it."

He looked away from her and said stonily, "Who said love? It could just be sex."

"It could be, sure. You've known Alini a lot longer than I have. You think that's something she'd do? Look, I think she's doing all this to try to get you to change. I could be wrong. But you need to change anyway. You're killing yourself."

Macsofo sneered. "Like my weak brother did?"

"Yes. Just like that." She saw him wince, and pressed her advantage. "You have to stop drinking. And you have to stop treating people like shit."

"You think I am like my brother the drunk, is that it?"

"No, I don't think you're like him. He was a lot nicer." She saw Macsofo's hands tighten on the table, the knuckles turn white. She swallowed. "Look, I don't know what happened with that Mendicant, and you don't either, but I do know that Darroti never insulted any of us, even when he was drunk. He never ragged on people for not earning enough money. He never spat on anybody, Uncle Macsofo. And you've got to stop blaming him and Alini and America for all your problems, and start taking some responsibility yourself."

"Well," he said, his voice icy. "Aren't you just the perfect little self-help American bitch?"

She was starting to shake; she could feel it. Behind her, she heard her father make a hissing sound, but he didn't say anything, and neither did Timbor or Harani. "Yes," she said. "Yes, that's exactly what I am. And you're an abusive alcoholic SOB, and if you threaten anybody in this family, or outside it, I'll call the cops on you so fast it'll make your head spin. Got that, Uncle Max?"

"Oh yes," he said. "I'm very scared." But he'd started to cry again.

"Good," Zamatryna said. "You should be." She turned to Timbor, who looked pale, and said, "I'm going to the hospital now. To see how Betty is. If Jerry calls, tell him I'll call him later, okay?"

The drive to the hospital calmed her down somewhat, and she was relieved to find Betty looking relatively comfortable in the CCU, despite all the beeping and buzzing. "Betty, how are you? I'm sorry I couldn't get here sooner. I was busy this morning. And they'll only let me stay for fifteen minutes now."

"Where's Jerry?"

"He's—at home, I guess. I haven't talked to him since last night. I know he's concerned about you. I'll call him later to tell him you're doing better." Zama squeezed Betty's shoulder. "You are doing better, right?"

"Jerry loves you."

Zamatryna sighed. Aliniana had always said that, too, although she'd only met him briefly a few times when he'd picked Zama up at the house—times Zama had carefully chosen because Max wouldn't be there. Zama had figured that Alini was just in hyper-romantic soap-opera mode, but Betty didn't have that excuse. "Well, I don't see how you can tell, after meeting him for ten minutes when you were having a heart attack."

"He told me. I asked him, while you were carrying my bags to the car."

"And what was he going to say, that he hated my guts? Betty, listen, I'm here to find out how *you* are, okay? Are you feeling better?"

Betty looked away. "Yes. For a little while. Zama, I'm scared."

"For a—what do you mean? Are they going to do more tests?"

"They did them. This morning, while you were busy. They woke me up at dawn. I need—to live a long time, I need an operation."

Zamatryna gave her shoulder another squeeze. "So you'll have the operation. That's scary, I know, but then you'll feel better."

"Won't have it. Can't afford it. Too expensive."

"What? Betty, they can't do that. They can't refuse treatment you need to live. Look, don't worry, we'll get this straightened out. I'll talk to the nurses and find out what this is about, okay? Please don't worry. You're going to be fine."

But her conversation with the nurse wasn't very reassuring. "Your friend needs triple bypass. At least triple: maybe quadruple. And she doesn't have any medical coverage. That surgery runs at least two hundred thousand dollars."

"Wait a minute. She needs it to save her life, right? You're trying to tell me that bypass is elective surgery?"

"She needs it to *prolong* her life. We *saved* her life by putting her in CCU: that's the extent of the legal obligation. The hospital's swallowing that bill because it has to. But you're not going to find anybody who'll do free bypass on her. Look, honey, this is going to sound brutal, but even if you got a surgical team to donate its time, you'd still have to pay for the facilities and equipment and drugs. And frankly, she's not a good risk."

"Medically?"

"Mentally. Don't look at me that way: I told you it was going to sound brutal. Anybody who donates that surgery will want to donate it to somebody who's going to be a productive member of society, okay? What was her quality of life like before she came in here? She's mentally impaired and she lives on the streets, right? Is that worth maintaining? Ask yourself."

"*What?*" Zama felt the floor spinning beneath her. "Who are you to judge her quality of life! It's her life! She's a person! She wants to live, just like anybody else does!"

The nurse sighed. "It sucks. I know it does. But unless you've got two hundred thousand socked away someplace, I don't think you're going to be able to do anything. Welcome to America, huh? I have to get back to her now. You can visit again tonight."

"Visit? And she'll be all right? You won't have cut her throat to save the hospital some money?"

"Hey." The nurse turned, her voice sharp. "Don't talk to me that way. I didn't invent this system, and I don't like it any better than you do. I'm taking care of her as well as I can."

Zama's mouth tasted like blood. "I'm sorry."

"Yeah, well, you watch your manners." But the nurse reached out and touched her arm. "Good luck. I know this is hard."

Now what? She stood gasping for breath by the nurses' station, and finally turned to walk to the elevators. She had to go back home, call Jerry, get ready to go to work. At least things couldn't get any worse. That was some comfort.

But when she got home, Lisa was sitting in the kitchen, two suitcases next to her and a newspaper on the table in front of her. It looked like no one else had moved since Zama had left. They looked like they'd been punched.

"What?" Zama said. "What is it?"

"Hi, sweetie," Lisa said. She sounded like she'd been crying. "Did you see the paper this morning?"

"No. I was distracted." Zama grabbed the paper. What in the world?

"Front page," Lisa said. "First column. See the headline? Camp clerk indicted on INS fraud?"

"Oh, no." Zama stared at the newsprint, but she couldn't seem to take it in. "Oh no. Is that—the clerk who—the one you paid—"

"Smart girl."

"But—I mean, do they know about us? Is there any way they could—we might be okay, maybe they don't know about everything, maybe they won't figure it out, nobody's called us or come knocking—"

"I don't know," Lisa said. "I'm wondering that too. But Stan figured it out. He figured it out right away. And he figured out I hadn't told him the truth." She smiled wanly. "So he kicked me out of the house. I'm going to be staying with you guys for a while, if that's okay."

11

Darroti

Every night, now, he watches over his father's shoulder as Timbor writes letters. He writes them in Gandiffran, in the graceful rolling script of home; he writes them in a blank book with a drawing of stars and a smiling crescent moon on the front. The letters always begin, "Dear Darroti," and at first Darroti thinks that this means Timbor knows he is here. But it soon becomes clear, from the letters themselves, that Timbor does not know that.

"Dear Darroti," the first letter begins, "I wonder where you are now, and whether your spirit is learning anything. A friend of mine said that it would help me to write you letters, because I have been having very strange dreams. He is a doctor; he treats people whose minds have betrayed them. He tells me that people who have lived through difficult things often have such dreams. Do you dream where you are now, Darroti? You lived through more difficult things than I have, I think. The most difficult thing I ever had to live through was your own death. That was even more difficult than your sentence, even more difficult than exile has been.

"But I am writing these letters to tell you, wherever you are, that we are doing fine here in America, in exile, although I will never be as fine as I would have been if you had not died. It is silly to write the letters, because I know you will never read them, but my friend thinks they will help me, and I respect him, so I will try. And so I will tell you what we are doing now."

And so Timbor tells Darroti about driving a cab, about how Harani is cooking in a casino and Erolorit is packing meat in a supermarket; he tells his son about everyone's job and about the children's school accomplishments, and most of all about Zamatryna, the family's joy. The letters never contain a word of uncertainty or discontent, and Darroti wonders whom his father is trying to fool. He wonders how his father can believe that lies will make anyone feel better: and then he remembers his own lies—all the lies that led him here, that led the family here—and realizes that lies are the province of the living.

For Darroti, who cannot hear speech, can nonetheless perceive the storm of emotions in the house, the currents which bounce and buffet him whenever he is not hiding in his father's bookcase. He feels Macsofo's fury and Aliniana's despair, his father's endless sadness, the pain and confusion of the cousins on the rare occasions when they are home. He senses Erolorit's joyless resignation and Harani's yearning for the past. He knows that Zamatryna suffers pain, although he does not know why, and he knows that she works to keep the others from seeing it, just as Timbor works to make his letters cheerful.

There are sometimes other people in the house: the woman Lisa and her husband Stan—whom Darroti has often seen before, and whose names he now learns from his father's letters—school friends of Zamatryna's and her cousins', men who come to repair the pipes or the television set. Darroti cannot read these people well, because they are not his family, not connected to his story. Stan and Lisa are the clearest, because they are the closest to the others. They care the most. And yet Lisa's kindness is also cocooned in lies, and Stan stumbles in the darkness of his doubt.

And then one day there is a new person in the house, only for a few moments: a large young man, sun-browned, with hair so pale it is almost white. And Darroti, who has ventured out from the bookcase for a little while, hoping to avoid a gale, feels an updraft of love so pure and potent that it nearly lifts him through the roof.

He knows that kind of love. It is what he feels for Gallicina. It is the world reformed, made new, each time the lover sees the beloved's face. It is the miracle which makes the cosmos dance, which keeps the planets in their courses, which fuels the fire of the stars. It is salvation.

And no one else in the house seems aware of it.

Who is this young man?

"Dear Darroti," Timbor writes that evening, "Zamatryna has a new boyfriend now, a football player named Jerry. He looks like a collection of tree trunks lashed together, and he is not very clever."

But he loves her! Darroti would shout this into his father's ear, if he could. Jerry loves her! He will save her; he will make her happy. He will save you all. He wants to shake his father's shoulders, but the pen still moves across the page, oblivious.

"Aliniana thinks that he is fonder of her than she is of him. Zamatryna says that he is just a friend and that it is nothing serious, but they have a good time eating food together, even if they do not bless it. Her sorority sisters are very impressed that she is dating Jerry, and that is mainly why she sees him, I think. Ah, she is a little American now, in ways I will never understand.

"Erolorit has gotten a raise at work. This will allow us to repay our debt to Lisa sooner. Harani burned her finger on some grease tonight, but we put a bandage on it and now she is fine." The letter meanders on, talking about money and utility bills and the glass Timbor broke this morning, and Darroti is helpless to bring it back to what he wants to know. Jerry. What of Jerry? There must be more about Jerry.

Darroti desires information, indeed is desperate for it. And so now he ventures more often from the safety of the bookcase, the security of the towel, which remains perpetually wet with his tears. No longer needing sleep, he watches ceaselessly for any sign of Jerry, but these are few indeed. Twice more Jerry comes into the house, each time for five minutes; each time his radiant love finds no reflection in Zamatryna's distracted indifference. Darroti invades Zamatryna's bedroom when she is not there, hoping to spot photographs, love letters, any sign that she realizes or returns the ardor she has kindled, but there is nothing: her bureau and desk are bare, fastidiously neat, the bed meticulously made, the closet always shut. The room looks as if no one lives there at all, and Darroti never stays long. Were he to penetrate the surfaces, creep into the drawers of the desk as he creeps into the towel, for instance, he knows he might discover more, but delicacy stops him. He barely knows this child at all. She was seven when he died. He has no real right to spy upon her secrets; and if once she realized Jerry's love, surely she would not keep it hidden.

So he searches Timbor's letters, which he knows he has permission to read, for any clue that the family understands the depth of Jerry's devotion. He finds none; he finds nothing else, either. The letters are tissues of fact containing no truth, surfaces as seemly and off-putting as the ones in Zamatryna's bedroom. Timbor describes his passengers and the routes he has driven; he talks about Rikko and Jamfret's prize in the Science Fair; he shares Aliniana's gossip about the mayor's cousin's fingernails.

Because Darroti now spends much more time outside the bookcase, he knows just how artificial Timbor's letters are. He watches Macsofo and Aliniana fight and fight and fight again. He watches Harani weep in the garden when she thinks no one can see her; he watches Timbor weep in bed and mumble to the clown on the wall, saying all the things, presumably, he will not say in his letters. Darroti strains to understand the words his father mutters, strains to read his lips, but he cannot. He watches Aliniana throw the costly, bejewelled clown at her husband, watches it shatter on the floor.

He watches her storm out of the house, watches Macsofo rage and weep, watches Zamatryna confront him the next morning. He watches Lisa arrive, also weeping, with the newspaper and her suitcases. He thinks that his towel, the one that never dries, is a fitting symbol for this weeping house.

He wonders how long it will take his father to start telling the truth in his letters, to the memory of his son, and not just to a painting of a clown.

It does not take very long at all, after Lisa comes. That same night, after everyone else has gone to bed—Lisa is sleeping in Poliniana's room—Timbor takes out the blank book and stares at it. He stares at it for several minutes, until Darroti wonders if he plans to write in it at all. But at last he opens it, his hands shaking, and lifts his pen.

The pen which used to roll so smoothly scrambles now, and skips. The handwriting looks broken. The sentences sound broken. All of Timbor's surfaces have broken. He does not begin by writing "Dear Darroti"; he simply writes.

"I cannot pretend anymore. All is wretched. All is misery. More misery than Darroti's death? No, but as much misery. From so many places. From everywhere and everything.

"Darroti, if you could read this, could you ever have imagined what you have done to us? I tell myself it is not your fault. But I do not understand. I do not understand why. Why this is happening. Why you killed the Mendicant. Why you killed yourself. Those things began it all.

"Your brother takes after you, and drinks. He works on the poison trains, and drinks. He curses us. He drove his wife away. She has gone away. She wants a divorce. She says—but I cannot write that, and Zama thinks it is not true.

"The clerk who sold us our fake papers has been caught. They say he will confess. He will offer information to spend less time in jail. What will happen to us? It will be the same questions: where are you from, and what direction did you walk in to get here? I remember Zamatryna saying, 'We walked forward.' We cannot go back. But the Americans will not believe that. Will they send us to Afghanistan, where we know no one?

"We are caught. Lisa is caught. Stan kicked her out because she lied to him. She is here now, in her mother's house. In the house where she grew up, where she is now our guest. Stan wants a divorce. Stan, who does not believe in divorce. Aliniana, who never heard of divorce before we came here.

"I went to the Auto Museum. It is Saturday. I always meet Stan at the Auto Museum. I wondered if he would be there. He was there. He was sitting on a bench near the De Soto. He was crying. He asked me why I had lied to him. He asked me how he could go on living, when he knew that his wife had lied to him. I thought he was angry at me, but then he wept in my arms. Like a child. Like Darroti did when he was small and had nightmares. He told me he could see no light anywhere. He told me God is dead. He told me Jesus is a joke. He told me forgiveness is impossible. He said he could not keep living. He said that twice.

"He is alone in his house now. I am terrified. I want to stay with him, to keep him safe, but I could not keep Darroti safe, even when we were in the same tent. I could not keep him alive when he did not want to stay alive. And I must stay in this house, to keep Macsofo safe. And to keep the others safe from Macsofo. I cannot be in two places at once. I cannot watch Macsofo and Stan at once, because Lisa is here too.

"Zamatryna said I should call the police. She said I should tell them that Stan was in danger. I told her please to call if that is what we must do. I do not know what to do. She knows what to do. What would we do, without her?

"Jerry called to ask how Betty was. Zamatryna did not want to talk to him; she says he is not important right now. She says there is no way he could understand what we are going through. She says she has too much else to think about. So I told him how Betty is.

"Betty is dying. She needs an operation on her heart. The Americans will not give it to her. It costs too much money. She has no money. People do not help beggars, here. No, some do. We do. Stan and Lisa do. Jerry did. But doctors do not. Or not doctors who operate on hearts. This is a terrible country.

"I hate it here. I hate everything that is happening and everything that has happened. I hate exile.

"I have told Macsofo that he must stop drinking. Everyone has told him that, but I told him again, tonight. I did not think he would agree. He never has before. But tonight he said he would try. He is frightened, I think. He understands our danger from the clerk. He asked me if Aliniana knew, if she had read the news, if anyone had spoken to her. It is the first concern he has expressed for her in months.

"He asked where his children are. I said I do not know. Zamatryna said they are probably with Aliniana, and Macsofo nodded. He said, 'We must stay together now.'

"No one answered. It is he who has driven us apart. After a little while he looked at his shoes, and said, 'I will throw out my beer. I will not go to those meetings, but I will throw out my beer. You must take care of me when the visions start.'

"Lisa said he must go to a hospital. Lisa said he could die. She said that people can die, if they stop drinking without medicine. She said it would be safer for him to keep drinking. But he said, no, no hospitals. He wants to be with his family. And Lisa told him he was crazy, and she told us that we are crazy if we do not take him to the hospital. But he will not go.

"At least he has remembered that he loves us.

"Everyone is dying. I do not know what to do."

Timbor closes the book. He puts the book away. He lies down in his bed and stares into the darkness. He does not talk to the clown, tonight. Darroti believes that Timbor does not need to talk to the clown because he has talked to the book. Timbor has told the book the truth. He has told the book that he does not know what to do.

And because Timbor has done that, Darroti does know what to do. Or, at least, he knows what he must try to do.

He remembers lying in Stini's apartment, raging and howling, his thirst for drink like knives and chewing worms all over his body. He remembers the visions he had then: of terrible flying lizards, of giant eyeballs with mouths at their center, seeking to devour him, of Gallicina performing obscene acts with other men. He saw venomous snakes slithering from holes in the walls; he saw his feet and hands detach themselves from his body and crawl away, transforming into purple crabs; he saw motes of dust become volleys of arrows aimed at his eyes and his genitals. He watched his clothing twist into ropes to strangle him; he watched the floor become a stormy sea in which he would surely drown.

He remembers how convinced he was that everything he saw was real.

People in Gandiffri do not believe in ghosts. Timbor has ignored his dreams because he knows, as everyone in Lémabantunk knows, that the dead cannot converse with the living, that the Great Breaking cannot be mended. But drunks foregoing drink believe their visions, and Macsofo is about to battle crabs and snakes and lizards of his own.

Very well, then. Darroti will give him something else to watch.

That is one thing he must do. There is another. For somehow Zamatryna must be made aware of Jerry's love, the love that is so much like Darroti's for Gallicina. Jerry must convince her to let him in, to think he is important. He must be made to understand more than she thinks he can. He must be made family.

If Darroti can do this, if he can help Jerry's love succeed, his own love will be redeemed. If Jerry can win Zamatryna, then all the pain and waste of exile will not have been for nothing. If Darroti sees them happy, then it will begin to be all right that he ruined his own chance of happiness. And then perhaps his memories will not torment him so.

Darroti has a plan. Darroti has several plans. Darroti's plans multiply like the slugs in the garden. But to do what he wishes to do, he will need to acquire new skills. Can the dead change, here? He has already learned new things. Can he do new things?

Well, he must try.

In Gandiffri, the spirits of the dead were contained: a spirit in a leaf could only move in the wind that blew the leaf. Darroti has believed that he is tethered to his family; he has believed that he is a discrete entity, a fixed and finite mass. But he no longer has a body, so maybe he is wrong. Perhaps he is not bounded, or bounded only by his own beliefs.

Darroti begins to experiment.

He practices taking different shapes. He spreads himself into a thin mist near the ceiling; he oozes through the cracks under doors; he succeeds, at last, in walking through a wall. He discovers that, indeed, he is not bound by the rules his body followed. He knew this before, in a puzzled kind of way—he sensed that he could creep inside Zamatryna's desk if he chose, just as every night he curls weeping inside the towel—but he did not realize the extent of it. The dead have powers here, however limited.

Darroti shapeshifts all over the house, navigating the storms of crisis. The family is oblivious, as always; if he creates any disturbance, how could they tell, in the midst of all their other troubles? And for now, for just a little while longer, he wishes it that way.

That is the first step, taking different shapes. Now for the second, much more frightening. Can Darroti break the tether to his family, to this house? And if he does, will he be able to return?

If he becomes lost, then all is lost. But if he does not try, then all is already lost.

And so he tries.

Darroti travels through the window, into the garden. It is a cool autumn day, the sunlight brilliant on the river, on the leaves, on the last flowers in the garden, goldenrod and purple aster. Darroti rises far above the house, swimming through the air. He feels the tether tighten; he pulls against it. It will not give.

In pain, he swims back down, through fragrant falling leaves. The tether slackens.

Back up. Pull, pull. Again the tether tightens; again Darroti's fear and caution yank him down again.

He weeps above the garden; his salt tears glisten on the goldenrod like dew. This cannot be. He cannot let it be.

And so he tries again. He remembers his love for Gallicina; he summons his love for his family, his love for Lémabantunk, his love for the boy Jerry, whose love will save Darroti. Darroti rises on a current of love, like the current of love he felt from the boy himself.

And the tether stretches. Warmed by the love, it softens like taffy, becomes endlessly elastic. It will not hold him now, and neither will it break. It will let Darroti go wherever his plans require him to go, and it will lead him home. It will not allow him to be lost.

Exultant, Darroti soars above the house, above it and around it, swooping like the hawks he sees flying above the mountains. Perhaps his plans will work. Perhaps, for once, something he attempts will reach fruition. Perhaps, for once, he will not be a failure.

But there is one more skill to learn, the hardest.

Darroti goes back into the house, back into the bookshelf, back into the towel. This is his safest place. Nothing bad can happen here. He goes into the towel, and there he becomes water. And there he pulls himself from himself, as a single water drop will separate in two.

It is very difficult, at first, very frightening. But at last, now, there: he has succeeded. He is in two pools, one on the right side of the towel, one on the left. Two pools of Darroti, joined by a tether of love. And now he moves the two sides of himself together again, flowing back into one pool.

Apart again. Together again. Apart again.

More confident, this time he tries to break the tether, to cut the bond between the pools, but he finds it will not break. He pulls and tugs, and still it will not break. He begins to believe that it would not break if he wanted it to.

Darroti smiles.

Darroti practices being in two places at once.

12

BLESSINGS

Zamatryna sat in the Pneumatic Diner on a Friday morning, eating eggs. The Pneumatic Diner boasted neon on the ceiling and amateur psychedelic art on the walls. The décor was guaranteed to induce migraine, but the food was excellent. Zama looked at the eggs so she wouldn't have to look at the walls or at Jerry, who sat across from her. "You do that a lot," he said.

"I do what?"

"You look at your food, instead of at me."

She glanced up at him. "Jerry, I'm sorry. And I'm sorry I didn't call you to tell you about Betty. I just—things got a little crazy. You know. Betty, my aunt and uncle splitting up, school starting again—"

"I know. It's okay. Your grandfather told me about Betty. Is she doing better now?"

"Well, I guess. Better's relative, isn't it? She got out of the hospital, went back in, and now she's about to get out again. Without that surgery, she doesn't—well, she doesn't have much time. It sucks."

She hadn't seen Jerry for almost three weeks. She'd dodged his calls, avoided him at school, ignored his messages. Finally, yesterday, she'd found him waiting outside one of her classes, holding a

bouquet of flowers. Sarah-Bee had been there too, and had nearly
fainted at how romantic Jerry was. "I guess playing hard to get really works, huh?" she'd said with a sigh.

Zamatryna didn't think Jerry was romantic, and she hadn't been
playing hard to get. Jerry was a pain in the ass, even though he'd
helped Betty—maybe because he'd helped Betty, because he'd seen
Zamatryna at her least competent—and Zama had been avoiding
him because she didn't have the courage or energy to break up with
him directly. She didn't know if he'd heard about the INS scandal, or
if he'd thought to connect it to her. The family was still waiting ner-
vously for an official phone call or a knock on the door, but so far
there had been only silence. They kept hoping they'd be overlooked.
Lisa said not to count on it. "That clerk was pond scum, frankly, and
I'm sure he still is. He'll sing like a bird to reduce his sentence. And
he can't have made many single deals much bigger than ours."

So, basically, they were going to be toast, although they didn't
know when. And in the meantime Macsofo had been struggling
with do-it-yourself detox: he'd start to dry out, have hideous DTs,
go back on the sauce again, and try to dry out again. He was on his
third attempt. Lisa kept demanding that they take him to a hospital,
but Max simply refused to go. So, Zamatryna thought grimly, they
might have another corpse on their hands soon.

They didn't know where Aliniana was. She called the house oc-
casionally to ask for things—clothing, cooking supplies—which
she picked up from Harani at work. She wouldn't say where she
was staying, or what her phone number was, or whether she was really having an affair. The cousins had arrived en masse one day, ig-
noring their father and his frantic questions, to pack up their
belongings. Zama thought, on the whole, that this was evidence
against the affair—the children couldn't afford to stay by themselves, and surely Aliniana wouldn't want them with her if she were
in the middle of a grand passion—but there was no way to know
for sure.

In short, everything was a mess. And the last thing Zamatryna needed on top of everything else was Jerry and his clueless questions; she couldn't possibly explain to him what was happening. But, holding his bouquet, he'd doggedly insisted on taking her to lunch; when she told him she had to work, he'd insisted on breakfast the next morning. She hadn't been able to think of any good ways to get out of that one, so here she was.

"So," she said, "how've you been?" Inane. Inane, Zama. You don't care how he is. Stop being nice to him: tell him you don't want to see him again, because shooting him between the eyes is the only message he'll get.

"Well," he said, "I've been having these really strange dreams."

"They have psychiatrists for that," she said coldly. Jerry's dreams were the last thing she needed.

He picked up a piece of toast and examined it thoughtfully before taking a bite. "The dreams are about you."

Oh, great. "You're obsessing about me? They have psychiatrists for that, too." She knew she was being bitchy: she didn't care. Maybe he'd get the message and go away.

Jerry shook his head. "They aren't dirty or anything. Not that—well, never mind. Zama, this is going to sound nuts. But are you and your family from, um, like, another dimension or something?"

She stared at him. For a moment she forgot to breathe. "Excuse me?"

"I told you it was going to sound nuts. But look, I know you're not from Afghanistan. At least, I don't think you're from Afghanistan. There's a guy from Afghanistan who works in my mom's office. I told him about you. He's never heard of kids in Afghanistan memorizing epic poems about geometry. He's never heard of kids *anywhere* memorizing epic poems about geometry. And I couldn't find any epic poems about geometry on the Net."

"Maybe you weren't using the right keywords," Zamatryna said. Her fingers felt glued to her fork, the same way they'd felt glued to her cell phone the night she and Jerry followed Betty to the ER.

"Maybe I wasn't," Jerry said. "But then—then that INS story broke, you know, the one about the clerk—"

"Yes. I know."

"I thought you would," Jerry said, taking a deep breath. "And I did the math, and the dates seemed right. And then the dreams started. And I've been having them every night. Always pieces of the same story. About how you and your family used to live in Léma-bantunk"—he pronounced it correctly, with a Gandiffran accent, and Zama felt a chill begin to travel up her spine—"only it was a city, not a village, and you lived together in a big house with lots of carpets and a courtyard, and there were lizards there, and your uncle killed someone, a woman, and so you had to walk through a shiny blue door, and you wound up here, in the camps, and your uncle killed himself on the fence and then when the bomb went off somebody smuggled you out in her van—"

"I'm leaving now," Zamatryna said. She was standing next to the table; her plate was in pieces on the floor. She didn't remember standing up. She didn't remember the plate falling. "I'm going. I'm not listening to this. You—you—I have to get out of here. I have to get some air. I—"

"Get all the air you want," Jerry said, "but I'm coming with you." He followed her as she stalked out of the second-story restaurant; she noted in a daze that he tossed money at the cashier as he went— honest Jerry!—and as she raced down the stairs and out the door, he stayed stubbornly next to her, talking. "I dreamed about a doll you brought from home, but then it lost its eyes. I dreamed about the INS people trying to figure out where you came from. I dreamed about how you were trapped in the camps because you couldn't tell them. I keep dreaming it, the same story, and it all fits together and— Zama, is it true? Is any of it true?"

"You're insane," she said, crossing First Street, heading toward the river. "Do you think anyone else will believe you if you say any of this? They'll have you committed. No one will—"

"I'm not going to tell anyone else!" He reached out now to grab her arm; he held her gently, but suddenly she couldn't seem to break away, although she'd fled before. "I wouldn't have told that guy in my mother's office if, if I thought, if I knew it might cause trouble, Zama, that's not what I want, Zama, would you please look at me? I just—these dreams are making me nuts. And maybe I am nuts. Maybe I need to be committed, just like you said. But I want to know, and you seem like the logical one to ask, and if it's true I won't tell a soul, I swear, I wouldn't do anything to get you into trouble. I want you to stay here. I love you. Zamatryna—"

"You *what?*" she said. He'd never used her full name before; she'd never told him what it was. Why did that bother her more than anything else?

"I love you."

"You do not."

He smiled. "Well, at least you're looking at me now."

She looked away. "Jerry, this is—"

"So is it true?"

She swallowed. "Is what true?"

"That your name's really Zamatryna. And that you're from another dimension. And that you walked here through a blue door."

She swallowed. She was sweating. He hadn't said anything about the beetle. Did that mean that the beetle itself was the only thing Zamatryna wasn't supposed to talk about? She didn't know. She couldn't work it all out. She didn't know how Jerry could be having these dreams. Her head hurt.

"I like Zamatryna," he said, holding her by both arms now. "It's prettier than Zama. I'd be happy if that were your name. And if everything else is true—if it *is* true, you can talk to me about it. I swear. And I won't tell a soul. I just want to know. If it's true, or if I'm crazy."

Stall. Buy some time. She looked up at him again, squinting, and said, "What do you think?" Something fell on her forehead. A raindrop. Where had that come from? There wasn't a cloud for miles.

She saw Jerry relax, saw something like wonder cross his face. "I think it's true."

"You think it's true," she said, as another impossible raindrop fell on her cheek. "And why do you think that, Jerry?"

"Because I dreamed about this, too. I dreamed that we were standing outside like this, and it started raining when it shouldn't have been. And I brushed the raindrops off your face, just like this, see?"

"Really," she said. She wanted to back away from his hand, the fingers tenderly smoothing the water off her skin, but she couldn't. Why couldn't she? "And then what happened, in this dream of yours?"

"And then I kissed you," Jerry said, and kissed her.

And now there was water on her face again, but it was tears, her tears, and she couldn't seem to stop crying, and Jerry guided her to a bench and sat her down and held her, saying "It's okay, it's okay, everything's going to be all right," and kissing her hair and her hands and her forehead. "It's all right, Zama, Zamatryna—"

"No it's *not*! It's not all right! What are we going to do? They won't let us stay here, and we can't—there's nowhere else to go and—I don't understand how this can be happening! How can you be dreaming about my life? How can you know about my doll and the door and my uncle?"

"I don't know," Jerry said, "but I do. Your uncle had a funny birthmark on his face, right? A mole like a starfish?"

"Yeah," she said, shivering. "He did. How can you know that? How can you know any of this?"

"Who knows? But I do know it. And I know something else, at least, I think I do. I know what we can do so you can stay here. We can get married, and then you can sponsor your family—"

"Jerry," she said, shaking her head, but somehow he was kissing her again and somehow she was kissing him back, enjoying it too much, she had to stop this, right now, before things got any crazier than they already were. She forced herself to pull away from him. "Jerry, no. Getting married wouldn't automatically make me legal, anyway. That's INS fraud all over again."

"Only if you don't mean it," he said, stroking her hair. "And it would help with the legal stuff, wouldn't it?"

She closed her eyes. "Jerry, look, I don't know how I feel about anything right now, too much else is happening—I—"

"I know," he said. "It's one of those things you have to be sure about. Like anchovies."

"Right," she said in relief, opening her eyes. "Just like anchovies. Marriage is like anchovies. I like that."

"Good," he said, smiling. "I finally said something you think is smart." And he kissed her again, and again she kissed him back, her body completely oblivious to the rational dictates of her conscious mind.

By the time she managed to extricate herself, she was sitting on his lap, and one of his hands was cradling the back of her head while another was halfway up her thigh, and she realized dimly that there was a series of warm, moist spots up and down her neck, where Jerry had been kissing her. No. No no no. This wouldn't do at all. She blinked, noting a series of moist spots on Jerry's neck—yes, she'd been kissing him too, fancy that—and said, "I think I'm getting carried away here."

"I'm heartbroken," Jerry said. She had to laugh. He grinned and said, "See, I made you laugh. When's the last time you laughed? I have my uses, right?"

"Oh, come on! You saved Betty's life."

He grimaced. "We both did. And the medics did. For the moment."

"Yeah."

"So let's talk about something happier. Tell me about marriage customs in Lémabantunk."

"Jerry. No. Let's not, okay? Because even if I did mean it, the INS wouldn't think I did. Not with the timing the way it is."

He shrugged. "You're probably right. Tell me about marriage customs anyway. Just so we don't have to talk about somebody dying."

She rested her head against his chest, and he put both arms around her and kissed the top of her head. She remembered Betty saying that he loved her, Aliniana saying he loved her. She remembered the plan she'd come up with several years before, of how she'd get married and use Betty as her Necessary Beggar and everything would be all right, for all of them. She realized that she was starting to cry again.

"Hey. Hey, Zamatryna, what is it? I was trying to cheer you up."

"Fat chance," she said, sniffling.

"Do you *have* marriage customs in Lémabantunk?"

"Of course we do! And I thought—I used to think—I had this fairy tale I used to tell myself. A couple of years ago. About how I'd do it that way and everything would be all right, because— well, it's hard to explain. There's this blessing, see, and—"

"Okay," he said, sitting her up. "Slow down. Start from the beginning. Tell me everything, okay?"

So she did. She told him about everything except the beetle. She told him about Mendicants, about the Necessary Beggar, about her daydream of using Betty as her Necessary Beggar so Betty would get gifts and the rest of the family would be forgiven. "But even if I did it that way, I couldn't give Betty that surgery, which is what she really needs. And I don't think—I'm not sure there's enough forgiveness in the world to fix my family, at this point. And anyway, I still think I'd have to mean it. For the blessing to take. And I just—I don't know. Everything's so confusing. An hour ago I was determined to break up with you, and now I'm telling you things I've never been able to tell anyone else. Plus making out like a crazed weasel."

"My parents have been married for thirty years," Jerry said, running his hand up and down her forearm. She wanted to melt. She couldn't let herself melt. She had to be a responsible adult. She really ought to get off his lap. "And you know what my mom told me once? She was terrified before they got married. She was afraid she'd wake up one morning and realize she'd made a horrible mistake. But if that's going to happen, it hasn't yet."

"Yeah, but I bet they'd been together longer than five minutes. And your mom was probably older than seventeen, right?" He was kissing her neck again. "Jerry, that's very distracting."

"Sorry." He stopped. "Okay, look, you're right. It's a little crazy. I know it is. But the question is, is it right? Is it true? These dreams I've been having are very crazy, but they're true. And I think there's a reason I've been having them. I think the reason is so I can marry you. Because that could—it could fix everything, if it worked."

And if it didn't, Zamatryna thought grimly, things couldn't get much worse. No, Zama, you'd better cancel that. Because the last time you thought that way, things got much worse. "Remind me again what this will fix?"

"Well, it might keep you from being deported to Afghanistan. Or at least slow things down. And if Betty gives that blessing, it might help your family. And—you know, I've been saving money. I inherited some from my grandparents, and I've been working since high school. I have about twelve thousand now. That's a start on the surgery fees, anyway. And we could tell people that as wedding gifts we wanted contributions to the Betty fund."

"You'd do that?" Zamatryna said, incredulous. "You'd give your life savings to Betty? You met Betty for about two seconds. Twelve thousand won't scratch two hundred thousand. Jerry, this is impossible."

"More impossible than the dreams? I'm only twenty: it's not like I can't save more. Lisa gave her life savings to you guys, didn't she?"

"Yeah, she did. But that's—that was religious. And we're paying it back." Very slowly. "Betty won't be able to do that."

"All right. So call this religious, too." He kissed her.

She pushed him away, gently. "Jerry, I'm sorry. This is way too crazy. It's too fast. We're too young. I need to wait until I'm sure."

"How long will that take?"

"I don't know."

He nodded. "Okay. And how long will it take Betty to die without the surgery? And how long will it take them to deport you to Afghanistan? And if you decide you're sure when you're in Afghanistan, then what do we do? Zamatryna—I'd rather get married and not have you be sure, but have you still be here, than have you decide you're sure and then not be able to get back into the country. You see? We're in Reno. We can get a civil ceremony in an hour, just in case it will help legally, and then arrange the other one. And if we really, really had to, if everything went wrong and we decided it was a mistake, we could get divorced in an hour."

"I don't want to hurt you," she said.

"I don't want you to hurt me, either. It's nice we agree on that."

"Jerry—"

"It's not like I'm not going into this with my eyes open. Please. Please, Zamatryna. Even if you don't love me—"

"Don't say that! I didn't say that. I—"

"Even if you don't love me *yet,* do it for your family. Do it for Betty."

"And when do I get to do something for myself?" she asked. She remembered Rumpled Ron telling her she was doing everything for the wrong reasons, for other people. This was a fine time to decide he'd been right.

Jerry gave her the sweetest smile she'd ever seen. "When you decide you love me," he said, and kissed her again.

She buried her head in his chest. "It's not going to work. Jerry, I don't believe in the Blessing of the Necessary Beggar. Maybe it meant something in Lémabantunk, but it doesn't mean anything here. I don't believe in any blessings. I don't think blessings exist. The INS won't buy it for a second, and Betty will die anyway, because we won't have enough money, and we'll decide we hate each other after a year and then I'll owe you your life savings in addition to owing Lisa hers, and—"

"You may be absolutely right," he said, massaging her neck. "And we could get hit by a truck in the next ten seconds, too. And since you've moved on to telling me how it *won't* work, instead of how it *wouldn't,* does that mean you've decided to do it?"

She shuddered. "I feel so trapped." Was this how Gallicina felt?

"Yeah, I know you do. If we went back to Plan A, which is sitting here on our rumps, making out like crazed weasels and waiting for the world to fall apart, would you feel less trapped?"

"No. But I'd feel less dishonest."

"You've been very honest," he said gently. "You've been painfully honest. You get big honesty points. No flies on you there."

"See?" she said miserably. "I've hurt you already. And Jerry, look, this is dishonest to everybody else, even if not to you. Does it count if you're the only one I'm telling the truth?"

"I don't know," he said. "But I know why you're telling me the truth. It's because the dreams told me the truth. And you know, there's no way either of us could have predicted the dreams. Which means there may be more surprises out there. Good ones. Zamatryna, I know blessings exist. Because the dreams do. And because you do."

"That's sappy," she said. She was frightened and angry now. Everything was wrong. This was all wrong. "That's beyond sappy. It's sick."

"I know," he said, and grinned. "So when do we tell your family that we're getting married?"

She took a very deep breath. "We might as well do it now. Everybody's home now, I think; it's everybody's day off. I just have to warn you, I don't think they're going to be very happy. And, uh, Jerry? Let's not tell them about the dreams. Not right away, anyhow. Let's just let them keep thinking that you think we're from Afghanistan."

"Okay. Why?"

"I'm not sure. Just—it's simpler. And they're freaking out about enough other things right now. Maybe later we can tell them. All right? Let's see how things go."

"Well, can I tell them I know about the Necessary Beggar? Will that help? If they know we're doing this to help Betty?"

"You'll have to tell them you know that. Just, like, pretend that you think it's an Afghan custom, okay?" Jerry was willing to give Betty his life savings. It occurred to her that she had to be crazy not to be in love with him. It also occurred to her that he was much too good to be true, and was probably an ax murderer wanted in fifteen states. What was she doing?

"What are you doing?" Lisa said an hour later, as the family sat around the kitchen table. Everyone was staring at Jerry and Zamatryna. "Kids, this is way too fast. You're too young. You're doing it for the wrong reasons."

"No," Jerry said firmly. "We're doing it for the right reasons."

"If you're doing it for the right reasons," Lisa said briskly, "do it right. Have a real ceremony, not one of those awful Instant Wedding Chapel things." Everyone else nodded, except Macsofo. Macsofo was busy retching into a plastic bowl on his lap. The family had tried to excuse him from the discussion, but he had insisted on being there, so now they had to listen to him vomiting like a dog.

"We *are* having a real ceremony," Jerry said. Zamatryna's tongue seemed to have cleaved to the roof of her mouth. "City Hall isn't a wedding chapel. We're having a ceremony with the Necessary Beggar, after the City Hall one. Zama told me about that. It's a beautiful custom."

Lisa blinked. "A what? A Necessary—what's that?"

"It's a custom from our country," Timbor said, frowning. "You told him about that? Zama? Why would you do that?"

"Why would you want one?" Harani asked. "Daughter, dear one, you are American now. It will not mean the same thing, here. It makes no sense."

"I want the blessing," Zamatryna said, her voice very small. "I want the Blessing of the Necessary Beggar."

Erolorit shook his head now. "Zama, this is not right. The blessing is part of home. It is a piece of home. We are not at home. It will not work here. It has no place in America. It will mean nothing to your husband."

"Yes, it will mean something to me," Jerry said. "I want to do it."

"He's the one who talked me into it," said Zama.

Jerry nodded vigorously. "Because it will help Zama—help all of you—make this home. Not just legally. Not just with papers. With your hearts."

"The Law of Hearts," Timbor murmured, sounding startled. "Did Zamatryna tell you about that, too?"

"No, sir. I figured it out on my own."

Macsofo looked up from his bowl. He was shaking like a dog now, like one of those toy terriers you could fit into a teacup. "Yes, that is right," he said hoarsely. "That is exactly right. This will help make America home." Now everyone stopped staring at Zamatryna and stared at Macsofo, who had spent years scorning both America and Gandiffri. What was he doing?

Timbor cleared his throat. "The family needs to discuss this privately. Jerry, I am sorry, but if we can ask you to—"

"Of course," Jerry said. "I can leave for a little while."

Timbor nodded. "Good. Thank you. And Lisa, I am very sorry

indeed, I know you are practically our family and Jerry is—is about to be our family, or hopes to be, and this is really your house, but—"

"No problem," Lisa said. She turned to Jerry and said, "Come on, kid. Let's go get some coffee. We'll be back in, oh, two hours. Will that be enough time, guys? Call me on my cell if it won't be." She squeezed Zamatryna's shoulder on her way out the door, and Jerry bent to kiss her.

"I love you," he said. "Do you need anything? While we're out?"

"Anchovies," she said bleakly, and he laughed and kissed her nose.

"Anchovies?" Harani said after they had left. "What does that mean?"

"It's a quaint German-Italian custom. Never mind. Look, I know—"

"You do not know," Erolorit said heatedly in Gandiffran. "You do not know anything. You are being a child. Zamatryna, this is not right. He is not right for you. He is not good enough for you."

"He is a very sweet boy and he is trying to help you," Harani said, "but that is not the right reason to get married." She glared at Macsofo and said, "I do not want you to have to break your marriage. One broken marriage in the family is bad enough!"

"Your parents are right," Timbor said. "You cannot love him. You have always said you do not love him, and you have changed your mind too quickly, and you are too young. And the marriage will not really help us with the border judges, if it comes to that."

"I need to do this," Zamatryna said. "I really do. And I want Betty to be my Necessary Beggar."

"No," Harani said. "I am your mother. I forbid it."

"It is wrong," said Erolorit.

"He is too far beneath you," said Timbor.

"You cannot use Betty that way," Macsofo said, and they all looked at him again. There was vomit around his mouth; he wiped it off on the back of his hand, looking ashamed. "Zamatryna, little Zama who is smart enough to be President, I have no problem with the rest of it. It is—it is a pretty story. The young man from a—let us call it a lower class. The young man who works hard to help you achieve something you want, do something you want, and in gratitude and because he is also sexy you fall in love with him, maybe even without meaning to, or maybe you cannot help yourself, and your family does not approve, but that does not matter. Because you are in love with him. Because he is the only person you can talk to about what is most important to you, and because your souls complete each other."

His voice was an odd sing-song. Zamatryna felt a chill on the back of her neck, like the one she'd felt when Jerry talked about his dreams. "Uncle Max, what are you talking about? Have you been watching soap operas?"

He smiled thinly. "It is very like another story I heard somewhere. Never mind. Zama, it is a beautiful story, but it can end very badly. Very badly indeed. Listen to me: the Necessary Beggar cannot be someone you know. It is terrible luck to seek a Necessary Beggar you know, even in jest, or even if you are trying to be kind. You must pick the first person you see."

"Yes," Harani said irritably, "that is how it works in Gandiffri, where there are Mendicants on nearly every corner, and where being a Mendicant is a holy calling. That is not how things work here. If she insists on the charade, she might as well use Betty. What difference will it make?"

"Max?" Zamatryna said. "What difference would it make? According to this story you aren't telling us? What happened, in that story?"

Macsofo looked down at his bowl. "In that story, the person seeking the Necessary Beggar sought someone he knew, someone he loved. And it all went wrong. And the Necessary Beggar—the Beggar died."

"He killed her," Zamatryna said quietly. "It's Darroti. It was Darroti and Gallicina, wasn't it? They were in love. I knew it."

"He didn't kill her," Macsofo said. "She killed herself, and he took the blame. He believed it was his fault."

Timbor was shaking his head. "What? What? They didn't know each other. They never knew each other! She was nobility! How—Macsofo, did Darroti tell you this? When?"

"During my, what does Lisa call them, my DTs," Macsofo said sadly. "Last week."

"*What?*" Erolorit said. "You are mad. Those are not real. They are hallucinations. You saw snakes, also."

"The snakes were quite real, brother, believe me. Even if you could not see them."

"No, Macsofo, I do not believe you. I do not believe—"

"I believe him," Zamatryna said. "I believe him because Jerry's been having dreams, too."

Harani squinted at her. "Jerry has been dreaming about Darroti and Gallicina?"

"No. Not exactly. He's been having dreams about—about us. The family. About Lémabantunk, and how we got here, and the camp. He knows things he couldn't possibly know, things I never told him. That's why—that's how—well, that's why we decided to get married. Part of it."

"Because he is the only person you can talk to about what is most important to you," Macsofo said.

She shivered. "Yes. Exactly."

Max nodded. "Just as Darroti was the only person Gallicina could talk to about her dream of being a Mendicant. Little Zama—be careful. Because if you do this right, if you fix the story, if it comes out right this time, it will be a blessing indeed. But if you do not, we will be cursed anew."

"Great," she said in English, her mouth dry. "Terrific. Thanks a lot. No pressure."

Timbor put his hands flat on the table. "I do not understand. Darroti is dead. How can he—"

"Ghosts," Zamatryna said. Should she tell them about Gallicina? But Gallicina had never stopped commanding silence. Be careful, Macsofo had said. "Grandfather, the dead can speak to the living, here. There was never a Great Breaking, I guess. Anyway, people here see ghosts. Some people."

"Ghosts speak in dreams?" Timbor said. "In dreams? Like the dreams I have been having since—since—but I thought they were just dreams. I—"

"Of course you did," Zamatryna said. "You're from Lémaban-tunk. Look, can I marry Jerry, please? Are we all agreed on that much, at least?"

"What else do ghosts do?" Timbor said. "Do they weep into towels?"

"What?" Erolorit said. He looked at Timbor. "Is that thing still wet?"

"Yes. It has never dried. I did not tell you because, well, it was too strange and I was afraid that Stan would think it was the Devil, and—maybe it is. I do not know. Do ghosts weep?"

"Darroti's does," Zamatryna said. She suddenly felt absurdly cheerful, the way she had when she heard about Aliniana's ridiculous affair. She felt like laughing. "Darroti's ghost cried on my face so Jerry would wipe the tears off and kiss me."

"What?" Timbor shook his head again, like an animal trying to rid itself of fleas. "When?"

"This morning. That's—well, it's sort of what started all this. Look, Darroti evidently wants me to marry Jerry, right? So can the rest of you get on board? For Darroti's sake? Because we want to make Darroti happy, don't we? Oh, Grandfather, please don't cry—"

"How can I help it? How can you expect me not to cry? And I still cannot believe—Macsofo, you must tell me the entire story. About Darroti."

"I will, Father. I was not sure I believed it myself, until now."

"I kept having dreams too," Timbor said, sounding bewildered.

"Has he been trying to speak to me, then, all this time? But I cannot believe that. About him and Gallicina. I still—"

"You will believe it when you hear the story, Father."

"I don't believe any of this," Harani said tartly. "And there is still the issue of this marriage. Zamatryna, even if you were older, Jerry is not good enough—oh, someone get the telephone! And if it's a telemarketer, tell him to shoot a rocket launcher up his ass!"

"Ooooh," Zamatryna said, reaching for the phone. "You're learning *excellent* idiomatic English at the casino, aren't you? Hello? If you're a telemarketer, I'm supposed to tell you—"

"Hey, sweetie, it's Lisa. You sound like you're in a good mood. Is everything okay there?"

"I guess so. A bit weird, but okay. Are you guys okay?"

"We're fine. But we're heading back to the house. I'm afraid there's a bit of a, well, a bit of a complication. We decided to call the hospital and see when Betty was getting out. She's already out. They discharged her today, right onto a bus headed for the camp. It's part of the first sweep."

Zamatryna's throat tightened. "That stinks. She won't get very good medical care out there, will she?"

"Better than she would sleeping by the river. That's not the issue. The issue is that, once she's in there, we can't go in to get her out. They've tightened security up a lot, not that it was all that loose before. We could fill out a bunch of paperwork and go through a bunch of rigamarole six ways from Sunday; I mean, it's not Dachau, there is contact with the outside world, but it won't be easy. And I don't know how long it would take. And we're kind of living on borrowed time here anyway."

"Right," Zamatryna said, uncertain where this was going. "So—"

"So Jerry and I figured we should drive out there now, see if we can maybe, I don't know, head off the bus or something."

"A high-speed chase of a county transport?" Zamatryna said.

"That's wonderful. What a great plan. That's really going to increase our credibility with the INS."

"I didn't say a *chase*. But if we can catch up with Betty before she disappears into the camp—look, if you think it's nuts, we won't do it. But then you may not see Betty again."

"I'll do it," Zamatryna said, resigning herself to the surreal. "It's no crazier than anything else that's happened today."

"Okay. We'll be in front of the house in, like, thirty seconds."

"Where are you going?" Timbor demanded when Zamatryna put down the phone.

"To the refugee camp." She was already pulling on a sweatshirt. "To try to intercept Betty. It's a long story. I'll tell you all about it when I get home, if we don't get arrested or something." If she got arrested, at least she wouldn't have to worry about getting married.

"What?" Erolorit stood up. "What are you talking about?"

Harani stood up too. "I'm going with you. What is this insanity?"

"We're all going," Timbor said.

Zamatryna shook her head. "Why? So we can all be arrested?"

Timbor glared at her. "Because we are family, and that is what we do! We go places together! Especially if there is any danger!"

"We may wind up back *in* the camp," Zamatryna said.

"Then we will be in the camp together. Is that Lisa honking out front?"

It was. She was in the SUV that she and Stan had bought after they gave the van to the family. It was big enough for all of them, and a good thing, too, because no one trying to follow them could have kept up with Lisa's driving. Lisa raced along at eighty-five miles per hour while Jerry filled the rest of the family in on the Betty situation; when he'd finished, Erolorit engaged Jerry in strained conversation about accounting. Macsofo, between bouts of heaving into his bowl, gave Zamatryna anxious instructions about the Necessary Beggar.

"You must pick the first person you see. Even if it isn't Betty. Do you understand?"

"Yes, Uncle Max. I understand. Can I blindfold myself, or just keep my eyes closed, and have someone tell me when we find her so I can look? Or would that be cheating?"

"That would be cheating. It is already cheating for you to be seeking someone you know. This is making me very nervous, Zamatryna."

"Okay," said Zamatryna, head pounding. "So if I see someone else first, that person has to be my Necessary Beggar? But can we still give Betty the money for the operation?"

"Yes, of course! That is how any civilized country would do it, anyway. And you can give the Necessary Beggar something else."

"With what money?" Harani asked. "Macsofo, just a little while ago, you would have been the one asking that question."

"Aye. I suppose I would." He was silent for a moment, running his finger meditatively around the rim of his puke bowl. "I wish Aliniana were here. She would know better than I how to advise you, little Zama."

"I wish she were here for many reasons," Harani said, her voice bitter. "And whose fault is it that she is not here?"

"Harani," Timbor said. "Enough. That will not help anything."

"Nonetheless, it is the truth. Macsofo, did these visions of yours teach you any lessons about mending your marriage?"

"Aye. Aye, they did." He looked out the window, and Zamatryna saw him shiver. "They taught me that drinking and jealousy are both terrible curses. Like exile, except that sometimes a person can return from them. If he is lucky, and if it is not already too late." He was quiet again for a few miles. When he spoke, his voice was almost too soft for Zamatryna to hear. "I must tell Alini that I am sorry."

"You should have done that a long time ago," Erolorit said.

"I know, brother."

"Hey," Zamatryna said, and touched his arm. "Hey, Uncle Max, she'll come back. I'm betting she will. Because even if she has a lover, like she says, she can't be real with him. She can't talk about Lémabantunk. She can't share her history."

"Unless Darroti is sending him dreams, also," Macsofo said grimly, and Zamatryna saw Jerry give them an inquisitive glance.

"You told them?"

"Yeah. It's okay. Uncle Max, somehow I don't think that's what Darroti's doing. Not that I'm an expert or anything." Zamatryna rubbed her eyes. There was still Gallicina, the wild card in this mix: what was she up to? Zamatryna didn't think that Gallicina's spirit, sent into the beetle's body back in Lémabantunk, could leave it now, but how could she be sure?

"All right," Macsofo said. "What has happened with Alini has happened. It will—it will be mended, or not. Right now we must think about you. Zamatryna, you must choose your Beggar properly."

"I know. You told me that. Look, Uncle Max, cheer up. I doubt I'll get the chance. We'll never get to the camp. We're going to be pulled over for speeding first."

"Oh, pshaw," Lisa called cheerfully from the front seat. "I'd have to be doing a hundred and ten to get pulled over, on this road." They were already on the long, desolate highway to Gerlach, the desert fading away into blues and browns in the distance. Zamatryna realized that she'd never seen this route before, because the last time she'd taken it, she'd been hiding under a blanket. She hugged herself. Their story was coming full circle, for good or ill. "Mind you," Lisa said, "I still don't think you kids should get married yet, okay? I'm doing this for Betty's sake, so we can get her out of there, take her home. Since we have room now. Since Alini and the kids aren't there."

"Right," Zamatryna said. "Objection noted and recorded." Jerry, in the front seat, turned and winked at her. She wondered what he and Lisa had talked about over coffee. Well, he'd tell her later. If they weren't all arrested.

Lisa gave a long, low whistle. "Hey, guys, look. Up ahead. Is that the bus? Am I good, or what?"

Zamatryna squinted at the speck on the road as Lisa accelerated. "It could be another bus."

"Come on, Zama. How many buses *take* this road?"

"Yeah, I guess you're right. So, um, how exactly are we going to convince them to let Betty come with us? Or were you planning to toss her into the SUV like firewood and take off, the way you did last time?"

"I don't think that will work," Lisa said drily. "I don't know. We'll just, well, we'll tell them the truth. That she can stay with us. That she'll be closer to the hospital that way. We'll do the best we can."

They were behind the bus now; Lisa really must have been doing a hundred and ten before, although now they had slowed to sixty. "Lisa," Zamatryna said, "I don't think getting pulled over for tailgating will be much better than getting pulled over for speeding."

"I'm not tailgating, sweetie. I'm keeping a good following distance."

"Yeah, but that's it. They'll know you're *following* them. They'll think we're terrorists or something."

"If we were terrorists, we wouldn't be so obvious," Lisa said. "Our best bet is probably to be as up-front as possible. Zama, relax. Jerry, would you tell her to relax?"

"Why didn't the hospital call us before they released Betty?" Zama said. "They had our phone number from when we brought her in. Don't they try to make other arrangements for people?"

"Who knows? Maybe the number got lost. Maybe she was too scared or confused to ask them to call. Look, it's a bureaucracy. All kinds of things can get screwed up, even when people know how to stick up for themselves. Which Betty doesn't. Which is why we're here."

Jerry turned around now, reaching into the back seat for Zamatryna's hand. "Don't worry," he said. "We've found her. We're in time. That's the first step, isn't it?"

They stayed behind the bus the remaining twenty miles to the camp. Zama worried the entire way. Betty wasn't going to be the first homeless person she saw. Zamatryna wouldn't be able to choose Betty as her Necessary Beggar. They might not be able to get Betty out of the camp at all. This was craziness. Nothing was going to work. What was she doing?

And when the camp itself came into sight, she felt her insides twist. She'd seen photographs of it, and it wasn't even the same camp they'd been in. She hadn't expected to have such a visceral reaction to the sight of the fences, the barbed wire, the cluster of low, drab tents. She glanced over at Timbor, who was clutching something. His towel, the wet one.

"You brought Darroti," she said very quietly, in Gandiffran.

"Families stay together, Granddaughter."

She squeezed his hand with the one Jerry wasn't holding. They were linked now, the three of them. She was the bridge between them, the bridge between Gandiffri and America. She looked at the fences and said, "I think Darroti would be here anyway. He doesn't seem tied to that towel anymore, if he ever was."

"Nonetheless," Timbor said. "It is—it is how he is visible, to me."

The bus pulled to a stop in front of them. Here were the gates, the guards going to meet the bus. Fighting déjà vu, Zamatryna got out of the SUV, into a brilliant autumn afternoon scented with sagebrush. Jerry was next to her. She had to keep her eyes on the bus. She couldn't stop watching it, in case she missed Betty and saw another homeless person first instead.

Someone in an Army uniform came up to them. That was all right, because he wasn't one of the homeless; he had a job, so she couldn't have chosen him as her Beggar anyway. "Excuse me, but who are you people?"

"A friend of ours is on that bus by mistake," Jerry said. There was movement inside now; the doors opened, and Zamatryna's stomach tightened. Please let Betty come out first. Please. "We have a place for her to live. She can come home with us."

"I don't know anything about that. I can't let you just—"

"Betty!" Zamatryna said. Here she was. She was the first one. She was the first one getting off the bus; a guard had reached for her arm to help her down the steps. She looked up and saw Zama, and smiled.

"You came to get me. I knew you would. God bless you, sweetheart."

Macsofo had coached Zamatryna on what to say, had impressed upon her the importance of saying it exactly right, and saying it as soon as she saw Betty. Feeling ridiculous, knowing that all the guards and everyone on the bus were watching her, she bowed and said, "Please grace my wedding, to remind me of the ground of my fortune."

Betty stared. "What?"

Zamatryna straightened up again. "I'll explain it later. And I'll tell you what you have to say back, okay?"

"This is highly irregular," the guard said, sounding bewildered.

"Right," said Lisa, behind them. "So who do we talk to, to fix it? Come on, buddy. This place is crowded, right? If we can take care of her so you don't have to, isn't that a good thing?"

It took hours. They had to answer questions, call the hospital to confirm that they were friends of Betty's, talk to her social worker at Sierra Regional Center. Lisa and Timbor, into whose custody Betty was being released, had to sign roughly ten thousand pieces of paper. But finally it was done. It had worked. They were taking Betty home.

On the way back to Reno, Zamatryna sat between Jerry and

Betty. Jerry's arm was around her, and her hand was on Betty's shoulder: another bridge. Betty didn't smell as much as usual. The hospital must have bathed her. She and Jerry told Betty what they wanted her to do, and why.

"I knew it," Betty said placidly. "I told you he loved you."

"Yes, you did. Do you remember what to say now? What I told you?"

"I will grace your wedding, to remind you always of the gifts you have received," Betty said. "Is that it? Did I do it right?"

"You did it perfectly," Zamatryna said, glancing at Macsofo. He didn't look any happier than he had before, but at least he wasn't retching anymore.

"That's pretty," Betty said.

"Yes," Jerry said. "It is. It's beautiful."

We did it, Zamatryna thought giddily. Everything's okay now. We'll be home soon, and Betty will be with us, if she doesn't just wander away again, and on Monday Jerry and I will get our marriage license and have the civil ceremony, and then we'll plan the other one, and we'll invite Alini, because she'd never dream of not coming to my wedding, and Max can apologize to her and—maybe it will all work out. Maybe we'll be okay. She put her head on Jerry's shoulder, wondering if she loved him yet. She couldn't tell.

But as they pulled up to the house, Lisa said, "Uh-oh. Trouble in River City. Who are those people on the porch?"

"It's Stan," Harani said, peering out the window into the dusk. "Stan and someone else. I've never seen him before."

"I have," Erolorit said. "He looks familiar. Where have I seen him?"

"On television," Timbor said bleakly. "And in the newspaper. That is Kenneth Glenrock. He is in charge of the INS investigation."

"Oh, *shit*," Lisa said. "Stan ratted on us? Stan called the INS? I'll kill him! I'll tear his balls off, that lousy good-for-nothing—"

"Calm down," Jerry said. "Lisa, just breathe, okay? Losing your temper isn't going to help. Let's just talk to them. Glenrock's not in uniform or anything. If he were here to arrest you guys, he'd have cops with him. He probably just wants to ask you some questions."

"We should have gotten married this afternoon," Zamatryna said, her throat tight. It hadn't worked. She'd jinxed everything after all, by looking for someone she already knew to be her Necessary Beggar, or by saying the formula in English instead of Gandiffran, or by not really loving Jerry. Now they were going to be sent to Afganistan, where they'd never lived in the first place, where they'd have to start all over. She'd never get to be a lawyer. She'd never see Jerry again, or Stan or Lisa, or the Truckee River.

They all got out of the SUV, and walked in a clump toward the porch. Jerry had one hand on Zama's shoulder and one on Betty's. When Stan saw them, he stood up and said cheerfully, "I didn't call him. Lisa, everybody, I swear I didn't call him. I had nothing to do with this. I got here and he was already here, waiting. We've had a nice chat."

"Yeah, I'll just bet," Lisa said savagely. But Zamatryna, looking at Stan, saw that he looked happy. When was the last time he'd looked happy? She couldn't remember. In fact, he looked more than happy. He was glowing. He looked like he was in love, or on drugs.

"Stan?" Timbor said, frowning. "Are you all right?"

"I'm *fine,* brother! I'm better than fine! I—"

"I'm sorry," Kenneth Glenrock said, "but do you mind if I talk to you folks for a minute? Inside the house?"

"Certainly," Timbor said. "Let us go into the living room. Mr. Glenrock, would you like coffee?"

"No. Thank you." They filed into the living room, perching on Lisa's mother's overstuffed furniture. Glenrock cleared his throat again. "Look, I think you know why I'm here."

"Yes," Lisa said. "Yes, we do."

Glenrock nodded. "Can I ask—may I just speak to the family, please?"

"We're all family," Lisa said, her voice cracking. "Everybody's family here. This is Betty, we're adopting her, and this is Jerry, he and Zama are getting married, and Stan and I, we've known these folks practically since they got here. So whatever you have to say, you can say to all of us."

Glenrock pushed his glasses up on his nose. He looked pained. "Well, all right. But I have to ask you a question, and—it may be painful. Did you come here with someone else? A man who died in the camp?"

There was a short silence. "Yes," Timbor said. "My youngest son. He killed himself. Why is that important, Mr. Glenrock, please?"

He looked at Lisa now. "Yes, I know you now. You don't remember me, do you? No, you wouldn't. That was ten years ago."

"Excuse me?"

"You came to our house," he said. "After my father died in the bombing. My father was Neil Glenrock. He was very upset, when—when Mr. Gandiffri's son died. He went to your tent, to try to help. Do you remember that?"

"Yes," Timbor said quietly. "I do remember, now. It was hot. His uniform was too hot. He stood there sweating, trying to be kind. And I was unkind to him. I am sorry."

"No," Glenrock said. "It meant a lot to our family that anyone remembered that, after he died. It meant a lot that your friend here came to the house to tell us about it. I just—I just wanted to see if you were the same people. I thought you were." He stood up and said, "You know, I have some leeway. In this investigation. We've got enough to nail the clerk, and you've been here long enough to be naturalized anyway. So have all the others, of course, but—well, some of them haven't been using their time here very constructively. That makes a difference. Anyway, we'll work with it. I'll try to work with it. I can't promise anything, but I'll try."

"Thank you," Timbor said. "Thank you very much, Mr. Glenrock. That means a lot to us."

When he was gone, Erolorit shook his head and said, "I don't believe it. I don't—I can believe in Darroti's ghost more easily than I can believe what that man just said. It can't be that simple. Can it?"

"We don't know," Timbor said with a sigh. "We have to wait to find out. He didn't promise anything. He only said that he would try."

Lisa turned to Stan and said, "Well? And in the meantime, what do you have to say for yourself?" He should be the one asking that, Zamatryna thought bleakly. She's the one who lied to him. But she's scared and hurt, and she's feeling defensive. "Stan, what the hell are you doing here? You kicked me out of the house. You said things—"

"I was wrong," he said, beaming. "Now I know how wrong I was, because Jesus came and told me so."

"Really," Lisa said, her eyebrows arching. "Is that so, Stan Buttle?" She didn't sound like she believed him.

Stan was oblivious. "Yes, that's so. I finally had a vision, Lisa, the thing I've wanted all my life, and it came when I was at my lowest point. I had a gun. I was going to—well, I wanted to die. Because the whole world was darkness, and nothing was right or true, and I thought God didn't exist anymore. And then Jesus came. He was wearing a white robe, just like he does in the picture we have in the kitchen, and there was a glow all around his head just like that, but his skin was dark, the way it really was, the way it should be. He looked like Timbor's folks."

Timbor and Zamatryna exchanged a glance, and Lisa said steadily, "Right. That's good. Jesus wasn't a white boy from California." Stan grinned at her, and Zamatryna had the feeling this was an old joke. "Go on. What happened?"

"He was crying because he felt so sorry for us," Stan said, his voice dreamy. "Because he loves us. He had a mole on his face that looked like a starfish." Jerry started to cough, and Zamatryna kicked him. Stan said, "I've never heard of that. I never heard of that mole before. I couldn't have made that up, Lisa."

"No," Lisa said. "I don't think you could."

"It made him seem more real."

"Sure it did. What did he say, Stan?" Lisa was leaning forward now, her eyes yearning: Zamatryna wondered if she was hungry for Jesus or for Stan himself, or for both of them.

"He told me love is the most important thing in the world," Stan said, his face shining. "He told me he forgave you for your lies, Lisa, because you lied to help Tim's family, and that I had to forgive you, too. And he told me that he forgave me for my anger against you, and that I had to ask you to forgive me, too. And now I know that Jesus is real, and that forgiveness is real. Because I've seen it. I've felt it. I've seen him. So how can I not believe? I'll never lose my faith again." He turned to Timbor and said, "Oh, Tim, I wish you'd seen him! I wish I could show him to you. Because then you'd believe in Jesus, just like I do."

"I believe in your Jesus," Timbor said, very gently. "And I believe in what he told you."

Stan looked back at Lisa. "So I'm here—to tell you I forgive you, and to ask if you forgive me. And if you love me. And if you'll live with me again. And—"

"Well, sure," Lisa said. Her face was wet. "All you ever had to do was ask. Come on, Stan. Let's go home and talk this all out. Can you folks—will all of you be okay without me? Will you excuse us, please?"

"Of course," Timbor said. "Of course we will."

"Good," Lisa said, wiping her face. "Betty can have Polly's room now."

Betty had been sitting in the most overstuffed chair, quietly watching everything; Zamatryna wondered how much she understood. After the kitchen door had closed behind Lisa and Stan, she looked at Zamatryna.

"Is it good, what just happened? What those two men said? That was good, wasn't it?"

"Yes," Zamatryna said, dazed. "Very good."

"I want to lie down now, Zama. I'm tired. Is there a bed?"

"Yes. We have an entire room for you. Come on, Betty, I'll show you."

Getting out clean sheets and making the bed steadied her somewhat, made her feel less crazy and unreal. Betty's labored breathing worried her, but at least Betty wasn't in the camp, or on the streets. One thing at a time. After Betty was tucked in, Zamatryna got some water from the kitchen—she'd suddenly realized she was desperately thirsty—and then went back into the living room. "Well," she said. "Our Darroti's been a busy boy, hasn't he?"

"I don't think he had anything to do with Mr. Glenrock," Timbor said.

"No, it doesn't sound like it. No starfish there." She sat down on the couch next to Jerry, who put his arm around her. She was exhausted. She was glad everyone was gone. She couldn't deal with anything else happening today.

"Now," Timbor said. "Macsofo, would you please tell me this business about Darroti and Gallicina? And would you tell me what makes you think that it was real, and not just a delusion, like the snakes?"

"I keep telling you, the snakes were real." Macsofo shrugged. "But I believed the story about Darroti because it explained the necklace he brought from home, for one thing. Of course, I suppose I cannot be sure that my mind was not just inventing the story. But after everything else that has happened, it seems less likely."

"I used to dream about the necklace too," Timbor said, frowning. "When I dreamed about Darroti."

"What necklace?" Zamatryna asked. She'd closed her eyes; Jerry was stroking her hair, lulling her to sleep. She was only vaguely following the conversation, which sounded as if it was happening underwater. There would be time enough to learn everything else, later. She was too tired now. She couldn't absorb anything else.

"You never saw it," Timbor said. "I never saw it, until Darroti died. The Army men found it. Darroti was wearing it. A black silk cord with a silver figure-eight on it."

"A what?" Zamatryna asked, opening her eyes. She sat up, pulling away from Jerry. "A figure-eight? It doesn't—Grandfather, it doesn't look like an X, does it?"

"Well, yes, I suppose it does. Except that the ends are closed."

"It is derived from an X," Macsofo said. "That is what my dream said."

"Oh my God. Grandfather, may I see it, please? Do you have it here?"

"Certainly," he said, and pulled it out of his pocket. Zamatryna looked at it. She was no longer even remotely sleepy. Yes, it was the right shape. She remembered all those hours she'd spent watching the beetle: the ends of the X had been connected, rounded like that, and she'd always thought it was because beetles weren't very bright and the insect couldn't figure out how to make a better X, and anyway the ends were connected when parents drew it in the air to silence their children, too—

"Macsofo," she said. "Uncle Max, can you tell me what it means? Do you know what it means? It's very important."

"It's a kiss," he said, sounding mystified. "It was their private symbol for a kiss. Darroti and Gallicina. Their symbol for their love."

"Oh my God," she said. "Oh my God. She's *kissing* him?" They were all looking at her as if she'd lost her mind. "I have to go get something. Everybody stay here. Nobody move. I'll be right back. Just—stay here!"

She got up and ran into her room, into the closet. There was the jar. There was the impossibly long-lived beetle in the jar. There was the pattern, the same figure the beetle had been making every second for the past eleven years. "Oh, you poor thing," Zamatryna said. "I'm so sorry. I didn't know!"

Clutching the jar, she ran back into the living room. "What," Erolorit said, "is that?"

"It's Gallicina," Zamatryna said. "It's her spirit, trapped in a beetle. She—she came into exile with us, to be with Darroti. She hid in my things. And she's stayed alive all this time, and I've kept her secret all this time because I thought it was an X, I thought she was telling me to stay quiet, but she wasn't. She was kissing Darroti."

They were all gaping at her. She didn't care. "Grandfather, is the towel here?" He handed it to her, and she opened the jar and dumped the beetle out onto the towel, and then there was a flash and the smell of lightning. Macsofo yelped, and Jerry grabbed Zamatryna, and a blue door appeared in the middle of the living room.

13

Timbor

The most grievous acts may be forgiven if the transgressor repents, and if the victim forgives; but the dead cannot forgive. That is what we believed in Lémabantunk, where the dead cannot speak to the living. At home, we knew that no murderers could ever return from exile, because those they had killed would never be able to forgive them.

We never thought that someone who had not really murdered would accept a sentence as a murderer.

The Judges are just. We believed that, in Gandiffri; and although we also believed that they did not choose the worlds to which they sent the exiled, I wonder now. Do the Judges have more power than they know, or claim? Or does the Door itself sense, somehow, where the exiled need to go? In the Tale of the Great Breaking, the Elements are exiled, and find what they are seeking in the very punishment imposed on them for having sought it. Is that, then, how every exile works?

For this much is certain. Only in a world of ghosts, a world where the Great Breaking never happened, could our story have unfolded as it did. Only in a world where the dead speak to the living could Darroti have made his truth known, at last, and been reunited with his love, and been forgiven by her as she was by him. For she needed his forgiveness even more, I think, than he needed hers. Her action was the one that sent us into exile. It is fitting that she followed us, because she sent us here. But only here could the sentence have been reversed, the exile revoked, the Door reopened.

When the Door reopened, we stood staring, all of us in shock. I saw Jerry hugging Zamatryna, clutching her; I saw the terror on his face. I think he feared that she would leave him, go through the Door back home, where he could never follow. None of the rest of us even thought that far: for while we stood there stunned, the beetle spread her wings and rose above the towel, and a mist rose from the towel to enfold her. And, still enclosed in mist, she flew then, through the Door, and vanished. And the Door did too. It winked from sight, gone just as suddenly as it had come.

And still we stared, until at last Macsofo walked to where the Door had been. He held a hand out, cautiously, and waved it through the air. "Nothing," he said. I saw him tremble. "It is gone." And then he looked at Zamatryna, who held the towel as tightly as Jerry held her. "That cloth is dry now," he said. It was not a question.

She looked down at the towel, felt it. "Yes," she said. "Completely dry." She looked at me. "Grandfather, I'm sorry."

"If he is home again," I said, "I am not sorry."

Would we have gone back through the Door ourselves, had it stayed open? We have discussed this question many times. Erolorit believes that it closed so quickly so we would not have that choice, which would have tortured us: for how could we have chosen? Lémabantunk is my home, still, but Zamatryna is American, and Jerry is American, and Alini and the cousins were not with us. We still believe that families must remain together: if not in the same household, at least in the same dimension. How could we have gone back to Gandiffri, and left them behind? And Jerry says, quite sensibly I think, that perhaps the Door that beckoned Darroti and

Gallicina home from exile could not do so for us. Perhaps we are, in fact, at home now, our exile tamed and turned to something else: if not yet quite to home, then to the hope of home.

For Jerry and Zamatryna did get married. The Monday after that fateful Friday, they had their civil wedding at City Hall. Civil: say invisible, for it took twenty seconds, and there was no rejoicing, not as yet. They did it to try to slow the INS, should Kenneth Glenrock find himself unable to spare us. But so far we have not yet heard from him, and so we hope we never will. And that was several months ago.

They do not yet live together, and they have not had their wedding with the Necessary Beggar: the Real Wedding, they call it. They will have that in the spring, or maybe in the summer, when Zama is eighteen and after Betty has recovered from her surgery. The surgery is scheduled for next week. The children have been working very hard, to raise the money. They got Betty in the Reno newspapers, and Stan and Lisa told many churches about her, and doctors and nurses came forward to donate their time, so that all the children need to pay for are the facilities and the equipment, and the many medicines Betty needs. It is still a huge amount of money, but Betty has become a celebrity. She has been in *People* magazine, and on TV, and now the money comes from many places, not just Reno. And so we hope that she survives her surgery, which terrifies us all, and terrifies her most.

I am glad about Betty. How could I not be? Watching her rest in Poliniana's old bed, her face sweaty from exertion if she has only walked across the room, is terrible. She barely has the energy to flap her hand, which always flaps. It has kept her with us, this weakness; it has kept her from wandering as she used to do, and I wonder if she will wander again when she is better, if we will once again have to search for her in the parks and by the river. And yet it troubles me, that she had to become a celebrity to get the help she needed, that help is not given to everyone here. There are still all those people in the camp, the ones we could not bring back with us when we brought her back. New people go there every week, on the buses. And so the parks are safe and seemly now, while the camp grows ever more crowded. The camp is out of sight. Most people can forget it. We cannot.

And so Jerry and Zamatryna's wedding will be unconventional, both for America and for Gandiffri. They will have their Necessary Beggar—if she lives—but they will already have given her their gift, for Jerry's savings are still the largest single sum she has received. And I suspect that they will receive other gifts, gifts for themselves, although they only plan to ask for help for Betty. Certainly Zamatryna will wear an American wedding gown, and carry flowers, although they will be flowers she has grown herself; and afterwards she and Jerry will live in an apartment by themselves, not with Jerry's family, as they would have done in Lémabantunk. At any rate they will live in Reno until she goes to law school. Since there is no law school in town, I do not know where she will be then. That will be terrible, to have her in a different city for three years, but many families live in different places here. I wonder how they can, how they can bear it, but they do. And after law school, Jerry and Zamatryna will come back here, where they are loved, to be with us.

And does she love him? She still will tell you that she is not sure, and yet I think she does. I see it in her face; always she notices when he comes into the room, or leaves it, and she begins to fret about his health and future, and her smile is brighter when he is the cause of it. And I grow fond of him, for he is not as simple as we thought. Jerry studies carefully, and if he does not learn as quickly as Zamatryna does, he learns deeply and well, and speaks thoughtfully, and steadies her. And there is no doubt that he loves her; she is his world. I begin to believe that she could do no better, although at first I thought she could scarcely do worse.

She will wake up one morning, or look up one evening at a sunset or a tree, and know that she loves him. This is my hope for her:

that she will find her love has grown in secret, as a plant grows underground before it flowers. And one does not poke at the plant before it lifts its head from the soil; one lets it be. And so I do not nag her about loving Jerry, or tell her what I see in her face when she looks at him or speaks of him. I let her chatter on about the wedding, and about her plot to reunite Macsofo and Alini.

Well, perhaps it could happen. I do not know. They speak now; she lets him see his children, who are sullen but polite enough. He has apologized, and she has said she needs more time to learn to trust him again, and that is fair. He is not drinking now. We all begin to hope he will not start again. He has stopped working on the poison trains and gone back to bricklaying, and that is certainly a relief. He likes his job more than he has in years. And if he is sad, I think it is a healthy sadness, the grief he never let himself express before. He is easier to be with now, far easier to love.

But whether Aliniana will fall swooning into his arms when she sees him in a tux, as Zama claims, I cannot say. I rather doubt it. I will be happy if they simply dance. The other day Alini told Harani she had dumped her lover, who only wanted her body; this news sent Zamatryna into ecstasies. "He never existed," she said triumphantly. "I told you! He was never real to begin with. That's why we've never met him, and why I can never get Polly or Rick or Jamfret to talk about him. He was just a story. But now she's ready to start thinking about coming home to Uncle Max, so she's clearing the decks. And when she sees him in that tux, she'll be a goner, I'm telling you."

"You can tell me all you want," I told her. "I will believe it when I see it."

"Oh, Grandfather," Zamatryna said, laughing. "Alini's an incurable romantic. And she loves him. She always has."

"If you say so. I still remember the night she threw the clown."

Zamatryna rolled her eyes. "Yes, but that's the sign of how

much she really loves him. The passion was going in the wrong direction, that's all."

"If that is love," I said, "I will take indifference."

"No, you won't. You're not indifferent, and neither are they. We aren't indifferent people. Everything will be fine, Grandfather. I promise."

"That is not your promise to keep," I told her, and she laughed and kissed me and danced off to get dressed for her date with Jerry that night. Her room has grown much messier, since she no longer has Gallicina to hide. But Zama tells me that Jerry is neat enough for both of them, and Jerry seems to agree, at least for the moment. We will see if he agrees once they begin to live together. If she is messier, she is also happier, for the weight of the beetle has been lifted from her shoulders. It was an awful burden, that peanut butter jar. I wonder how she bore it for so long, beginning when she was so little. I wonder how she hid it from us all. She moves more lightly now, so much so that it seems impossible we never saw her heaviness before. And yet, how could we? We had no basis for comparison except the old days, in Gandiffri: and exile and the camp, and Darroti's death, would have been weight enough, if we had seen her weariness and questioned it. Instead, we thought her flawless. We saw the child we wanted her to be, not Zama as she was. I like her better now. She shares her flaws now, and her fears, and so I also trust her joy. I think it is no longer a clown's joy, hiding the tears inside. I think it is real, and growing.

Stan and Lisa are back together, of course. I think that was Darroti's kindest act. We thought at first that we would not tell them what had really happened, but at last I told Lisa: secrets had hurt us so, and I feared to keep any more.

"Oh, I already knew," she said. We were in the kitchen, where we always seem to have important conversations: only Lisa and I, for everyone else was gone. "Jerry told me about his dreams, over coffee that day. He told me about your city, and about the door. He thought I'd already known; he was horrified when he realized I didn't, poor kid, thought he'd spilled the beans and broken his word to Zama. But you know, Timbor, it was okay. I already knew it had to be something like that, the way you guys could never tell anyone where you were from. And it doesn't matter. You're here now. That's the important thing. So anyway, Jerry told me about Darroti, about that funny mole he had, and then when I heard Stan talk about his vision, I figured out what was going on."

"But if Stan found out," I said, "his faith would be broken again. And we must not let that happen."

Lisa shook her head and put her hand over mine. "Timbor, you know what? If he found out, it wouldn't make any difference. It doesn't make any difference. Jesus comes to us in other people, always. That's the way it works. Stan always knew that with his head: he just couldn't wrap his heart around it. The trick is learning to see Jesus everyplace, learning to see Christ in whatever poor schlub is walking down the street. Stan can talk about that to beat the band, but he was never very good at doing it. Because he was too afraid, you know, afraid of the other people he knew it was his job to love. Afraid that he'd get hurt, or that he'd go to hell for loving somebody who'd done something wrong, even though that's the entire point, that's what we're supposed to do, because everybody does things wrong. So if Stan learned to see Jesus in a ghost, well, then, that's fine. Because now he's learning to see Jesus in the check-out kids at the supermarket, too, even when they shortchange him or break the eggs or take too long loading the cart because they're gossiping with their friends."

"But you don't believe in ghosts," I said, frowning.

"I'm saying ghost because that's your word, honey. I'd call Darroti an angel, myself."

"No," I said, shaking my head. American angels are nauseating. "He had no harp or wings."

Lisa snorted. "I didn't say he was a Hallmark angel. I don't believe in those any more than you do. Angel means messenger. And he certainly delivered messages, didn't he?"

Perhaps Lisa is right, that it wouldn't make any difference if Stan knew about the ghost. I still have never told him; I will let her do that. Instead, I let him tell me about Jesus, which he does every Saturday when we go to visit the De Soto. We sit on the bench by the beautiful car with the plastic sunbursts on top, and Stan tells me about his vision, about how Jesus came and gave him hope. He never tires of telling me, and because I know it was my son who gave him hope, I never tire of listening. I would surely lose my patience otherwise, for Stan's sermons now are much more fervent even than they were when first we came here. I wonder sometimes how Lisa can stand it. And yet she is happy, and Stan's church has begun to grow again: he has found his fire, Lisa says, and its light is drawing others.

"Come to worship tomorrow," he tells me, every Saturday. "Come and join us, Timbor. Listen to the Word of God."

"Friend," I always tell him, "I get your Word of God every Saturday, from you. I do not need it on Sunday also."

"But it's different with a group of other people. It's different when we all pray and sing together. You still don't believe, Timbor, I can tell you don't; you're just being polite and listening to me. You were always polite, but I want you to be happy—"

"Stan," I tell him, "I am so much happier than I used to be that you would not believe me if I told you. I could not make you believe it. And I believe in the vision you had, because I have seen how it brought you and Lisa back together."

"The Fruits of the Spirit," he says, beaming.

Yes, I think, and the Spirit was Darroti's. "And Stan, tomorrow is my day to spend with Jerry and Zama. You know that."

This always placates him; he loves the children. And, indeed, I treasure my Sundays, the days they save for me. We go to movies, or we walk along the river. We talk about the wedding. I answer Jerry's questions about Gandiffri, for he is endlessly curious, and indeed, there is much that Zama also does not know. I tell them about the Elements and the Great Breaking, about the Great Market and the Judges, about the regions of Gandiffri and the carpets in each one. Jerry tells me that one of his sisters-in-law is a weaver, and he has asked her to make a carpet with the colors of the Elements. It will be his house-warming gift to Zama, when they get their apartment. It is a lovely thought; he is a lovely boy.

And sometimes we talk about Darroti and Gallicina, puzzling over the story Macsofo told us, the story that explains so much I never really noticed at the time. I think back now on Darroti's struggles with liquor, on his odd excitement some days at the Market and his deep despair on others, on the nights he spent away from home, when we simply thought that he was with his friends. I think about all the people who came to buy carpets from us, and wonder if I ever saw Gallicina in the crowd. Sometimes, still, I torment myself, wondering if I could have made the story end a different way if I had noticed more, said more. And yet there is no way for me to know: and would I want a different ending, a story where we never left Gandiffri, never met Stan or Lisa or Jerry? It is unanswerable. I am glad I cannot make that choice.

But I make the children promise not to keep such secrets, ever. I tell them: "When you have children of your own, pay attention. Take nothing lightly, nothing for granted. Always let them know that they can talk to you. Always love them." And yet I think they would do that anyway; and Darroti's story has taught them that they must not keep their feelings from each other, that they must not let jealousy or anger grow.

Zamatryna wears Darroti's necklace now. She and Jerry love the fact that the sign that means a kiss also means forever, in mathematics. I was startled when she began to wear it; I thought the symbol would bring her too much pain, remind her of all those years hiding the beetle in the peanut butter jar. But to her it is a symbol of reunion and hope. And so she always wears it, as Lisa always wears her cross, although Zama has replaced the black silk cord, which had begun to fray, with a fine silver chain. And sometimes when she sees me looking at it, she hides it, tucks it into her shirt. "It's making you look sad today, Grandfather. I know how much you miss him."

Aye, I miss him. I shall always miss him, my youngest child, the boy who toddled around the garden in the sunshine, pulling the wagon I made for him. Darroti, my clown, the last fruit of my love for Frella, whom I also miss. The family keeps Zamatryna's doll, the wooden one, on the hutch in the dining room now, where Lisa's fancy clown used to be. Harani has given it new yarn hair, and eyes of blue beads: it looks happy at last. It is a beloved reminder, but it is not my son.

And yet he visits me, in dreams, and now I know to listen. I listen to his tale of how he read my letters, how they told him what to do. Am I inventing that? I will never—can never—know for sure, and yet I think that I am not. I think that my Darroti, who learned how to be two places at once, is everywhere now. I think he left a part of himself behind with us, when he went through the Door; I think the family still remains together, and always will.

And I dream of him in Lémabantunk, a Lémabantunk different than the one I knew, and yet the same. I dream that the city goes on without us, still vibrant, still beautiful with banners and flowers and festivals. I dream that Darroti and Gallicina dwell now in a tree. It is a lovely elm in one of the ceremonial gardens on the edge of the city, not far from the park where they had their first private meeting. Birds nest in their leaves, and children climb on their branches. I dream that they grow and learn together in death as they did not do in life. The Elements are gracious, to permit them to be together now.

That is a good dream, and I have it often, but it is not my favorite. My favorite is the dream that I had only once, the very night the Door appeared among us and disappeared again.

In that dream, Darroti watches Zamatryna bring the jar out from her bedroom, watches her open it. He feels the beetle land upon the cloth containing him. And then he feels the beetle trace its figure-eight, its kiss, and he knows that Gallicina tried to make the sign before she died. He knows, at last, that she heard him, heard the tale he tried to tell her, sobbing, while her life ran out upon the stones. She heard him say he loved her: she heard and understood that he had been with Stini only to go to the place where he would keep his promise to his love, to forfeit drink.

With her last strength, Gallicina tried to trace the kiss upon his wrist, to tell him she had heard. That strength failed her; she could not complete the pattern.

It is completed now, at last. The pattern is completed, and Darroti knows himself forgiven. His soul rises from the towel to embrace her, as he has yearned to do each moment since she died. And the Door opens, and they fly through it. They fly home, through the blue tunnel, into the glorious sunshine of an autumn day in Lémabantunk, where they will dwell in love forever.